OUT OF ASHES OF LOVE

Chy Anne Autumn Osborn

LifeRich PUBLISHING

LifeRich Publishing is a registered trademark of
The Reader's Digest Association, Inc.

LifeRich Publishing books may be ordered
through booksellers or by contacting:

LifeRich Publishing
1663 Liberty Drive
Bloomington, IN 47403
www.liferichpublishing.com
844-686-9607

ISBN: 978-1-4897-4682-5 (sc)
ISBN: 978-1-4897-4683-2 (hc)
ISBN: 978-1-4897-4684-9 (e)

Library of Congress Control Number: 2023906200

Print information available on the last page.

LifeRich Publishing rev. date: 04/13/2023

We are Pilgrims in a strange land
We are so far from our homeland
With each passing day it seems so clear
This world will never want us here
We're not welcome in this world of wrong
We are foreigners who don't belong
We are strangers we are aliens
We are not of this world....

Not of This World words and music
by Bob Hartman performed by Petra

If the world hates you, keep in mind that it hated me first. If you belonged to the world, it would love you as its own. As it is, you do not belong to the world, but I have chosen you out of the world. That is why the world hates you.

John 15: 18–19, NIV

Dedication

This book is in part dedicated to the Nez Perce people, the great Nimipu. The information they provided during my trip to Idaho was invaluable. In return, I have done my best to make the telling of this story as accurate as possible. Special thanks to Scott Gilbert and Sam George of Kamiah, Idaho.

The rest of my dedication belongs to those in my life who never gave up on me or my writing, even when I doubted myself. Thank you to my long list of editors, friends, and cheering section. And most especially, thank you to my daughter, Tashina, who has never stopped believing in me or the stories I love to tell. May God use them to change and inspire those who read them.

Prologue

1978 - Idaho

As the sun sank slowly behind a ridge of mountains, a young Indian warrior of eighteen summers and his prized spotted stallion lay side by side in an Autumn field. The stallion was dead from a bullet through the brain. The warrior might well have been dead himself, for he stirred not, and his life's blood stained the prairie grass. Yet his heart continued to beat despite his bruised and beaten body, as well as the mass of bloody flesh his back had become when laid open by a cruel whip.

His enemies had surprised him with their abrupt arrival, their hatred, and their brutality. Just that very day, the warrior had made a vow to love, forever, the fair-skinned woman who possessed his heart—the woman claimed without reason by the one who'd held the whip.

Now, with but one sunrise between he and his beloved, the warrior had been beaten, warned, and told to stay away. To make sure that he'd listen, his enemy had threatened the same for the very woman the warrior loved. The circumstances being what they were even in this mid-twentieth century, there was no doubt his enemy had all the advantages.

Through the haze of pain that nearly consumed him, the warrior concluded the only way to keep his vow of love was to do as he'd been told. He was to leave the woman of his heart, his Morning Light, and live with the great sorrow of her loss for the remainder of his days.

It's a view that brings forth the heart and soul of people
who have chosen to live in a different culture.
A culture that has a different beat
than the rhythm of the Reservation.
Each has chosen a path that only they
can achieve and feel content.
They speak from their hearts and
soul so others may follow
a path that will lead them into two cultures....

Laverne K. Morrissey, Paiute

1

1992 - Minnesota

The brick two-story home was old, at least one hundred years. But it had been faithfully cared for throughout its lifetime. The pine floors shone with polish, the walls were newly papered, and every room radiated the efforts of proper cleaning. Even the grounds surrounding the house spoke of stately elegance in the way of hundred-foot maples and row after row of lilac bushes, their array of color currently hidden by fall.

The house itself had many rooms. One of them, a bedroom, rested at the rear of the house on the second floor. It was a large room, with bookcases built into two walls, the shelves lined with classics by Charles Dickens, Sir Arthur Conan Doyle, and Shakespeare. At least one bookcase was given over to books on astronomy, while star graphs carefully framed in glass hung on several of the walls.

The central focus of the room was a full length Indian headdress made of eagle feathers, and the king size bed over which it hung. The bed resided well off the floor on a captain's pedestal, and spread out upon it were several quilts lovingly made by a mother's hand and stitched with Indian sign. Beneath the spread of quilts, lay a man.

Phoenix Yellow Wolf Stargazer woke to the sound of his calico purring contentedly atop his chest and the aroma of brewing coffee floating up through the open floor vent from the kitchen below. With his eyes still closed, he reached up and stroked the contented Esmeralda, who so thoughtfully greeted him each morning. She purred louder, rubbing her face against his hand. With great tenderness, Phoenix rubbed her ears. She was fourteen years old compared to his thirty-two years young.

Despite the warm welcome to the morning from his aged friend, Phoenix felt incredible loss, knowing once again an emptiness he'd tried to bury in the past. For he had dreamed about her again. *Aerielle.* He shouldn't be surprised. It was fourteen years to the day since he'd done the hardest thing in his entire life. It was the day he'd given up Aerielle Buchanan, the woman he loved.

Opening his eyes, Phoenix shifted to a sitting position, cradling Esmeralda's rumbling body against him. September morning sunshine poured through the beige curtains of two windows gracing the wall to his left. The rising sun's bright radiance warmed the padded seat of the old rocker sitting near the far window. Cleopatra, the black Persian, had chosen this spot for her morning ablutions, while Sheba sat inside the window curtain on the sill, her tail twitching back and forth, parting the curtains with its gold length.

Gold. Spun gold. Hair like corn silk spilling over shoulders that shook with amusement. Aerielle.

Setting Esmeralda down into a nest of rumpled blankets, Phoenix swung his legs over the side of the large bed, reaching for the pair of jeans that lay at the end of it. He put them on, listening as he did so, to the hushed sounds coming from the kitchen below. He glanced at his watch. Seven o'clock. Sofia, good friend and coworker, was early this morning, not for the first time, and not that it mattered. Phoenix was generally up by now, and his brother Hawk, asleep across the hall, could remain unconscious through almost anything.

From a nearby drawer, Phoenix retrieved a red T-shirt and pulled it on, conveniently hiding a multitude of white scars that laced his back. Reaching up, he slid his long hair free of the T-shirt, letting the length of his tangled mane fall freely. He'd comb it later. Right now the aroma of fresh-brewed coffee was beckoning.

Lifting Esmeralda into the crook of one arm, Phoenix started for the open bedroom door. Spock and McCoy, his two German shepherds, sprang off the braided rugs they slept on, eager to follow.

"Mornin', boys," said Phoenix, reaching down to pat each of them on the head and rubbing an ear or two. Their tails whipped back and forth in greeting, thumping the door frame as they left the room. Thankfully they got along better than their namesakes.

Spock was first down the enclosed stairwell, the sound of his paws muffled on the carpeted steps that followed the dark pine railing to the large foyer below. Then his nails clattered across the wood floor as he made for the kitchen at the rear of the house.

When Phoenix entered the room with McCoy at his side, Sofia had already let Spock out into the backyard. The door was once again held open, and McCoy glided out to join his brother.

Twenty-seven-year-old Sofia Bendetti turned from the door, black curls dancing about her shoulders. Her hair was the color Phoenix's should have been had he received more of the Nez Perce blood from his mother. But like Crazy Horse, the Cheyenne chief of old, his hair was wavy and a dark muddy brown. His eyes, on the other hand, were the color of obsidian, unlike Sofia's, which were brown and decidedly warm.

Warm and inviting. A smile that welcomed you like morning sunlight. Aerielle.

"Sleep well?" Sofia inquired. She studied Phoenix closely as he leaned against the old fashioned, gold-specked linoleum counter with white painted cupboards.

"Well enough," he replied, pouring himself a steaming cup of coffee one handed, while still cradling Esmeralda with the other.

"You seem a little blue this morning."

Blue. Eyes the color of a cloudless summer sky. Aerielle.

Phoenix pulled away from his persistent thoughts, slopping coffee over the rim of his mug as he unintentionally jerked away from the counter as well.

"That's answer enough," continued Sofia. "Just have a seat and play the silent Indian while I fix you a bagel."

But being silent was part of Phoenix's problem. It allowed his thoughts to wander. "So what do we have on the agenda today?" he asked, sitting down before the small oak table and nestling Esmeralda in his lap.

"You mean besides Mr. Danvers' cow?" Sofia replied, setting a glass of orange juice before him.

Phoenix smiled for the first time that morning. Mr. Danvers was just one of the clients to avail himself of the veterinary services provided by the veterinary team with the help of Sofia. Hawk handled most of the domestic cases at their in-home office, while Phoenix dealt mostly with farm animals, including Mr. Danvers' cow. There was most likely nothing wrong with the cow. There never was, but Phoenix was out there twice a month to soothe the old man's nerves. Mildred was his prize possession, providing the old man not only company but "the best darn milk in the state of Minnesota."

Phoenix looked up at his and Hawk's long-time secretary and receptionist. Sofia was grinning at him. "I knew I could get you to smile."

With this pronouncement, she turned her back and proceeded to plop a bagel into the toaster.

Phoenix didn't know what he and Hawk would do without her. She was their right hand, ever present, ever loyal, and the only person Phoenix didn't mind referring to him as an Indian in any way, shape, or form.

Her voice, low and husky, calling him "Half-Breed." Aerielle.

Well, Sofia was the only one in the last fourteen years, anyway. She was also in love with Hawk Pale Horse Stargazer, unbeknownst to the twenty-nine-year-old.

Phoenix could well understand why Sofia didn't reveal her feelings. She was a practical, down-to-earth kind of girl—not the type Hawk normally went out with. And Hawk went out with more than his share of women, most of them polished and chic. His brother was certainly an epicure of women. The problem was, if they weren't packaged with a fair amount of elegance, he often failed to discover the rich bouquet within.

This was one of many aspects separating Phoenix from his brother. Hawk dated women who were smooth and sophisticated, while Phoenix dated no one at all. Another difference between them was their appearance. Hawk had inherited traditional black hair, unlike Phoenix, and he even had the dark eyes, but his skin didn't have that sun-bronzed look to it, and his features didn't announce their heritage like Phoenix's with a sharp nose and high cheekbones. Hawk could have passed for one of Sofia Bendetti's brothers, while his easy charisma drew people to him, especially women, like a well-baited line. It wasn't an assumed kind of charm either, but a natural attraction about him that even their younger sister Sparrow had inherited.

Phoenix glanced over at the doorway to the foyer, sensing Sheba and Cleopatra's entrance into the room. The felines looked at him expectantly. Getting up from his chair, Phoenix poured two saucers of milk, one for Esmeralda and one for the other two. Setting the saucers and Esmeralda onto the new linoleum floor, he returned to his seat just as Sofia served up the toasted bagel, smothered in strawberry cream cheese.

All at once there were two warning barks from outside, and then a doorbell rang, the particular sequence of chimes informing Phoenix that someone was at the veterinary entrance at the rear.

"Little early for office hours," announced Sofia, heading beneath the stairs through the rear passageway that lead to the office waiting room.

Phoenix remained seated, biting into his bagel. He knew from experience that if an emergency awaited, the party at the door would be leaning on the bell. There had been just one ring.

Phoenix heard the dead bolt release and the door open.

"It's about time you answered the door," said a commanding voice Phoenix recognized as Mrs. Wellington's, one of their older and more ostentatious neighbors.

"Mrs. Wellington," greeted Sofia. "I'm afraid office hours don't start till nine."

"Oh, but this is an emergency," proclaimed Mrs. Wellington with an authoritative voice, and Phoenix heard her step inside. "Baronessa has just had the most unpleasant morning. Couldn't hold her breakfast down."

Phoenix nearly choked on his bagel at this announcement. The old woman had probably fed the Pekinese too many donuts. He felt sorry for the dog.

"She must see the doctor," Mrs. Wellington continued. "Baronessa could be gravely ill."

There was a brief pause before Sofia replied. "I'll see if the doctor can help you."

"I don't want that long-haired Indian, now. You get me the other one."

Phoenix shook his head in disgust as he took a sip of coffee. What'd she think his brother was? Italian?

"Mrs. Wellington," began Sofia with an edge that only those close to her would recognize. "Hawk Stargazer is not currently available."

"Then Baronessa will just have to wait." The back door slammed abruptly.

So much for her emergency, thought Phoenix.

Sofia re-entered the kitchen with an amused expression on her face. "Quite a piece of work, isn't she?"

"Did I hear the vet bell?" questioned the aforementioned Hawk Stargazer, appearing in the kitchen.

The vet bell was one of the few things that could wake his brother who, Phoenix noted, had thrown himself together quite quickly in a pair of Dockers and a sweater.

"Mrs. Wellington and Baronessa," Phoenix explained. "Couldn't hold her breakfast down."

Hawk grinned and then winked at Sofia. "I assume you mean the dog?"

Sofia grinned back while Phoenix just grunted and bit into his bagel.

"Probably too many donuts," continued Hawk, running a hand through his short uncombed hair. "You know, breakfast does sound good, and it smells great."

"With coffee and orange juice?" offered Sofia, reaching for the package of bagels.

"Definitely," Hawk agreed, leaning against the counter. "I suppose we owe you lunch in return for making breakfast."

Sofia eyed him with raised brows. "Not if either of you is cooking it."

"She's awfully insulting this morning, don't you think?" asked Hawk, glancing at his brother as Phoenix got up from the table and carried his empty plate to the sink.

Phoenix nodded in agreement, meeting his brother's gaze. "Pretty accurate, too. Try dinner at Leeann Chin's. You might find her a little more agreeable."

"But you're not big on eating out," returned Hawk.

"I didn't say invite me. I said invite her. Now if you'll excuse me...."

Leaving his brother to go from there, Phoenix left the kitchen, headed where, he wasn't sure. Moments later he ended up in his study, a large room on the second floor at the front of the house. Moving around the large oak desk in the center of the room, he sank into the waiting chair, the leather cold against his back despite the T-shirt. And though he knew it was his imagination, it seemed he could feel his scars throbbing, which was always the case after an encounter with Mrs. Wellington. People like her brought back memories of excruciating pain and bloody wounds inflicted by those who felt American Indians were beneath contempt. Phoenix often felt bitter in return, but he knew better than to think one race was better or worse than another, for the same race that had taught him hatred, had also taught him love.

With his thoughts again filled with Aerielle Buchanan, Phoenix pulled open the top right drawer of his desk. Lifting up a business card folio and a sheaf of papers, he pulled forth a worn photograph. It was his one and only picture of Aerielle, taken by his mother during Sparrow's ninth birthday party.

In the photo Aerielle was laughing, unlike in Phoenix's dreams where she never even smiled. Usually she was in danger from some unseen enemy, while he was unable to save her. Phoenix rarely dreamed of her now, unlike the first few months after he left. But that had been Idaho, fourteen years past, and the last he had heard, Aerielle had left his family's ranch to start nursing school. Idaho was a long way from Minnesota, and fourteen years a long time. Despite this, Phoenix knew he would forever be tied to her. He had loved her. She had loved him. And because of Aerielle, he had experienced God's love as well.

Leaving her had been the most painful thing he had ever done. Back then he had thought it was the right thing to do. But with the passage of years, Phoenix no longer believed this to be true. Had he been closer to God at the time, would he have been instilled with some inner wisdom? And what if he had told Aerielle his true reasons for leaving? Would she have received some knowledge he had not?

Phoenix continued to study Aerielle's image in the photograph, noting the laugh lines around her eyes. At eighteen she had been full of joy and spontaneity and, as pale skinned as the typical white girl came. She was as far from being Indian as he was from being white, despite being his father's son.

How he had despised her when she first came to live with his family. Though the purpose of her coming was to be a sign language tutor for six months, Phoenix figured she wouldn't have taken the job but for the exorbitant amount of money his step-father Nevin had had to offer. But Sparrow, suffering from progressive genetic deafness and slowly losing her ability to hear, had needed Aerielle's skills desperately.

Phoenix could remember the day Aerielle arrived as if it were yesterday. Could still feel the sweat trickling down his back from the heat, taste the salty moisture that collected on his upper lip, and smell the combined odor of fresh hay, horses, and manure.

→→→

Pausing before the third stall on the left side of the barn, Phoenix wiped the sweat from his forehead with a brush of his arm. It was inordinately hot today, even for mid-June, and the heat made the job of mucking out the stalls all that much more unpleasant. Phoenix's long hair, loosely plaited in a single braid, clung to the damp flesh of his back, while the handle of the shovel he leaned upon was difficult to grip with moist hands.

But Phoenix would rather be doing almost anything, anywhere, than sitting inside the house trading niceties with the just-arrived Aerielle Buchanan. He'd heard the pickup pull into the yard almost an hour ago, his step-father, Nevin Stargazer, attorney-at-law, returning with the "honored guest." Yet Phoenix made no effort to greet her. She was here to teach them sign language. Fine. He would start tomorrow. In the meantime, there were still twelve more stalls to clean. Two dozen or so appaloosas made quite a mess.

Taking up the shovel, Phoenix began on the next stall. His movements were powerful and driven as he thrust the shovel into the soiled hay, the muscles in his shoulders bunching with each movement. He had just finished the current stall when he heard her enter the barn. It had to be her. Sparrow's footsteps were light and hurried, Nevin and Hawk's heavy and firm, and his mother rarely came inside. These footsteps were light, yet cautious like a stranger's.

Phoenix turned to face her, resting one hand on the shovel, the other hand on the sliding stall door. He was not impressed with her innocent blond, blue-eyed looks. Bangs brushed her eyebrows, and she was taller than he'd expected, around five foot eight, but still shorter than his six foot. Her casual jeans and tee were name brand, while her complexion was flawless and without make-up, and her teeth perfect. Yes, she was smiling, despite the scowl Phoenix leveled in her direction.

"You're Phoenix. I'm Aerielle," she announced, clearly not put off by his silence. "I was told you were the one to thank for my sleeping quarters. It seems you've been forced to room with your brother for six months."

Phoenix shrugged. "No problem." But it was, and not because he was forced to share a room with Hawk. It was a problem because she didn't belong here. She was an intruder. She wasn't "Indian."

"Looks like you've got your work cut out for you," she said, glancing around the large red barn with its abundance of spacious stalls. "Would you like some help?"

Phoenix raised an eyebrow in disbelief, the buzzing of flies filling the surprised silence. "This is manure in case you hadn't noticed."

The smile on her face turned contemplative as she tilted her head to the side. "Oh, I noticed. I notice a lot of things."

Phoenix's anger rose as he took in her relaxed stance and devil-may-care attitude. He'd love to see her shovel manure, but tempted as he was to hand over the shovel beneath his grip, he had to think of Sparrow, and scaring away the tutor was out of the question.

"You're here to teach sign language. You aren't expected to help with chores," Phoenix said at last, still leaning against the stall door.

She didn't move. "Nevertheless, the offer is genuine. If you have another pair of those," she added, nodding down at the black rubber boots he wore.

She had to be nuts. No one volunteered to muck stalls. No one except himself, that is. But there she was, her large blue eyes never leaving him as she waited for an answer.

Five minutes later, wearing his brother's boots, Aerielle worked in the stall next to Phoenix. As he lifted another load into the wheel barrel, he glanced in her direction. She worked steadily, but without hurry, like she wasn't out to prove anything. She also worked in silence, which amazed Phoenix, and he waited apprehensively for her to begin some needless chatter. But her

> lips remained silent, and in some respects, so did her eyes, for not once had Phoenix caught a glimmer of disgust or even fear, something he'd learned to expect as a Nez Perce.

→→→

Giving the photograph of Aerielle one last look, Phoenix slipped it back beneath the papers in the drawer, closing it gently. It was time to put away the past—again, at least for one more day. Leaning back into the cushioning softness of the chair, Phoenix swiveled around so he looked out the large French doors that faced the south Minneapolis street and the bright rippling lake. There were over ten thousand lakes in Minnesota; he still found it ironic that of all lakes he could have chosen to live on, he had ended up on one of those named for an Indian—Lake Nokomis.

→→→

Aerielle Buchanan smiled down at her young patient in the hospital bed before her. Ten year old Lisa smiled back, looking as undefeated as ever. Aerielle was pleased, if not surprised, for just recently the girl's right leg had been amputated below the knee to stop the spread of cancer. Knowing the girl's busy foster-mother wouldn't be stopping in until later that day, Aerielle had decided a special visit was in order.

"How am I doing?" questioned Lisa, gazing up with sparkling hazel eyes.

"You're doing just fine," assured Aerielle, resting her hands on the railing of the bed. "Did you get to see the piglet they brought into the playroom this morning?"

Lisa nodded. "I got to hold it, too."

"You be sure and eat all your lunch today, okay?"

"Even the jello?" grimaced Lisa.

"Even the jello. And then I'll see about getting you some extra special ice-cream this afternoon."

"Really?"

"Really."

"Chocolate and marshmallow?!"

"Chocolate and marshmallow," confirmed Aerielle.

"Okay, I'll eat my jello. Thanks Dr. B."

"You're welcome. Now I have some other duties to take care of, Lisa. Don't give the nurses too hard of a time."

Lisa just smiled.

Aerielle left the girl and made her way to the nurses' station where she examined several patients' charts.

"Dr. Buchanan?"

Aerielle turned with clipboard in hand to face her favorite nurse, Heather Finch. The young woman was in her late twenties, and aside from the head of thick red hair, she also had a generous smile.

"I put the x-rays you've been expecting on your desk," Heather was saying. "I also have some papers for you to sign."

"Bring them to me," replied Aerielle, replacing the patient chart she held. "I'll be in my office for a while."

Ten minutes later, after being stopped repeatedly in the wide corridors, Aerielle reached her small office. Closing the door behind her, she shut out the general hospital hubbub and the smell of antiseptics. She seated herself at her cluttered desk, and finding the x-rays, Aerielle snapped them into the display screen behind her and switched on the light. It was just as Aerielle had suspected, and she shook her head. Eric Lopez would need surgery within the week.

There was a knock on Aerielle's door, and then Heather stepped in bearing a short stack of papers. With the pile set before her, Aerielle began to sign. Heather stood beside the desk in silence as Aerielle made short work of the job at hand.

"Here you go," Aerielle said, shuffling the stack back together.

Accepting the papers, Heather paused, her expression somber. “I’m sorry about Michael Todd. You doing okay?”

“Yeah, sure.”

But as Heather departed, Aerielle felt anything but sure. Ten-year-old Michael Todd, most recently a patient of four weeks, had died that morning. And though Aerielle told herself, this was life on the cancer ward at the Children’s Medical Center, she never got used to losing one of her patients...one of her children.

Frustrated, Aerielle turned to the x-rays and pulled them free of the display. Sliding them back into the envelope, she tossed it onto the desk, where it knocked over a five-by-seven frame resting there.

Aerielle reached out, carefully picking up the frame and returning it to its original position. Her eyes took in the photograph that was enclosed in the wooden frame. Her thoughts went back to the day it was taken and beyond, back to the day she met Phoenix Stargazer. She smiled as she remembered the very first thought she’d had when she’d seen him. What a hunk. Not only had she admired his physique, but he had had an incredibly bold face, with glorious cheekbones and a perfectly straight nose. He also had a skin tone that made tanning unnecessary. His resentment in her coming, however, had been equal to his attraction, and Aerielle had found herself respecting the wall he’d put up. This feeling had been intensified when she’d seen his room, her room for six months.

→→→

It was unlike what she’d normally have expected from someone her own age, she decided. Seated on the bed where she’d taken a moment to relax, Aerielle glanced around Phoenix’s room. She would have predicted posters on the walls, but there were none, and the room was meticulously neat. After meeting

Phoenix, Aerielle doubted either of these conditions was out of the ordinary. And as for what did line the walls, Aerielle was impressed with the array of ancestral pieces, including a floor length headdress, a shield, and a bow that appeared to be made of bone.

Obviously proud of his heritage and possibly resentful of non-Indians, Aerielle suspected Phoenix would be a challenge to get along with. Apparently it mattered not whether one lived on the reservation or off for a person to be resentful of the "white man," for the ranch was located in Shaman Prairie, population 1,892, its acreage spread across the eastern reservation line, occupying both Indian and non-Indian land. As for the rest of Phoenix's family, they were welcoming, and nine-year-old Sparrow had eyed Aerielle with a look of awe on her face.

Suddenly, there was a knock on the bedroom door and Aerielle called, "Come in."

The door opened slowly, revealing Phoenix, his thoughts well hidden by a sober expression, his muscles unsuccessfully concealed by a black T-shirt. Aerielle was surprised to see him.

"I left a book I needed," he explained.

Aerielle wondered what Phoenix was reading a month after high school graduation. She'd traded her calculus book in for historical romance.

"Help yourself," she said, nodding casually. "After all, it's your room."

"It's behind you," said Phoenix reluctantly, pointing toward the headboard. Aerielle turned to see the book lying where he'd directed, the old bow hanging on the wall above it. Reaching out, Aerielle grasped the book, unable to resist looking at the cover before handing it off to Phoenix. The book was on astronomy, which Aerielle found interesting, but the name written below on the white label at the bottom of the cover, surprised her. "Phoenix Weston?" she said handing him the book. "I thought your last name was Stargazer."

She knew immediately it was the wrong thing to say, as his dark eyes narrowed and a muscle on one side of his jaw began to pulse. "It is, now that Nevin has adopted us. But my birth father was white." Phoenix spat the word out as if it disgusted him. "He left my mother when I was eight and Hawk was five. Our parents became one of the few one-in-twenty divorces that Idaho lays claim to."

"I'm sorry. That was thoughtless." Reaching for anything to say to make up for her blunder, Aerielle brought up the first alternate subject that came to mind. "That bow," she began, pointing back at the wall behind them. It looks old."

She thought he was going to leave without another word, but he seemed to collect his anger and, taking a deep breath, he answered her. "It is. More than a century as a matter of fact."

"Wow." Aerielle glanced at the bow with even more respect. "What's it made of?"

"Sheep horn."

"And the headdress? Is it made with real eagle feathers?"

"Yes. It, too, is very old. It would take a long time to get enough feathers to make one since collecting eagle feathers is illegal."

They were illegal, his words said unspoken, because the white man had hunted the bald eagle nearly to extinction. "Where do you get them, now?" Aerielle asked anyway, her curiosity speaking for her.

"The U.S. Fish and Wildlife Service collects dead eagles that are found, and we obtain the feathers legally from them."

Aerielle nodded, absorbing the information. "And what about that, um, 'satchel,' hanging beside the door? Is that like a medicine bundle or something?"

Phoenix studied her intently. "You're not from here, are you?"

"Minnesota. Minneapolis actually. My family moved out here a year ago."

Aerielle saw Phoenix pause before the next question, as if his curiosity was arguing with him. "How do you know ASL?" he finally asked, using the abbreviation for American Sign Language.

"My father's deaf. I was raised using it. Kinda bilingual, if you know what I mean. Your sister Sparrow gives the impression she's eager to learn." Aerielle wasn't sure she could say the same for the girl's brother.

This time Phoenix nodded, and then he turned and strode to the door. He paused on the threshold, glancing at the "satchel," a leather pouch with a rawhide string before glancing back at her. "It was for the wyakin, what you would call a guardian spirit. After a quest for a personal wyakin resulted in its revelation, the Nez Perce would then place a talisman of his wyakin in the bundle and carry it with him. Since the wyakins were usually animals, the bundle might include

> such things as a feather or a tuft of fur. One's wyakin was never revealed to another, though its power might have been."
>
> "Power?" questioned Aerielle.
>
> "One might receive protection against bullets, or the ability to know when one's death might come."
>
> "Do you have a wyakin?"
>
> Phoenix stiffened and Aerielle realized she'd said the wrong thing—again. But he did answer—in a way. "My people no longer make a practice of seeking a guardian."
>
> Maybe they should, thought Aerielle as Phoenix departed in silence. Maybe she would tell Phoenix about her guardian—her God—and her faith in Him.

→→→

Aerielle pulled her thoughts back to the present. It was hard to believe that fourteen years had passed, and Phoenix was now thirty-two like herself. They had been so young. Briefly, she wondered where he was now, what he was doing with his life, and if he had left his anger behind. She had certainly fought to leave hers.

Brushing away the memories, Aerielle opened a desk drawer and pulled out her lunch, which consisted of a peanut butter and jelly sandwich, an orange, a thermos of milk, and a book to read. Aerielle glanced at the title of the book she'd grabbed that morning. *Love's Sudden Splendor.* She smiled ruefully and shook her head. She had about five minutes to read, and that's about all the time she'd had for romance over the years. Shrugging, she picked up the book. As long as she didn't have a romance going, she might as well read about someone who did. The only problem with the book was that it was historical, and Aerielle was living in the present. She could no more conjure herself up a romantic cavalry lieutenant than she could bring Michael Todd back to life.

Fresh anguish washed over Aerielle, and she felt exhaustion take hold of her heart. Forget the hospital, her lunch, and the book at hand. She'd give anything to be at her apartment right now. At least tomorrow was Sunday. A day off would do her good. Maybe she'd go out and sit by the lake—Lake Nokomis.

I sat down in a fat and beautiful country. I had won my freedom and the freedom of my people. There were many empty places in the lodges and the council, but we were in a land where we could not be forced to live in a place we did not want.

Chief Joseph, thinking himself safe, just before the last battle at Little Bear Paws less than fifty miles from the Canadian border--as quoted in *Chief Joseph of the Nez Perce* by Robert Penn Warren.

2

Mildred was fine, just as Phoenix had suspected. He patted the cow congenially on the rump as he turned towards the door of the otherwise empty barn. Now that Phoenix was through with his exam, Mr. Danvers would probably put Mildred out to pasture for the day.

And what a perfect day for it too, Phoenix decided as he stepped out into the sunlit autumn morning. A light breeze swirled a multitude of leaves about the dirt driveway, and the air tasted crisp. Phoenix paused, letting his gaze travel the acres of Mr. Danvers' property now bare of their summer harvest of hay. Phoenix felt a rush of longing for a place such as this, with an existence as bare of other people as possible, surrounded by nature at its best, and plenty of animals. Phoenix's biggest struggle with being a vet was dealing with some of the animals' owners.

In the case of Mr. Danvers, this was never a problem. But there were other occasions when the nonjudgmental temperaments of his patients did not extend to those to whom they belonged. In spite of this, and despite the scars of prejudice Phoenix bore, both emotional and physical, there remained a deep yearning for a world where he fit one hundred percent. There was no doubt he was more Nez Perce than "white" if for no other reason than his tribe was more accepting of mixed blood. Even so, there were times when he felt tainted.

Feeling movement against his leg, Phoenix glanced down and discovered a large black cat rubbing its head against his jeans. Phoenix grinned, and setting his medical bag on the ground, he scooped the purring fur ball into his arms.

"Hey, Jack," murmured Phoenix into one scarred ear. "How you doing, bud? Staying out of trouble?"

Jack responded with a friendly bat of his paw as Phoenix gently probed the cat's body for recent battle wounds.

"Let me see that," said Phoenix, catching the large playful paw in his hand. Examining the calloused pads, he noticed two fresh cuts. "What'd you get yourself into? Why don't you let me take care of this?"

Jack purred as if giving his approval, and Phoenix grabbed his bag and went to sit on an old barrel resting near the barn. Jack stretched out on Phoenix's lap as if preparing for a nap, his head lolling back over the edge of Phoenix's thigh.

"Some tough guy you are," remarked Phoenix, pausing a moment to rub the big cat's stomach. "If my Sheba or Cleopatra could see you now, they'd be offended by your lack of decorum. Esmeralda, now, she'd probably understand, having been raised in similar surroundings."

Phoenix continued to ramble on as he proceeded to disinfect Jack's wounds. The cat remained unaffected by the procedure, more interested in the undivided attention he was getting. Phoenix enjoyed the trust Jack continued to put in him since the day they'd met almost three years ago when Phoenix had started coming to Mr. Danvers'. Though the cat didn't belong to the old man, he was often at the farm. Sometimes Phoenix suspected the cat knew his schedule and came to visit intentionally. Phoenix enjoyed their time together.

Though it was God who gave Phoenix's life meaning, it was moments like these that gave it joy. They helped fill the void left by Aerielle Buchanan's absence in his life, gave him a goal other than "surviving without her."

Reluctantly, Phoenix set Jack back on the ground. He often

wished he could take the cat home, but even if he were free to do so, Jack would fit into Phoenix's world about as well as Phoenix did at times.

Getting to his feet, Phoenix watched as Jack ambled off towards the back of the barn, the cat's mind on what to explore next. Briefly, Phoenix's thoughts went with him, but the honking of geese overhead drew his attention back. He stood a moment, watching the large flock of Canada geese fade into the blue horizon.

Turning away from the barn, Phoenix placed his medical bag into his black, four-door pickup. He then strolled past his two German shepherds resting comfortably in the dirt and on toward the white farm house. Availing himself of the wide front porch, old Mr. Danvers sat rocking in a wooden chair as old as himself. A pitcher of icy lemonade and two glasses sat beside him on a small table—it looked like a scene from a TV commercial.

"How's Mildred doing, Doc?" questioned Mr. Danvers, never ceasing in his perfect rhythm with the chair.

Phoenix mounted the wooden steps, a smile forming on his lips. "Healthy as can be."

Mr. Danvers' old withered face crinkled into a smile. "That's my Mildred. How 'bout you wash them there paws a yers off, and then sit with me fer a spell. Got fresh lemonade. Squeezed the lemons meself just this mornin'."

"Sure thing," agreed Phoenix, stepping in through the screen door.

Making his way to the kitchen counter, he set about cleaning off his "paws" in the old porcelain sink, just as he did every two weeks. Mr. Danvers loved to chat, and Phoenix looked forward to their visits. If it were up to him, he wouldn't even charge Mr. Danvers for looking after his cow, but the old man wouldn't hear of it. He paid Phoenix every two weeks whether Phoenix liked it or not, right out of the ceramic cookie jar that sat at the end of the spotless counter. The cookie jar itself was shaped like a cow, and Phoenix thought it fitting.

Rejoining Mr. Danvers on the porch, Phoenix settled into a chair on the other side of the small table. Reaching out, Mr. Danvers poured him a fresh glass of what Phoenix had come to decide was the best lemonade he'd ever tasted.

"How's that there truck a yers runnin'?" questioned the old man.

"About as well as Mildred I'd say."

"That's good to hear. That old heap of mine's been spittin' and sputterin' somethin' fierce just recently. Old man Grady's son down the road said he'd be takin' a look at it fer me come this weekend."

"Will you be needing transportation before then?" asked Phoenix, taking a deep swallow from his glass.

"No, no," assured Mr. Danvers, shaking his head. "Me and Mildred ain't be needin' nothin' right now."

The late morning breeze whispered across the porch, stirring the cow-shaped wind chimes that hung nearby. They tinkled joyously.

"Ain't it just a beautiful time a year?" remarked Mr. Danvers, continuing his steady rocking.

Phoenix only nodded in agreement as he took another sip of refreshment.

"Course it can be a lonely time a year, too," added Mr. Danvers. "My Mildred—my wife Mildred—she just loved the fall, the smell of the air, the cool days, bakin' lots a pumpkin pies.... You'd think after fifteen years I'd be used to havin' her gone, but it just ain't so. Ya know she was only seventy when her heart gave out. We'd been married fer more than fifty years."

"She must have been some woman," said Phoenix softly, as he thought of his own lonely autumns.

"Oh, she was, son. She was. A good wife can sure make the years fly. So how come you ain't hitched yet, Doc? You ain't even had yerself a girlfriend in the three years you been comin' out here."

Phoenix was not given a chance to reply even had he been prepared to, for Mr. Danvers continued. "I know yer Indian an all, er, Native American, but not all women mind any more than I do. We are on the last decade of the twentieth century."

Phoenix finished off his lemonade without responding. Equally silent, Mr. Danvers lifted up the pitcher and refilled Phoenix's empty glass.

Picking up the motion of his rocker again, the old man nodded knowingly. "So who was she, this one who obviously stole yer heart and ruined you fer every other woman out there?"

Phoenix eyed Mr. Danvers, not surprised by the wise old man's question. "Her name was Aerielle."

"Ah, and was she as perty as her name sounds?"

Phoenix paused, visualizing the woman he'd dreamed about only last night. "More so.... Her eyes were the color of the sky and her hair like sunlight."

Mr. Danvers sipped from his glass. "And where is she now?"

"I haven't a clue."

"No chance a yer meetin' up again?"

Phoenix shook his head. "Not outside of a miracle."

"Well, you hang in there, Doc. You never know what the Almighty has in store."

"Of that I'm well aware."

"Oh, I suppose I should pay ya before I up and ferget."

Phoenix didn't respond as Mr. Danvers entered the house to retrieve his payment from the ceramic cow. By the time the old man returned, Phoenix had finished off his second round of lemonade, depositing the empty glass on the table.

"Here you go, Doc," said Mr. Danvers, shoving a ten into Phoenix's hand as the latter stood up. "And take some eggs, too," he added, handing over a small basket with at least a dozen.

"Mr. Danvers, this isn't necessary—"

"Now don't argue with me, son. I know darn well you ain't charging me enough fer Mildred's checkups. The least you can do is take these here eggs as extra payment. Them hens been layin' up a storm this week, anyway."

"Thank you," said Phoenix, giving up the useless argument.

"Now go on. Get with ya. I'm sure you got other patients to see. Can't spend the whole day jawin' with an eighty-five year old man."

Oh, but he could, thought Phoenix, making his way to the pickup. He'd enjoy it too, spending an entire day talking with Mr. Danvers. The old man and his knowledge were priceless. One thing Phoenix had learned growing up in the tribe was to revere the old ones and their experience.

"See you later," Phoenix called back as he and the dogs jumped into the truck.

The old man simply nodded.

→→→

The sun was setting, leaving the mid-September day in crimson. Aerielle soaked in the view as she walked her Australian shepherd, Idaho, around the lake. Often they had to side step off the paved path to make way for bikers or joggers.

Tilting her head back, Aerielle inhaled deeply. Oh, how she had missed the changing seasons after having lived in Texas for so long. She felt like raking a pile of leaves together and jumping into them. Idaho apparently had the same idea, for suddenly he made a lunge for a pile swirled into a colorful leaf pool around an old oak tree. Due to Aerielle's inattention, the determined dog managed to pull the leash from her relaxed grip. She ran after him, catching up as he circled the tree as if attempting to roundup the leaves. Said leaves flew in all directions as Aerielle stomped into the pile and onto the end of the leash. She started to laugh, and Idaho nipped at her heels.

"Cut that out," she demanded with a grin, as she sidestepped the herding dog. "Do I look like a sheep to you?"

Idaho danced along beside her, looking all the while as if he was grinning.

"I think you like Autumn just as much as I do." Reaching down, Aerielle rubbed the dog's ears. He looked up at her with knowing eyes. One of the most intelligent breeds there was, Aerielle had trained him as a therapy dog, which enabled him to accompany her to the hospital fairly often.

He'd been *her* therapy dog first, for he had helped fill a terrible rift in her heart. Now, he was her best friend, especially since moving to MN. She'd had to start making friends all over again, but there was little time for that. Loneliness, unfortunately, was her second best friend.

Idaho yipped at her and plunged through the leaves, insisting she let go of such thoughts and join him for the remainder of the walk not yet taken.

They continued on the path around the lake, while the sun sank lower. Eventually they reached another open stretch of grass and trees. People lingered alone and in groups, talking, reading, and—

Abruptly Idaho was off again. For a moment Aerielle couldn't believe it, for this time he'd left his leash behind, clenched firmly in her hand. Aerielle started after him breaking into a run. She never saw the person making a mad dash for a Frisbee. She certainly felt the impact, though, when the two of them collided. Both were knocked to the ground, which was not quite as soft as it appeared.

Aerielle started laughing, despite the small bruise she'd just incurred on the side of her head. She pushed herself up into a sitting position, brushing at her clothes. "My mother used to say I should find new ways to meet people."

Warm masculine laughter followed her statement, and then immediately it stopped.

Aerielle glanced up to see what had happened. The guy she

had run into sat just a few feet away, staring at her. Their gazes locked, and for a moment, the world went silent.

"Hawk?"

"Aerielle."

They spoke in unison, Aerielle's use of his name as a question, Hawk's a statement of disbelief, both signing the other's name as if they'd last spoken yesterday.

And then the silence again.

Aerielle rubbed at her head where it stung from the recent head-on collision.

Hawk must have taken it as a sign of disbelief, for his response was not one of concern, but of amazement.

"What are you *doing* here? I mean...in MN, not, not right here."

The dog! That's what she was doing here! Aerielle jerked her head about, and then sighed in relief to see Idaho on his way back to her. He had a Frisbee in his mouth, and his expression said he did not regret abandoning her. Aerielle, however, regretted moving her head so, and rubbed at it again.

Hawk saw the move for what it was this time and slid across the grass, closing the few feet separating them.

"Are you hurt? Let me see." And as if he'd just wiped out the last fourteen years, Hawk reached for her head, and with surprising intimacy, brushed her hair away from her injury. "You're bleeding. What'd you hit your head on, anyway?"

"Besides you?"

"Funny," he grinned, dabbing away the blood with his thumb before wiping it off on his grass stained jeans.

Idaho arrived then, thrusting his head between them and dropping the Frisbee proudly into Aerielle's lap.

Idaho wasn't alone, having been followed by one of the other Frisbee players, come to retrieve the disc Hawk had been attempting to catch. Without a word, Hawk picked up the Frisbee and held it up for his friend.

"Hawk, don't you know running a girl over isn't the best form of introduction?"

"Or reintroduction," mumbled Hawk, still looking at Aerielle's injury as his friend walked off. "At least you won't need stitches."

"Is that a professional opinion?"

Hawk grunted, dropping his hand as Idaho used his tongue to clean the injury. "Well, sort of, I am a vet. Of course, after that "licking" you just took, you might need some disinfectant."

As if knowing he was being referred to, the dog turned to gaze at Hawk, appearing to decide whether he needed a tongue washing, too.

Hawk patted him. "Nice catch there."

"A vet," repeated Aerielle with surprise. "I knew...I knew Phoenix was interested," she said forcing the name between her lips, "but I had no idea you were. Congratulations."

"What about you? You were headed off to nursing school when you left Idaho. Did nursing turn out to be the right fit?"

"No, actually, it didn't."

Hawk's hand stilled on the dog. "Oh. I'm sorry."

"Don't be. I became a doctor instead."

Hawk looked at her with admiration, and Aerielle suddenly found his gaze slowly taking in the whole of her. Aerielle discovered she was doing the same. Hawk Stargazer no longer appeared the younger brother. He had grown up, filled out, and the hair that used to be longer than hers was now cut short in a very contemporary and somewhat rakish style.

"You've changed," she said, before she realized how stupid she sounded.

He didn't seem to notice. "Is that good or bad?"

"Neither. Just an observation."

"Well, you *haven't* changed."

Aerielle smiled. "Is that good or bad?" she parroted.

"Neither. You were always stunning."

Aerielle's eyes widened at the unexpected compliment.

"Hey, I was fifteen, not blind. I'm not blind now, either."

Aerielle felt herself blushing, something she rarely did. Distractedly, she reached out to pet the dog and her hand ran into Hawk's.

As if sensing her discomfort, Hawk raised his hands and signed his earlier question. "What are you doing in MN?"

"I did grow up here you know," replied Aerielle aloud, as Idaho plopped down beside her.

"Yes, but the last I heard, you were living in Houston."

"Sparrow told you?"

"Well, no. Actually I overheard her talking to our parents. Despite the letters you two wrote, she never spoke of you."

Picking up the open collar, Aerielle replaced it where it belonged, around Idaho's neck, firmly snapping the latch before speaking. "That was one of the conditions related to our letter writing."

"*One* condition? Let me guess, the other condition was not to tell you about the evil oldest brother, I must have been part of the first condition at the very least, but I suspect the second as well."

Aerielle nodded, sadness filling her expression. "I didn't want Phoenix knowing anything about me, and I couldn't risk you telling him, intentionally or not. I thought it would be easier for Sparrow to make you both off limits no matter which direction the mail flowed. She was only nine, after all."

"I guess those conditions were why *you* didn't know *we* were here."

We? thought Aerielle. Did he say we?

But of course he had. And there was no question in Aerielle's mind as to whom Hawk was referring. Phoenix. Phoenix whom she'd loved. Phoenix who had broken her heart.

Trying not to show the melee of her thoughts, Aerielle replied evenly. "I assume by we you mean Phoenix?" She really didn't need to ask.

Hawk nodded. "We've been here four years now."

"Have the Brothers Stargazer opened up a Vet Clinic?" guessed Aerielle.

"Right on the mark. That's been the biggest change in our lives. What about you?" continued Hawk, glancing at Aerielle's left hand resting on the dog's back. "Any other changes in your life?"

Aerielle followed the direction of his gaze. "No weddings or divorces."

"Speaking of weddings, you must know Sparrow got married last year."

Aerielle smiled, momentarily forgetting Phoenix. "She sent me pictures. It's been special writing to her. I feel like I got to hear her grow up through the words she writes but no longer hears."

"She certainly has grown up."

"So what's this fellow's name?" asked Hawk changing the subject and nodding toward the Aussie.

"His name's Idaho."

"Idaho?"

Aerielle shrugged. "Idaho changed my life, and so has he."

"Have you ever been back? I know you and your mom left Idaho just after your dad died the spring following your time at our place."

A wave of loss washed over Aerielle. "Only once. My mom moved around with us—Idaho and me—until she died in a car accident five years ago. I was in Crystal Springs just for a day so see her ashes buried next to my dad. I didn't even write Sparrow that I was coming. I knew she'd want to see me, and well...."

"I'm sorry," said Hawk. "Come on," he urged, "let's walk and you can tell me more."

Reaching for Aerielle's hands, he stood up, pulling her with him, and Aerielle suddenly found herself looking up at him in surprise.

"Yeah," said Hawk, reading her mind. "I've got two inches on Phoenix, now. I told you I wasn't fifteen anymore."

→→→

Yawning, Aerielle brushed out her thick long hair as Idaho watched her sleepily from his perch on her bed. He looked happy and serene, kind of like Aerielle was feeling. She'd hated to see Hawk go. They'd walked and talked a long time, and it was well past dark when he escorted her home to her Victorian turned apartment building. She and Idaho rented the second floor, but she had said goodbye to Hawk outside…reluctantly. She couldn't remember the last time she'd had such a long conversation with anyone, let alone not having the hospital stealing a majority of the conversation. As much as Aerielle loved what she did, she also loved her time away.

After Aerielle had shared more about the death of her mother, Hawk had steered the conversation to calm, safe waters. No shop talk, no Phoenix. He was gallant, easy to talk to, and oh, so easy on the eyes. Fifteen he was not. Closer to thirty. It was hard to believe Hawk had almost doubled in age since she had seen him last. Tonight, for the first time in a long time, Aerielle had loosed hands with loneliness.

And she wouldn't be lonely on Friday, either, thought Aerielle grinning as she set her hairbrush down. Hawk had asked her out to dinner. He hadn't exactly declared it a date, but if the look in his eyes was any indication…. Aerielle knew she should be considering the wisdom of accepting Hawk's invitation. After all, there had been Phoenix. But what of Phoenix? He'd abandoned her and the love they'd shared fourteen years ago. Fourteen years. A lifetime.

→→→

The grandfather clock out in the foyer was striking nine when Phoenix left his shepherds in the yard and stepped through the back door to the kitchen. When the clock ceased its chimes the house was still and silent, Phoenix briefly wondered where his brother was off to this evening. But then as always, Hawk was often off to something or someone.

Making his way up the creaking stairs to his room, Phoenix yanked off his T-shirt. So that neither his hair nor his clothes got in the way of his job, he almost always wore short sleeves and a braid to work in. And he had certainly worked today. Hours later than normal. He'd run into two separate emergencies, which had exhausted his time and his body. Peeling off the rest of his clothes, Phoenix showered and dressed in clean jeans and a hooded, long sleeved sweat shirt, the whole while trying not to think about anything.

Returning to the first floor, his damp hair now hanging loosely down his back, Phoenix started up the coffee maker. He stood at the counter, his coffee mug in place of the pot, waiting for that first reviving cup of hot liquid to come.

Phoenix had just replaced his full mug with the empty coffee pot when he heard the front door of the house open and close. Sipping at his coffee, he waited for his brother to make an appearance in the kitchen.

"Thought I smelled coffee," remarked Hawk, entering the room with a contented smile on his face. Phoenix wondered what her name was, but then as Hawk drew closer, Phoenix realized his brother smelled like the outdoors. "You play Frisbee tonight?

Hawk ignored his question. "Must have been a long day," he said instead, reaching into a cupboard for a mug. "You weren't home when I left at five."

"Just got back." Phoenix went on to explain his emergencies, and Hawk nodded in sympathy.

"Things have been pretty hectic lately. We really should consider getting some help, Phoenix."

Phoenix ignored his brother's comment. Hiring another vet or a technician was a sore spot for discussion.

Hawk noted the silence and sipped at his cup of coffee while avoiding Phoenix's gaze. "I started the evening playing Frisbee, but I spent the rest of it catching up."

"Catching up?" repeated Phoenix. "Catching up on what?

"More like with whom."

When Hawk didn't finish, Phoenix demanded impatiently. "All right, I'll play. Catch up with wh—"

"Aerielle," blurted Hawk, his gaze abruptly meeting that of his brother's.

Stunned, Phoenix felt as if all the air had left the room. Hawk couldn't have said her name, but he had. Phoenix set his coffee down as calmly as he could, making every effort to hide the effect the news was having.

All at once a thousand questions began to flood his thoughts. Where did Aerielle live? Had she become a nurse? Was she married? Have a couple of kids? These last thoughts only aggravated the renewed pain Phoenix had known upon waking that morning, and he fought against acknowledging them.

"Aerielle. Here," he said at last, her name whispered in near reverence. The syllables felt loved and familiar on his tongue, and he could almost smell the scent of hyacinths, feel the touch of her hand within his as he stared into those blue eyes.... But, oh, God, it had been fourteen years.

"She lives on the other side of the lake in that blue Victorian we drive by," continued Hawk, exchanging his coffee for a banana on the counter. "She's, get this, not a nurse, but a doctor. A pediatric oncologist. Pretty awesome, huh?"

Phoenix allowed himself a smile. His Aerielle. A doctor. Why wasn't he surprised?

Hawk bit into the banana, mumbling out of the side of his mouth at the same time. "I'm having dinner with her Friday."

Phoenix's smile faded, and he was glad he'd already set down his coffee. Turning away from his brother, he opened the fridge as if he, too, was looking for something to eat. Of course, his real intention was to hide the anger that caused the telltale tick in his jaw.

So what if they had dinner. That's what old friends did, wasn't it?

"Got any problems with that?" inquired Hawk from behind him, continuing to talk and eat at the same time.

After fourteen years Phoenix wasn't about to tell his brother the truth, the whole truth and nothing but the truth. "Not at all."

Hawk seemed to accept his words as fact. "Good," he replied.

"She must not be married, or at least not now," remarked Phoenix, continuing to keep his voice as casual as if he were asking about Sofia.

"Never been. Sounds like med school had her attention. And she's only been back in Minnesota for six months."

Phoenix finally grabbed a hunk of cheese from the fridge and began searching for a knife.

"Hair still long?" he questioned.

"Yeah, about two thirds as long as yours."

Phoenix needed to change the subject, needed to be alone. He searched frantically for something else to say or do. "Oh, by the way, Sofia left you a note. It's stuck in the frame of that big mirror in the foyer. I think it has something to do with dinner at Leeann Chin's. You know. In exchange for breakfast."

"Thanks," said Hawk, throwing his banana peel in the garbage. Grabbing his coffee, he turned and left the kitchen.

Phoenix abruptly leaned back against the counter. Tossing the cheese aside, he buried his head in his hands. *God, what am I gonna do? Hawk's got a date with Aerielle.* My *Aerielle.* But she wasn't his anymore, at least that's what Phoenix told himself. Conversely, he knew in his heart of hearts she would always be his. Unfortunately, Hawk had no way of knowing the state of Phoenix's heart. As far as he was concerned, Phoenix and Aerielle's teen-age romance ended like so many others. And as for Aerielle, with his unannounced departure fourteen years ago, Phoenix had given her plenty of reason to believe that his feelings were immature and easily forgotten. Neither his brother nor Aerielle had any way of knowing the true state of Phoenix's heart and the scars it bore.

What had Phoenix said to Mr. Danvers about his chance of seeing Aerielle again? "Not outside of a miracle." Phoenix groaned, wishing he could rip out what remained of his heart. *He* hadn't actually seen her yet. Hawk had. What kind of twisted miracle was this?

Their honesty is immaculate and their purity of purpose and their observance of the rules of their religion are most uniform and remarkable. They are certainly more like a nation of saints than a horde of savages.

Jean Baptiste Le Moyne De Bienville as quoted in *Chief Joseph of the Nez Perce*
by Robert Penn Warren.

3

Standing in the storage closet filled with medical supplies, Phoenix counted the store of syringes for the third time. He couldn't seem to keep his mind on things this morning. Knowing his brother was taking Aerielle to dinner tonight was having a terrible effect on his concentration. It would be different when office hours began and patients started arriving, but checking inventory wasn't the most mind absorbing project in the world.

Logging the correct number of needed syringes away in his head, Phoenix began counting the boxes of gloves, wondering at the same time where his brother was taking Aerielle.

"You could always ask," Phoenix mumbled sarcastically, his frustration rising. But it didn't matter where, it mattered why. Giving Aerielle up himself was one thing. Allowing Hawk to take her out was another. But what was he to do? Tell Hawk that the girl Phoenix dumped fourteen years ago was off limits? That'd go over about as well as two stallions in a herd of broodmares.

"Leave it," muttered Phoenix, using the same command he used on his dogs to tell them something was off limits. Now if he could only convince *himself* that Aerielle was off limits.

By the time he entered the reception area ten minutes later, Phoenix had decided he was getting out of the house that night. His determination must have shown, for Sofia eyed him closely as he came to stand beside her desk.

"What's up?" she questioned.

"Inventory's kinda low," he replied, knowing that wasn't what she meant. "We're gonna have to put in a special order."

"No problem," said Sofia, reaching for a pad of paper and a pen. "I'll check it out."

"I already checked the totals," offered Phoenix, reaching for the newspaper sitting unread on the desk. "Probably need a half order. By the way, how's your grandmother doing?"

"About the same, I guess.... So what do we need?"

"Syringes and gloves.... She been to a doctor yet?"

Sofia shook her head, the pen moving across the paper. "She refuses to go. She refuses to do anything I or anybody else tells her, like slow down, relax, you don't have to make homemade pasta every day of the week."

"Suture and antiseptic swabs," continued Phoenix glancing through the ads. "If you think some time off would help...."

"Thanks, but I'm afraid that would only make things worse. Grandma would make me into a project, too."

Angry, Phoenix closed the newspaper and folded it with much crumpling.

Just then, Hawk entered the room. "Morning, guys. Did I *hear* the paper in here?"

Gripping it tightly, Phoenix shifted positions and handed it over without comment.

"Wanted to see how our ad looks," continued Hawk, rifling through the pages until he found it.

"May I remind you that it's *your* ad, placed without *my* permission?!" snapped Phoenix. "May I also remind you we can't handle any more clients right now?"

"And may I remind you, Phoenix, our business is such that we'll have to hire someone whether we gain more clientele or not. So the sooner you quit being pig-headed about the whole thing the better."

Frustrated, Phoenix knew darn well their schedules were getting out of hand with many evening hours added on to already full days. He knew they needed to hire a vet technician.

He also knew that person was Sofia, but she wouldn't be done with her schooling for a while longer. However, Hawk was not aware that she was taking any classes. Sofia's accomplishment was being saved as a surprise.

"There's plenty of work, but nothing we can't handle," soothed Sofia, her calm voice filling the angry silence.

Hawk's only response was to refold the paper just as noisily as Phoenix, and stride from the room.

Sofia leaned her elbows on the desk, casually tapping her pen on the pad of paper. "Maybe we should tell him, Phoenix."

Phoenix shook his head "Let's wait a little longer, okay? Maybe things will blow over."

It was obvious Sofia didn't believe his words any more than he did as she leaned back in her chair with a skeptical air. Phoenix decided it was time for a change of subject. "So Sofia, what are you doing tonight?"

"Tonight? Nothing. Need some help here?"

"Actually, I was wondering if you'd like to have dinner tonight."

Sofia stared at him as if he'd grown two heads; she didn't answer right away, as if evaluating the question.

"I'd say 'surely you jest,' but you don't make jokes. So, does this have anything to do with what Hawk told me, about going out with one of your old girlfriends?"

Make that his *last* girlfriend, thought Phoenix. "Maybe. Probably. Forget I asked."

"Oh, no," said Sofia getting to her feet. "You can't take the invite back. I accept. As long as you know that maybe, probably, it's because your former girlfriend is going out with Hawk."

Phoenix refrained from responding for but a moment. "Sounds fair."

"So where are we going?" asked Sofia.

"Like I would know. You pick, I'll pay."

"Oooh, I like the sound of that," she replied, walking around the desk. "You know the new mall's open. I've heard it has some great restaurants."

"You're going to drag this country boy to The Mall of America?" Phoenix demanded.

"Oh, I'll pick some place calm and quiet. I know how you feel about crowds. I have learned *something* about you over the years. Maybe I'll even dress up," continued Sofia, her eyes thoughtful. "Heaven knows I've had little opportunity to do so in a while."

"Just keep in mind that my idea of dressing up is a pair of jeans with no holes in the knees, and a turtleneck."

Sofia's eyes lit with a smile. "Really, Phoenix, with your face? No one will be looking at your clothes. The guys will be jealous of your good looks, and the gals will be jealous of me. You've got a face fit for a modeling career. Hasn't anyone ever told you how beautiful you are—in a very masculine way of course."

Phoenix couldn't believe what he was hearing. Never in his life would he have expected a woman to call his face beautiful. Except Aerielle that is. And he had thought her opinion colored by her feelings for him.

Dumbfounded, Phoenix just stared back as Sofia.

"I'm sorry. Did I embarrass you?"

"'Stunned' would be a better word."

"I feel honored, then. I haven't seen you stunned in the three years I've known you."

→→→

Aerielle was just returning to her office at the hospital after being reprimanded by her superior for racing Lisa down the hallway in wheelchairs. It had seemed like a good idea at the time. Lisa had laughed and lit up with joy. It would be a while before she received her prosthesis, and Aerielle wanted her to learn that a wheelchair could be fun, not just restrictive.

Just as Aerielle sat down, her door opened and Heather Finch stepped in. "Aerielle," the red head began, dropping the "doctor" in private as Aerielle had requested. "I'm afraid Timothy Wallace was re-admitted this morning...."

Her voice trailed off as Aerielle winced. Timothy Wallace had leukemia, and at this stage, if the three-year-old had been re-admitted, it wasn't likely he'd be going home again.

"His mother's going to be here a while this morning," continued Heather. "She asked to speak with you."

"Of course," agreed Aerielle, feeling the muscles in her shoulders tightening up.

"I know it's hard, but you need to try not to get too attached, Doc. You'll burn out. Then you won't be any good to anybody."

"Shut the door, Heather," said Aerielle, rubbing her temples, "and then tell me how you do it. How do you stay detached? How do you not feel like each one of these children is your own?"

Letting the door close behind her, Heather walked to the front of Aerielle's desk and sat down in one of two comfortable brown leather chairs. "It's not easy."

"I went to school for twelve years, Heather. My whole world has been medicine. I've lived and breathed little else."

"And you're still living and breathing little else," put in Heather. "That's the problem. You've heard the expression, 'get a life.' You have to have something else besides this hospital, Aerielle. You need to fill your spare time with friends, hobbies, a man."

"A man?" questioned Aerielle, a smile touching her lips. "You have someone in mind?"

"My brother's available," replied Heather, her blue eyes twinkling.

"Oh, yeah? And how old's your brother?"

"Nineteen. But he likes older women."

Aerielle grinned. "As it so happens, I am having dinner with someone tonight."

"What's this?" demanded Heather, leaning forward. "Aerielle Buchanan has a date? Must be a lucky guy."

"I don't know that it's really a date," began Aerielle, and then her expression sobered. "It isn't important. With Timothy here—"

"That's exactly why it is important. Listen to yourself, Aerielle. You're making the hospital your life. You can't. Everything that can be done for Timothy and any of the other patients is being done or has been done by you or somebody else.

"Go out, date or not. Do something outrageous. That shouldn't be difficult for you. Try flirting with the guy. Do anything that will make you forget about this place, or any other problems you may have. And then of course, you have to report back to me on how the evening went."

Aerielle nodded her head reluctantly. "I guess you're right. I'll give it my best shot. Right now, though, I'd better talk to Mrs. Wallace."

→→→

Sofia managed to stun Phoenix twice in one day. When Phoenix went to pick her up at the home she shared with grandmother, he barely recognized the Sofia who answered the door. She'd traded in her casual wear for a simple, yet stunning red dress with a wide black belt that accentuated her waist. She also wore sheer black nylons, red heels, and her mane of curls and been tamed into a stylish chignon.

Phoenix said nothing at first, just stared, and then remarked. "I'm sorry. I must have the wrong house. I was looking for the Bendetti residence."

Sofia rolled her eyes. "It's just a sweater dress."

"I don't think I've seen a sweater of any type look that good on anyone."

Sofia abruptly stepped outside, pulling the door closed behind her. Grabbing Phoenix's hand, she pulled him down the steps toward the sidewalk. "Come on, we have to leave, or Grandma's going to hall you inside for interrogation."

Surprised, Phoenix followed without saying a word. They

were almost to the truck when Sofia stumbled. "Dog gone it," she mumbled, clutching Phoenix's hand for dear life as he steadied her.

"You okay?"

"Yes, mortified, but okay. My heel got caught in the sidewalk crack. I'm out of practice wearing heels."

"Hope you're not drinking tonight."

Sofia glared at him, humor evident in her eyes. "You be nice, or instead of going to the quiet restaurant I promised you, I'll drag you through the amusement park at the mall and make you wait in a long crowded line to ride the Camp Snoopy rollercoaster."

→→→

Aerielle examined her image in the mirror over the bathroom sink, adding a touch of blush before applying Rogue Red lipstick to the curve of her mouth. Taking in the finished product of her appearance, she met the troubled blue eyes of her reflection. She'd gone casual, not wanting to put too much stock in the evening with Hawk. He was due in just a few minutes, and Aerielle continued to wonder if it was wise going out with Phoenix's brother. Her thoughts the last week had been filled with the past, bringing back painful memories she had thought were long ago left behind but for a few bruises. What would Phoenix think about Hawk taking her out? Did he care? Did he even know? Was this even a date?

"Shut up!" Aerielle scolded herself. "Please God, I don't know what I'm doing. Don't let me go alone."

That was the point, according to Heather Finch—not being alone—but of course she hadn't been referring to God. Aerielle took a deep breath and let it out slowly. She had to forget, or at least ignore, what had happened years ago, and concentrate on the evening at hand. After all, it would be Hawk at the door, no one else.

Just then Aerielle heard a soft yip from Idaho followed by

a knock. Aerielle glanced at her watch. Well, the young Hawk had grown up to be punctual. That was promising.

Before opening the door, Aerielle told Idaho to sit, which he promptly did, but his eyes were eagerly glued to the door. Taking another deep breath and glancing toward Heaven, Aerielle opened it.

She stared. Some guy from GQ had just shown up at the door. Hawk had somewhere acquired a bit of fashion knowledge. He looked dressed up even without a suit or tie, in some layered ensemble that included an array of autumn colors, including a stylish jacket, that said anything but sports coat. This was definitely a date.

"I think you've come to the wrong place," Aerielle announced, continuing to look him over. "Or at the very least I'm under dressed for the occasion," she added, looking down at her red sweater and jeans.

"You look fabulous to me," replied Hawk, checking her out. "And I am of the opinion that red is one of your best colors."

Aerielle realized then that he was admiring her lips and not her sweater.

There was a whine from beside her, and she was grateful for the distraction. She had forgotten Idaho was sitting there. "All right, boy. Go ahead and greet."

At the sound of the familiar command, Idaho "greeted" Hawk, sitting down in front of him and holding out a paw.

"Oh, that's good," said Hawk. Leaning down he shook Idaho's paw and then rubbed his head and ears.

Aerielle still felt she ought to put on something else, and maybe Hawk sensed it, for he said, "If you're wearing a coat, get it. If not, let's go. You are *not* changing."

Aerielle didn't argue.

→→→

Sofia kept her word, not about the rollercoaster, but the restaurant. After parking on level five of the east side parking ramp, they'd taken the elevator down to the first floor of the mall. The Napa Valley Grill was not far inside the entrance they chose, and was as quiet and uncrowded as an elegant restaurant should be. The waiter had shown them to a table for two, leaving them with both menus and a wine list.

Phoenix studied the menu and got hungrier just reading the descriptions. "Clearly, I've haven't been eating out enough."

Sofia looked up and smiled. "Well, if you two bachelors would fix something besides macaroni and cheese, and pizza...."

"What can I say? When I was growing up, I was too busy cleaning stalls, managing horses, and fixing fence line to learn how to cook."

"Well, then, what are you going to have with so many abundant choices?"

"Hmm. I don't think I can resist the walleye."

"Well, I'm having the rosemary chicken."

As if on cue, their waiter magically appeared and took their orders. "Would you like wine with your meal?"

Sofia responded in the affirmative, ordering a single glass of Pinot Noir.

"You sir?" the waiter inquired of Phoenix.

Phoenix looked helplessly at Sofia and shrugged. "The same?"

"Belay that," said Sofia. "He'll have a glass of Chardonnay."

After the waiter had departed, Sofia spoke. "I'm sorry, I couldn't let you drink Pinot Noir with fish."

"Clearly, I needed assistance. I didn't know we had a wine connoisseur working for us."

"Me?" laughed Sofia. "Hey, I'm Italian, we have wine with most of our meals. While you were out behaving more like a cowboy than an Indian, I was growing up learning what wine went with what foods, especially pasta and its various sauces."

"So tell me more about growing up Italian."

And Sofia did. They enjoyed a long conversation about

family life, siblings, and busybody grandmothers, their conversation changing briefly when their food arrived.

Phoenix would have described their plates as works of art; the food smelled delectable. Sofia's meal had one unique feature that left Phoenix perplexed. Sofia saw him looking at her plate and shook her head. The pearls dangling from her ears reflected a suffused light. "Don't ask. I have no idea why there's a pine tree sticking out of my mashed potatoes."

Phoenix laughed at her description, because it was a fairly accurate picture. It really did appear to be at least a part of a pine tree. "I wonder if it's edible."

"I don't know that, either," Sofia replied with a smile. Pulling it from its decorative stance, she offered it to him. "Care to try it?"

"Not me," he said, waving it away. "I wouldn't dare. I have no idea what wine goes with pine. Now, Hawk, he would probably know what that is, if it's edible, and what wine goes with it."

Phoenix could have kicked himself for bringing up his brother, but it was better than talking about Aerielle, or so he thought. The brief flash of anguish on Sofia countenance said otherwise.

"What is it?" he asked

"What's what?"

"Don't give me that. I saw the look in your eyes. What is it?"

"It's nothing. I'm not going to spoil our evening."

"If it's spoiled, then it's my fault. I'm the one who stupidly mentioned his name," added Phoenix, reaching across the table to cover Sofia's hand with his. "Now out with it."

She didn't meet his gaze, just stared at the miniature pine tree she twirled between the fingers of her other hand. "I guess I've often wondered if Hawk isn't interested in me because I lack class."

"What?!"

"I mean really, just tonight I've managed to trip over my

own feet via a sidewalk, I still live at home, even if it is just Grandma and me, and I don't know what plant is sticking out of my food. I bet he likes his dates to have more panache."

Leaning forward over the table, Phoenix pulled the "pine tree" from Sofia's hand, leaving it on her plate as he now took both of her hands in his. "Listen to me, Sofia. You are a fabulous person, a great co-worker, and a beautiful woman, and I mean from the inside on out. Your only problem is that you happen to be human like the rest of us. If my brother is truly looking for "perfection," and I'm not saying he is, he certainly doesn't deserve someone like you."

Sofia looked at him, searching his eyes. "You mean that, don't you?"

"Yes. I do. And if you ever need reminding, you come see me and I'll tell you again."

Sofia smiled. "You know, Phoenix, I think there's a lot more to you than meets the eye."

→→→

An hour later, Hawk and Aerielle were seated in the middle of the Rainforest Cafe, located on the first floor of the south end of the Mall of America. Their table sat next to an aquarium, one of many, including an arch of water with large fish swimming overhead as people entered into the eating area. Periodically, elephants trumpeted, monkeys chattered, and thunder clapped overhead while "rain" fell around the outer edges of the restaurant, sending up a mist. Overhead, tropical trees perfected the illusion of eating in a rainforest.

Taking the last hot wing off the Raging Thunder appetizer platter, Aerielle peeled the chicken off with her fingers and popped it into her mouth, enjoying every morsel.

Hawk shook his head with an amused grin, glancing at the empty plate. "Are you going to have room for dinner?" he teased. "I remember you always liked to eat, but I thought you might save some room for the main course."

At that very moment, a waiter was approaching their table with their food, carefully avoiding a near collision in the crowed aisle of the busy restaurant. Aerielle hungrily eyed her entree of Tribal Salmon, served on a cedar plank and topped with roasted hazelnut and Frangelico butter. Hawk's dinner, a Taste of the Islands, looked just as tantalizing with its coconut shrimp and blackened tilapia topped with a mango salsa and dynamite scallops and shrimp.

As the waiter departed, Aerielle finally responded to Hawk's remark, a guilty smile coming to her lips. "I must admit, eating is still one of my favorite pastimes."

"You wouldn't know it," replied Hawk, his gaze appraising.

Aerielle smiled as she noted Hawk's compliment, Heather's encouragement of harmless flirtation coming to mind. Forget it, she told her image of Heather before speaking to Hawk as she glanced at his plate. "Are you going to let me sample what *you're* having?

Hawk responded by preparing a forkful of tilapia with a piece of shrimp. "You ready?"

Aerielle stared. Was he actually going to feed it to her?!

Hawk motioned towards the table. "You're going to have to move your plate closer than that or I'll have it all over."

Aerielle breathed a silent of sigh of relief, and eagerly reached for her plate. She slid it over as Hawk deposited the luscious looking mouthful.

"Now all's fair in love and restaurants, you know," he said eyeing Aerielle's plate as she slid it back over. "Don't I get to sample the salmon?"

Aerielle smiled, quickly cutting a piece of the coveted item. Hawk held out his plate. With smooth precision, Aerielle proceeded to lift her fork but failed to clear the lip of her water glass. With a ping and then a plop, the salmon promptly fell in, settling to the bottom.

Both stared at their unexpected personal aquarium.

Hawk spoke first. "I hope you don't expect me to drink

that. Salmon is, after all, a salt water fish." Abruptly he began to laugh.

Aerielle burst into laughter as well, and for the first time that evening, she truly began to relax.

→→→

By the time Phoenix and Sofia left the restaurant, everything on the first three floors of the mall was closing up, and the huge corridors throughout were quickly emptying. Phoenix and Sofia had to stop at one of the many eight-foot pillars displaying all four levels of the mall, including an icon showing them where they were now, and the best way to get where they were going. The movie theaters were on the fourth floor, but the fourth floor was a partial, leaving most of the mall with three. As they reached the nearest escalator leading from the third to the fourth floor, Phoenix realized he had no idea what they were seeing.

"Did you say what movie we're going to?" He was feeling quite relaxed after the pleasant conversation and great food. He hoped the movie had some action, or he might do the unthinkable and dose off on his "date."

"No, actually, I forgot to mention it," said Sofia turning toward him as the escalator carried them upward. "We're going to Batman Returns which is probably a good thing. I'm so relaxed; I think I would fall asleep."

"That boring, am I?" teased Phoenix, despite his similar thoughts.

"I didn't mean it that way," said Sofia in defense as the escalator prepared to deliver them to an empty corridor. "You carry on quite the conversation when you wish to."

The escalator leveled off and they both stepped away at the same time, only for the second time that evening, Sofia's heel got caught. She cried out in fear, but Phoenix was already responding as he grabbed her upper arms and pulled her toward him, saving her from a dangerous fall backwards. Abruptly she was free, the momentum carrying her forward against him. Sofia gripped Phoenix in terror and then she began spewing angry words in Italian, her forehead resting against his chest.

Phoenix wasn't about to ask her to repeat herself. He just waited for the words and the fear to subside. It didn't take long, but it was long enough. Long enough for Phoenix to realize he was holding a flesh and blood woman in his arms. Her scent captivated his senses and silenced his tongue. A decades worth of loneliness and empty arms swept over him with such force, Phoenix's reaction was instinctive, and his comforting hold tightened into an embrace.

Sofia looked up, surprised, but before she could utter a word, Phoenix kissed her, long and hard, his mouth persuasive against hers. She did not resist. When Phoenix finally broke the kiss, Sofia said nothing. Hoping she wasn't upset over the liberty he had taken, he tried to think of something to say.

Sofia beat him at finding speech. "That, um, took me a little off guard. Now that I'm better prepared, would you, uh, mind doing it again?"

This time his kiss was met with equal fervor, and Sofia wrapped her arms around his neck, as if she feared she'd dreamt the first one. Phoenix made sure the second kiss was more memorable than the first.

When at last the kiss ended, they drew apart slowly, reluctantly. "We better be on our way," murmured Phoenix, "or we'll be late for the movie."

Sofia nodded, still dazed. "I'll need my shoe."

"What?!" Glancing down, Phoenix realized that one foot was bare. Glancing at the escalator, there rested the red shoe, amazingly enough sitting upright as if on display.

Phoenix retrieved the shoe and kneeling down slipped it on Sofia's foot.

"Should I call you Prince Charming?" she laughed as he stood.

"More like I should call you Cinderella. At least the 'slipper' wasn't glass."

→→→

Later, as Phoenix pulled up to the curb near the Bendetti home, Sofia turned to him, a wry smile on her face. "I better say goodbye here."

"The Gestapo still up?" inquired Phoenix.

"I fear so, or at the very least sitting in the front room pretending to be asleep. Thank you for the wonderful evening, Phoenix. All of it."

"I couldn't have done it without you," he said, unable to hide a smile.

"You know, I learned something about you tonight."

"What's that?"

"I discovered you have a sense of humor hiding inside."

"Occasionally it escapes."

"I also found out you're a really good kisser." Without waiting for a reply, Sofia leaned over and kissed *him* this time. "Goodnight, Phoenix," she murmured, pulling away and reaching for the door handle. "See you Tuesday."

Phoenix waited until she'd entered the house and closed the door before he headed home.

→→→

When Phoenix arrived home ten minutes later, it was all he could do to keep his *dogs* from kissing him. Spock and McCoy danced around whining with excitement as they competed to see who could slobber on him first.

"All right, boys," soothed Phoenix with a firm voice. "You know the rules. If you want attention you need to sit." The two shepherds sat in choreographed obedience, and Phoenix gave each of them a chest rub and an ear scratch. The dogs continued to share their happiness, their whines escalating into a mini-howling contest.

"I was only gone for," Phoenix paused, looking at his watch, "six hours?!" Good grief, it was after midnight and he hadn't even noticed.

Urging the dogs along, Phoenix eventually ushered them to the back of the house and outside.

He turned to stare at the empty kitchen and suddenly realized his brother wasn't home. No car? No Hawk. Well, if he'd taken Aerielle to dinner and a movie, he'd probably be home at any time.

Phoenix was still telling himself that an hour later as he sat in the front room like Sofia's grandmother, only he wasn't pretending to be asleep. Phoenix knew he wouldn't sleep until Hawk came home. And so, after he'd changed out of his "good" clothes, which Hawk would have noticed, he'd ensconced himself in a high-backed leather chair and fortified his waiting with a Veterinary magazine. Two of the cats had found him, and now besides the shepherds at his feet, Sheba was resting on the back of his chair, and Esmeralda was warming herself in the crook of Phoenix's arm closest to the small table lamp.

She looked at him as he shifted uncomfortably. Phoenix slapped the magazine closed, having just read the same page for the umpteenth time. Where was Hawk?! And what were he and Aerielle doing? Phoenix's mind went exactly where he didn't want it to. Hawk wouldn't, would he? But Aerielle wasn't the type, at least she didn't used to be. But what did he know of her now? The Aerielle he'd known back then had guarded her virtue like a prized possession, her passion belonging first to her God. Had her faith changed? Had it grown or had it been wiped away by the crazy world they lived in? And how would he feel if what he'd done to her all those years ago had effected that kind of change.

→→→

The sound of light snoring woke Aerielle and, half asleep, she reached out a hand and caressed his head. He stirred, then woke, his dark eyes opening to gaze at her with affection.

"You're snoring," she mumbled, staring back at him. "Since when do you snore and what are you doing sleeping up here with your head on my pillow?"

The expression on the dog's face turned guilty. "You are supposed to be at the end of the bed, you naughty dog." But her voice held no edge, and Aerielle stroked his ears. Idaho leaned hard into her hand as if having his ears scratched was more enjoyable than herding.

Aerielle smiled. Aside from her beeper going off at the end of the evening, her date with Hawk had worked out remarkably well. He had incredible charm, and Aerielle had even managed to forget the hospital.

She had been a little nervous when it had come time for him to leave, hoping he wouldn't try to kiss her goodnight—something she was not ready for. But, just as he had been the rest of the evening, Hawk remained a perfect gentleman. When he'd walked her and Idaho back to the door after walking around the lake, he'd asked if he could see her again. Aerielle had nodded her ascent, while terrified she might have to rebuff a kiss. But Hawk simply clasped her free hand in his and raised it to his lips briefly before setting it free. "Goodnight, Aerielle."

And then he'd left even as she said goodnight in return.

Wide awake now, Aerielle sat up on the edge of her bed and reached for the Bible on her nightstand. Her eyes paused over the photograph that rested nearby, a duplicate of the one she had at work.

Abruptly she dropped her hand as her thoughts were forcibly filled with Phoenix and her memories of him. Could any two brothers be more different? Phoenix had been anything but "charming." He'd been a determined young man, possessive and protective of those he loved. Aerielle had reveled in the strength of his presence and the assurance she'd felt in being with him.

And then he'd left, leaving excuses Aerielle had found hard to accept. She wondered what kind of man he had become.

Glancing at the photograph on her nightstand once more, Aerielle experienced a fresh renewal of pain. "Not tonight," she groaned, reaching for the picture and placing it in the top drawer. What she had let go of through the passage of time and God's grace, she fought against taking back.

Grabbing up her Bible, Aerielle clutched it to her chest. How had she managed to end a pleasant evening with Hawk by torturing herself with things better left behind?

Frustrated with herself, Aerielle held tightly to her Bible and swung her legs up onto the bed and slid down into a comfortable position. She tried to read the Word daily, but it was more like every other day that she actually managed to, and she hadn't read before going to bed. Tonight was every other, and Aerielle opened to the book of Psalms. The scripture soothed her aching heart, touching the hurt with Psalm 119:49–50 "Remember the word to your servant, for you have given me hope. My comfort in my suffering is this: Your promise renews my life." God *had* renewed her life, and He continued to offer comfort in her times of need.

After reading for a short while longer, Aerielle took a few minutes for prayer. Tonight, those prayers included her job, two of her patients, wisdom for her tentative relationship with Hawk, and in the end, Phoenix, who in her memories remained forever eighteen.

→→→

With a start, Phoenix heard his brother's car. "Everybody up," he declared getting to his feet with cat and magazine in hand. Hurriedly he bounded up the stairs, the dogs torn between following him or greeting Hawk. They had identified the sound of the car as easily as Phoenix had. Phoenix didn't care either way; he just didn't want Hawk knowing he'd been waiting for him. There were more subtle ways to interrogate someone.

Phoenix waited in his darkened bedroom after setting Esmeralda down next to a sleeping Cleopatra. Knowing his brother's habits, Phoenix knew it would be but a couple of minutes before his brother ascended the stairs.

Down below he could hear howling whines as the dogs greeted Hawk. Not long after the noisy trio made its way up the stairs.

"Quiet, you two," said Hawk as rowdy dog tails slapped the railing and shepherd vocals continued to clamor for attention. "You guys are gonna wake Phoenix up."

"Too late," announced Phoenix coming to stand in the darkened doorway. *Too late for you to be getting home tonight of all nights.*

Hawk jumped, stopping in front of Phoenix. "You scared me."

Was there any guilt to be heard in that voice, but then Phoenix smelled the fresh scent of the outdoors again. "Sorry," he replied. *Sorry I didn't tell you to stay away from her.*

Spock and McCoy had finally calmed down some and had begun a serious nose inspection of Hawk's clothes. "Don't worry. I didn't bring home a new dog. I was just visiting with one."

Phoenix knew he was missing information, because despite all his faults, Hawk wouldn't refer to Aerielle or any other woman as a dog.

"I may be tired," said Phoenix, realizing he really was, "but what dog are you talking about?"

Hawk glanced at him. "Oh, that's right. You wouldn't know. Aerielle's got an Aussie. His name's Idaho."

Idaho? Aerielle named her dog Idaho? What—No, better not to ask.

"Anyway," continued Hawk, "Aerielle was going to walk

him after I dropped her off. I asked if she wanted company and we walked Idaho clear around the lake."

So that's what took you so long. Phoenix felt relief settle over him, but he couldn't let Hawk see. *So what's she look like?* "So what's he look like?"

"He's a red merle, beautiful coat. A little past his prime, but he doesn't act like it. Also, he has one pricked ear."

"It stands up?"

"Yeah, it makes him extra cute with one ear up and the other down. He couldn't be a show dog, but he's smart enough. Course, most Aussies are. Since it was so late and there was practically no one around, Aerielle let him off leash. He tried to round up some Canada geese that thought they'd settled in for the night."

Phoenix couldn't help but smile at the image. "I think I like this dog." And then, looking down at the two dogs who had sprawled on the floor he asked, "Did you hear that? Her shepherd actually herds something. All you two do is chase squirrels."

"And eat leftovers," put in Hawk. "And I have no leftovers for them from dinner for a change, either. Food was too dang good, and I'm still stuffed. We ate at this great restaurant at the Mall of America."

"You ate where?" Phoenix's voice was deadpan, but he felt as if his heart stopped.

"Place called the Rainforest Café."

"At the Mall of America?"

"Yeah, you been there yet? You should try it. Great restaurant choices. They even have a movie theater."

Movie theater? "Did you see one?"

"A movie? No. We went to Camp Snoopy. That's the amusement park."

"I've heard about that." Phoenix closed his eyes as if to block the image of four of them potentially running into each other just hours ago. How close had they come?

"Well, I can see you're tired," said Hawk. "I'll let you get back to sleep.

Sleep? How was he going to sleep, now? "Yeah, goodnight Hawk."

"Night, Phoenix."

→→→

Surprisingly, Phoenix did sleep, but his dreams were torn from him well after three by the sound of McCoy shifting on his rug. There were times when Phoenix hated being a light sleeper. Tonight he abhorred it. Groaning, he rolled over on his stomach, burying his face in his pillow. The sweet dream that had been stolen from him this night had been of Aerielle. And in this dream, she hadn't been in danger.

Turning again beneath the warm quilts, Phoenix sat up, the covers sliding to his waist as he leaned forward. Dark tangled hair spilled over muscled arms as he cradled them on his knees, his head down. In his mind, he reached for the fading dream, his heart aching to recapture it. Aerielle's tender kisses had been so real, the love present in her eyes reaching to his soul.

Moonlight rippled across the bed, the partially leafless trees outside Phoenix's window shifting in the unseen breeze. How many similar nights had he and Aerielle spent together searching the sky for stars and counting the hours left in each other's arms. So innocent had their relationship been by today's standards, but Phoenix longed for those simple nights where their lovemaking involved no more than whispered endearments, sweet embraces, and tender kisses.

Phoenix could remember the way the soft silk of her hair felt beneath his fingers and the gentle caress of her hand upon his face. It seemed as if she had been his just yesterday. Instead, she was going out with his brother, and Phoenix had kissed Sofia.

The fact that he'd dreamed of Aerielle after spending an evening with Sofia suggested many things, but Phoenix blatantly ignored the obvious. Separating the two women, Phoenix thought only of Aerielle, longing to cling to his memories, but trying to face the fact that her life had changed now, and most likely she had too. He wondered if she still loved to eat, especially hot, spicy foods. Were her feet still ticklish? Did she still wear Hyacinth? Was her faith in God as strong as it had once been?

Of all the things Phoenix hoped hadn't changed, the last was the most important, for it was her faith in God, which she had given of to Phoenix. It was also that which Phoenix had clung to so tenaciously through the years that followed.

McCoy shifted on the floor, drawing Phoenix's attention. He met the sleepy dog's gaze before the German shepherd laid his head back down. Sleep. That's what he should be doing, thought Phoenix, running a hand through his hair.

Getting comfortable, Phoenix nestled into the sheets and pillows, heaping the blankets on top of him. He'd grown cold sitting there in the dark. Closing his eyes, he willed his thoughts to clear, but as slumber overtook him, Aerielle continued to linger in his mind.

"Made by the same Great Spirit, and living in the same land with our brothers, the red men, we consider ourselves as the same family; we wish to live with them as one people, and to cherish their interests as our own."

Thomas Jefferson: To the Miamis, Powtewataminies, and Weeauki as quoted in *Chief Joseph of the Nez Perce* by Robert Penn Warren.

4

Rain drummed steadily on the farmhouse roof as Phoenix sat across from Mr. Danvers in the old man's kitchen. The old man was in the process of serving up two pieces of homemade apple pie to go with the ice cold milk already waiting on the table. Mildred's milk of course. Companionable silence had settled over the two, and Phoenix waited as Mr. Danvers set the pie tin back down and grabbed up his fork.

"Dig in, Doc. Not as good as my wife Mildred used to make, but it'll do."

"It'll more than do," assured Phoenix swallowing a forkful. "This is great."

"My Mildred, she used to add some secret ingredient, I'm sure, fer my pies never taste like hers. Won her share of pie contests, ya know."

Phoenix thought about the secret ingredient the old man was so positive Mildred used and wondered if it might possibly have been just a pinch of love.

"Yer lookin' tired, Doc," announced Mr. Danvers, eyeing Phoenix over the rim of his milk glass. "Yer either workin' too hard or havin' somethin' on yer mind."

In silence, Phoenix consumed another bite of the warm sweet pastry, listening to the rain as it pounded into his pain-filled thoughts. A muscle twitched in his jaw as he followed up with a large sip of milk.

His glass still in hand, Phoenix studied the old man's fork as it pushed through layers of apple. "Aerielle's living in Minneapolis."

Abruptly their eyes met, Mr. Danvers' a knowing blue, Phoenix's, expressionless midnight skies.

"You seen her then?" questioned Mr. Danvers, resting his fork on the table.

Phoenix's grip tightened on his glass. "No.... Hawk ran into her and she's been seeing him."

"I take it Hawk ain't be knowin' yer current feelin's towards the young lady."

"What's for him to know? Fourteen years ago we 'dated,' and then I up and left."

"A decision yer still regrettin'."

Phoenix didn't answer. Instead, he dug his fork back into his pie.

Mr. Danvers did the same, finishing his own piece off in silence. Washing his last bite down with a slug of milk, Mr. Danvers glanced at Phoenix who sat motionless over his empty plate. "If you could tell her anything you wanted to right now, what would it be?"

Phoenix stared at the table a moment before he glanced up, his dark eyes unable to hide the pain this time. "I'd tell her I never, never meant to hurt her."

→→→

Later that same day, Phoenix sat hunched over the large oak desk in his study. His dark brown hair, released from the confines of a braid, hung in waves down his blue sweatshirt. Placed on the desk in front of him was the photograph of Aerielle. He examined it, wondering again how the years had changed her.

He wouldn't be able to avoid her forever. Those had been Mr. Danvers' words many hours earlier, and Phoenix knew the old man was right, but he had no desire to find out if his present turmoil would be made worse by actually seeing Aerielle. The irony of the whole situation was not lost on Phoenix. He had intentionally moved to Minneapolis knowing it his only chance of ever seeing Aerielle again, that chance being very low indeed. However, God was in charge of miracles, and Aerielle had told Phoenix she was planning to work here. For the last four years Phoenix prayed that God would bring about a reunion, and had well imagined various scenarios of their meeting. But none of those scenarios had included his brother running into Aerielle first or asking her out to dinner. Unplanned and unexpected. That's how Phoenix had pictured it. Forewarned was not leaving Phoenix forearmed, but instead unarmed and fearful. Just the fact that Aerielle was having dinner with Hawk told Phoenix she wasn't anxiously awaiting their own reunion.

Phoenix's thoughts were interrupted by a knock on the open door. Without being obvious, he covered the photograph with some papers as Hawk strode in.

"You gonna be around tomorrow?" questioned Hawk, stopping in front of Phoenix's desk.

"What's up?"

"Well, we have those two dogs staying over from surgery. Someone will have to check on them, and I kinda have plans."

Phoenix heard the words Hawk didn't speak. He had a date with Aerielle. Before Phoenix realized what he was doing, he found himself questioning his brother about it. "Where you going?"

"Vikings game and then dinner."

Phoenix nodded, biting his tongue for having asked. "Well, I'll check on our patients, not to worry."

"Thanks."

"Sofia go home then?" asked Phoenix, getting to his feet.

"No, actually. I've been negligent in taking her to Leeann Chins, so we're finally going tonight. You wanna come?"

Phoenix shook his head, walking over to the large French windows and gazing into the dark street. "Not tonight. You two have a good time."

Phoenix shook his head again as his brother left the room. How had things gotten so mixed up? Hawk was dating a girl Phoenix's heart still clung to, and Phoenix was dating a girl who'd been carrying Hawk's torch for years. Not that he and Sofia had had more than one official date. That in itself had been almost as awkward as their *first* evening together at the Mall of America. Phoenix had to admit he didn't see a future in it. Even now, Sofia and *Hawk* were having dinner—Phoenix's most likely ineffective plot to get his brother to notice her. Phoenix could only dream that it would work. Could only hope that Hawk would find some reason to stop dating Aerielle.

"Phoenix?"

Phoenix turned at the sound of Sofia's voice.

"You sure you don't wanna come?" she asked, closing the distance between them.

"Things are complicated enough," he replied, taking Sofia in with eyes not accustomed to seeing her as more than just a good friend.

She looked particularly appealing this evening in a bright pink and black skirt/top combination. She also wore a smile that lit up her eyes. His brother must be blind.

"Before I forget," she began, waving a hand. "My grandmother wanted me to invite you to dinner after church tomorrow. I told her I didn't think—"

"I'd love to," Phoenix agreed abruptly, ignoring the possibility he might be avoiding a chance of running into Aerielle.

"You would?" Sofia returned surprised.

"I would," said Phoenix. "Just let me know what time. I just have to make sure I check on our patients."

"Well, great. Grandma will be thrilled. I warn you, though, you'll get the third degree."

When Sofia was gone, Phoenix turned back to the view of the street below and the not so distant shimmer of the lake. Aerielle lived just on the other side of that lake. So close. So near. What would he say if he actually ran into her one day? Phoenix had no wish to find out, for as much as he longed to see her, he was afraid. Afraid of the wound that might re-open in his heart. Afraid of the recrimination he might see in her eyes—or worse, the indifference.

The lake shimmered as the breeze touched it in the moonlight, and Phoenix shivered in the suddenly cold room. Unconsciously, he folded his arms over his chest as if to protect the heart within.

→→→

Driving home from church on Sunday, Phoenix figured by the time he took care of his patients, he'd arrive at the Bendettis' right of schedule. If Mrs. Bendetti was going to give him the third degree, at least he'd be on time for it. As Phoenix rounded the corner of the street the house was on, he was met with the sight of Hawk's car parked at the curb. Glancing at his watch, he found the time to be just after eleven. His heart stopped beating; at least it felt that way. Hawk had to have left by now. If he was back, then Aerielle was with him.

Phoenix drove past the house, his thoughts and emotions in turmoil. What were they doing here? How long would they be? Phoenix couldn't just keep driving around the block, and the animals needed attention.

Not knowing what else to do, Phoenix pulled into the driveway and parked his truck in back of the house. What else could he do? The animals were waiting. *Sofia* was waiting. Getting out of his vehicle, Phoenix resigned himself to the possibility of seeing Aerielle. Barely acknowledging Spock and McCoy, who greeted him inside the fence, Phoenix trudged toward the backdoor.

→→→

"I still can't believe I forgot the tickets," exclaimed Hawk as he pulled his sports car over to the curb in front of the Stargazer house.

Aerielle smiled at him encouragingly from the passenger seat. "Things happen. Look at me. I overslept today."

"Well, I'm lookin', and you don't appear to have gotten ready in a hurry," assured Hawk, his black eyes glinting appreciatively. "You want to come in while I find the tickets?"

Aerielle glanced at the beautiful brick home and manicured lawn. If Hawk was inviting her in, then most likely Phoenix wasn't home.

"Do you happen to have food inside that house?" questioned Aerielle, turning back to Hawk with a grin. "I missed breakfast."

Hawk grinned back, shaking his head in amusement. "Plenty."

Moments later the two entered the large foyer. "The kitchen's that way," announced Hawk motioning towards the back of the house. "The pantry's to the left, and it's full of munchies. Help yourself."

Left alone, Aerielle remained standing in the large foyer, her feet seemingly riveted to the spot. So this was where Phoenix lived now. Though she was surprised to find him living in a city, from her view, she felt the house suited him. What else she felt at that moment was unexpectedly little considering her emotional state a week past. But Aerielle had given up loving Phoenix long ago, and it was only the memories that remained, haunting her, taunting her with their "what ifs." And contemplating what might have been, got one nowhere. The present was all too real to be worrying about the past. Right now that present included finding something to eat and going to a football game.

Pulling out of her reverie, Aerielle headed for the kitchen to find the walk-in pantry. It was an easy enough task. However, finding the light switch was another matter. There had to be one, she determined, glancing at the light bulb in the center of the ceiling. But she quickly gave up her futile search, deciding the light from the kitchen would be sufficient. Making her way past a case of pop, Aerielle found a shelf filled with chips and crackers to choose from. She had just about made up her mind when, without warning, the pantry door slammed shut with a loud crash, and she was left standing in complete darkness.

Muttering polite obscenities such as "drat blasted" and "darn fangled door," Aerielle attempted to find her way out. She knew she was heading in the right direction when she stubbed her toe on the case of pop. Uttering another exclamation and jerking back, she knocked a can of something off the shelf and was thankful when it missed her feet.

Almost immediately Aerielle's hand was on the door. Reaching for the knob, she tried to turn it, but it wouldn't budge, as if someone had hold of it from the other side.

"Hawk you'll pay for this," declared Aerielle, shoving at the door with her hands just as it was opened from without.

She abruptly found herself falling forward into space and then being caught in a masculine embrace. Aerielle felt the back of her arms cradled by firm hands while she glanced down at her own pressed against an unyielding black sweatshirt-clad chest. Aerielle knew without a doubt whose arms held her, whose heart pounded beneath her touch, whose dark waves of long hair lay crushed beneath her palms. This was not what she had in mind for their reunion, had she a reunion in mind at all.

"And what if it isn't Hawk?" Phoenix suddenly asked, referring to Aerielle's threat of moments before.

His voice, though huskier than normal, reached past the years, and Aerielle felt its tug on her heart. She found her head lifting, her gaze following the length of his hair to the familiar features of his face. Her hands, still pressed to his chest, felt his sharp intake of breath when at last his searching gaze met hers.

Aerielle had forgotten how incredibly handsome he was, at least to those who saw past the harsh angles of his face. He had a warrior's countenance, whether it be Nez Perce Indian or Scottish Highlander. With those piercing eyes and his striking alabaster-like bone structure, he could appear incredibly dangerous, either as an enemy or a knight in shining armor. He had been both to Aerielle. Right now he was neither. He was just Phoenix, her Phoenix, with the arresting cheekbones that longed for her caress, the soft hair her hands begged to freely stroke, the mouth—Aerielle wrenched away from the thought, her gaze shifting elsewhere. It was then she noticed his nose, and the very slight change that had been effected since the last time she'd seen him.

"It's crooked," she declared, her surprise made more evident by the odd timing of her comment. "Your nose. It's crooked," she repeated.

"I broke it," responded Phoenix calmly. "Well, actually, somebody else broke it."

Phoenix's reply sounded just as strange as Aerielle's question, considering their first topic of conversation after fourteen years was his nose. But neither seemed to notice the incongruity of their dialog.

Aerielle's thoughts shifted from Phoenix's nose as she came to realize he was staring at her with even greater intensity than she had been with him. She immediately questioned whether her hair was in place, her lipstick on straight, and if the purple and yellow Viking sweatshirt she wore looked all right. She also wondered if what Phoenix saw made him regret leaving her. But what did *she* care? Why should it possibly matter? But it did matter. Despite the current situation, it was unbearably painful to know that this man she had loved so deeply had given her up so freely. How could he?

How could he? It was a question Phoenix was asking now and had been asking for most of those missing years. How could he have left her? Lied to her? Hurt her? And gazing into those vivid blue eyes of hers, he was confronted with his most recent wrongdoing. His vow. He had broken his vow. And though Aerielle remained innocent of the truth hidden within his heart, the fragments of that broken vow seemed to glisten from her eyes. Phoenix felt shamed, unworthy, and yet at the same time he longed to run his hands through her halo of corn silk gold, to crush her body to his, and kiss her soft moist lips. But reality was all too prevalent, and Phoenix realized they couldn't stand there all day, each caught in their own turmoil and, in each other's arms. The only way such a meeting between them could be more awkward was if Hawk walked in.

With that thought, Phoenix stepped back, releasing Aerielle so quickly that she stumbled. He reached out, but she caught her own balance, the expression on her face seeming as dazed as Phoenix felt.

"What are you doing here?" he found himself asking stupidly as he moved another step away. "I mean I thought you and Hawk were going to a game."

"He forgot the tickets...and then I was hungry."

Always hungry, thought Phoenix. She hadn't changed. "That's why you were in the pantry."

"But how did the door close if you didn't—"

"The air suction from opening the back door. I wouldn't even have known you were in there except you were making such a fuss."

Aerielle smiled and then a giggle escaped her lips. "My big toe may never be the same again."

"I heard you were a doctor. Congratulations."

"Thanks."

"Speaking of doctorin', I have some patients to check on. It's good seeing you again."

Phoenix made his quick and awkward escape through the door leading to the foyer. The last thing he wanted was an encounter between Aerielle, Hawk, and himself. Facing one at a time was difficult enough.

Mounting the old stairs, Phoenix contemplated his last words to Aerielle. "It's good seeing you again," he mimicked under his breath. It was more like hell.

"You talking to me?"

Phoenix glanced up as Hawk descended the stairs. They stopped on the same step, Phoenix gripping the hand rail for more than one form of support.

"Just mumbling to myself," he offered.

Hawk nodded, his expression unrevealing. "Misplaced the tickets," he explained as if he needed to break the sudden silence.

This time *Phoenix* nodded.

"You see Aerielle?" asked Hawk.

Phoenix was tempted to lie. "Yeah, she's in the kitchen. Have a good time at the game." Leaving this casual suggestion behind, Phoenix continued on up the stairs as if nothing unusual had happened that morning. As if he hadn't thought about kissing Hawk's "girlfriend." He knew his brother's eyes followed him, and Phoenix wondered what Hawk was thinking. Most of all, though, he wondered what Aerielle was thinking. Did she hate him?

Did she hate him, Aerielle asked herself as Phoenix slipped from the kitchen. At that moment, yes, because for some reason she felt she'd just been rejected all over again.

Aerielle brushed an agitated hand through her fringe of bangs. What had she expected from him? An explanation? She had gotten that in the form of a note the morning after he left. An apology so weak compared to the strength of the man, that Aerielle had always felt there was more to his exodus, such as that he hadn't really loved her. But that answer was just as hard to believe or accept as the one he had written. As a result Aerielle had been left angry and bitter, desolate and heartbroken. And though the years had healed many wounds, and Aerielle had successfully gotten on with her life, this sudden reunion had done damage to her heart. Did she still love him? Not likely. Did she hate him? Probably not. But could he still hurt her? Oh, most definitely.

Caught up by her voluminous emotions, Aerielle stood unmoving, seeing nothing of the here and present, hearing only the first words she'd spoken to Phoenix in fourteen years. *Your nose is crooked.* What an unremarkable, meaningless, stupid thing to say. She had imagined all kinds of encounters with him over the years, and none of them included comments about his nose—hitting it maybe. Aerielle remembered well their first argument and how she'd been tempted to slug him herself.

→→→

Aerielle marched towards the barn, determined to speak to Phoenix whether he wanted to listen or not. She'd been here almost a month now, and he hadn't shown the least bit of interest in learning the sign language, which was so essential to Sparrow's future.

With the appaloosas running loose in the corral, the barn was eerily quiet, and Phoenix was nowhere in sight. Aerielle checked all the stalls, the smell of horses and hay surrounding her.

Unsuccessful in her search, Aerielle mounted the ladder to the loft. Doors at one end led to a deck where Phoenix kept a telescope set up. In inclement weather, the telescope was stored just inside the loft, and Aerielle took a chance that Phoenix might be up here.

Following the narrow path between the bales of hay that lined the loft, Aerielle walked to the end of the barn where the telescope stood in an uncluttered spot. She failed to discover Phoenix, but Aerielle found her attention drawn by the shrouded piece of stargazing equipment.

Carefully removing the large soft dustcover protecting the telescope, Aerielle admired the intricate unit. It looked expensive, very expensive, with numerous handles and knobs for adjustment. Reaching out, she ran a finger across the sleek surface of the scope, wondering what it would be like to view the night sky through its powerful lenses.

"I would appreciate it if you'd keep your hands off."

Aerielle jumped at the sound of his voice, hard and unforgiving. She was surprised to find him standing so close without having heard his approach. Just a few feet away, Phoenix stared at her with cold eyes. And with his glorious dark hair falling well past his shoulders, the vision of the magnificent yet angry warrior couldn't have been more evident had he been wearing buckskins and carrying a bow. The impact of that image was more than effective. The message was also doubly clear. *Keep your hands off my belongings, your person away from mine, and tread lightly where my family is concerned.* Right now, Aerielle was breaking the first two commandments.

But Aerielle was not about to be intimidated by his air of cool regard. *She* was angry too, and her fingers fisted over the fabric of the dustcover still held in her hands. "Actually I was *looking* for *you.*"

No response. Not a muscle on his exemplary specimen of a body moved. Not a glimmer of interest touched the depths of his incredible eyes. Did a heart beat within the powerful frame Aerielle admired despite the demeanor that came with it?

"It's about Sparrow," she continued.

There was a twitch in his jaw. "What about Sparrow?"

Score one for her side, thought Aerielle. "In a short period of time, Sparrow's going to be relying on sign language as a major form of communication, and you've shown no interest in learning it yourself. This can only be detrimental to her ability to adjust."

Aerielle paused, the silence in the barn broken by the sound of horses' hooves and other activity going on outside.

Phoenix's lips moved. "Are you through?"

It was then that Aerielle could have slugged him, or at least passed a sharp hand over the beautiful cheekbones highlighting his face.

"No, as a matter of fact, I'm not!" she exclaimed, taking a step forward. "I think it's about time you give up your selfish prejudices, if for no other reason than your sister. Obviously you don't think too much of us 'pale faces,' and I agree there are some that are enough to make a person sick. But let me tell you something Phoenix Stargazer, you've got a competitive edge on all of 'em at being a jerk. And now. For your information. I'm through."

Striding forward across the wooden boards, Aerielle slammed the covering from the telescope against Phoenix's chest. The contact was brief as she marched on past, and Aerielle failed to note anything beating other than the rhythm of her own hot tempered pulse.

→→→

"You find anything?"

Hawk's voice brought Aerielle's thoughts back to Minnesota with such abruptness that for a moment she had no idea what he was talking about.

"Oh. Yes. No. I'm not hungry anymore," Aerielle added when Hawk's eyebrows went up. "Find the tickets?" she continued, trying to get back on track.

Hawk raised one hand waving the tickets before putting them in an inside pocket of his leather jacket. "Shall we?" he asked, gesturing toward the front of the house while closing the pantry.

Aerielle led the way, neither of them speaking aloud, but both fulminating with unspoken thoughts. Closing the door behind them, they started down the steps. As if choreographed, they both burst into speech, Hawk turning to Aerielle who was one step above him.

"Hawk, why did you—"

"I know you just saw—"

Both their voices trailed off as they faced each other, literally eye to eye, now that Hawk stood below Aerielle. Their lips held the unfinished questions, while their gazes held the surprise at finding themselves so close. Neither spoke or moved.

Without thought, Aerielle began to study Hawk's features, comparing them to his brother's, which she had so closely studied just moments before. His face would be considered eye-catching by anyone's standards, with a strong jawline, recently unshaven, unlike Phoenix, who as she recalled, never needed to shave. And while Phoenix's cheekbones were one of his most prominent features, Hawk had attractively hollowed cheeks, as well as a hint of a smile to his lips, and eyebrows with a questioning arch. His hair was truly black unlike Phoenix's, his eyes also a liquid obsidian.

Aerielle looked into those eyes now, just mere inches away, and felt her heart stop. How had she not noticed before? Their eyes, from the shade, size, and shape to the generous thickness and length of their ebony eyelashes, were identical. And right now, Hawk's eyes were studying her with an intensity that matched his brother's from minutes ago.

Hawk's lashes lowered thoughtfully. Oh, crap, was he going

to kiss her? Well, why not? Neither of them owed anything to Phoenix or the past. Hawk seemed to hesitate a moment, as if giving her an out. Instead, Aerielle met him halfway, their kiss as gentle and tentative as Hawk's hand that lifted to caress the back of her neck. Aerielle tried to block out everything except that tender kiss and the pleasurable time Hawk was taking with it. Against all odds, Aerielle's thoughts fought to forget what Phoenix's kisses had been like. Yet his face filled her mind's eye and Aerielle cried out within. *Nooo! Leave me alone, already. Haven't you hurt me enough?! Get out of my thoughts!*

It was too late. Hawk was releasing her, and Arielle let him go reluctantly. He at least seemed to have enjoyed the kiss, for he was smiling. "We keep that up, we'll miss kickoff."

Hawk took her hand as they continued down the steps. "What were you trying to say before, on our way out of the house?"

Aerielle shook her head. "Another time." She no longer had the energy to find out why the brothers were living in Minnesota. "What about you? You were trying to ask me something."

"After that, um, kiss, it doesn't seem to matter."

Aerielle wondered what he meant, but she didn't have the energy for *that* question, either.

"I remembered all the insults I had endured
and my blood was on fire."

Chief Joseph as quoted in *The Nez Perce*
by Virginia Driving Hawk Sneve

5

Monday morning sunlight dappled the sink and gold countertop through white eyelet curtains. But its greeting barely reached the slumped-shouldered figure sitting at the kitchen table, and its caress did little to warm Phoenix or dry the waves of long damp hair that clung to his back. His dark eyes were closed, and a cup of warm coffee sat discarded in front of him. The taste was bitter on his tongue this morning, no matter how much sugar he added.

It had been a horrendous night, plagued with haunting dreams of Aerielle and reminders of a broken vow. And even after seeking God's forgiveness in the early hours of the night, Phoenix had been unable to find his own. As a result, his shower that morning had been scalding in an attempt to wash away his own self-disgust.

He had lied to Aerielle fourteen years ago, and now, he was breaking vows. Had nothing changed? Had he not learned anything through the passage of time?

Absently, Phoenix reached down and stroked the old calico curled up in his lap. Esmeralda had been a gift from Aerielle.

The back door opened, and Phoenix glanced up as Sofia entered.

"Phoenix, you look awful!" she exclaimed, her eyes searching his face. "Are you sick?"

Sick at heart, maybe. "I didn't get much sleep."

"What happened?" asked Sofia, joining him at the table. "Is it Hawk? How 'bout the animals?"

Phoenix shook his head. "They're all fine...Sofia, we need to talk...I need to talk."

"I'm listening."

Without thought Phoenix reached for his coffee, taking a small sip. He winced.

"Yesterday," he began, setting his cup down, "when I came to check on the animals, Aerielle was here."

Understanding dawned on Sofia's face. "That's why you left so quickly after dinner yesterday. Grandma was worried the lasagna gave you heartburn."

Phoenix ignored Sofia's attempt at humor. "I can't go out with you anymore, Sofia."

Sofia nodded as if that's what she'd expected to hear. Her black curls brushed her shoulders as she tilted her head in question. "Are you in love with her?"

"I don't know," Phoenix answered honestly, not attempting to hide the turmoil he was experiencing inside. "But the decision not to date has nothing to do with emotions. It has to do with a vow. One I broke when I started dating you. Sofia, I'm sorry."

She shrugged. "Don't worry about me. Grandma might be upset, but she'll get over it."

More humor. Phoenix only stared.

"Hey, look," Sofia continued. "I don't mean to make light of this. It's just that no guy's ever broken a vow over me before. At least not that I know of."

Appearing disgruntled, Sofia jerked to her feet and strode over to the counter. Hurriedly, she poured herself a cup of coffee. Gulping down a quick swallow, she choked on the scalding liquid.

It was obvious to Phoenix that he'd made her uncomfortable. He stood to his feet, Esmeralda cradled against his chest, his unfinished coffee clasped in his other hand. Moving to the counter, he dumped the brew into the sink. Beside him, Sofia sipped from her steaming mug, more careful this time.

"I didn't mean to lay anything heavy on you, Sofia," Phoenix offered, glancing her direction.

She looked at him, her brown eyes thoughtful as she surveyed his face. "You know you're a pretty complex person, Phoenix. This Aerielle must be really special if she managed to figure you out."

Phoenix grunted and turned around, leaning with his back against the counter. "I've been meaning to ask you how dinner went with Hawk."

It was Sofia's turn to grunt as she, too, turned and leaned against the counter. "Pretty good. Hawk seemed a bit surprised to see me dressed in something other than my standard fair, and we talked easily. Maybe if he hadn't already been dating Aerielle...."

Sofia's sentence trailed off, leaving Esmeralda's purring the only sound in the silent kitchen. Phoenix studied Sofia as he continued to stroke the old calico's head, and a thought abruptly came to him.

"Today's Monday," he stated, the realization surprising him. "It's your day off. What are you doing here?"

Staring straight ahead, Sofia gave an amused smile that was almost a grimace. "Yeah, well, get this. I thought maybe we needed to talk."

This time both of them grunted.

→→→

Early Wednesday evening, the doorbell for the clinic began ringing incessantly, drawing Phoenix from his second floor study in a hurry. He hoped it wasn't Mrs. Wellington. His brother wasn't home. As he flew down the stairs, Phoenix glanced at what he was wearing. He wasn't exactly dressed for office hours. The jeans he wore were old, with tears in both knees, and his sweatshirt looked like he'd painted in it, which he had.

Opening the vet clinic door, Phoenix found a boy in his early teens standing with a sheltie pup held gingerly in his arms. The dog's left rear leg was bleeding from a gash.

Before the boy had a chance to speak, Phoenix reached for the injured puppy, taking the animal gently in his hands as the boy released him. The puppy's eyes followed his master even as he left the boy's arms.

"He doesn't look too bad," offered Phoenix, heading back towards the rear door of the waiting room. "Why don't you have a seat."

"I'd rather watch."

Phoenix stopped, turning back towards the sandy-haired boy. His stance was firm, his green eyes unwavering. It was almost as if he were daring Phoenix to say no.

"You squeamish?" asked Phoenix.

"No."

"What's your name?"

"Tyler."

"Okay, Tyler. You can watch. I might even need your help. But you'll do exactly as I say, is that understood?"

"Yes, sir."

"And if you even *think* you might get sick, you leave."

"Got it."

Phoenix proceeded to the general office and then on into the operating room, Tyler behind him. Setting the wide-eyed puppy down on the operating table, Phoenix ordered Tyler to hold him there while he prepared a hypo.

"What's his name and what happened to him?" asked Phoenix, returning with the anesthesia.

Tyler straightened from whispering something in the dog's ear.

"His name's Boba Fett, and I don't know what happened to him. He got loose, and when he came back, he was like this."

Phoenix stroked the puppy's head. "It's okay, Boba Fett. You're gonna go to sleep for a little while, and when you wake up, you'll feel a lot better." Inserting the needle, Phoenix pressed the plunger, at the same time glancing in Tyler's direction. The boy didn't wince.

Nor did he wince through the procedure that soon followed after Phoenix had briefly departed to change into a set of blue scrubs. As a matter of fact, Tyler barely appeared to blink as Phoenix sewed the dog's leg up. He seemed fascinated, watching Phoenix's every move as if to memorize each one.

The stitching job completed, Phoenix laid the sheltie in a small kennel and then scrubbed up for the second time. "He'll wake up in about an hour," Phoenix explained, drying his hands off. "You live far from here?"

"Not far," said Tyler noncommittally, squatting down in front of the kennel.

"You want to stick around and have something to drink?" offered Phoenix, pausing beside the boy.

Tyler stood up, shrugging his shoulders. "Sure."

While leading the way to the kitchen through the hallway beneath the stairs, Phoenix freed his hair from the braid he'd put it in.

"How many years did it take you to get it that long?" questioned Tyler.

Phoenix thought about it for a moment. "Not really sure, actually."

"So when's the last time it was short?"

That question required no thought at all.

"Fourteen years."

"You must have a lot of girlfriends. They really get into hair like yours. Of course that's assuming they don't mind you're American Indian."

Phoenix glanced back at Tyler as they entered the kitchen. He realized by the expression on the boy's face that he was giving him a hard time in a friendly sort of way. "I take it you don't mind?"

"No way. I think it's kinda cool. I'm just a boring 'melting pot' of mumbo jumbo. I think it'd be more interesting to be one or two things than ten."

A half-smile touched Phoenix's lips as he stopped in the middle of the kitchen. "How old are you, Tyler?"

"Almost as old as your hair. I'll be fourteen next spring."

Despite the urge to laugh at Tyler's adding six months onto his age, Phoenix's only response was to nod. "So what do you want to drink?"

"How 'bout some coffee?"

"It's decaffeinated...."

Tyler's eyebrows shot up. "You'd actually give me some?"

"Why not? Can't be any worse than the other stuff you probably drink."

"Never thought about it that way. I guess I'd rather have pop. What da ya got?"

"What we *have*," began Phoenix emphasizing the 'have' "is diet coke and diet root beer."

"What is this, a health food store? Decaf, diet...."

Phoenix just stared, waiting for an answer.

Tyler grinned. "Guess I'll haaave root beer."

Stepping over to the fridge, Phoenix retrieved a couple of root beers, tossing one to Tyler who caught it one handed.

"So where do you live?" inquired Phoenix.

"At the moment, next door...."

Phoenix's pop tab snapped open loudly in the abrupt silence. "Next door?"

"Dorothy Wellington's my grandmother," confirmed Tyler, snapping open his own can of pop.

Phoenix swallowed a slug of root beer, while managing not to choke. "She know you're here?"

Tyler grinned for the second time. "Are you kidding? She warned me about you. Thinks Indians are only good for running gambling casinos."

For some reason Phoenix found himself grinning back. The kid certainly had audacity.

"So what exactly are you, anyway?" questioned Tyler. "I mean, what kinda Indian?"

"My mother is a full-blooded Nez Perce."

"Hmm. Nez Perce. Not from around here?"

"Idaho."

"So what about your dad? If he's not Indian...."

"Well, to quote someone I recently met, he's a 'melting pot of mumbo jumbo.'"

Tyler sipped at his root beer, studying Phoenix past lashes that were darker than the sandy blond of his hair.

"So why are you staying with your grandmother?" asked Phoenix.

"My mom and dad are havin' some problems. Mom and I moved in with Grandma to give the situation some 'breathing space.'"

"Are you worried your parents might get divorced?" The question was not one Phoenix asked lightly, for he could well remember the day his father had chosen to leave, though Phoenix had been much younger than Tyler.

"A little, I guess," shrugged Tyler. "But they're going to start marriage counseling, and Mom thinks they ought to be able to work things out."

"Speaking of working things out," continued Tyler, settling into a chair at the table. "You haven't asked me how I'm going to pay you for taking care of Boba Fett. I don't have much money. At the moment, I've got about seven bucks."

Phoenix nodded thoughtfully. He hadn't been concerned in the least about receiving payment, but he admired Tyler's willingness to make some kind of restitution. "Maybe you could work it off," he suggested, sitting down opposite the boy.

Tyler's eyes lit up. "Whatcha got in mind?"

"How about a couple hours each afternoon next week, starting Tuesday? There's a lot of stuff that needs to be done around the clinic."

"You gonna be here?" questioned Tyler, sipping his pop.

"I spend quite a bit of time in the field."

"Well, then, how 'bout afternoons at the clinic, and one day in the field with you? You do work Saturday's don't you?"

Phoenix smiled at the boy's persistence. "Yeah, I work Saturdays.... All right, it's a deal. But you need to get your mom's permission first."

Tyler groaned.

Phoenix raised his eyebrows. "Is that a problem?"

"Not with my mom, but I'll never hear the end of it from my grandmother."

Grinning in understanding, Phoenix nodded. "That I can well believe."

"Hey, would you mind if I went and checked on Boba Fett?"

"Not at all," assured Phoenix, knowing the pup would still be sleeping. He watched in silence as the boy left the kitchen, contemplating the sudden realization that Tyler reminded him of Aerielle. They were both annoyingly frank, and just a tad mouthy.

→→→

The bright July day was reminiscent of spring. It was the kind of day that soothed and caressed. Phoenix enjoyed it's intoxicating effect as he stood grooming the horses...and watching Aerielle. She was in the garden pulling weeds beside his mother. At the moment she was sitting on her heels, her back to the corral. Phoenix found his eyes continuously drawn to her despite the brush in his hand and the appaloosa standing beside him.

Pulling his attention back to the horse, Phoenix ran the brush over the animal's back, ignoring the compulsion to glance up from his work again. Aerielle was certainly the most aggravating female he'd ever met, but he had to admire the way she'd stood up to him the day before. She'd been down right furious with him, and those blue eyes of hers had been ablaze with angry fire. After she'd stormed off, the memory of those fiery eyes had burned away any and all calm thoughts for the rest of the day. By morning his temper had ebbed, but there remained a warmth, a reminder, that seemed to emanate from the location where her hand had made contact with his chest. Absently, Phoenix raised a hand, pressing his fingers to the spot where she had hit him. His beating heart greeted him with its steady rhythm.

"You planning on breaking yourself a filly?"

Phoenix was startled by the sound of his brother's voice, but attempted not to show it. Slowly, he once again pulled his traitorous gaze from Aerielle. Resting his arms on the warmth of the Appaloosa's back, he glanced at fifteen-year-old Hawk who was leaning against the corral fence.

"I don't think that's any of your business," he replied, leveling his brother with a deadly stare.

Hawk ignored the warning. "Maybe not, but even I know a purebred when I see it."

Phoenix didn't deign to answer, but Hawk grinned smugly before turning towards the barn.

"Phoenix. Phoenix."

Phoenix turned at the sound of his name to find Sparrow running up the dirt drive calling for him. Her long black braid bounced against her back one last time as she came to a breathless stop beside the fence. Grinning profusely, she waved a sheet of paper up at him.

"An A!" she exclaimed. "I got an A!"

Tossing the brush to the ground, Phoenix carefully accepted the fluttering paper from the excited child. He gave it his full attention as she looked on, noting the neatly written work and the big red A at the top. Nevin and his mother had enrolled Sparrow in a special summer school class to give her a jump on what would be a difficult year ahead. She seemed to be enjoying the classes, and apparently was doing well, as her test grades continued to indicate.

"Good job," said Phoenix, signing the words with his hands despite the hindrance of the paper.

"I have to show it to Mom," Sparrow went on excitedly.

"She's in the garden," offered Phoenix, simultaneously making the hand movements.

Sparrow reached for the paper.

"I know you're excited, Sparrow," continued Phoenix, signing some words, skipping others, "but don't forget to use sign language, at least for the words you know."

Sparrow nodded, accepting the paper. "I will," she replied, signing this time.

Glancing at the paper, Sparrow grinned again and headed in the direction of the garden. Phoenix turned, following his sister with his eyes, only to discover Aerielle headed towards him, something orange grasped in one hand.

Phoenix waited, his face revealing nothing as Aerielle approached.

"I'm new at his gardening stuff," she spoke/signed, meeting his expressionless eyes. "I pulled out a young carrot instead of a weed," she went on, holding up her mistake. "I thought Mirage here might enjoy it."

"This isn't Mirage," signed Phoenix, knowing Aerielle had seen him use ASL with Sparrow. Reaching up, he patted the rump of the appaloosa beside him. "This is Morning Dew."

Aerielle shook her head, briefly breaking eye contact in order to feed the carrot to the horse. "I'm afraid I'm no good at telling those two apart."

"My ancestors used to mark the ears to keep the herds separate," Phoenix remarked off-handedly, attempting to sign the words.

"Your ancestors used to mark the ears to keep the herds separate," repeated Aerielle, demonstrating the signs. "There must have been many horses. I read somewhere that the appaloosas were once called Nez Perce horses."

"True, but the Nez Perce did breed other horses, as well."

"It's also true that I was wrong in accusing you of not learning ASL. I was under a false impression, obviously."

"*Obviously*." Phoenix signed the word only, his tongue remaining still, yet even in the silence his sarcasm was evident.

Aerielle raised her eyebrows at the silent reply, apparently recognizing the humor in it, for they both knew he had been intentionally deceptive. Phoenix felt a smile attempting to overtake his lips. He fought it briefly and then grinned.

"Why, Phoenix," exclaimed Aerielle in mock surprise, "your mouth can smile as well as bite."

Phoenix suddenly realized his mouth wanted to do something else at that moment, like kiss the self-satisfied smirk off her face.

"Well, I must get back to the weeding," continued Aerielle, tossing her head saucily. "Now be a good boy and keep practicing your ASL, and maybe teacher will give *you* an A."

Phoenix shook his head in disbelief as Aerielle turned and strolled off. Maybe his brother wasn't so wrong. She was as high spirited and sassy as any purebred filly he'd ever dealt with.

"My people, what have you done? While I was gone you have sold my country. I have come home and there is not left me a place on which to pitch my lodge."

Chief Looking Glass, June 9, 1855 as quoted in *Chief Joseph Country, Land of the Nez Perce* by Bill Gulick

6

Aerielle tugged at her stethoscope as if she were loosening a tie. With her other hand she rubbed at her eyes. Her shift was almost over.

"Late night?"

Aerielle opened her eyes to find Heather Finch watching her.

"You were ten minutes late this morning," continued Heather, grinning across the counter of the nurses' station.

Aerielle smiled back. "Hand me Jimmy Denning's chart would you? I was late because of construction."

"Too bad. I was hoping you had a late date last night."

When Aerielle failed to respond, Heather jumped to her own conclusion. "You did, didn't you?" she demanded, reaching for the requested chart and handing it over.

Aerielle studied the results of Jimmy's latest tests as an announcement went over the paging system. "Jimmy's improving. And it was just dinner and a movie."

"There's no such thing. It was with Hawk again, right? What'd you see?" demanded Heather, leaning conspiratorially forward and tapping a pen firmly on the counter.

Though shaking her head to dismiss the seriousness of the situation, Aerielle answered Heather's eager questions. "We saw Batman Returns."

"Hawk. What an unusual name. I think I like this guy. And

if he's half as sexy as his name.... He doesn't happen to have a brother available, does he?"

Color rushed to Aerielle's face when an image of Phoenix as she had last seen him in his kitchen intruded upon her thoughts. The shock of seeing him that day had eventually worn off. Even so, she found the thought of him with another woman, even one as sweet as Heather, uncomfortable.

Aerielle shook her thoughts free, prepared to defend her lack of reply, only to discover that Heather's attention had been momentarily drawn away by another nurse.

Heather glanced back at Aerielle, a smile reappearing. "You wouldn't happen to have a pet of some kind you could take in to see this Hawk? You did say he was a vet."

"Idaho *is* in need of an update on his shots. But, I don't need an excuse to see this guy. I told you, it's nothing serious."

"Well, then, maybe you need to be dating his brother."

Heather ended her statement with a wink, letting Aerielle know she was well aware of her blush and the brief silence that had passed at the possibility of Hawk having a brother.

→→→

Stopped at a traffic light, Phoenix leaned forward, pulling his hair free of its braid while loosing his thoughts of the work day. The light turned green, and he settled back into the seat. A contented sigh escaped as he directed the truck towards home.

It was Friday, and though he worked tomorrow, the scent of "weekend" hung in the air. It was 3:30, and once he processed the blood tests he'd taken at the Sanderson Kennels, he'd have his evening free.

Maybe he'd take the dogs around the lake. It was fairly cool. Hopefully, the lake wouldn't be crowded. The more deserted the better. Phoenix missed having mile after mile of land to himself.

As if sensing his thoughts from the back seat, Spock stuck a comforting wet nose in Phoenix's ear.

"Yeah, boys, we're almost home."

→→→

Idaho's vaccinations completed, Aerielle rubbed the dog's head and stood up as Hawk disposed of the used hypo.

"Thanks for adding us to your afternoon schedule," she said, walking with Hawk toward the door. "You didn't tell me Idaho'd be your only patient." Aerielle paused in the doorway, glancing into the empty waiting room.

"Not my only. Just my last. We work a lot of hours, but normally on Fridays we wrap it up by three. Sofia needs time off, and I like my Friday nights free."

The question of what Phoenix did with *his* Friday evenings passed through Aerielle's mind.

"So...." began Hawk, his professional tone changing to one of teasing as he leaned back against the door frame. "Are you planning on paying for this visit now or charging it?"

Aerielle raised an eyebrow. "And what's the going rate for office visits?"

"Hmm," said Hawk with mock seriousness. "I'd say the shots are worth about two kisses. Of course, that's if you pay today. If you decide to charge, it'll cost you three."

The glint in his eyes told Aerielle that the kisses he had in mind would not be like the brief few they'd shared after a certain football game or the two dates since. They would probably be more in line with their kiss before the game—their first kiss, when she'd seen Phoenix in his eyes and had tried to forget him. Maybe this was the opportunity to find out what she really thought. After all, Aerielle hadn't stopped thinking about *either* Hawk or Phoenix since that day. She'd found herself unable to stop comparing the two in every way there was to compare. But that kiss with Hawk—the first one—it hadn't been long enough. This was one comparison she wanted to make before their relationship got any more serious.

Aerielle leaned back against the opposite doorframe, feeling in need of its support. She smiled at Hawk invitingly. "I make it a practice never to go into debt, especially when the interest rate is 50 percent."

"I was hoping you'd feel that way," grinned Hawk, stepping closer and pressing a hand to the doorframe that Aerielle rested against.

"Before I pay the bill, do you give out lollipops?"

Hawk eyed her quizzically, his face just inches away. "Lollipops?"

"I give lollipops to *my* patients."

"Would you settle for a milkbone?"

"Well, I've never *had* a milkbone before—"

Aerielle's reply was cut short by Hawk's silencing kiss, followed by the opening of the vet clinic door.

And across the distance of the waiting room, Phoenix Stargazer's pleasant afternoon was being cut short by the sight of Hawk kissing Aerielle—*his* Aerielle. Fury welled up inside and it was all Phoenix could do to maintain his control. He managed to keep his emotions from his face, but his fists longed to do damage to his brother's. Instead, he remained motionless, his heart seeming to cease its beating in the eternity of seconds which followed.

Three shepherds, two German and an Australian, danced about in the waiting room, greeting each other with snorts and sniffs and two wagging tails, but Aerielle failed to notice. She was only vaguely aware of Idaho's excited barks as McCoy nosed the other dog in a way that most humans found embarrassing.

Palpable tension filled the room, Aerielle feeling as if she'd been caught with her hand in the proverbial cookie jar, Hawk pulling away in frustration, mumbling something about timing, and Phoenix looking on, the familiar tell-tale muscle pounding out a rhythm against his jaw. Aerielle read the rhythm and knew—he was livid.

As if signaled, Aerielle's own anger exploded within. What gave him any right to disapprove?! He'd been responsible for ending their relationship years ago, and Aerielle had fought and scratched her way into the future without him. She would not be made to feel guilty by his unreasonable jealousy now.

Hawk was the first to speak, though it failed to break the steel-like tension. "I see you got your business done early today."

"I have lab tests to run for the Sanderson Kennels. If you two will excuse me, I had better get to it." Phoenix kept his voice void of emotion. What else was there to say? What *could* he say? All of this was his fault.

Phoenix started forward. His steps carried him between the two still standing in the doorway. Inadvertently, his arm brushed Aerielle's, and in that brief contact he realized she was as tense as he. Despite his every effort to hide his emotions, she had read his anger and reacted to it.

Phoenix swore softly in the language of the old ones as he entered the tiny lab just off the exam room. He wanted desperately to slam the door behind him, but closed it almost without a sound. Unfortunately, the emotional tumult inside him was such that he found himself in the dark, having forgotten to flip the light switch that lay on the wall outside.

Phoenix stood motionless with his back against the thick wooden door, unable to see, not caring if he did. The perfect darkness surrounded him, engulfed him, filled him, but offered no comfort for the pain, which came from knowing he'd given up his greatest gift—Aerielle. And though he repeatedly told himself it had been a long time ago, it seemed like yesterday that he had last held her, kissed her, and told her of his love.

Sliding slowly to the floor, Phoenix bowed his head against bent knees, his hair brushing the floor. "Oh, God, what have I done? What do I do now?"

→→→

Hawk insisted on walking Aerielle home, but both were quiet as they started around the lake. A breeze had sprung up and it seeped through Aerielle's thick sweater. It cooled her blood in more ways than one, and she felt her anger sucked away with the warmth-stealing wind. Normally, Aerielle would have enjoyed a walk such as this. Brilliant colored leaves whirled about in a fall frenzy, while a myriad of carved pumpkin faces greeted passers-by from creatively decorated porches across the street. Yes, any other time. Well, why *not* now? Was she going to let Phoenix ruin a perfectly splendid afternoon?

"What a beautiful day it is," Aerielle declared, sliding her arm through Hawk's.

He glanced at her, a smile coming to his lips. "Why yes. Yes it is."

Idaho seemed to think so as well, for at that moment he pulled hard on his leash and yanked Aerielle off the sidewalk, his nose working overtime. Aerielle let him lead her and he pulled her and Hawk about ten feet into the leaf carpeted grass, the crunch of autumn beneath their feet almost loud enough to drown out Idaho's yip of joy.

"What is it, boy?" laughed Aerielle as the dog buried his nose in the leaves, searching with canine accuracy.

Suddenly his head popped up and he turned to them, showing off a nice sized stick he had discovered.

Hawk laughed. "We must have passed a dozen other sticks by now. What's so special about this one?"

"All I know is, he's particular about the sticks he chooses."

As if he'd been announced, Idaho brought the stick forward, but instead of coming to Aerielle, he went to Hawk, his back end wiggling in excitement.

"You're supposed to take it, admire it, and give it back to him," encouraged Aerielle. "Then rinse and repeat. He'll do this about a half a dozen times before he's satisfied."

Hawk did as instructed, grinning almost as much as the dog at the repeated gift exchange. Finally satisfied, Idaho promptly lay down in the leaf-laden grass, happy as a clam with his stick resting between his paws.

"I've never known a dog to do that," said Hawk.

Aerielle smiled fondly. "He's done it since he was a puppy. But not normally with others. He must really like you."

Hawk smirked. "Well, what's not to like?"

What *was* not to like, thought Aerielle. He was handsome, kind, charismatic, and he had a great sense of humor.

"You know," said Aerielle. "I believe I still owe you payment for Idaho's vaccinations."

Hawk eyed her, humor in his expression. "Really. I thought maybe I was going to have to comp that visit."

"Well, you're getting paid one way or another, so it's either cash or kisses."

"Hmm." Hawk appeared to think on it. "Cash or kisses.... Get over here, you."

When Hawk reached for her, Aerielle went willingly, determined to give Hawk her full attention.

The payment was supposed to be two kisses, but Aerielle wasn't sure there would be time for a second as the first one increased in tenure and tenacity, Hawk clearly putting as much effort and persuasion into it as she was. Aerielle slid her arms about his neck, stroking his short cropped hair, determined to block Phoenix's face from her mind. There was no telling how much longer the kiss might have lasted, how much more energy would have been put into it, if not for a passing stranger's footsteps drawing them apart. It didn't matter. Aerielle knew it hadn't worked, because despite all her efforts, as well as Hawk's, she hadn't stopped thinking about "him," hadn't stopped seeing "his" face through her closed lids.

Hawk released her regretfully, but no more regretful than Aerielle, for despite the lifetime between them, Aerielle was not free of Phoenix, and likely, never would be.

Hawk stared at her as the cool air rushed between them, separating them by more than form. "I failed, didn't I?"

"Failed?" repeated Aerielle, still gathering her scattered thoughts.

"It was a test, wasn't it? Either that, or you've suddenly become extremely fond of me."

What was it about these brothers, thought Aerielle. They both had the same sense of discernment as their mother. How rare in a man, let alone two. "What if I'd just been holding myself back and couldn't keep my emotions in check any longer? Was the kiss that unconvincing?"

Absentmindedly, Hawk ran a thumb over his lips. "Oh, it was convincing alright. Apparently it was *my* effort that wasn't. I've seen the way you look at me sometimes, Aerielle, like you're seeing someone else instead of me. What I don't get...we don't look anything alike."

Aerielle dropped all pretenses, honesty filling her expression. "You have one identical feature. Your eyes."

"The old windows to the soul, huh? Why couldn't it have been our noses? Even if that were true, they wouldn't look alike anymore."

Aerielle smiled lightly, but worry filled her eyes. "I'm sorry, but I had to know before...before—"

"Before I got too attached?"

Aerielle nodded. "Am I too late? Do you hate me?"

Hawk laughed, reaching out a gentle hand and stroking her cheek. "I could never hate you, Aerielle. And no, it's not too late. I won't expire from unrequited love."

"What is it?" he continued, dropping his hand as he studied her expression. "I'm the one who didn't just have his heart broken, but you look like you're going to shatter into a million pieces. Are you that upset we couldn't make you forget him? I mean I'm always open to more practice—"

"You're awful."

A smile tugged at Hawk's lips. "I'm sorry. Really. What's wrong?"

Aerielle took a deep breath. "I know this is going to sound

like the oldest question in the book. And even when people do say yes, they're usually lying, but...."

"But?"

"Can we still be friends?"

"Is this a trick question? You're serious, aren't you?"

"Never mind. Just forget I asked." Aerielle turned away from him, determined not to look back, terrified of what might happen when she went back to "having no life" outside of the hospital.

But Hawk had grabbed her arm, and she was forced to face him again. Tears brimmed in her eyes.

"I'm sorry. That was a stupid way to respond," he admitted. "I only meant why wouldn't I be your friend? I'm an adult... mostly. I knew 'we' as a couple was iffy. But for the record, I like hanging out with you."

"You do?" Aerielle looked into his Hawk's eyes, saw he was telling the truth. "You do."

One tear, now in relief, spilled over and down her cheek.

"You're crying." Reaching out, he ran a comforting hand down her arm. "I promise. Friends it is. As long as you can put up with me."

Aerielle let out a laugh. "You have no idea how much I need you, Hawk, how attached I've become in such a short period of time. I know I must seem more like a child than an adult right now, but—"

"You seem like you're human, Aerielle. That's not something that needs explaining. Has it occurred to you maybe I would miss *your* friendship if you just walked away?"

"You wouldn't just say that to make me feel better?"

Hawk placed his hands on her shoulders, his gaze penetrating. "No. I wouldn't. No lies. No lies between you and me, Aerielle. I will always tell you the truth."

Unlike Phoenix, thought Aerielle. Hawk didn't need to finish the sentence.

"Deal?" demanded Hawk.

Aerielle felt a deep sense of gratitude well up within her. "Deal."

"Good."

"Now I have to tell *you* the truth."

Hawk eyed her warily. "What truth?"

"I'm cold. Can we go home?"

Hawk grinned. "Home it is."

→→→

As they continued to follow the sidewalk toward Aerielle's place, her thoughts were once again consumed by Phoenix and what had happened at the clinic. She speculated about the reasons behind his anger that afternoon. The years hadn't kept her from reading the fury inside of him and knowing it was caused by jealousy. But jealousy of whom? Hawk? Would Phoenix have reacted similarly if it had been another man, or was it simply brotherly rivalry? And what did any or all of it have to do with Phoenix choosing Minnesota to live?

Aerielle shook her head in confusion, pulling Idaho aside to allow room for someone riding a bicycle. The Aussie paused in the grass, snorting loudly while Aerielle shivered in the breeze that suddenly whipped up off the lake. With her free hand she rubbed her opposite arm roughly, trying to create some warmth. A strand of hair clinging to her sweater caught between her fingers. Lifting the strand to set it free, she immediately recognized it wasn't one of hers. It was too long, too dark, too wavy. It belonged to Phoenix. Raising her hand, Aerielle released the memento to the wind, wishing it was similarly easy to loose herself of him. But that single strand of hair was like their relationship. No matter how long or brief an encounter with Phoenix was, no matter how much or little passed between them, he always left something behind.

→→→

Aerielle's night of sleep was only two hours old when she was drawn from it by the sound of her name spoken low but firm. Her slow-to-open eyes widened in surprise when she realized Phoenix was standing beside her bed. Certainly they'd formed some sort of truce over the sign language issue that afternoon, and previously she'd assured him his room would always be accessible to him, but a midnight visit to her bedroom was not what Aerielle had in mind.

Clutching the blanket to her chest, Aerielle quickly shifted into a seated position. "Can I help you?" she questioned with just a touch of sarcasm.

The darkness cloaked his face, but Aerielle could have sworn he smiled. She had a sudden vision of the white female captive being ravished by the young Indian warrior. *Get a grip, Aerielle.*

Phoenix was speaking. "It's a good night for the Northern Lights. If you're interested in seeing them, meet me in the loft."

With those words he was gone, not waiting for Aerielle to respond. Realizing this was an opportunity to sign a peace treaty with said Indian warrior, she quickly got out of bed and changed into some clothes.

Minutes later, Aerielle joined Phoenix on the deck just off the hayloft. When she arrived he was peering into the telescope and adjusting one of the knobs.

Aerielle proceeded to the railing, deciding to let Phoenix set the mood for peace negotiations. Her attention was immediately caught by the spectacular view spread out upon the heavens. More stars than she'd ever seen before, claimed the night. The sight was unlike anything she'd seen in the light polluted skies of Minneapolis.

"See anything you recognize?"

Aerielle turned to find Phoenix watching her. "The Big Dipper," she responded, motioning in its direction. "Isn't it also known as Ursa Major?"

Phoenix shook his head. "Not exactly. Ursa Major, also known as The Great Bear, is a constellation, and the Big Dipper is part of that constellation. It makes up the tail and hind quarters of the bear."

Aerielle turned her eyes back towards the Dipper, studying it with a new perspective, but it was hard to picture a bear. Maybe she needed to work on her imagination. "So what else do you know about the Big Dipper?"

Phoenix's footsteps were light as he joined Aerielle at the railing. Though she refrained from looking his direction, she felt his presence, for his stature cut off some of the gentle breeze, which had been playing with her hair. There was silence between them for a moment, the sound of crickets Aerielle hadn't noticed before, filling the void.

And then Phoenix spoke, his voice thoughtful. "The Big Dipper is made up of eight stars."

Aerielle counted. "I only see seven."

"You see the second star in the handle?" said Phoenix, stepping closer to Aerielle and pointing.

For a moment Aerielle thought his shoulder brushed hers, but then realized it was a length of his hair blown against her by the breeze. With it came the subtle scent of musk which Aerielle found appealing.

It occurred to her that Phoenix was waiting for an answer. "The one in the middle that's higher?" she spoke at last.

"That's right. Only there's two stars not one. They're known as twin stars."

Aerielle studied the sky and found the second star.

"The one most people see, the brighter of the two, is Mizar, which means to cloak, or veil. The other star is Alcor. In ancient Arabia, the sultans chose their archers dependent upon who could see both stars."

Aerielle laughed. "Guess I wouldn't have gotten the job if I'd had to notice it myself."

She sensed Phoenix's nod of agreement. "That makes two of us."

Once again Aerielle found herself distracted by the scent of musk. She determined to ignore it, just as she was attempting to ignore the touch of Phoenix's hair against her skin just below the sleeve of her oversized T-shirt.

"So what's over there?" waved Aerielle, forcing her thoughts back to the sky at hand.

"Taurus for one," said Phoenix, motioning once again.

"Well, I don't see any bull." Hearing her words aloud, Aerielle started to laugh. She had seen plenty of bull from Phoenix in the last month. Including the deception about the sign language, something neither was using now.

"What's so funny?" asked Phoenix.

Aerielle shook her head. "Oh, nothing. I'm just getting slaphappy." She paused. "You really know your stuff when it comes to stargazing. It's more than just your last name. I'm impressed."

Phoenix made no reply, and Aerielle lost herself to the thousands of stars overhead. "I'm impressed with God, too," she added. "He did a pretty fantastic job of putting the stars there."

"You say that as if you know him," said Phoenix, his attention remaining on the display before them.

Aerielle was silent for a moment, feeling the continued brush of Phoenix's hair as she tried to put her thoughts into words. "Well, in a way I do. I mean, having a relationship with God is kind of like having a relationship with someone else. He shares with me through his Word, and I make sure I get back to him every day."

"And how does one talk to God?"

"Same way I'm talking to you."

"And do you tell *Him* off, too?"

Aerielle smiled, laughter filling her voice. "Sometimes. Only *He* doesn't deserve it. But He understands."

"Did you tell God about the phone call you got tonight?"

Startled, Aerielle turned. For a second time that night she found Phoenix watching her. Unconsciously, she stepped back, trying to read his face by the light of the stars and partial moon.

"Sparrow told me," Phoenix continued, revealing his source. "She said you got a call from a guy tonight. She thought he was being mean to you because you got angry and told him where to go. What were the words....'Go jump in a lake, and if there aren't enough choices in Idaho, try Minnesota?'"

"I said that, didn't I?" grinned Aerielle. She tried to read the expression in Phoenix's dark eyes, but they were hidden by the night. She didn't need to see them, though, to know his interest in her phone call was a result of concern. Not that he'd be willing to admit it of course.

"His name is Jim Peterson," continued Aerielle, knowing she wasn't required to explain. "We went out the last three months of our senior year. I dumped him on prom night after he got drunk and I had to call my parents for a ride home. He was not pleased, and since then has failed to accept the fact I no longer have any interest in him. This phone call is just part of his continued harassment. I was hoping if I ignored him, he'd go away."

"*I* ignored you, but you didn't go away."

Aerielle didn't know how to respond, her voice lost to her, just as her gaze was lost in his. Once again the crickets grew louder, playing their harmonies in this latest silence. The breeze picked up, and Phoenix's hair whipped about his shoulders. Trapped by those dark eyes, all Aerielle could think about was this white Minnesotan female having her lips claimed by the captivating Nez Perce warrior.

→→→

Two hours later, as Aerielle returned to her room alone, she still had no idea how either of them had broken that gaze. It hadn't been Aerielle's idea, that's for sure. But Phoenix apparently had an iron will and had forcibly turned his eyes away and found a falling star for Aerielle to concentrate on.

"Meteor," Aerielle grumbled aloud, using the correct term. "Drat blasted, interfering meteor," she continued, as she angrily peeled off her jeans and tossed them into a heap on the floor.

Still grumbling, Aerielle got into bed, hauling the covers over her. Turning on her side, she rested her head on her arm and determinedly closed her eyes. And then opened them. She could have sworn Phoenix was once again in her room, his room, whatever. It was the scent of him, the musk, and then Aerielle realized it was her T-shirt that smelled of him, his hair having continuously brushed her sleeve. So, he used musk shampoo. Aerielle smiled, and buried her nose against her shoulder, greedily taking in the scent he'd left behind.

→→→

Phoenix didn't know how long he sat in the dark, but he'd determined he wasn't moving until he was sure he was alone, however temporarily. He couldn't face either Aerielle or Hawk right now. It wasn't too long before he heard one of the outer doors closing. Even if Aerielle departed the house alone, Phoenix could leave the clinic area before his brother returned.

As he made his way to his study, Phoenix determined he was alone, aside from the four-legged creatures. Clearly Hawk had walked Aerielle home.

Unable to resist, Phoenix stood before the balcony windows in his study, his eyes drawn to the forms of Aerielle, Hawk, and Idaho. Just thinking those words together caused Phoenix to grimace with the irony. Why had she named that dang dog Idaho?

The threesome was far enough away now that Phoenix couldn't make out the details, but close enough that he noticed the Aussie tug Aerielle off the walk and into the grass. Hawk followed and for a moment the three just stood there. And then

Hawk was wrapping Aerielle in his arms and she seemed more than eager to accept his embrace.

Phoenix tore himself away from the window, his chest feeling as if a hole had been carved out of it. He couldn't stand to watch if Hawk kissed her again. How long ago had Phoenix stupidly told Hawk it was okay to take Aerielle to dinner. A month? Most of Hawk's relationships didn't last more than twice that, sometimes even less. And the only reason Phoenix knew, was because Hawk made a habit of bringing his dates to the house eventually. Why should Aerielle be any different? Hawk liked to play the field. Aerielle was too good for him anyway, at least the Aerielle Phoenix had known…still thought he knew. It turned out *he* hadn't been worthy of her either.

Phoenix groaned, angry and frustrated. There were no words to express the tumult inside him, though how it could stay inside with the terrible hole in his heart, Phoenix didn't know.

"Idaho counts hundreds of square miles of lakes and fifteen thousand miles of rivers, and embraces lava craters, sage plains, waterfalls, cedar forests and sand dunes. Idaho enfolds the deepest canyon in North America. It is all here on a pelagic scale and, in comparison to the rest of the country, as uncrowded as the high seas."

Cort Conley, excerpted from Light on the Land
as printed in *Oh! Idaho* - premier issue

7

Phoenix's heart was heavy. Aside from the disaster his life had been reduced to lately, he'd lost a foal in birth that afternoon. He felt tired, empty. All he wanted to do was sleep, but 6:30 seemed a bit early for bed. Besides, his desk was piled with paperwork. Paperwork he'd been ignoring in exchange for the view of the lake outside his study window.

Hearing Sofia's footsteps on the stairs, Phoenix turned his chair to face her as she entered the room.

"The report's finished," she said softly, placing the document in the center of Phoenix's desk.

"Thanks, Sofia."

Silence followed as Sofia studying him. "I'm sorry about the foal, Phoenix. I'm sure you did all you could."

Phoenix stared at Sofia, but failed to see her. "I tell myself that, but it doesn't help...the image of that young girl's face when she was told the colt died...I can't seem to shake it...." Phoenix's eyes focused. "Did you tell Hawk, yet?"

Sofia shook her head. "Haven't had a chance. It was busy this afternoon, and now Tyler's with him. I didn't want to spoil the boy's first day with bad news."

Phoenix nodded. "Understood. How's Tyler working out, anyway?"

"Oh, he's great! Seems real interested in everything."

"I have this feeling we've a vet in the making."

"I think you're right," smiled Sofia.

"You on your way home?"

"In a minute. Can I get you anything before I leave?"

"You've done plenty."

"There's still some coffee in the pot I made at three. You want a cup?"

"That'd be nice, Sofia. Thanks."

Sofia left Phoenix to his brooding, but it was only momentary as Hawk marched in, his feathers obviously ruffled about something.

"My ad's missing from the paper," Hawk declared.

Phoenix leaned back in his chair, though his frustration over the foal was making it hard to ignore his brother's anger. "That's right. I had it removed."

"What gave you the right?!"

"What right had you to place the ad?" returned Phoenix, shifting forward. "I never agreed."

"Agreed?! Since when do we agree on anything?! You think because you own a majority share of the business that you get to make all the decisions!"

Phoenix took a deep breath, then let it out slowly. Enough was enough. Hawk needed to be told about the plans concerning Sofia. "Hawk, I—"

"And you know what else I think?" continued Hawk, firmly placing his hands on Phoenix's desk and leaning forward. "I think you canceled the ad because you're mad about me and Aerielle."

The immediate silence which followed was laced tighter than the string on the bow hanging on the wall. Phoenix stared at his brother, their dark eyes a clash of wills. Hawk's nostrils were slightly flared, and Phoenix could feel his own jaw signaling his anger.

"Get out," said Phoenix, his voice as even as a smooth sheet of ice.

Hawk's eyes narrowed. "I'm not going anywhere until we talk."

"Fine. You can have the room to yourself," announced Phoenix, rising to his feet.

Moving around the desk, he headed for the door, a definite purpose to his steps. He passed Sofia on the stairs without a word, and as he reached the foyer, he could hear her demanding to know what Hawk had said to him. Grabbing a jacket and a pair of leashes out of the front closet, Phoenix proceeded to collect the shepherds from the back yard and head for the lake.

It wasn't until Phoenix was almost halfway around the lake that he noticed the two leashes he carried weren't attached to the collars of the dogs who walked faithfully at his side. Phoenix promptly slid the leashes into the right pocket of the jacket he didn't remember putting on.

Thankful for the somewhat concealing darkness, Phoenix shook his head in disgust and continued along the walk. He had come mighty close to losing control with Hawk tonight. It seemed as each day passed, it was getting harder to keep his emotions in check.

He knew he should be more logical about this whole dating thing with Hawk and Aerielle, but since when had he ever been logical when it came to Aerielle? Phoenix truly believed Hawk and Aerielle's so-called relationship would lead nowhere, yet his belief did nothing to ease the intensity of his pain.

He felt ripped apart by the desire to run from the past and, the need to face his brother with the truth of what he was feeling. But instead of telling Hawk what his seeing Aerielle was doing to him, instead of telling his brother it was tearing him up inside, Phoenix would probably end up warning him to "stay away from her, or I'll beat you to a bloody pulp."

Phoenix winced at his own thoughts, remembering the night someone felt that same way about him. Of course, Phoenix wouldn't actually carry out his threat. Other than the usual roughhousing, Phoenix had never struck his brother in anger.

The wind stirred, rustling the few remaining leaves on the trees. Phoenix slowed to a stop to get his bearings and realized he was just across the street from Aerielle's small apartment building.

"It figures," he mumbled aloud, glancing down at Spock and McCoy who both looked up inquiringly. "Females. They make a man stupid."

Spock sat down, wagging his tail.

"You know, boys, it's no wonder Hawk's a bit ticked off. First I tell him I don't mind if he takes Aerielle out, and then I act teed when he does. That's what you call giving mixed signals. And it ain't the first time I've been called on the carpet for it. Of course, that other time it was linoleum...."

→→→

In contrast to the hot August day, the linoleum felt cool against his bare feet as Phoenix stepped quietly over to the oven and peered through the glass window. Not getting a good enough view, Phoenix cracked the door, wincing at the seemingly loud creak it made. He'd been doing his best to avoid Aerielle since the night they'd spent stargazing, and there was no way he wanted to get caught nosing around the cookies, no matter how wonderful they smelled or looked. The sight of the chocolate chips melting into the cookies made Phoenix's mouth water.

Abruptly, the buzzer went off. Phoenix jerked back, inadvertently releasing the oven door and allowing it to slam shut. Then he heard the screen door and knew Aerielle and Sparrow were on their way back in to remove the cookies.

Phoenix headed in the opposite direction, toward the dining room, only to discover his escape route blocked by some chairs his mother had moved so she could vacuum. He couldn't go back. He couldn't go forward. The only place of hiding was the alcove nestled between the two. The five by seven "room" had a narrow arched doorway and was pretty well hidden in shadows. Inside, his mother kept a spare kitchen chair and a telephone stand with the said telephone.

Darting inside, Phoenix went for the chair, but instead of just sitting on it, he crouched down on its worn wooden surface so that his feet were off the floor. He was not a moment too soon. He even found himself holding his breath as Aerielle and Sparrow entered the kitchen.

"Are they done?" asked Sparrow excitedly.

Phoenix heard the oven door open, pictured Aerielle's hair spilling forward as she leaned down to look. Or was she wearing her hair up today?

"They sure are, honey. Why don't you grab some paper towels, and we'll lay the cookies out on the dining room table."

"The dining room," Phoenix muttered under his breath. He'd be more visible from that direction.

"Aerielle?" came Sparrow's voice as a chair was dragged over to the counter.

Aerielle's "Yes, honey?" was accompanied by the sound of paper towels being unrolled.

"Is it true that the way to a man's heart is through his stomach?"

Aerielle laughed and Phoenix could picture her blue eyes lighting up.

"Well, I suppose that depends."

Uh oh, Aerielle was passing the alcove on the way to the dining room.

"On what?"

Phoenix saw Aerielle stop as she encountered the barrier of chairs. "Why don't we put the first batch of cookies in the kitchen, Sparrow. Then we'll move the chairs back."

"What does it depend on?" reminded Sparrow, still out of sight.

Phoenix couldn't even remember what the question was. Oh yeah. The way to a man's heart.

"What it depends on," continued Aerielle, turning back towards the kitchen with her tray of cookies, "is the man."

Phoenix pressed back in his chair, wishing he had the ability to disappear like his ancestors were supposedly given to doing.

"I mean men are—" Aerielle stopped, stared, those blue eyes Phoenix had pictured moments before meeting his.

He gave her his best "Are you going to make something of it?" look, while at the same time noticing how the hair she wore up, trailed wisps about the smooth pale flesh of her neck.

"Men are," continued Aerielle, her eyes never leaving Phoenix, "the most unpredictable, irritating, wishy-washy creatures God ever put on this planet."

"What does 'unpredictable' mean?" came Sparrow's voice.

"It means you never know how they are going to act from one moment to the next."

"That sounds like Eddie, all right."

Aerielle turned her attention to the kitchen. "Who's Eddie?" she questioned, as Phoenix wondered the same thing.

"A boy in my summer school class."

Phoenix followed with his ears as Aerielle disappeared from view. "And does he act different from one moment to the next?"

"All the time. He likes me one day and ignores me the next."

Phoenix heard Aerielle laugh over the sound of clanking cookie trays. "Men can be that way. Doesn't matter whether they're eight, or eighteen."

"My brother's eighteen."

Phoenix didn't need his little sister to tell him whom Aerielle was referring to.

"Yes, I know," assured Aerielle, cynically.

"Yes, I know," mimicked Phoenix in silence.

"So what do you do?"

"Well, honey. If I were you, I'd have lots of patience and hope he gets his act together."

"No food?" asked Sparrow, seriously.

"Well, it certainly can't hurt to try. Maybe Eddie's just waiting for the best chocolate chip cookies he's ever had. Why don't we wrap up two of the biggest ones you can find. You sneak 'em into his desk when no one's looking. Just make sure he knows they're from you."

Many hours later, close to midnight, Phoenix found *his* two cookies resting on his telescope. Oh, he got the message all right. So maybe he had been a little unfair, ignoring Aerielle the way he had. *Tananisa*, she was more then he'd ever bargained for! He'd almost kissed her the other night. Phoenix didn't want to think about where that might lead. He was Nez Perce. She was white...and what tempting white skin she had.

There he went again, thinking about Aerielle. Avoiding her obviously wasn't working, so what was the point?

"It's all your fault, you know," grumbled Phoenix, glancing up at the barn roof. He wondered if Aerielle's God heard him. Maybe Phoenix should ask Aerielle. Grabbing up his cookies, he headed for the house.

Arriving at Aerielle's door, Phoenix knocked gently, just as he had a couple of weeks ago. And as before, there was no answer.

Tentatively, he turned the knob and opened the door, using the light from the hallway to see by.

He was surprised to discover Aerielle sitting cross-legged on the bed, dressed in jeans and a T-shirt, and apparently waiting for him.

Phoenix remained in the doorway, and for lack of knowing what to say, he bit into one of the cookies, the taste of chocolate bringing his taste buds to life.

Aerielle spoke, breaking the silence. "I won't ask why you've been ignoring me."

Phoenix suspected she knew.

"I won't even ask why you were hiding in the alcove."

Phoenix suspected she knew that, too.

"What I will ask," continued Aerielle, her tone serious, "is how are the cookies? And remember, your sister helped make them."

She grinned.

Phoenix smiled reluctantly. "They're wonderful."

"Good. I have another question for you. This powwow coming up in a few weeks, would you prefer I didn't come?"

"It's open to the public," he shrugged, taking another bite of cookie.

"But I'm not exactly the general public. If you would prefer I not be there, I won't come."

Phoenix once again found himself amazed by the many facets of Aerielle's personality. "You're more than welcome to come, Aerielle. Besides, Sparrow adores you, and she'll want you to see her dance." Phoenix made a point of not mentioning his own performance.

"I'll be there," assured Aerielle, and for a moment Phoenix felt she had read his thoughts.

"So what's in the sky tonight?" questioned Aerielle, sliding off the bed and heading towards the door.

Phoenix swallowed the last of his second cookie, following Aerielle with his eyes. "About anything you want to see. I thought we'd ride out a couple of miles. The whole sky'll be visible."

Aerielle paused before him, her eyes sparkling. "I can't wait to see God's handiwork from a better vantage point."

"So your God is responsible for the stars?"

"What god do *you* serve, Phoenix?"

Her question was tentative, wondering if he would find it offensive, but his eyes remained silent, and no telltale sign showed at his jawline.

"I have no god."

Aerielle was surprised, wondering at the loneliness that thought invoked. "And your ancestors? I assume they followed some religion depending on what side of the treaty they were on."

"They were nontreaty Indians, and yes, most followed the dreamer religion. My great-uncle Yellow Wolf was twenty-one when he fought beside Joseph and Looking Glass as they retreated toward Canada."

Aerielle knew the basic story of the last Indian war in U.S. history. Famous Chief Joseph—who was known for the words "I will fight no more forever"—and several other chiefs and their bands, had attempted to escape to Canada, only to be stopped short of their goal, which was where Joseph had given his popularized speech.

"I was named after him," continued Phoenix.

Aerielle was confused. "Named after whom?"

"My great-uncle. My middle name—my Nez Perce name—is *Hemene Moxmox*. Yellow Wolf."

→→→

Aerielle pressed a little harder on the accelerator of her truck, trying to speed her escape from the hospital. But there was nowhere to go. Rush hour surrounded her. Her apartment and the soothing walk she planned around the lake with Idaho were hundreds, if not thousands, of slow moving cars away. It was times like this Aerielle longed for the open-emptiness of Shaman Prairie, or even the endless forested roads that wound through the mountains of Idaho. And of course there was the Clearwater River Valley and Kamiah.

→→→

Phoenix had said the trip from Shaman Prairie to Kamiah was somewhere between an hour and an hour and a half, but it seemed considerably longer to Aerielle. The prairies had disappeared quickly as the family truck Phoenix drove was swallowed up in foothills thick with pines. The road had twisted and turned through the dense wall of deep green, allowing them the occasional view of another rising mountain of pine steeples. They had soon swept into the river valley on Hwy 12, now on reservation land, driving south toward Kamiah, the Clearwater River off to their right their sole companion.

With her window cranked down in the late morning August heat, Aerielle could hear and feel the river's sweet serenade of welcoming coolness. She was grateful for its almost human company, for the Phoenix beside her was as silent and stiff as a bronze statue. For the umpteenth time, Aerielle glanced over at him, but as usual his attention was staid on the road, his work-worn hands wielding a tight grip on the steering wheel. She wondered if the muscle on the left side of his jaw was revealing as much tension.

She also wondered at the wisdom of convincing Phoenix to give her a complete tour of Kamiah just days before the Looking Glass Powwow, or *any* time for that matter. Kamiah, was, after all, the heart of his people, their "Garden of Eden" so to speak, and despite Kamiah being somewhat of a tourist attraction, Aerielle had asked for a sharing of its past by one of those still effected *by* that past. Though the division and "enslavement" of the hearts and souls of the Nez Perce had taken place over a hundred years ago, some of their descendants were still wearing chains. Had Aerielle, on insisting this trip be taken, tightened those that Phoenix wore?

"I'm sorry," she blurted, her words filled with deep regret.

For the first time since they'd left, Phoenix looked at her. "What for?"

"For pressuring you into this sightseeing trip. I could tell you really didn't want to play tour guide, but I didn't listen."

Phoenix returned his gaze to the road, and Aerielle sensed he was struggling for a response. "It's not that I mind playing tour guide. The role is just an unfamiliar one. I'm usually forced to bear the burden of being a tourist *attraction*, not a guide."

Aerielle stared at Phoenix's profile, surprised by his admission, and fearful she was as guilty as the rest. "Have *I* made you feel that way?"

Her question was greeted with silence.

"We can go back if you'd like," she offered.

"No," said Phoenix abruptly, his gaze lost to the road. "No, you have not made me feel that way. I'll show you whatever you want to see."

How 'bout your soul, wondered Aerielle.

"Where would you like to start?" asked Phoenix.

Aerielle bit back her unspoken question, turning her eyes away lest she reveal her thoughts. Taking a deep breath, she let it out slowly. "How 'bout at the beginning?"

The beginning, of course, was the Heart of the Monster, a large grassy mound fifty feet in diameter, around fifteen feet high and surrounded by a decorative wooden fence to keep people off.

It was located past Kamiah proper, just off of Highway 12 in an open field next to the Clearwater. A stand of trees offering shade to several picnic tables made up the visitors' nearest scenic view. Here, throughout the summer, forest rangers came and told the Nez Perce legend of how they—the Nimipu[1]—and all others came to be.

There were but a few visitors scattered throughout the historic spot. Phoenix and Aerielle paused in a small amphitheater-style visitors' shelter a short ways before the picnic area, but with a clear view of the Heart.

"Kamiah was the winter home for many of my people," explained Phoenix, as Aerielle began to read information displayed on the walls.

Aerielle turned to him, found his gaze, not on the informational tidbits, but on the panoramic view available from the open sides of the shelter. She moved up beside him, letting her gaze take in the greens and browns of surrounding foothills, which to Aerielle's Minnesotan eye, looked more like mountains. The river rumbled softly in the background. The scene was peaceful and calming, inviting one to rest a while.

[1] Nimipu is the name the Nez Perce originally gave themselves. It is pronounced Nee-mee-poo. The name Nez Perce (Pierced Noses) was bestowed by the French after supposedly seeing one of the Nimipu with a pierced nose. There are conflicting opinions whether this custom was ever carried out by them, but the name remains.

Aerielle blocked out the sound of cars on the road, tried to rid her vision of houses, electric lines, and the signs of modern life. "It's beautiful here," she announced, "but it must have been magnificent in its untainted state of a hundred years or so ago."

At her words, Phoenix stared at her, his expression unrevealing, yet intense.

The moment was interrupted as they were joined by another couple, obviously tourists evidenced by their camera equipment. They glanced at Phoenix curiously, and then the woman stepped forward and pressed a button on the shelter wall for a recorded message. They listened as a group to the best known legend of Itsiyiyi—Coyote, that of The Heart of the Monster.

Aerielle tried to concentrate on the words, but it was difficult. The other couple was studying Phoenix without being obvious, while he, bereft of any hesitation or covertness, continued to stare at Aerielle. Finally, it must have occurred to him he might be making her uncomfortable, and he glanced away, if but briefly.

Aerielle's attention was divided by Phoenix and the story of how Coyote created the Nimipu and all other people. According to legend, creation of the human race took place at the end of the age in which animals spoke and acted as humans do now. At this time, a great monster, "Koos-Koos-Ki," came and swallowed up all the animals, all of course except Coyote. *And maybe a wolf*, thought Aerielle, feeling Phoenix's unsettling attention on her once again. *He's just masquerading as a human to get by.* Right now,

Aerielle felt like she was being watched by the beast—Yellow Wolf.

Suddenly, Aerielle realized she'd missed how the Coyote had saved all the animals. She only knew they were free, and the Coyote had destroyed the monster, tearing it apart and throwing pieces of it in all directions. Each part became a different people—a different tribe. When he was done, Coyote realized he hadn't created a people for the Kamiah Valley. And so, taking up the heart of the monster, Coyote squeezed out some blood and sprinkled it over the land. It was this blood which became the great Nimipu. And from that day forward, the animals spoke no more.

No wonder he's so quiet, thought Aerielle, glancing at the masculine profile Phoenix currently presented her.

The other couple left as soon as the recording was completed, leaving Aerielle and Phoenix alone again.

"So what is it?" asked Aerielle, turning to face him directly. "Why were you staring at me like I'd just stepped in horse manure?"

Phoenix looked at Aerielle, the same intense light to his dark eyes as he studied her yet again. "What you said...about the valley a hundred years ago...it was as if you were reading my mind.... Of course, it seems you're always reading my mind."

Aerielle was amazed by this declaration—his admission—but kept her surprise to herself. "So what made this time different?"

"This time you not only read my mind, you spoke my exact thoughts, as if I myself had spoken them aloud."

Aerielle took a moment to absorb this information. "And when else have I read your mind?"

Phoenix brushed at a strand of hair the breeze had blown across his face. "This morning you knew exactly what I was going to have for breakfast and even started making it before I got to the kitchen."

Aerielle bit back a smile. At eighteen, Phoenix was already a creature of habit, and she had learned that on the days he showered early, he had a larger breakfast, taking more time and allowing his hair to dry somewhat. She also knew that on those same days, he almost always had French toast, fresh orange juice, and a slice of ham. No mind reading there, just time honored observation.

"Yesterday," continued Phoenix, "you knew I was worrying about one of the mares though I hadn't said anything."

Once again, Aerielle had recognized the signs forthcoming from him, the slight nuances one often learns after living under the same roof with someone.

Aerielle nodded, keeping her secrets to herself.

Phoenix was shaking his head. "That same day, you even knew when I was hungry. You told me to go eat something. That I was driving you crazy."

Unable to contain herself this time, Aerielle burst out laughing. "That was easy. I could hear your stomach growling six feet away."

Phoenix laughed, and Aerielle felt her resulting pleasure deep inside. It wasn't often

Phoenix laughed, or even smiled, in front of her—in front of anybody.

"Seriously," said Phoenix, the laughter quickly gone, "If I'm not already telling you something I hadn't planned to say, you have this uncanny ability to say what I'm thinking anyway, and even express it when I don't know how."

"Does it bother you?"

Phoenix's gaze penetrated hers, as if he longed to see within her as he thought she saw into him. "I don't know.... This ability you have, do you suppose it's your God's way of getting to me?"

Aerielle smiled. "Well, I can't say as I'd put it past Him."

"What am I thinking now?"

Aerielle's first response was to laugh. "Probably that you're grateful those tourists didn't strike up a conversation and ask a bunch of questions."

Phoenix's lashes lowered, hooding his eyes. "I see I'm going to have to watch what I think about around you."

"Not on my account," said Aerielle, her attention drawn by something fluttering on the ground. She stepped away from Phoenix and retrieved a brochure possibly dropped by their previous company. The brochure turned out to be a visitor's guide, with the words "Welcome to Kamiah" printed on the cover.

Aerielle felt Phoenix's presence behind her as he looked over her shoulder. "Welcome to Kamiah," he said, reading aloud.

Was it her imagination, or had Aerielle "read" a groan in the way Phoenix spoke those words.

"I suppose you'll want to see everything listed there," said Phoenix, sounding somewhat resigned.

So, there *had* been a groan.

"I have a better idea," replied Aerielle, glancing back at Phoenix. "What's *your* favorite historical spot?"

Phoenix's expression grew contemplative, almost distant. He stepped away from her, shadows of leaves hiding his features, making Aerielle wish she truly *could* read his mind.

"It's a place many go, but not a place I've ever taken someone."

There was reverence in his voice as he talked, as if he spoke of something holy. Yet again Aerielle wondered if she was treading on "sacred ground."

Phoenix turned to her, his face declaring a decision. "White Bird."

White Bird. Aerielle liked the sound of it. "What is White Bird?"

"A battlefield. *The* battlefield. The one on which the Nez Perce war began. It was named after the chief who occupied the land there."

"Will you take me there?" The question was irrelevant, for Aerielle knew Phoenix had already made the decision.

"Yes. I'll take you," replied Phoenix. "But you knew that, didn't you?"

Aerielle smiled. Phoenix shook his head.

At about the same time the Civil War began in 1861, another war of division had begun in the West. Only the division had not to do with freedom from slavery, but another form of enslavement—the reservation.

In 1863, the Nez Perce were left with but 750,000 acres of reservation land, having given up 13 million more. Whether this was done willingly or unwillingly depended on which side of the Nez Perce division one was a member of—the treaty Indians or the non-treaty Indians—those who'd signed and those who hadn't. Unlike the white man's president, there was no one leader for the Nez Perce. Each band with its own chief was a government unto its own.

The treaty of 1863, often referred to as the Steal Treaty, was an agreement made by only some of the Nez Perce and the white man. It was written as a result of the discovery of gold on the Nez Perce reservation as it stood from the original treaty of 1855. Those chiefs who stood upon the non-treaty side numbered five, including the well-known Chief Joseph, also known as Heinmot Tooyalakekt, Thunder Traveling.

Yet even before the 1863 treaty, the white man had begun dividing the Indians with the introduction of "religion." I say religion and not Christianity, for no group who behaved as many of the missionaries did to the Nez Perce should have had the right to claim the sacrificial name of Christ, for where Christ's heart was forgiving, their' s was filled with judgment.

By the time the treaty of 1863 was signed, the
Nez Perce had been divided not just into treaty
and non-treaty Indians,(upper and lower) but
Christians and heathens, the heathens also
known as long hairs and blanket Indians. Christian
Indians were known by their white man's clothing,
Biblical names, and for the men, short hair.

But in the end, it mattered not what they wore, who
they worshipped, or what agreements they may or
may not have made—in the end, all the Nez Perce,
rendered apart as they might be, were ordered to
live together on a fragment of their original land,
their freedom gone, their captivity begun.

Chy Anne Autumn Osborn

8

The drive to White Bird Battlefield, though taking them off the reservation, was in itself worth the effort, for they passed through Grangeville which was surrounded by some of the most beautiful "amber waves of grain" in the country. The shimmering golden land appeared to stretch forever, challenging the eye to find the end of it. Aerielle was amazed by the endless beauty. There was nothing to compare it to in Minnesota.

Yet, despite the loveliness of the view, it did not come close to White Bird.

As Phoenix pulled into an overlook that was part of the eleven mile road tour that wound through the White Bird hills, Aerielle found herself in awe of this new vision of endlessness. Her gaze reached out to the gently rolling hills of prairie gold, the rounded grassy ridges, the steep slopes and rocky ravines, all against the backdrop of the pure pastel blue of the sky. It was a view that caught at one's imagination of eternity. Aerielle felt herself holding her breath as she attempted to etch this piece of paradise into her memory.

She got out of the truck as if in a trance, unable to take her eyes off the view. This was not what she had pictured for a battlefield, but then, what were former battlefields supposed to look like.

Phoenix joined her near the edge of the overlook, he equally as silent as she. A soft breeze brought the scents of nature and a quickening of the soul. Aerielle could not envision a battle here, didn't want to.

"So what happened here and why?" The questions asked themselves. Aerielle glanced at Phoenix, not even sure she'd spoken aloud. The breeze blew his hair back from his face, allowing Aerielle an unhindered view of this modern warrior's noble face.

The warrior began to speak. "It was 1877, fourteen years after the Steal Treaty was signed. The white government ordered the nontreaty Indians onto the reservation on punishment of death if they refused. They were given thirty days to gather all their stock and cross a river flooded from spring melt off and move inside the boundaries. The chiefs agreed, but there was a lot of rebellion among the younger warriors."

"Am I to understand they didn't do as they were told?" she asked wryly.

Phoenix gave a false laugh, continuing to gaze at the empty battlefield. "The day before the 30 days were up, while the chiefs were away from camp, three warriors rode off and killed several whites known for certain atrocities against the Nez Perce. When they returned to camp, they gathered a bigger party which went on to kill another ten. In all, fourteen whites were killed. Of course, no one bothered to keep track of the number of Indians killed on reservation land after the first treaty."

Despite the sarcasm to his words, Aerielle sensed Phoenix was not in turn condoning the death of the fourteen.

"Anyway, the chiefs expected reprisal from Howard's Troops, so their bands retreated to White Bird's Village, all in all, about 700 people, maybe 200 warriors. Then on June 17, 1877 the last Indian war began with the firing of a white man's gun."

"I take it that this was not the battle where Chief Joseph gave his famous speech?" said Aerielle, running her hands over her arms as if to brush away the vision.

"No. Though Joseph was here all right, along with two other chiefs and their bands. They were White Bird—an old man—and Toohoolhoolzotes. Looking Glass didn't join until July when his village was attacked. Joseph's brother Ollokot was there, though, and a another well-known warrior named Two Moons."

Aerielle nodded thoughtfully, "What about Yellow Wolf? Or was it Chief Yellow Wolf?"

"He was there, but as a scout, as well as one of Joseph's guards. He wasn't given the status of a chief until much later, but he never used the title."

"And what qualifications are required for this rank of chief?"

Phoenix glanced at her briefly. "Some say ten successful horse stealing raids."

Aerielle laughed. "Not exactly what I expected to hear."

"Maybe it would help to know that becoming a chief did not make one a war chief. Neither Joseph nor White Bird were war chiefs, more like peace chiefs and administrators. Now, Looking Glass, he was a war chief, and one of the best, despite the battle of Big Hole where so many were lost."

"Ah," said Aerielle. "The reason for the Looking Glass Powwow."

Phoenix nodded.

"Tell me more about your namesake," said Aerielle.

Turning toward Aerielle for the first time, Phoenix gauged the sincerity of her interest. He was apparently satisfied with what he saw. "Yellow Wolf was second cousin to Joseph. He was twenty-one when the war started, and known as a great horseman. He was also one of the few survivors when the fighting ended.

"By the time Joseph made his speech at Bear Paw Battlefield in Montana, most of the chiefs were dead. Looking Glass died of a stray bullet in the last few days. Ollokot, too, was killed, and Toohoolhoolzotes and Hahtalekin—whose band joined later—were also killed at Bear Paw. Joseph was worried about those who had survived and could not go on, so he surrendered. Yellow Wolf and White Bird and several hundred more tried to escape, continuing on toward Canada. They should've all made it. It was only fifty miles away."

"Did Yellow Wolf?" asked Aerielle, wondering what had become of his name sake.

Phoenix's eyes reflected the earnestness in Aerielle's question. "Yellow Wolf and White Bird, and some of their followers."

"You must take great pride in not only knowing your heritage, but from where and whom your name comes."

Phoenix shrugged. "Our Indian names are supposed to be kept in the family, but it's good when the history of that name is kept as well. It also helps when your namesake leaves a biographical book behind, like *Yellow Wolf, His Own Story.*"

"You don't see too many of those around. I'll have to read it." Aerielle glanced back out over the steep rolling slopes and grassy knolls. "So what makes this your favorite place in spite of it's birthing a war?"

There was no answer, and Aerielle turned to find Phoenix staring at the same view, a slight twinge of muscle making it presence known along his jaw line. When he finally spoke, he did not look at Aerielle. "I was hoping you would know...and I would not have to tell you."

The intimacy of Phoenix's words amazed her—stirred her. He wanted her to read his mind. He was pleading for her to read his mind. He might often act as if he wanted nothing to do with her, but there was a part of him in rebellion, hungering to open up, to give—to receive.

Aerielle felt the urge to take whatever he desired to give, to share with him all he wished to receive. In the few months that had passed since their first encounter, she had learned so much of him. She knew many of his habits, his loves, and even a few of his dreams. And now, slowly, she was being permitted to know his soul. With that knowledge came the pressing need to feel the beating of the heart she now knew thrived within the chest she'd claimed was empty. She longed to know the warmth of his lips against hers, and most of all to caress the waves of hair that made him who and what he was—Phoenix Yellow Wolf Stargazer, descendant of the Nimipu.

Aerielle was shocked by this sudden rush of tenderness and urgency she felt for Phoenix. Totally gone were the feelings of alienation she had known just months before.

Suddenly, Phoenix was looking at her, his eyes haunting and dark. Aerielle was forced to push away her self-revelations and face the moment at hand. Why was White Bird Phoenix's favorite place?

Aerielle tore her gaze from Phoenix's sharp boned features and let her eyes absorb the vision of beauty, which brought to mind the unblemished purity of a virgin bride. "I think," she began, her thoughts struggling for words, "that despite its past, this land remains uncompromised, its beauty untainted even as it holds on to a history of struggle—of survival. And no matter in what direction you look, the hills and slopes roll on into the edge of the sky. You can lose yourself here, can't you Phoenix?"

Silence greeted her, a Yellow Wolf silence, and Aerielle knew she'd spoken the words he needed to hear. She had "read his mind."

The breeze picked up, bringing to Aerielle the familiar scent of Phoenix's recently washed hair. She saw movement out of the corner of her eyes as Phoenix reached up and brushed back his hair. If but the hand were hers.

Aerielle felt a brief touch of his gaze, and then it was gone as he turned once more to feast on the expanse before them. When he spoke, his voice held a note of something Aerielle would not have noticed a month earlier—confusion. "I knew you'd understand. You seem to understand a lot, including somehow, me. I don't know why I care whether you do or not...but I do."

Phoenix continued before Aerielle had a chance to respond. "I want to own land here some day, Aerielle, a good 5000 acres maybe. And I'll build a house in the center of it all.... There'll be one room with walls made of glass. The room will be my hideaway, and wherever I look, I will see paradise."

Aerielle gathered Phoenix's words together like delicate flowers, attempting to create a garden—an image—of that which he envisioned. What she found, was paradise indeed.

→→→

The sky had clouded up, and it had begun to mist by the time they had completed their auto-tour of White Bird and gotten more than half way back to Kamiah. Aerielle casually flipped through the pages in her Welcome to Kamiah brochure. Something caught her eye. Phoenix noticed.

"Is there something you'd like to see?" he asked glancing over.

Aerielle eyed him in return. "Would you mind?"

"How could I? You just spent two hours at White Bird with me."

"Do you know where the bluffs with the Indian writings are?"

"I've been there. The writings aren't Nez Perce, you know."

"Oh, I understand that. I've just never seen any 'writings' before."

A short while later as they drove through the small town of Kamiah, Phoenix pointed out a few places, including the Nez Perce Trading Post, owned and operated by the Nez Perce tribe. It looked similar to convenience stores everywhere.

"Can anybody shop in there?" asked Aerielle, feeling ignorant.

"Anybody. Of course, unless you have Tribal ID you'd have to pay taxes."

"And of course, you don't."

Phoenix grinned, turning down a side street. "I don't have to pay taxes anywhere on the reservation."

"Well, then, I'll just have to have you do all my shopping."

Phoenix snorted. "That ought to offer some interesting insight."

"So how much of an Indian do you have to be to qualify as one?"

"Twenty-five percent—Here's where the powwow will be held," added Phoenix, pointing to what resembled a school building. "There's a field on the other side of the Wa-a'Yas."

"The what?"

"The Wa-a'Yas Nez Perce Community Building. It includes a restaurant, medical services, the BIA, a gymnasium. The gym is where they hold winter powwows or rained out powwows.... Did you know that only about 15% of the reservation is actually owned by individual Nez Perce or the tribe?"

Aerielle glanced at him in horror. "After all your people went through? That's abominable."

"The tribe's working on getting it back."

"How big *is* the tribe?"

"Between 1800 and 2000 people."

"And how big is the reservation?"

"About 750,000 acres. We lost more than thirteen million."

Aerielle shook her head in disbelief, unable to find a response.

Minutes later, after traversing a small residential neighborhood, they took a lonely road along the river edge. Shortly, they pulled off and parked the truck in a patch of gravel.

"People like to fish off the rocks up here," said Phoenix, jumping down from the truck.

The low hanging afternoon clouds were still loosing a mist over Kamiah, but it wasn't enough to dampen the adventurous spirit.

Phoenix led Aerielle down a grassy path to a line of railroad tracks which they began to follow. Neither said anything, and the quiet gave Aerielle time for a bit of computation. "Twenty-five percent, huh? It only takes a couple of generations of intermarriage with Non-Nez Perce to disqualify the family line. Is there a lot of pressure?"

"To keep the blood?" said Phoenix, as they followed the track between tall green grasses and an assortment of trees. "Yeah, a fair amount, I guess. But much is lost on my generation."

"I'm not sure which is worse," remarked Aerielle, "having to worry about 'keeping the blood' and your past history alive, or not having any past or history to remember. I mean, me? I'm just an American, a blood mix that contains more nationalities than I know of. I have no stories of ancient times, no history I can claim or pass on—other than "American History"—and no traditions of a nationality or race type, at least none that I know the roots of. I do things because I was taught to, but not why. I'm just a white American.... I wonder how long it will be before those race questions they have on different tests and forms will be unanswerable by most. In the end, of course, I don't suppose it will matter. We humans worry so about things that will have no place in God's kingdom."

"As always," said Phoenix, veering off the tracks and down a faint trail. "You see life's complexities so simply. If only I had a moment to see through your eyes."

Aerielle did not respond, having no inclination as how to allow him to do so. Without words, she followed Phoenix towards the bluffs rising up on their left that overlooked a rocky boulder-strewn river's edge on the right.

Phoenix's long hair glistened with mist. Damp spirals clung to one another in a thick veil down his back. Aerielle admired his crowning glory anew, secretly wishing her own hair would grow that long.

The muted world around them slowly gained a musical strain with the sound of rushing water against the river rocks. Aerielle found her attention drawn three different ways at once, toward the melodic sound of water, the history afforded cliffs, and the alluring figure before her.

To say that Aerielle was not watching where she was going was an understatement. The ground suddenly slipped from beneath her feet, and Aerielle instantly found herself sitting in the wet grass, her right ankle crying out from the bump it had taken on a rock in the path.

Phoenix turned instantly as Aerielle drew her knees up to her chest and reached for her ankle.

"How bad is it? Let me see," ordered Phoenix, crouching down beside her.

Aerielle was surprised by the gentleness of Phoenix's touch as he carefully probed her ankle. So there really was magic in his hands, she decided, as the momentary pain quickly faded.

She stared at him, his hair spilling forward like a rippling waterfall, hiding his face from view as he examined her. The light scent from the dark cascade was delicate yet overwhelming to Aerielle's senses.

"How does it feel?" he asked.

"Uhm, fine. I think it's fine." Aerielle stumbled over the words, her eyes fixed on the tempting, damp spirals of Phoenix's hair.

"Are you sure it's okay now?" Phoenix asked, as if from a distance.

Aerielle nodded though Phoenix couldn't see. "Uh huh, fine."

Without having determined to do so, Aerielle raised a hand, reached out.

Phoenix looked up, Aerielle's hand, previously just inches from his hair, now just inches from his face. Stunned, she jerked her hand back, shocked by her own temerity. She fumbled for words of explanation, finding her tongue tied in knots by the question in his piercing glance.

Aerielle took a deep breath, determined not to break down into a pool of adolescent tears. Let him stare and question. At eighteen she ought to be able to speak for herself. "Your hair," she began huskily, her voice determined not to sound normal. "You have the most beautiful hair. It befits you. It's like a window into your soul."

Phoenix did not respond at first, and Aerielle thought for sure she'd die of embarrassment yet. He must think her a melodramatic twit.

And then without speaking, Phoenix reached out his own hand and took Aerielle's offending one. With little effort he slid his fingers into her palm, releasing the fist her hand had become. Slowly, he drew her hand toward him, closing her fingers anew over a length of the mane she revered.

As if welcoming her with an embrace, wisps of curling waves wrapped about her fingers. Phoenix's luxuriously thick hair was neither exceedingly soft nor coarse, but somewhere in between.

Aerielle's heart was pounding so loud in her ears, she was amazed she could hear when Phoenix began to speak. "What is it that you *see* through that window into my soul Aerielle?"

"I see...I see someone full of boldness, courage, and pride. But I also see bitterness and anger, and a longing to know something different. Something without blemish or stain. You not only want to live on White Bird, you want to live *in* it, too."

"And what are my chances?"

"Living on White Bird would take much time and money, but having the peace you seek...it's yours for the asking."

"You have great faith in this God of yours, Aerielle."

Phoenix's words were spoken as he rose to his feet. Despite the clinging tendrils, Aerielle's hand slid from his hair, only to be taken in one of his while he helped her to stand. He released her hand almost instantly, as if he found the contact more immediate than expected.

"Your ankle?" he questioned, glancing downward.

Aerielle tested it without hesitation. "It really is okay."

"Good. Now follow me—carefully. And while you introduce me to this God of yours, I will show you the writing on the wall."

→→→

A half hour later, as Aerielle stepped out of her apartment building with Idaho at her side, she laughed, recalling once again how that excursion at the bluffs had ended. They had been on their way back to the truck when Phoenix had casually pointed out the "writings" on Aerielle's jeans, or more accurately, the grass stains streaked across her rear-end as a result of her fall.

Aerielle laughed again, lost in the memories encouraged by the crisp night air that surrounded her with its peacefulness. She took a deep breath, letting it out as a sigh. She might have continued to stand there, but Idaho was tugging on his leash, eager to explore.

Stepping forward, Aerielle headed towards the lake that glimmered beyond the road. So lost in her thoughts was she, that when she spotted the figure standing near the lake, Aerielle thought she was imagining things. She stopped abruptly, studying the apparition in the starlight. But even at this distance there was no question that the figure with his back to her was Phoenix.

Aside from the shepherds on either side of him, she could see the light breeze tug at the length of his hair. Hair that seemed to symbolize everything he was and everything he stood for. It hung like a manteau, cloaking his back in dark waves. His mane was as much a part of him as Aerielle's memories of him were to her.

Maybe that was why she found herself deeply relieved he hadn't cut his hair off. Maybe it would have been easier if he had. She could still remember the feel of it against her hands, and the scent of musk lingered in her memory like a tempting lure.

At that moment Phoenix raised an arm, motioning towards one of the dogs that had wandered too far. The jacket he wore was fringed and as he lifted his arm the silhouette reminded Aerielle of a feathered wing. Without warning she was overtaken by the memory of many feathers and much long hair.

→→→

Feathers and long hair. Aerielle hadn't seen so much of either at one time before. Then again, she'd never been to the Looking Glass powwow. Of course feathers and long hair were not all that there was an abundance of. She had also seen her share of Native American clothing, beadwork, moccasins, crafts, and art work. The air was festive, the tourists fascinated, and the drum beats never ending. To a trained ear one drum beat was sure to sound different from another, but to Aerielle they all sounded the same.

By now, halfway through the hot August day, they seemed a part of her, pounding along with the rhythm of her pulse. Aerielle enjoyed the sound of the drums, and had watched fascinated, as the "fancy dancers," including Hawk, had performed. And during the rest of the morning and early afternoon, locals and visitors from bordering states had displayed their skills proudly, performing a variety of dances to the beat. A lot of work and training went into the bright beautiful costumes and the exacting performances.

Scanning the crowd, Aerielle searched for Sparrow. She spotted the child heading in her direction, clothed in a buckskin dress decorated with bells and beads which she had worn for the cape dance.

Aerielle waved at Sparrow. The girl smiled back, signing something Aerielle missed through the crowd.

Finally Sparrow reached her side, and Aerielle began signing immediately, speaking at the same time. "You were wonderful. I'm really impressed."

Sparrow beamed. "Did you see the applause?" she asked, obviously pleased with her word choice. Aerielle had been teaching her to "see" the things she would no longer be able to "hear."

"I sure did, honey."

"Come on," said/signed Sparrow. "We have to hurry and get a good view. Phoenix is next."

The two began to work their way through the crowd, and Aerielle was glad of the sign language. It meant they didn't have to work hard to hear each other. "Where's everybody else?" asked Aerielle.

"Mom went to find Dad, and Hawk's helping Phoenix get ready for the dance. He needs help with his roach."

Aerielle had seen most of the articles of Phoenix's costume, and the piece Sparrow referred to went in the hair and looked like a mohalk of died porcupine quills. The rest of his "traditional" outfit included a knee-length breechclout, moccasins, short angora leggings that went from below the knee to his ankle, a breastplate of bone and beads, and a bustle made with an array of eagle and hawk feathers.

Aerielle and Sparrow found a place with a clear view, and minutes later, the "traditional" dance began. To Aerielle's unskilled eyes, it appeared little different than other dances she had seen that day. On the other hand, Phoenix did not look as the other dancers. Though his hair was braided like many of those with the long hair, it was lighter, and the expression on his face was intensely serious.

He also showed off his costume rather well, admitted Aerielle, once again admiring Phoenix's build, much of it currently on display and highlighted by unforgiving sunlight. But then, Phoenix had nothing to forgive, his body honed and his muscles taut from his extensive work on the ranch. Not all the dancers were so lucky. Yet one thing they all seemed to have in common was their darker skin tone.

When Phoenix's group was done, there was the usual round of applause. Sparrow attempted a whistle for her brother, but was only partially successful. She looked at Aerielle and shrugged, and Aerielle kindly completed the whistle for her. It was sharp and loud, louder than Aerielle had intended. People stared and Sparrow started to laugh. Phoenix and several other dancers glanced in their direction, and Aerielle wanted to sink into the ground. Maybe they wouldn't know it was her. Fat chance, thought Aerielle, Phoenix's gaze locking with hers. Aerielle shrugged as Sparrow had done. There was no obvious response from Phoenix as she watched him head off the field.

Moments later, he started toward the front of the Wa-a'Yas when a man about his height stepped in front of him. Aerielle couldn't see the man's face, since his back was to her, but Phoenix's was plainly visible, and Aerielle could read his anger. Anger that spewed forth in words as Phoenix spoke to the man briefly. Aerielle didn't know what the man said in return, but Phoenix ignored him. Stepping around him, he stormed off in the opposite direction toward the street that ran between the Wa-a'Yas and the residential area.

The man turned, his eyes following Phoenix with a look of resignation, and the resemblance which was there shocked Aerielle. The man could be none other than Phoenix's father. It was the eyes, the shape of the jaw, the color and wave to his hair.

Aerielle's heart went out to Phoenix, recognizing the turmoil he must be going through.

"I'm gonna go change into regular clothes and find Mom," cut in Sparrow, tugging at Aerielle's sleeve before motioning with her arm.

Aerielle glanced in the direction the girl was pointing and nodded her head. "Go ahead. I'll meet you later." After I meet with Phoenix.

Hurrying her way through the crowd and rounding the side of the building, Aerielle saw Phoenix across the street as he disappeared behind Nevin's truck. The topper was on today, and the back window was flipped up. Aerielle ran across the street. Phoenix's back was to her when she came from around the side of the truck. He was attempting to remove his head roach after it had become tangled with his hair, which he'd prematurely tried to unbraid.

Apparently, he'd begun removing any encumbering pieces of his ensemble once out of view of the field, for his bustle hung over the tailgate, and his breastplate lay on the truck bed. His actions had become thwarted at that point.

Phoenix's muscles flexed, rippling the smooth flawless skin of his back as he fumbled with the combs that held the roach in his hair. Unsuccessful, he uttered something under his breath. Then he tossed his head back in an effort to shake his hair loose. The movement reminded Aerielle of an animal. Phoenix muttered something else.

"And what language is that?" she inquired.

Phoenix became still, but he did not turn to face her. "Shahaptin," he said, his voice even. "The Nez Perce are also known as Shahaptin."

"Well, I don't think I'll ask you to translate, but would you like some help?"

Turning at last, Phoenix faced her, his lingering anger evident in his jaw. He stood without moving, saying nothing, his dark eyes absorbing her.

Aerielle barely recognized the man who stood before her now. They'd spent countless hours together in the last couple weeks, mostly under a star-laden sky. And yesterday, yesterday had been like a dream with Phoenix opening up to her like he'd never done before. But this Phoenix was different. This was the Phoenix she'd told off and decided had no heart. This was the closed and angry warrior, ready to defend whatever he deemed needed protecting, including himself. Yet despite all this, Aerielle felt drawn to him just as she had the day before. His defensiveness was but a facade, and Aerielle felt a rush of tenderness for the man beneath.

Aerielle had asked if he wanted help. There had been no answer. Ignoring his lack of reply, she moved to his side. His jaw gave evidence to his tension, but he didn't pull away. As Aerielle reached up, she could see the strands of hair twisted around the teeth of the combs. She did her best to make swift work of the problem, but found herself with a sudden case of nerves. She wasn't used to standing this close to him, or touching him so casually. She could feel the heat radiating from him, smell the scent of musk that lingered from his shampoo.

Aerielle's fingers slipped, yanking on Phoenix's hair. He didn't make a sound, but Aerielle felt the need to apologize anyway. "Sorry," she murmured, glancing forward. That in itself was a mistake, for Aerielle's cheek brushed against a hard muscular shoulder.

At last Aerielle worked the tangle free. "That was your father, wasn't it?" she abruptly asked, taking a grateful step back, the roach of quills in hand.

Phoenix's eyes narrowed as he turned to face her while running a soothing hand through his hair. "He had no right to come here."

"What did he want?"

"To appease his conscience." Phoenix enunciated each word, tingeing them with anger. And then a bitter laugh escaped. "He said he wanted to talk."

Aerielle nodded thoughtfully. "Maybe he deserves a chance to be heard."

"And maybe it's none of your business!" snapped Phoenix.

Aerielle's eyes flashed as her anger erupted. "Maybe you're right! Maybe I should just keep my white nose where it belongs!"

Turning, Aerielle stalked off, still gripping the headpiece.

"Aerielle. Aerielle, wait," ordered Phoenix, his voice insistent.

Aerielle ignored him and would have kept going, but suddenly he had hold of her arm. Unceremoniously, he jerked her around, the roach flying from her grip. And then he kissed her, his right arm sliding like smooth iron around her waist, holding her to him while his left hand caught in her hair.

Aerielle hadn't even seen the kiss coming and found one of her own hands crushed between them against his chest. His lips were hard, demanding. Kissing Phoenix wasn't supposed to be like this. Aerielle lifted her free hand to attempt escape, but when she went to push against his shoulder, her hand slid into the rippling waves of the hair she had barely touched moments before.

The feel of his hair against her palm, and the sudden realization that a heart beat powerfully beneath the hand pressed to his chest, tore away her anger. And despite the temper she knew had brought about the kiss, Aerielle was forced to respond by the strength of her own emotions and desires.

But her heart prevailed too late, for just as the tension drained from her body, Hawk's voice intruded upon them from some distant point beyond the truck.

"Phoenix? You out here?" he called.

The angry, yet passionate moment that might have been, was gone. Phoenix started in surprise, releasing Aerielle like a poisonous snake as if he'd just remembered who and what she was. Aerielle stumbled backwards, nearly falling.

"There you are," said Hawk, appearing at the back of the truck. "What happened to you? You disappeared faster than a frightened colt."

Phoenix ignored his brother, his stunned gaze on Aerielle. She stared back, the truth behind their first kiss overwhelming her, filling her with anguish. She turned away, lest Phoenix see her pain.

"Aerielle," he whispered, his voice filled with his own torment. "I'm sorry."

Aerielle started running, dodging Hawk who stood there with questioning eyes and his mouth half open.

Phoenix's words echoed around her. *I'm sorry*, he'd said. So was she.

"In a wide country of rolling hills and sweeping prairies, beautiful valleys threaded with silvery streams gushing from canyon gutted mountains, through whose craggy pinnacles the wind ever sings canticles to the gods, were found the Nez Perce people."

McWhorter, as quoted in Hear Me, My Chiefs.

9

Phoenix, still facing Lake Nokomis, glanced over at McCoy who had wandered too far. Raising his arm, he motioned for the dog to return.

"Good boy," he murmured gently, reaching down to scratch McCoy's ears. "Don't want you getting into trouble. I'm in enough of it for the both of us."

And he was, Phoenix realized, in a deep doodoo of a mess. The moccasins he wore on his path in life were soiled with lies and hidden truths, and memories that tore at his heart. And the innocent woman whom he'd loved, and then grieved.

"Dear God," Phoenix whispered aloud, "forgive me. Forgive me for my ignorance and the mess I've made of things. Forgive me for Hawk...for Aerielle. Help me to know what I should do, what direction I should take.... Please, I beg you, give me guidance."

"Phoenix?"

The dulcet sound of her voice filled him. Aerielle.

Was he imagining things? Phoenix turned. She stood a dozen feet off, her dog straining at the leash. Idaho.

"Am I intruding?" she questioned.

Phoenix wanted to laugh. "No. No, not at all."

Aerielle stepped closer, or was she *pulled* closer by the eager Aussie?

Phoenix introduced his German shepherds to Aerielle. Both

beat their tails against the air when Aerielle leaned down to flirt with them and fondle their ears.

"And this is Idaho," she announced, shaking her head at the Aussie who was busy sniffing the other shepherds.

But Phoenix wasn't looking at the dogs any longer, he was looking at Aerielle. *Really* looking at her, taking in the changes of time.

Aerielle felt his scrutiny and wondered what he saw. Wondered if it pleased him. Knew that she cared. How could she not, when she knew her own reaction at seeing *him* was more than simple curiosity?

And so she studied him in turn, observing the differences time had wrought. His hair was as she remembered it, but he was slightly taller, and his forehead revealed new lines of worry. What had he worried about those fourteen years?

Phoenix had worried about Aerielle. Year after year he had wondered what kind of life she lived and how she had changed. Now, at last, she stood before him, and though he couldn't pinpoint any specific changes in her general appearance, the innocence he remembered about her was gone, as if she'd experienced one too many setbacks in life. Phoenix felt guilt wash over him. How much of that loss had he been responsible for?

The silence between them grew, becoming uncomfortable. They both started to speak at once, then laughed nervously. Phoenix nodded. "You first."

"I just wanted to know how the vet business was doing these days," she began.

The painful memory of the foal he'd lost surged through Phoenix, bringing with it the urge to deny the hurt inside. But this was Aerielle, the woman who'd taught him that it was all right to express the emotions which churned within him. And though he didn't practice what he'd learned very often, he hadn't forgotten how.

"I lost a foal today."

"Oh, Phoenix, I'm sorry." Aerielle felt his pain, stepped forward to offer a touch of comfort. But the years were like a wall between them and the moment strained. Awkwardly, she dropped her hand before contact was made.

"Let's walk," she said instead. "A night like this can soothe the ragged edges."

With Idaho on Aerielle's right, the shepherds on Phoenix's left, and the years between them, they started along the path following the lake. The night air surrounded them with a gentle breeze that hinted of the winter soon to come, yet neither were aware of anything but each other.

The memory of musk which suddenly pervaded Aerielle's senses urged her away from thoughts and into speech. "So...." she began, well aware of how lame a beginning that was.

"So, what?" repeated Phoenix.

"So, why don't we forget about the past for a few minutes and concentrate on important things. How are you and God getting along?"

Phoenix smiled, the burden on his heart lifting slightly. Aerielle's question told him much of what he had been wondering about her and wouldn't have known how to ask. She was still as straightforward as she'd always been, and apparently, God was still very dear to her heart.

"Well, we're on speaking terms. And I haven't told Him off recently," answered Phoenix. "Of course, He's told *me* a thing or two...."

"And are you listening?"

His expression serious, Phoenix met Aerielle's inquiring gaze. "I'm trying."

Aerielle found the honesty in his eyes almost overwhelming, amazed that he wasn't trying to hide from her as he had years ago.

"How 'bout you?" inquired Phoenix. "You and God that is."

"We're okay," replied Aerielle, tugging on Idaho's leash.

"We talk, I read my Bible when I can...and a few StarTrek novels."

"So you're still into StarTrek, huh?"

"It's about the only thing I use my VCR for, StarTrek first runs, reruns, and movies. What about you? Seen any good movies lately?"

Phoenix fought back guilty memories of Sofia, and quickly brought up the name of the last "good" movie he had seen. Their discussion soon turned to other movies and TV shows, and then on to books. The barriers between them slid away, and Phoenix became lost in the moment. He was unaware of how long they walked. Neither did he notice the evening become cooler and the breeze pick up. He couldn't even say if they'd passed anyone, let alone what time it was.

Eventually, when they grew tired, they settled onto a bench across from Aerielle's building, the dogs at their feet. The discussion of books soon brought them around to StarTrek again.

"Have you read any of the StarTrek novels?" inquired Aerielle, burying her hands deeper into her pockets.

"Can't say that I have."

"I'll loan you some if you'd like. I have them all."

Phoenix nodded. "I'd like that."

"Can you imagine," continued Aerielle, glancing out at the lake and then up at the sky, "what it would be like to travel among the stars? You could trace out the pattern of the big dipper. Find out how far Alcor really is from Mizar, I mean close up."

Phoenix watched the animation light Aerielle's face, finding himself remembering...regretting...wishing.

"Where would you travel first?" asked Aerielle, her attention remaining on the view while the wind tousled her hair.

"The Pleiades." Phoenix's answer came without hesitation... without thinking.

Aerielle's rapturous expression died instantly, confusion

replacing it. She turned her face toward him, but her eyes did not meet his. "I think it's time I go in," she said, getting to her feet.

Phoenix could have kicked himself. How could he have mentioned the Pleiades? The memories attached to them were endless. "I'll walk you back," he said, standing.

"I can manage just fine."

"I'll walk you, nonetheless."

Aerielle knew there was no point in arguing. She simply nodded and started off in the direction of the apartment building. As they crossed the dew-laden grass, she kept her eyes straight ahead even as she battled the need to turn and look at him. Why had he brought up the Pleiades? For a few brief hours the past had been no more, and they had simply enjoyed each other's company.

Maybe it was better that he had. What hope was there for a future between them, anyway? Aerielle knew better than to think they could ever be just friends.

As they reached the apartment building, Aerielle paused on the walk. She'd only planned on saying a quick thank you and running in, but the need to meet his eyes one last time was overpowering. She found herself drowning in the depths of them. "Thank you for walking me home," she managed at last.

"Good night, Aerielle." It was all Phoenix could do to say those simple words and walk away. And as he turned his back on her, he felt the agony of the first time he'd left her revisit him with a force that left him desperate for oblivion.

Behind him, Aerielle stared at his departing form, fighting the urge to call him back. Tears she could not hold in spilled onto her cheeks as she mourned for what might have been.

→→→

When Phoenix returned home a short time later, he found Hawk seated at the bottom of the stairs waiting for him. His brother rose as Phoenix shut the front door and stepped slowly forward. The shepherds beat him to Hawk, greeting his brother with affection while Hawk patted them absently. Repentance was evident in his manner, and Phoenix paused before him.

"Phoenix, I'm sorry," began Hawk. "Sofia told me about the colt. How'd the Taggart girl take it?"

"Not very well, I'm afraid."

"I'm sorry."

"Thank you."

"Look, Phoenix. Sofia also told me about why you've been putting off hiring someone. I mean about her getting her vet tech license and all."

"I should have told you sooner," offered Phoenix.

"I shouldn't have been so bullheaded."

"I only waited because it was supposed to be a surprise."

Hawk smiled. "Well, it was definitely a surprise. A very nice surprise."

"I'm just glad it's out, now," returned Phoenix. "One less thing for us to argue about."

Silence suddenly took over. It was an awkward moment as they continued to stand there at the bottom of the stairwell. Both were avoiding the subject of Aerielle. Phoenix was well aware Hawk hadn't apologized for accusing him of being jealous. He knew his brother wasn't about to admit the inappropriateness of his accusation. Nor was Phoenix yet willing to admit part of what his brother had said was true. He *was* jealous.

"You going to bed now?" questioned Phoenix, cutting through the silence.

"Yeah," nodded Hawk. "How 'bout you?"

"Think I'll do some paperwork."

"Don't stay up too late."

Small talk. It was all small talk. And it quickly died as the two made their way up the stairs. Hawk disappeared into his bedroom as Phoenix entered his study. But instead of sitting down at the desk, he made his way over to the French doors that faced the lake.

The night once again closed about him as he stepped out onto the balcony. Moving over to the railing, Phoenix glanced to his left, his gaze searching the night sky for only an instant before he found what he was looking for. The Pleiades. The small group of stars glittered like Christmas tinsel, their familiar light reaching out to Phoenix. Every year during the time of the Pleiades, Phoenix watched them, studied them. He had always taken comfort in knowing that no matter how far away Aerielle was from him, these same stars shown over her.

→→→

The dining room clock chimed midnight as Phoenix stared down at the head roach resting on the table. Several quills were broken off, others dirty, some bent. The roach was damaged, just as Phoenix's relationship with Aerielle was. She had dropped the roach because he'd manhandled her; she wasn't speaking to him because he'd behaved like a jerk. So, now, she had two jerks in her life. Jim Peterson had called again tonight, apparently abusive, and Aerielle had stormed off to her room furious.

Phoenix ran a finger over one of the broken quills. It would take time to repair the hair piece, but the time was negligible. How did he repair things with Aerielle? He doubted the two cookies he'd left for her would have much effect, and not because they were store bought. Phoenix ran a hand through his hair in frustration and then slammed his fist onto the table.

How did he get into this mess anyway? She was white. He should have kept his distance from her, but no, yesterday he'd gone and told her things he'd never told anyone. He'd cracked the door to his inner sanctum, and she had slipped inside. Now the door had been tightly closed again. Phoenix should just leave it that way. Yet even as he formed these thoughts, Phoenix rose to his feet, headed towards Aerielle's room.

His knock on her door was greeted by silence. This scenario was becoming familiar. Phoenix wondered if on this night he should just pound on the door and forget about waking the household. Of course there wasn't much of a household to wake up. Nevin and his mother were in Boise, and Hawk was sleeping in the barn as one of the mares was showing signs of foaling early.

In deference to Sparrow, Phoenix knocked quietly again and then reluctantly pushed the door open. He could see Aerielle lying on the bed, her back to the door.

"Aerielle?"

There was no movement, no sound except the brush of denim as Phoenix shifted nervously.

"I know you're awake." He didn't, but felt it was a good assumption. "Aerielle, I'm sorry.... I shouldn't have talked to you that way...or kissed you like I did."

"You're right. You shouldn't have."

Phoenix let out his breath at her reply. At least she was talking to him. "I'm sorry," he said again, knowing how weak the words sounded. "Please. Come with me tonight. Perseus should be sending us a spectacular meteor shower. Maybe up to a hundred meteors an hour."

Phoenix paused, his pain building with the silence. But enough was enough. He'd apologized the best he could. Standing around pleading for forgiveness like a chastised puppy wasn't his style. Just as he was about to turn away, Aerielle spoke.

"You think I'm going to get dressed with you standing there?" she demanded, her voice filled with sarcasm.

Phoenix knew relief and apprehension at the same time. What was he doing? "I'll be waiting outside with the horses."

It couldn't have been more than five minutes before Aerielle emerged from the house, but for Phoenix it seemed like hours. And now he had no idea what to say. He simply handed Aerielle the reins to Morning Dew, waiting to see that she mounted without mishap before doing the same with his own horse, a stallion named Steel.

Glancing over to see if Aerielle was ready, Phoenix noted her stirrups were too long. Someone taller had obviously used her saddle in the horse parade. Phoenix was about to comment when Aerielle started Morning Dew forward. Using his legs to signal the saddleless Steel, Phoenix followed suit.

They rode for twenty minutes before pulling up at one of Phoenix's favorite spots, a grassy plain well beyond a stand of pines with a view of the foothills to the west of them. Dismounting, they dropped the reins free and let the horses wander unfettered, the plenteous supply of thick grass drawing forth the animals' appetites.

Removing the extra blanket he'd brought along on Steel, Phoenix spread it out on the grass as he always did to protect from the dew. Aerielle sat down, wrapping her arms about her knees as she studied the northern horizon.

"You've been telling me about this meteor shower for the last couple weeks," she began. "I'm getting impatient."

Phoenix joined Aerielle on the blanket, leaving a comfortable distance between them. "I've never known you to be the impatient type."

"You'd be surprised," replied Aerielle, glancing over at him. "I just hide it well. Do you hide things, Phoenix?"

She knew darn well that he did, and Phoenix was quite aware he was being baited, but he wasn't biting. "So, have you memorized the constellation chart I gave you?" he asked, changing the subject.

Aerielle laughed. "Hardly. You gonna throw a pop quiz at me or something?"

Suddenly there was a streak of light in the sky, and they both motioned at once. The meteor shower had begun. Soon the pace picked up, offering a splendid view, with each streak of light being quickly pointed out.

But even with the display the night sky offered, Phoenix could not free his thoughts of the woman so near. The breeze brought to him the scent of her perfume, and the movement of her arm drew his gaze more to her than the meteors she pointed out. Worst of all, his memory betrayed him, bringing to mind the urgency of her response as she'd so briefly returned his unplanned kiss that afternoon.

Good grief, how she'd gotten under his skin. How she'd gotten into his blood. It was all foolishness. No doubt the starlit summer night only encouraged such thoughts. Yet even knowing this, Phoenix could not chase away the longing to know the sweetness of her lips once more, and to experience the pleasure of her embrace.

The next hour and a half was turmoil as Phoenix fought himself over his feelings and his desires for Aerielle. He tried to concentrate on the hundreds of meteors cascading through the backdrop of night, but their appeal had become dim in the presence of the one beside him. For Aerielle was like the light of sunrise, reaching out in the darkness to touch the world with her warmth.

Much to his relief, the remnants of Perseus slowed their display, and the decision was made to head back. Once on their feet, Phoenix grabbed the blanket and threw it over Steel who stood leisurely next to Morning Dew.

Phoenix didn't know if the horses had been aware of the meteor shower, but as always, they seemed intent upon the night. Their ears twitched at the sound of crickets, and their nostrils were busy taking in the wondrous scents of summer, like the abundant yellow display of wild Mules Ear blooming nearby.

Pausing for another look at the sky, Phoenix caught a last streak of light before he turned back to the horses. Aerielle stood between them, fiddling with one of her stirrups, obviously having some difficulty. Phoenix moved in to help, the distance between the horses seemingly small now that he was standing next to Aerielle. He reached past her, his fingers brushing hers as he took over the job of adjusting the stirrup.

Aerielle became still beside him and then spoke with excitement. "There's a set of stars I've never noticed before."

Phoenix glanced up from his work and over Aerielle's shoulder to see what she was pointing at.

"Do you see them?" she asked, glancing back at him.

As she turned, Phoenix felt her hair brush against his arm.

"They seem to have a sparkle all their own," continued Aerielle, her attention returning to the sky.

Phoenix found it difficult to concentrate and was beginning to feel effectively corralled by the large warm bodies of the horses on either side of them. Letting go of the stirrup strap, he took a step back, giving himself breathing space. Forcefully, he turned his attention heavenward.

Stars came into focus, their glittery light every bit as beautiful as Aerielle thought them to be. "You're looking at the Pleiades," he informed her.

"A constellation?"

"Open star cluster, part of Taurus."

"It's beautiful."

"They're beautiful. The stars are the seven daughters of the mythical Atlas and Pleione. Supposedly the daughters were transformed into stars."

"Do they have names?"

"Electra, Maia, Taygete, Alcyone, Celaeno, Merope, and Sterope."

Aerielle shook her head, a smile evident in her voice when she spoke. "You never cease to amaze me, Phoenix."

Phoenix's gaze dropped to caress Aerielle's hair, and instantly he began berating himself for his continued distraction. He should never have brought her out here. He should never have knocked on that "tightly closed door." Stupid, thought Phoenix, his anger with himself growing.

Suddenly, Aerielle turned to face him, her eyes locking with his. So much for the physical space he'd put between them. Frustrated, Phoenix lowered his head, grabbing for the stirrup, but Aerielle stopped him, grasping his jaw between her fingers and forcing him to look at her. The touch of her hand against his jaw intensified his anger even as it set fire to his skin, but he didn't pull away, remembering how he'd treated her that day.

"What are you afraid of, Yellow Wolf?" Her tone mirrored Phoenix's own impatience.

His dark eyes narrowed. "Nothing," he replied adamantly. Pulling away at the same time, he bumped Steel who side-stepped a half dozen inches.

Aerielle's gaze was unrelenting. "You deceive yourself."

Phoenix stared back, the muscle in his jaw stirring to life. "And what have I to be deceived about?"

"Me," declared Aerielle, stabbing him in the chest with her finger. "The feelings you have for me."

Phoenix searched for something biting to say, found nothing.

"Personally," continued Aerielle, "I think you ought to kiss me again. And do it right this time."

Phoenix was amazed at her audacity. She had left him with few options. Either kiss her as he longed to do, or mount Steel and ride away as his stubbornness told him he should.

The decision was made for him as Aerielle stepped closer, brushing a gentle hand against his face. Phoenix's breath was torn from him at her touch, and he could feel his blood pounding as she leaned forward and up to tease his lips with hers.

It was not enough. Phoenix's arms crushed her to him. His mouth seared hers. He knew his actions were rough, but there was no anger this time. Instead, there was a desperate need to tear down any remnants of the door that had separated him from this woman who consumed his thoughts as well as read them. Aerielle buried her hands in his hair and Phoenix thought he'd drown in her arms. He didn't care if he did. He knew his view of whites—of Aerielle—would never be the same again. Nor would his view of the Pleiades.

As if from a great distance Phoenix heard a rhythmic pounding, and slowly he realized he was hearing hoofbeats. Aerielle heard them as well, and they pulled apart, Phoenix feeling as if he'd been drugged.

Phoenix stepped forward from between the horses as Hawk pulled up before them. His face was a mix of worry and excitement. "Sunlight's restless. I think she's gonna drop the foal."

"Blast!" exclaimed Phoenix, grabbing for his reins. Suddenly he paused, glancing at Aerielle.

"Well, go on!" she ordered. "You're faster without me, and I know my way back."

Phoenix accepted her assurance and vaulted onto Steel, but as he tore out behind his brother, he knew already that he'd left part of his heart behind.

Let me be a free man--free to travel, free to stop, free to work, free to trade where I choose, free to choose my own teachers, free to follow the religion of my fathers, free to think and talk and act for myself--and I will obey every law or submit to the penalty.

Chief Joseph, as quoted in *The Nez Perce Tragedy* by David Lavender

10

"Mooooo." Mildred's loud complaint filled the barn as Phoenix finished up her rectal exam.

Beside him, Tyler shook his head. "That's disgusting."

"You don't want to try?" asked Phoenix, pulling the latex glove off his right hand.

"Milking a cow is one thing. I didn't even mind checking her teeth, but this?" Tyler waved a hand in the general direction of Mildred's back end. "Not today."

Phoenix studied Tyler sitting beside him on a stool in Mr. Danvers' barn. The boy had said "not today" like he was planning on coming again. Technically, today was Tyler's last day helping out in payment for Boba Fett. But Phoenix decided right then to offer Tyler a permanent job after school helping at the clinic. As for Saturdays like today, Phoenix enjoyed his solitude, but there was something pleasant about having the boy around. Maybe Tyler could come on a "now and then" basis.

"How do you feel about stethoscopes?" inquired Phoenix, pulling one from his bag.

"No problem. We gonna listen to her heart?"

"Her stomachs."

"Stomachs?" Tyler repeated. "You mean as in more than one?"

"Cows have four," explained Phoenix. Pressing the stethoscope to Mildred, Phoenix used his other hand to tap against her side. He continued to move the stethoscope, tapping and listening. "Well, she sounds all right."

"Can I?" asked Tyler, holding out his hand.

Phoenix gave Tyler the stethoscope, showing him where to place it. Tyler tapped away, listening intently, a grin on his face. "Cool."

"When it doesn't sound like that," explained Phoenix. "Something's wrong. But it looks like Mildred's passed her physical today."

"Why is she called Mildred?" asked Tyler, handing the stethoscope back to Phoenix.

"Mr. Danvers named her after his departed wife."

"And why does he call you son?"

Phoenix paused in repacking his bag. "Probably because he's older and wiser."

"So why don't you call me son?"

"I think it's a generational thing," replied Phoenix. Besides, he didn't feel very wise. He certainly didn't have much wisdom concerning Aerielle. Closing his bag abruptly, Phoenix stood up. "I think we're done here."

→→→

Shutting the back door on the cold November wind, Phoenix turned towards Mr. Danvers who stood at the kitchen counter placing cookies on a plate.

"Mildred's fine," announced Phoenix, washing his hands in the sink.

"Have a seat, Doc. Hot coffee and cookies coming up."

Phoenix slipped off his brown work coat and placed it on the back of his chair before sitting down.

"So where's the boy?" continued Mr. Danvers.

"In the barn playing with Jack."

The old man walked to the table, setting down a plate of homemade peanut butter cookies and a pot of coffee. As he sat down, Phoenix poured, the room filling with the inviting aroma.

"How's your truck running these days?" asked Phoenix, before biting into a cookie.

"Mike Grady fixed it up right quick. Nice young man he is."

Sipping his coffee, Phoenix reached into the pocket of his red pullover and retrieved a photograph. He held it out for Mr. Danvers who took it in his wrinkled hand.

"Aerielle?" he inquired, glancing from the photo to Phoenix.

Phoenix nodded, seeing in his mind the picture he'd been keeping in his desk drawer. He'd slipped it in his pocket at the last minute that morning.

Mr. Danvers studied the photograph a moment, chewing on a cookie. "She changed much?"

"Not much," Phoenix replied, not surprised by the old man's assumption that he'd seen her. "She's aged some of course, but I swear she's more beautiful now than she was fourteen years ago. We actually managed to spend a couple of hours together before I put my foot in my mouth."

Mr. Danvers grunted. "You still love her?"

Thoughtfully, Phoenix studied the back of the photograph. "I'm beginning to think I never stopped."

The old man nodded, reaching for his coffee as Phoenix continued. "I can't stop thinking about her. The hours together I mentioned. It wasn't planned. And yet somehow it was."

Phoenix paused, reflecting on how his prayer had been answered the other night with Aerielle' appearance at the lake. Some would have called it coincidence, but Phoenix believed in something more.

The problem was, what did he do now? He couldn't exactly start over with her and act like nothing ever happened. He couldn't keep the lie he'd told her a secret forever. And then there was the vow....

"But?" said Mr. Danvers, questioning the long silence.

Their eyes met, Phoenix's clearly asking for advice.

"But what now? Aerielle's going out with Hawk, however temporary a situation I believe it to be. I mean he goes through women faster than a mare and a bucket of oats. Should I wait till the bucket's empty or offer a different bucket?

"I guess it depends on what you fill your bucket with," said Mr. Danvers reaching out to return the picture. At that moment the back door flew open and then slammed with a thud.

"Hey, what you got there?" asked Tyler, standing in the kitchen. His cheeks were ruddy from the cold, his sandy hair tousled by the wind, and his bright green eyes were fastened on the photograph now in Phoenix's hand. "Wouldn't be a picture of your girlfriend, would it?"

So young, so inquisitive, so honest, thought Phoenix. He couldn't help the smile that touched his lips. "Wash your hands and I'll let you see it.

Making quick work of the request, Tyler joined the men. Taking the photo in one hand and a cookie in the other, he sat down at the end of the table.

"Kinda young for you, isn't she?"

"It's an old picture."

"Ah," said Tyler, nodding with seeming wisdom beyond his years. "An old picture of an old girlfriend you still like."

Phoenix sipped his coffee, amazed at Tyler's observation. "Something like that."

"Well, she's got it going on," mumbled Tyler past a mouthful of cookie. "So what's the problem?"

"She's going out with Hawk."

"Oh. Now, that's a problem."

Mr. Danvers smiled at the boy's comment, but continued to drink his coffee in silence.

"Any suggestions?" asked Phoenix, leaning back in his chair.

Tyler chewed thoughtfully.

"You want some milk with that, son?" questioned Mr. Danvers.

Nodding, Tyler bit off another chunk of cookie. "Let's see.

You've got a thing for a girl whose dating someone else. And you want to spend some time with her without cluing in the competition, and maybe not even the girl herself. At least not yet. Clearly she sees something in the loser. Oh, sorry. Hawks not a loser. Might help if he was, but *Eric's* a loser and *Nicole* hasn't noticed yet.

"Who're Eric and Nicole?" asked Phoenix in surprise as Mr. Danvers returned with the boy's milk.

"Nicole's the girl *I* like," admitted Tyler. "And Eric's the competition.

"So what's your advice, Tyler?" inquired Phoenix, a grin on his face.

Tyler eyed the two men wisely. "I make it a habit of running into her a lot. Not literally of course, but that is a thought."

"You mean show up 'accidentally' wherever she happens to be?" Phoenix couldn't help but think about the accident of his and Aerielle's last encounter, or the literal run in of their first encounter.

"Yeah, man. Eric has no idea how much time I've been spending with Nicole."

"Is it working?" asked Mr. Danvers, joining the conversation.

"Hey, a little bit at a time goes a long way. I know what her favorite classes are, what her favorite color is, what books she's into, even what movies she likes. If I give her some time, and, Eric a chance to mess up....

More likely he himself would mess things up, thought Phoenix. If he could just use what he already knew about Aerielle in order to not say or do something stupid.

"Yer awful quiet, Doc," said Mr. Danvers. "Might you be thinkin' 'bout givin' Tyler's idea a try?"

"Maybe," Phoenix hedged. "If I can figure out how to turn a lake into a school."

Tyler grinned, gleeful, and Mr. Danvers smiled thoughtfully.

"I can give you some ideas," said Tyler.

"And I can be yer prayer warrior," agreed the old man.

Phoenix stared at the other two and laughed. What an unlikely trio they made.

→→→

As it turned out, seeing Aerielle was easier said than done. Running into her accidentally was one thing. Planning to run into her was another. It took perseverance and a bit of audacity, and Phoenix found himself running low on both as the days wore on.

Something had to be done, though. His brother was still pursuing the lovely Aerielle, and if anything, with greater effort, as he had been away from the house a lot lately.

After having finished a few errands Monday afternoon, Phoenix headed for home. The road following the lake was fairly deserted as he drove the last two blocks. Suddenly, a cat darted out into the street. Phoenix swerved to miss it. The reflection of the frightened yet unscathed animal appeared in his rearview mirror as Phoenix straightened out the truck. At the same moment, he spotted Tyler walking along the sidewalk, his head bowed to the cold November wind. Turning the wheel the opposite direction, Phoenix swiftly pulled the truck over to the curb. Leaning across the seat, he pushed open the passenger door.

"Cold enough for you?" he asked.

Tyler looked up at him, amusement lighting his eyes. "Oh, no, not at all," he assured, shaking his head adamantly.

"Get in. I'll give you a ride."

Tyler climbed into the cab, sliding his knapsack from his shoulders.

A minute later, they were home. Phoenix asked Tyler to come in for a chat. The boy was quick to accept the invitation, as well as the can of pop Phoenix offered him when they got inside. The shepherds, having properly greeted them, lay down beneath the kitchen table.

"I've got a patient to check on," said Phoenix, tossing Tyler a root beer. "While I'm doing that, why don't you give your grandmother a call and let her know you're here."

The patient, an orange tabby named Garfield, was recovering nicely from the emergency surgery Phoenix had performed that morning to remove crystals blocking his urethra. It appeared that Garfield would be ready to go home in a couple of days.

Returning to the kitchen, Phoenix found Tyler at the table munching on a bag of potato chips he'd found in the pantry.

"I'll have some too," said Phoenix, reaching for the bag as he sat down.

Tyler slid the potato chips across the table. "So how was the patient?"

"Just fine."

Phoenix explained what had been done while Tyler listened intently.

"Are you saying he couldn't go to the bathroom?" asked Tyler.

Phoenix nodded, thinking that this was a strange conversation to be having with a thirteen-year-old over potato chips and pop.

Tyler winced. "Ouch."

"He would have died in another twenty-four hours, but he'll get better now. And he should stay that way if they put him on a proper diet. How's Boba Fett doing? Is he leaving his stitches alone?"

Tyler nodded, sipping his root beer. "He's great, thanks to you. And behaving himself."

"Did you get your mom's permission to start work again tomorrow?"

"No problem."

Seeing that the potato chip bag was empty, Phoenix wadded it up, careful to keep the crumbs inside. "How was school today?"

"A problem."

"Nicole? Eric?"

Tyler shook his head. "English. It's my worst subject. I can't seem to keep the parts of speech separated."

Phoenix leaned forward, setting his pop on the table. "Do you know what a noun is?"

"Person, place, or thing."

"Name one."

Tyler grinned. "Nicole."

"Tell me something about her."

"Nicole has—"

"Keep it clean," warned Phoenix, seeing a suspect glint to the boy's eyes.

"—blond hair," finished Tyler.

"What is 'has?'"

Looking thoughtful a moment, Tyler shook his head.

"It's the action word," hinted Phoenix.

"The verb?"

Phoenix nodded. "That's right."

"Not much action in *that* verb."

"Nevertheless, it's still a verb. Now, what's 'blond?'"

"The hair color of your old girlfriend."

"It's an adjective," said Phoenix, ignoring him. "What's 'hair?'"

Tyler eyed him over the rim of the pop can he sipped at. "You haven't seen her yet 'accidentally,' have you?"

"No."

"Why not?"

Phoenix considered his answer, wondering how to best express his thoughts. "Many truths remain unspoken between us."

"You mean you lied to her?" demanded Tyler. "You didn't strike me as the lying type."

Guilt he did not attempt to hide swept over Phoenix. "There were mitigating circumstances," he said simply.

At that moment the front doorbell rang. Spock and McCoy stood to attention, their ears rotating like radar.

Telling the dogs to stay, Phoenix headed for the foyer.

Seconds later he opened the front door, surprised to find two uniformed police officers standing there. One of them he knew quite well. He was a dark-haired man a few years older than Phoenix by the name of Shawn Pleasant. Phoenix always thought it an unusual name for a cop.

"Hello, Phoenix."

"Hello, Shawn. This looks official."

"I wish I could say it wasn't."

A cold wind suddenly whipped through the porch and in the door, tugging at Phoenix's loosely plaited hair. "Why don't you come in and we'll talk."

The officers accepted Phoenix's invitation, stepping into the large sparsely-furnished foyer. Shawn introduced the younger man as Peter Denton.

"Do you know Tyler Hanson?" began Shawn, obviously uncomfortable.

"Yeah. Is he in trouble?"

"His grandmother claims she saw you driving like a 'drunken maniac' before forcing Tyler into your truck."

Phoenix's eyes widened as he stared at Shawn in surprise. "She said what? Never mind. I heard what you said." Phoenix shook his head in disbelief. "Well, I suppose she may have seen me swerve, but there was a cat in the middle of the road. But I didn't force Tyler into anything. Look, he's in the kitchen. Go talk to him."

As if on cue, Tyler appeared in the foyer, his curiosity triggered by the voices. The boy's eyes widened. Stepping forward, he directed his curious questions toward Phoenix. "What's up? You get caught doing a rain dance?"

Shawn grinned, glancing at Phoenix. "Where'd you find this kid, anyway?"

"He found me. Tyler, I want you to meet officers Shawn Pleasant and Peter Denton."

Tyler nodded, glancing from one officer's face to the other's and back again. "You guys know Phoenix?"

"*I* do," said Shawn. "He teaches Sunday school to the hearing impaired at church. My daughter's one of his students."

Tyler's gaze fixed on Phoenix with amazement. "You teach Sunday school *and* you know sign language?"

"Yeah. You got a problem with that?"

"Uh, no. Not at all."

"So what brings you to see Phoenix today, Tyler?" asked Shawn.

"We're buds. And he was helping me with my homework."

"What kind of homework?"

"English," muttered Tyler, but then his grimace turned to a smile. "We were using Nicole."

"Nicole?!" demanded Officer Denton, jumping into the conversation.

"You know. As in 'Nicole has blond hair.' Nicole and hair are nouns, blond is an adjective, and has is a verb."

The two officers looked at Tyler doubtfully.

"Yeah, I know," continued Tyler, "not much of a verb, is it?"

"Your grandmother seems to think Phoenix forced you to come here," explained Shawn.

"I thought you called her," said Phoenix, suddenly remembering.

Tyler looked chagrined, answer enough.

"You *didn't* call her!"

"I kinda couldn't," said Tyler, studying the hardwood floor. "She doesn't know I was here *last* week. I told her I was going to Mark's house."

"Did you bother asking your *mother* about last week?"

Tyler looked up at last. "I *did* do that."

"I think there's been a misunderstanding," cut in Shawn, "just as I suspected."

Phoenix glanced at the two watching him and Tyler, and shrugged. "I would agree with that statement."

"Nevertheless, I think we should take Tyler home. Better get your things, son."

Tyler grinned, turning toward the kitchen. "He called me 'son.'"

"Why'd you go and do that?" demanded Phoenix jovially.

Shawn looked confused. "What'd I do?"

Phoenix didn't bother to answer. They waited in brief silence as Tyler gathered his belongings and returned to the foyer. The officers and Tyler had just reached the front door when the boy turned back toward Phoenix. "Look, I'm really sorry. I didn't mean to get you in trouble."

Phoenix was quick to meet Tyler's troubled gaze. "Apology accepted."

"What am I gonna tell my grandmother?"

"The truth. Lies only separate."

The words he spoke applied to someone other than Tyler, thought Phoenix. He could be looking in a mirror.

"One more question," said Tyler pausing at the door. "Is kiss a verb? As in 'kissing Nicole'"

Phoenix rolled his eyes, but not without a smile pulling at the corners of his mouth.

Tyler grinned. "Now that's what I call an action verb."

As Phoenix shut the door behind the three, he couldn't help but think about Tyler's verb choice. That was one verb Phoenix liked, too, only with his and Aerielle's names together with Hawk's nowhere to be found.

But he was a long way from that much action. The verb truly fitting the situation was "lied." He wondered if he got around to telling the truth sometime in the near future if he could be the object of the verb "forgive."

→→→

The late afternoon sun was lowering itself toward the horizon. As Phoenix approached Aerielle's small apartment building that Friday, his fringed jacket was unzipped, his hands ungloved. It was a pleasant change from the winter-like weather earlier in the week, especially since this was his third "accidental" trip over since Monday afternoon. Not that he'd been successful. He had yet to find Aerielle at home or somewhere around the lake, and the one time he'd known she was home, Hawk's car had been parked in front.

All was quiet as Phoenix mounted the few steps at the entrance of the brownstone. Unfortunately, all remained silent in response to his pressing of Aerielle's apartment buzzer. Phoenix shook his head in frustration, turning back toward the sidewalk. At this rate, he wouldn't see her until next year. But what was he supposed to do, call her up and ask if she was home so he could come over and say he was just passing by? Or maybe he was supposed to call and hang up like some pre-teen adolescent.

Well, he'd picked a perfect day for a walk, anyway, thought Phoenix, glancing toward the lake. The water's mirror-like surface beckoned, and the naked trees crooked their arms invitingly, beckoning him to surround himself in a last breath of Autumn. If he'd known Aerielle wouldn't be home, he'd have brought the dogs. As it was, he'd just have to enjoy it alone.

His decision made, Phoenix started down the cement steps, his eyes on the scenic view as a pickup pulled up to the curb. He glanced at it briefly, liking the burgundy color. It had a king cab, and Phoenix suddenly realized Aerielle was driving. He paused on the walk as Aerielle parked, not appearing to have seen him. Starting across the grass towards her, Phoenix was struck by the incongruity of the large truck being driven by a woman dressed in heels and a fashionable suit, as was Aerielle when she stepped down. Of course, a truck was exactly what Phoenix would have expected her to drive. It just didn't seem to go with the designer label clothes or the fancy briefcase gripped in her left hand against the folds of a brown woolen cloak.

Unaware of Phoenix's presence, Aerielle's head was down as they approached each other. She would have side-stepped him if he had not spoken her name. Startled, she glanced up, her face marred by exhaustion, her eyes revealing the remainder of recent tears.

"Phoenix."

The way she said his name made Phoenix think she wouldn't have been any more surprised if he'd been Santa Claus. Her lack of equanimity pulled at his heart. "Are you okay?"

"Phoenix," she said again, as if having trouble believing he was really standing there. "I...I'm fine."

"Are you?" Phoenix stepped forward, searching her face for the truth, shocked by the idea that Aerielle would ever be less than open about her thoughts and feelings.

Her "cloudless-summer-sky" blue eyes fixed on his, and then filled with rain as tears surfaced. "No. No, I'm not.... It was *my* turn to lose a patient today."

Phoenix felt his own pain revisited from the previous week. Knew it was nothing compared to what Aerielle must be going through now. "I'm sorry, Aerielle."

Tears brimmed in her eyes, but Aerielle seemed to be making every effort to hold them back. "I know I shouldn't get attached to my patients, but sometimes it's so hard. And Timothy...Timothy Wallace was special."

"How so?" Phoenix prodded gently.

Aerielle's eyes grew sadly tender. "It was because of a little boy a lot like him that I became a doctor. I thought I could help others like him."

"I'm sure you *are* helping."

Aerielle shook her head. "Sometimes I have trouble believing that. I've spent a third of my life studying ways to help these kids, only to end up watching them die."

"They don't all die, Aerielle," assured Phoenix.

But his words only brought fresh tears to her eyes, forcing the flood already there to spill over. "Just one is too many."

Phoenix nodded. "You're right. It is."

"He was only three," she continued, her eyes pleading with him to understand. "I did everything I could."

Phoenix longed to take her in his arms, caress her trembling lips, kiss away her tears. But it was not his place, not his right. Her helplessness became his own as he fought for a way to respond, a way to soothe her pain.

"Walk with me," he said, motioning toward Nokomis. "Maybe it'll help 'soothe the ragged edges.'"

Aerielle glanced in the direction of the lake, seeming to see it for the first time since returning. "I should change. And get Idaho."

"I'll wait."

"I'll hurry."

But the Indians, free and independent as the air they breathed or the wind that blew, could not brook the restraint which the whites were always affecting to exercise over them.

Alexander Ross, 1812 as quoted in *Chief Joseph Country, Land of the Nez Perce* by Bill Gulick

11

Aerielle rushed up the stairs to her second floor apartment, fleeing from the urge to pour her innermost thoughts out to Phoenix. Running from the overwhelming desire to have him hold her and "soothe the ragged edges" in a way more natural to their former relationship.

She shouldn't have accepted his invitation to walk. She shouldn't be seeing him at all. The memories his presence evoked were all too powerful, too sensuous, playing havoc with more than just her heart. He was way too attractive. Aerielle remembered thinking once that he was deceptively good looking. Of course that had been before she'd discovered what lay beneath that protective bronze skin and the shielding chill of his eyes—a heart so tender, and yet so guarded, that only a rare few were privileged enough to be changed by it.

Pain, longing, and desire clung to her even as Aerielle attempted to free herself. It was only that she was weak today. Weak in the soul from losing a patient. Weak as Phoenix had been six days ago when he had lost one. It was folly. If only it had been Hawk waiting for her—waiting for her? What was Phoenix doing here?

No. Aerielle would not contemplate the possibilities. Forcing her key into her apartment lock, she demanded that the door open. She closed it just as roughly before wrapping Idaho in a desperate hug. But the dog was excited and refused to be still, and Aerielle had to release him. Standing, she froze, her eyes glued to the window and the normally innocuous view of the street. For the scene now encompassed the man who followed her thoughts as silently and persistently as any Indian ever tracked that which he chose to hunt.

His back was to her as he moved around her truck examining its features. His movements were liquid, alluring, and Aerielle found herself studying him just as closely as he studied her vehicle. She took in the way his faded jeans fit his long legs, the way his hair whispered against his jacket, the way the fringe on that jacket tantalized her once again with the memory of a proud Indian warrior who fought that which was not even against him.

God help her, thought Aerielle, tearing her gaze away and heading for her bedroom. What dangerous foolish thoughts. It was over between them. Why couldn't it have been Hawk here today? Hawk. Hawk, Phoenix, and Aerielle. There had been a time when the three of them had fought for a patient's life together without a single medical degree between them. It was the night Phoenix and she had shared their first official kiss beneath the Pleiades.

→→→

As Aerielle hurried Morning Dew in the direction of home, her thoughts were torn between the somewhat early arrival of Sunlight's foal and Phoenix's impassioned kiss that still tasted on her lips. Would it signify a change in their relationship, or would he act as if nothing had happened?

Arriving at the stable, Aerielle quickly tied Morning Dew outside and rushed into the barn. Two voices were raised in urgency, though the words remained a mystery since neither Phoenix nor Hawk were speaking English. Coming to a halt in front of Sunlight's stall, Aerielle found the brothers completing a successful attempt at getting a reluctant Sunlight to her feet.

"Walk her," ordered Phoenix in English before turning toward the stall door. He seemed surprised to see Aerielle standing there.

"What's wrong? What can I do?"

"Come with me." Striding past her, Phoenix started for the front of the barn, peeling his sweatshirt off as he went.

Momentarily, he disappeared into the tack room, reappearing seconds later with the phone in hand, it's long cord stretched out like a clothes line. He gave the phone to Aerielle. "I want you to call the vet," he explained, stepping over to a large wash tub. "Tell him Sunlight's foaling and the foal is backwards. I'm gonna try and turn it around."

There was worry in his voice if not on his face, and Aerielle quickly dialed the number he gave her. It seemed forever before a voice came on the line, allowing Aerielle to explain the emergency. Beside her, Phoenix began to lather his hands and arms with soap. He was just rinsing off as Aerielle hung up the phone.

"He's on his way," she said, wondering what to do next.

"Good. Turn the water off."

Twisting the faucets to cease the flow of water, Aerielle followed after Phoenix who was already on his way back to the stall.

Hawk brought the horse to a stop as Phoenix approached. Both began speaking softly to the horse while Aerielle stood by, amazed, as between contractions Phoenix slid one hand

and then the other into the mare. Aerielle had heard of such things, but never seen them. As she planned a future in nursing, she was fascinated by what was happening.

Phoenix's face became a study in concentration as he appeared to push, pull, and maneuver the unseen foal into proper position. Sweat glistened on his forehead and on the smooth plains of his back revealed through the length of his unbound hair.

Hawk continued to soothe the mare while keeping a tight hold on the halter. He looked worried, though Aerielle was sure that even at fifteen he had seen his share of foals brought into the world.

"This foal is huge," grunted Phoenix, straining, his efforts rippling through the muscles on his shoulders and back. "No wonder she can't wait to drop it."

At last he pulled his arms free, wet with fluid and blood. "Let Sunlight have another try."

Hawk released the halter. Soon, the mare was once again on her side in the straw. The three waited with anticipation, watching for the first appearance of a hoof. Phoenix sat behind the horse, prepared to help at the first sign of need. Aerielle could have sworn they'd all stopped breathing, for the labored efforts of the mare were the only sounds she heard. That is, until the three of them let out a concerted sigh as the inner amniotic sac appeared with one hoof leading. A second hoof appeared inside the sac and then a nose, resting on the forelegs.

The mare struggled to produce the head, and Phoenix reached out, grasping the foal's legs.

"The shoulders are caught," he uttered under his breath. Waiting for another contraction, he pulled gently on the foal. The head emerged, along with a vaginal tear.

"God, help us," murmured Phoenix, speaking both of the tear and the size of the foal.

"Man, it's big!" exclaimed Hawk in amazement.

The mare rested briefly, and Phoenix took the opportunity to cut open the sac and peel it away from the foal's nose and face. No one said anything else as the mare once again began to labor. The length of the tear and the amount of blood increased with each push/pull effort to deliver the foal. Aerielle knew that all was not as it should be. Even Phoenix's face revealed his fear.

An eternity of short minutes later, the foal slid free. But not before another tear appeared, as well as an inordinate amount of blood.

Hawk immediately reached for the foal, tearing away at the sac.

"Give me some rags," urged Hawk, motioning towards the clean pile at Aerielle's feet. She began handing them over, and Hawk quickly wiped out the foal's nose and mouth. Then Phoenix was demanding rags as well. The placenta delivered, he tied up the foaling membranes and began applying pressure to the mare's vaginal tears, hoping to stem some of the blood.

"Where's the blasted vet?!" he demanded of no one in particular.

"Phoenix, it's not breathing."

Phoenix jerked his head around toward the foal, lying motionless in the straw.

"What can I do?!" Aerielle pleaded, feeling helpless.

Phoenix reached up, placing a bloody hand on her arm. Pulling her down beside him, Phoenix put her hands where his had been. "Keep the pressure up."

He turned to the foal, his back hiding Aerielle's view of the lifeless form.

"Wait!" exclaimed Aerielle, as the mare she attended suddenly attempted to rise.

Hawk dived forward in the straw. Grabbing hold of the Sunlight's halter, he forced her down.

It was at that moment that the vet arrived, his middle-aged hands pulling open his medical bag before he kneeled in the straw.

"Worry about the mare," said Phoenix.

Aerielle felt herself go numb. The foal....

"The colt's gonna be just fine," Phoenix continued.

Still applying pressure to the mare, Aerielle turned, her hopes rising. Sure enough, she saw the foals nose shift in the straw. So it was a colt, a very *large* colt.

The vet began giving orders with knowledgeable assurance, even as he prepared a sedative for the horse. Phoenix's hands once again replaced Aerielle's, and his words urged her to the sink to wash up and retrieve a pan and what looked like a large baby bottle.

"The mare's not gonna be able to feed her colt right away," explained Phoenix, as Aerielle stepped out of the stall. "That'll be *your* job."

While Aerielle was gone, Hawk removed the rest of the amniotic sac from around the colt, rubbing the foal dry with towels. Phoenix began assisting the vet with repairs and attachment of an IV with fluids and medications. Soon, Hawk was milking the mare as Aerielle looked on, fascinated with the proceedings.

Some thirty minutes later, the partially-spotted colt had managed to stand and take a few wobbly steps. The umbilical cord proceeded to break off naturally, and Aerielle was told to clean the end with iodine. At that point, Hawk handed her the large bottle filled with the precious colostrum he had secured from Sunlight. Offering the bottle to the mare's hungry son, Aerielle was overwhelmed by another of the seemingly endless miracles as the fragile-looking colt fed eagerly.

Hawk had just begun to replace the soiled straw with fresh bedding when Phoenix and the vet finished up, swathing the mare with antiseptic one last time.

"I think she's gonna make it," announced the vet, rising to his feet. "I'll clean up and then sit with her awhile. You guys look like you could use a break."

Aerielle glanced down at her blood spattered T-shirt and silently agreed with the vet about their appearances. She then turned her gaze toward Phoenix, who had risen following the vet's momentary departure. Getting her first full view of Phoenix since the ordeal began, her eyes widened in shock.

There was blood everywhere. It stained his jeans, as well as his flesh. It was streaked through his hair and smeared on his arms, his chest, and even his face. He had saved Sunlight's life and wore the evidence to prove it. Aerielle was struck by the incredible picture of love he portrayed, reminding her of the compassionate death of Christ who had given his life and blood for her.

Abruptly, Aerielle realized Phoenix was aware of her gaze upon him. At once his face hardened, his obsidian eyes grew cold, and he turned, striding out of the barn. Aerielle knew he had misinterpreted her relentless stare as a look of disgust. She wanted to run after him, but the colt suckling at the bottle in her hand demanded she remain. Phoenix would have to wait.

An agonizing hour later, showered and refreshed, Aerielle located Phoenix fixing coffee in the kitchen. He, too, had recently showered. His long hair clung damply to his naked back, and his feet were bare beneath the hems of his clean jeans. Sunrise streamed through a nearby window, trailing over his hands as he scooped coffee into the coffee maker.

"How about some breakfast?" suggested Aerielle, retrieving a container of eggs from the fridge.

Phoenix slammed the basket into the coffee maker. "Not hungry."

"Of course you are. Do you want your eggs scrambled or fried?"

"I want nothing from you."

Aerielle stood before a different stretch of counter, listening as Phoenix poured water into the coffee maker and flipped the switch. Setting her eggs down, she took a deep breath and turned to face his back. "I know you don't want to talk, so just listen to me. Back in the barn, when I was staring at you standing there covered in blood, I knew I'd never seen anything so awful or so beautiful before. You were wearing the blood of life. You saved them, Phoenix—both of them."

Continuing to stare as his long wet hair, which had started to tighten into waves, Aerielle paused, not quite knowing how to continue. "You were a mess. I was a mess. But all I wanted to do was wrap my arms around you, blood and all, and share in the triumph of what you accomplished."

Silence followed Aerielle's words. Heart-wrenching silence. He didn't believe her.

"You're right about one thing," said Phoenix at last. "I don't want to talk to you."

Aerielle closed her eyes, biting her lip to block the pain.

The familiar scent of musk was her only clue that Phoenix was near. Startled and hurt, she turned abruptly, "What?!"

The eyes that met hers were tender, the hands that cupped her face, gentle. "This." And then his mouth covered hers.

→→→

The walk around the lake was a quiet one, with Aerielle not speaking and Phoenix respecting her silence. He studied her discretely, unable to get enough of the vision of his memories. He longed to take her in his arms and kiss her—he'd have settled for making her laugh. But Phoenix was no longer sure how to accomplish such a thing. Change had come like the seasons.

Once upon a time making Aerielle laugh had not required thought, and kissing her had not been something he resisted. Would it ever be that season again?

→→→

Phoenix took a deep breath of September night air mixed with the scent of Hyacinth. The perfume, he'd discovered over the weeks, was Aerielle's favorite. She wore it tonight as always, the scent of it teasing him as she lay beside him on the blanketed deck off the loft. Lifting an arm, she pointed heavenward, naming several constellations Phoenix hadn't asked her to point out.

"Well, teach, how am I doing?" she asked, glancing at Phoenix with a smug expression.

"You appear to have very good study habits."

Aerielle sat up, looking offended. "That's all you can say?"

"I wouldn't want your head to get any bigger than it already is."

"Well! And how are *your* study habits? Have you been reading the Bible I loaned you?"

"But of course."

"So tell me, oh humble one, what book have you been perusing?"

"The Song of Solomon."

Still sitting up, Aerielle snorted. "Are you telling me you've been reading love songs?"

Phoenix rolled onto his side, grinning. "You don't believe me?"

"Should I?"

"You wish me to prove myself?"

"By all means," insisted Aerielle.

Phoenix captured her gaze with his eyes, determined she would not doubt him again. "Let her kiss me with the kisses of her mouth. For your love is more delightful than wine. Pleasing is the fragrance of your perfumes; your name is like perfume poured out—"

"All right, I believe you," cut in Aerielle, her attention riveting on the deck railing.

For the first time, Phoenix sensed he was seeing Aerielle Buchanan embarrassed. "You wouldn't be blushing, would you?"

"Smart mouth, you changed some of the words."

In fact, Phoenix had changed only two. "Tell me how it's supposed to go," he teased.

"You're just looking for an excuse to kiss me."

"I didn't think I needed one."

Aerielle turned to face him, laughter replacing the embarrassment in her eyes. "You don't."

"Good." Phoenix reached out, pulling Aerielle back down beside him.

She offered no resistance, and their banter was quickly chased away by passion, their levity lost to desire. Phoenix kissed her more than once, offering no excuses for the breath he repeatedly stole from her lips.

She reached up, stroking the length of his hair that spilled around them. Her hands were like the sweet caress of moonlight, reminding Phoenix of the gentleness he often heard in her voice. A voice that could set him afire as easily as the long, lingering kisses they shared now.

He wanted her. He wanted her like no one and nothing he'd ever wanted before.

He wanted her heart, her soul, and yes, her body too. He had never claimed or won any of these from a woman before. No heart had ever seemed so full, no soul had ever touched his like Aerielle's. As for the physical, Phoenix knew that Aerielle was waiting for marriage, and what Phoenix had been offered by other girls he had refused. He was unwilling to take even a chance of fathering an unwanted child. His own father had been responsible for two of them and then deserted his family. Any children Phoenix produced would be cared for by a father that loved them. A father that loved his children like God loved His. And that was another gift from Aerielle. The knowledge of her God, which she had shared with Phoenix so willingly.

Phoenix pulled his lips from those of the woman who changed his life daily. He studied her widened eyes. Even in the darkness the color of blue was evident, as well as the smolder of passion. His body suddenly all too aware of hers and his thoughts filled with images belonging to the marriage bed, Phoenix pulled away. He sat up, running a hand through his tangled hair.

"It's getting late," said Aerielle, obviously having similar thoughts. She stood up, walking over to the telescope and peering through the lens. Raising a hand, she adjusted the scope. "The heavens have moved."

Phoenix smiled to himself. "That's a poetic way of putting it.... What time would you say it is?"

Aerielle studied the starlit sky longer than Phoenix would have had to. "Four, maybe?"

"Should have been in bed an hour ago."

"Phoenix, it's Hawk."

Phoenix glanced up to see Aerielle staring toward the house. He stood, joining her at the railing as Hawk approached. His brother looked as if he'd been awakened from a deep sleep despite the fact that he'd taken the time to throw on some clothes.

Hawk stopped below them, his face wary, his arms crossed over his chest as if to keep out the cool night air. "I thought you guys should know that Jim Peterson just called."

Aerielle's shoulders slumped. "That's the fourth time this month."

"It's four in the morning," announced Phoenix like that would change anything.

"He sounded kinda drunk. And I think there was a party going on. Lots of music, and there were some guys egging him on."

"What about Mom and Nevin?"

"I got to the phone first. I told them it was a wrong number."

"What'd he say?" demanded Aerielle.

Hawk shrugged. It was obvious he wished Aerielle hadn't asked. "He just kept asking if you were here, and telling me I'd better keep away from you.... I guess he thought I was Phoenix."

"Were those his exact words?" asked Aerielle.

Hawk looked away. "Not specifically."

"Tell me!"

"I'd rather not."

"Blast it all, Hawk! I have a right to know!" demanded Aerielle, shouting down at him.

"He called you an Indian lovin' slut and Phoenix a frickin' half-breed! Are you satisfied?!"

Angry, Hawk turned and marched back to the house. Aerielle stood without moving, her face expressionless. For the first time that night, Phoenix was cold. Anger rose within him, but he stifled it for Aerielle's sake.

"Hawk's not mad at you, Aerielle."

"I'm sorry I made him repeat it. I forget sometimes he's fifteen."

"He's strong. He'll get over it."

Aerielle turned, her expression concerned as she looked at Phoenix. "And what about you?"

"I've been called a lot worse than a half-breed."

"I kinda like the name," said Aerielle, greeting Phoenix's surprised expression with a tired smile. "As far as I'm concerned, it means you're made up of two special races. It allows me twice as much pleasure in knowing you. You can be my half-breed anytime."

Phoenix shook his head in wonder. "Never thought I'd hear that name as an endearment."

"As for me being an Indian lover," continued Aerielle, stepping closer. "I kinda like that term, too."

"You're taking this rather calmly, aren't you?" asked Phoenix, wondering where the usual angry reaction had gone.

Aerielle laid her head against his shoulder, sliding her arms about his waist even as Phoenix lifted his to enfold her. "I'm tired of getting upset over his calls," she said softly.

"Maybe it's time we notified the police."

"And tell them what? My old boyfriend calls us names?"

Phoenix had no answer, no solution to the problem. They didn't teach you how to handle these kinds of things in high school. He wasn't sure they taught you anywhere.

Aerielle shifted in his arms, brushing her face against his hair. "I love the way your hair smells."

Phoenix sensed a smile in her voice and waited for her to continue.

"It reminds me of a certain piece of scripture."

"Oh, it does, does it?" he said, wondering where she was leading.

"'Let him kiss me with the kisses of his mouth'," began Aerielle, using the correct pronouns which Phoenix had changed. "'Your love is more delightful than wine. Pleasing is the fragrance of your perfumes; your name is like perfume poured out.' Phoenix Yellow Wolf Stargazer. What a wonderful name for a half-breed."

"And what a wonderful excuse to kiss an Indian lover."

→→→

Aerielle was aware of little other than Phoenix as they circled the lake. She knew he watched her. Very few would have noticed, but Aerielle had developed a sixth sense to his subtle observation back in Idaho. Apparently, she had not lost the gift. Why did he watch her so closely? Was he concerned by her silence? It would be like him.

Aerielle was forced to leave her questioning thoughts as Idaho came to an abrupt stop in front of a favorite tree. Phoenix glanced at Aerielle, but she averted her gaze, studying his and Hawk's house now in clear view. Not for the first time, she admired the immaculate grounds, having no doubt as to who did the majority of the work. There was a gift in Phoenix's hands when it came to living things, be it plant or beast.

Turning her attention to Idaho, Aerielle caught sight of a young teenage boy approaching Phoenix from behind, his hands filled with leaves. Phoenix either heard him or sensed his presence, for he turned—but not before the sandy-haired boy showered him with leaves.

"You'll pay for that, Tyler," Phoenix declared, running after the fleeing boy. A leaf battle was soon in progress, and Aerielle was caught up in the splendor of the companionable autumn moment. Soon, she was laughing as the boy named Tyler pushed Phoenix over while he was in the process of scooping up more leaves.

Landing in the grass, Phoenix began to laugh as well. He glanced at Aerielle and then back at Tyler. "What are we doing this to each other for?" he asked, his gaze returning to Aerielle.

"Oh, no," she began.

But it was too late. They were on her in seconds, leaves cascading over her head. It became a free-for-all, everyone out for himself. Even Idaho got into the act, dancing excitedly and barking at each of them in turn.

Breathless at last, Aerielle collapsed on the grass. Phoenix and Tyler sprawled out beside her, laughter erupting periodically.

"You should see yourself," grinned Phoenix, pointing toward Aerielle's hair.

"Me? What about you?!"

Leaves clung to the length of Phoenix's hair, and Aerielle reached a mirroring hand to her own, feeling a crisp crunch beneath her fingers.

Phoenix laughed at the sound, and it suddenly occurred to him that he and Tyler had made *Aerielle laugh*. Phoenix didn't mind the boy's help at all.

"How do you sign 'You guys look ridiculous?'" asked Tyler, looking from one to the other of them as he rubbed Idaho's ears.

Phoenix was about to respond when Aerielle beat him to it, signing the words fluently.

Tyler was clearly surprised. "Hey, she's good."

"Who do you think taught *me*?" said Phoenix.

"You never told me it was—uhm—I mean you never told me where you learned it."

Phoenix glanced at Aerielle to see if she'd picked up on Tyler's blunder.

"Phoenix is teaching you ASL, I take it?" she inquired, seemingly unaware of the implication that Phoenix had been discussing her with Tyler. Phoenix breathed a sigh of relief.

"Not exactly," replied Tyler, "but he does use it to teach Sunday school to deaf kids."

Now it was Aerielle's turn to look surprised. "Really?! Wow!"

Phoenix felt uncomfortable under Aerielle's amazed stare and began picking leaves out of his hair. "By the way, Tyler, this is Aerielle Buchanan and her dog, Idaho. Aerielle, Tyler Hanson. He works at the clinic after school three days a week."

Aerielle acknowledged Tyler with a nod, asking him how he liked the work. Phoenix studied her as she continued to pull leaves from her hair, watching her fingers glide through the veil of gold and wishing the hands were his.

Aerielle felt his continued gaze, did her best to ignore it. But it was impossible. Despite her discussion with Tyler about the medical field, she was all too conscious of the pools of obsidian fastened on her. Why had he come to see her today? And what was he seeing now as he looked at her? Was he remembering their past? Was he regretting? Did she care?

Did she care about him at all, wondered Phoenix. Or did she only regret their time together? The only thing *he* regretted was the lie that separated them now. At least he hadn't told her he didn't really love her. That would have been the greatest lie of all. Not only had he loved her, he still loved her. And if he told her the truth to his lie now, he'd probably lose her all over again. But then, how did one lose what one didn't have?

Unable to stand the intensity of Phoenix's gaze any longer, Aerielle jumped to her feet, brushing herself off. "I think it's time I was on my way. I have things to do."

Liar.

Well, she'd *find* something to do. Being around Phoenix was a mistake. She might actually fall for him again.

"I'll walk you," said Phoenix, standing.

"That's not really necessary."

"Oh, but it is. Idaho, here, might be distracted by a flock of geese and then who will protect you from squirrels."

In spite of herself, Aerielle smiled. "You're making fun of my dog."

"Hey Tyler, where is Boba Fett, anyway?" asked Phoenix.

"Grandma made me take him to the groomers to be 'properly bathed and groomed.' Speaking of which, I better get home. We have to go pick him up."

"See you Tuesday, then, if not before?"

"Yeah, Tuesday."

"Have a good weekend."

"Nice meeting you, Tyler," called Aerielle to his retreating form. "Come on, Idaho. Let's head home. Phoenix will protect me from the dangerous wildlife should you get distracted."

If it came down to it, Aerielle knew he would protect her from anything and anyone. She was as confident of this as she was of her salvation. Some things about Phoenix had clearly not changed. Just like Aerielle's response to those qualities.

In other ways, Phoenix was a different man. And as they walked toward home, once again in silence, it was Aerielle's turn to observe, with Phoenix the object of her study. Fourteen years ago, she couldn't have imagined him teaching Sunday school. What a change that must have been for him, to step far enough out of his protective shell to help others. She studied his profile with wonder, recognizing admiration within herself similar to that which she had known the night long ago when he'd delivered Sunlight's foal. The stubborn yet hurting Phoenix had become a teacher, as well as a healer. He must have learned something through the years enabling him to reach out at church. The question was, had he also been healed of the pain inside himself?

Phoenix was well aware of Aerielle's gaze. Unused to being on the receiving end of such scrutiny, he found it disconcerting. He did his best to ignore her attention, in addition to his reaction to it, but at last he could stand it no longer.

"A penny for your thoughts," he said, verbally retaining his calm as he turned to meet her penetrating blue eyes.

"I was just thinking how amazing it is to find out you're teaching Sunday school."

"Do you hate me so much for what I did in the past that you begrudge me the effort?"

Aerielle came to an abrupt stop at the base of a leafless maple tree, her eyes widening in shock as if he'd hit her. "Of course not," she assured, unconsciously reaching out and placing a hand on his arm. "I admire what you're doing."

Phoenix felt his fears ease somewhat. "It's no different than what you did for us in Idaho."

"Yes it is. I got paid for that."

"You gave us more than sign language skills, Aerielle."

Their gazes locked in a time capsule of memory, each of them longing for an era that had past, a season that had ended. The connection formed by Aerielle's hand upon Phoenix's arm became electrical, and she drew away abruptly.

"That was a long time ago," she said huskily, glancing away.

"Yes. Yes it was."

"I have to go." Aerielle bolted, startling the snuffling Idaho into a run.

Phoenix said nothing, did nothing, as Aerielle retreated to her apartment building across the street from where they'd stopped. He waited and watched until she disappeared inside, and then, feeling very much alone, he turned and started for home.

Husband dead, friends buried or held prisoners. I felt that I was leaving all that I had but I did not cry. You know how you feel when you lose kindred and friends through sickness-death. You do not care if you die. With us it was worse. Strong men, well women, and little children killed and buried. They had not done wrong to be so killed. We had only asked to be left in our own homes, the homes of our ancestors. Our going was with heavy hearts, broken spirits. But we would be free.... All lost, we walked silently on into the wintry night.

Ollokot's Wife, as quoted in *The Nez Perces, People of the Far West.*

12

"I am so glad it's Saturday night," said Phoenix falling into a kitchen chair.

Sofia plopped down beside him, while Tyler stood at the counter consuming an apple, and Hawk retrieved a can of pop for each of them.

Opening a Mountain Dew, Hawk sat down across from Sofia. "All I want to do tonight is something that doesn't take any thought. Like maybe a movie."

"And a pizza," agreed Phoenix.

Sofia regarded them and smiled. "So why don't we rent a couple movies and order in?"

"Sounds like a good idea to me," said Tyler. "If I'm invited."

There were three nods of agreement, but Phoenix was the only one without his mouth full. "Of course you are.

"Hawk, why don't you go for the movies. You know what to rent. And of course, nothing over a PG13," he added glancing at Tyler.

Tyler rolled his eyes, mumbling under his breath.

"While you're gone, Tyler can go square it with his mother and tell his grandmother."

"And *I'll* call for the pizza," announced Sofia.

Their plans for the evening set, Hawk left to get movies, Tyler went next door, and Sofia placed a call for a large supreme with pineapple, as well as a basic cheese. As she hung up the phone, she turned to give Phoenix the total, but she never got a chance to say anything.

At that moment, the front door seemed to explode with sound as someone began pounding on it with violent determination. It resonated clearly all the way back in the kitchen. The shepherds bolted for the foyer, their deep voices bellowing out a continuous loud warning. Phoenix and Sofia were right behind them, stunned by the barrage continuing on the front door—someone *kicking* the front door. Phoenix briefly wondered what he could use for a weapon if needed, but then above the barking of the dogs, Phoenix could hear someone repeatedly screaming his name. Aerielle.

He yanked open the front door, yelling for the dogs to be silent as he did so. His eyes widened at the sight of Aerielle standing on his porch in a blood stained T-shirt, an unmoving Idaho weighing down her arms, her foot lifted as if to kick the door again.

Phoenix reached for the Aussie as a frightened Aerielle exclaimed he'd been hit by a car. Gently, Phoenix took the dog in his arms, surprised Aerielle had even been able to pick him up. He headed for the back of the house, toward the clinic and then the operating room, Sofia running ahead to get the door.

"Wait here, Aerielle," ordered Phoenix, and before she could protest, he kicked the door closed behind him.

Before Aerielle could even move, the outer clinic door flew open, and the boy who helped Phoenix bolted inside, his eyes wide with horror.

The two gazed at each other, momentarily wordless. "I…I was out there," the boy mumbled, experiencing his own form of shock. "Idaho. Idaho, he—Oh, crap. It was bad."

Despite the panic Aerielle was attempting to stifle within herself, her medical training came to the surface. "Tyler. Your name is Tyler, right?" she asked, closing the distance between them.

He hadn't stopped staring at her. "Yeah. Tyler."

Aerielle placed a hand on his shoulders, guiding him towards a chair. "Come. Sit down. Are you feeling dizzy at all? Nauseous? Cold?"

He sat numbly and Aerielle squatted down, eyeing him closely, having seen the look on facies like his too many times in her lifetime.

"No," he said, and then more forcibly, "No, I'm not cold, or any of the other stuff. I'm just—" He shook his head, his shaggy brown hair falling into his eyes.

Without thought, Aerielle raised a hand and brushed back his hair and caressed his face. "It's going be okay, honey." And then she realized what she'd just done, just said, but if the junior high boy noticed or was bothered by the attention, he kept it well hidden.

"I'll get you some water," assured Aerielle, getting up.

She went over to the water cooler beside Sofia's desk and yanked a Dixie cup from the dispenser and filled it up. Turning back towards Tyler, she realized for the first time his jeans were torn over one knee, and his skin was scraped and bleeding. He hadn't even mentioned getting hurt.

She hurried back to him, handing him the water while she re-examined his face. His eyes met hers, reality definitely residing there now, confirming her determination he was not in physical shock.

Squatting down, she examined his knee, perversely glad for something to do. "Does it hurt?" she asked, knowing knees could often be more painful than the injury implied. She picked at a few pieces of gravel, relieved. It didn't look too bad. She could probably find what she needed in one of the exam rooms.

Glancing again at Tyler, she found him shaking his head again, sipping dutifully at the water. "No, it doesn't hurt. I didn't even notice it until you said something."

Resisting the urge to stroke his hair again, Aerielle stood. "I'll go grab a couple things and we'll have this cleaned up in no time."

Finding antiseptic, as well as some gauze and tape, in the closest exam room, Aerielle quickly set about cleaning Tyler's knee. She ended up having to borrow Sofia's scissors to cut the jeans open farther.

"Hey," said Tyler, watching her. "If you do that to both knees and spread some of the blood around, I can probably sell these jeans as some kind of new fashion."

Despite her own anxieties over what was happening with Idaho, Aerielle smiled, looking up at Tyler. So he used humor in times of crisis.

"Maybe we could sell your jeans, too," he added, nodding at her.

Her jeans? Aerielle glanced down. "Idaho."

"Dang,' said Tyler. "I didn't think. I guess I thought it was yours for some reason."

"Well be glad it's not, or I might have passed out. I can't stand the sight of my own blood."

"Really? That's kinda funny when you think about it."

"More inconvenient than anything," she responded, taking up the gauze and the tape. It was a little awkward trying to hold the gauze in place while ripping tape. And she couldn't wrap it around his leg, either, at least not without cutting off the bottom of the pants. And that would reduce the resale value, according to Tyler.

"All done," she announced, standing and tossing the extra supplies on Sofia's desk. *Now* what did she do?

"How do you feel now?" she asked the boy, hurrying back to sit at his side.

"I'm better, thanks," he said, not looking at her. "I'm just—what about Idaho?"

What <u>about</u> Idaho?! Aerielle screamed inside her head. Without any more thought than the first time, she reached for Tyler, wrapping an arm around his shoulders. "He's going to be alright," she declared, ignoring the panic rising in her voice. "Phoenix has a gift. He can fix anything."

"Of course he can," agreed Tyler with sudden assurance. And then Aerielle felt *his* hand on *her*, as he patted her awkwardly on the back. "He fixed up my dog, Boba Fett just fine."

"He did?" Aerielle knew she was starting to sound unglued, and when Tyler jerked his head up to meet her gaze, she knew he knew.

"Yeah, he did," agreed Tyler, still patting, his halfway grownup expression studying hers. "He's still wearing a bandage, but he'll be fine."

Abruptly Tyler was offering her the remains of his water. "Here. Drink this."

Aerielle stared into his beautiful green eyes, took the water with her spare hand without question, and wondered exactly how old Tyler was.

Of its own accord, the arm she rested across his shoulders moved until her hand was once again stroking his hair. A painful silence filled the room. "Uhm," began Tyler, filling the emptiness, "Phoenix told me *you're* a doctor, too, and you work in a hospital. Only *your* patients are kids. I bet you you're just as good at being a doctor as Phoenix is. I suppose someone my age would still be classified as a kid, huh? Well, that'd be a drag, having to hang out with all the little kids. Of course, if it meant being able to play video games and stuff, there might be some benefit to it. I don't suppose they let pets come, though."

Tyler abruptly stopped speaking as if sensing the topic was leading to what he was avoiding—dogs.

Suddenly, the door behind which Idaho had disappeared re-opened and Phoenix stepped out. His black sweatshirt with the sleeves rolled up was soiled with blood. Even the length of his hair, unbound and untamed, had blood in it.

Instantaneously, Aerielle was standing in the barn fourteen years past with Sunlight's foal and Phoenix standing before her, covered with the blood of life. But now, as Aerielle's eyes met his, she knew this time he was wearing the blood of death.

Across the room, Phoenix was surprised to discover Tyler in

the waiting room with Aerielle. Even more unexpected was the tableaux playing out. Aerielle was tenderly stroking Tyler's hair with no negative reaction on the boy's part, while at the same time, Tyler appeared to be comforting *her*, his arm behind her back, a hand patting her reassuringly. It wouldn't be enough.

Moments before, hidden behind the door in the sterile surroundings of stainless steel and surgical white, death had come. Phoenix and Sofia had stared at each other over Idaho's forever lifeless form. It had been "over" five minutes ago in the middle of pressure bandages and resuscitation attempts, but Phoenix had been unable to let himself give up. How? How could he tell Aerielle? Idaho had come in with his heart still beating, and now, it was still forever.

Glancing down at Idaho's battered body, Phoenix had wanted to weep. Instead, he'd bitten back the pain and peeled off his bloody gloves, tossing them into the trash.

Sofia pulled her own gloves off, looking from Phoenix to the closed door. "Phoenix, maybe I.... No I guess not. This is something you have to do, isn't it?"

"Yes.... God help me."

Sofia reached out, placing a hand on Phoenix's arm. "I can at least come with you."

"No. Just cover everything except Idaho's head so she…so she can see him. I'd better get this over with." Silently, Phoenix pleaded for help from his creator as he headed for the door.

Now, watching the two in the waiting room, Phoenix's thoughts concerning Idaho lasted but a split second, but it was long enough for him to see the light of hope in Aerielle's eyes go out. Before he could even speak, her hand closed over a Dixie cup in her hand, crushing it and causing the water to erupt and spill over her hand.

"Aerielle, I'm sorry," began Phoenix, saying the right words, knowing they wouldn't help either of them. Instead, now Tyler looked as horrified as Aerielle. She got up, looking at Phoenix with frightened eyes.

Phoenix started towards Aerielle. Clearly she was the first priority.

"I tried, Aerielle. I really tried, but I couldn't save him."

She was shaking her head as if still hoping to fight off the truth.

"But you saved Sunlight. And her foal. And Tyler's dog. You saved all of them. Why didn't you save Idaho?"

Phoenix swallowed—hard. If he hadn't hurt her enough fourteen years ago—hadn't been witness to her pain—he was certainly crushing her now, and his witness of it was crushing *him*. "His heart stopped," explained Phoenix. *And now mine is.*

"Then why didn't you restart it, blast you?" she demanded, her voice rising with a note of hysteria as tears gathered in her eyes.

"I tried, Meyui."

Phoenix heard the endearment leave his lips before he could stop it, but he wouldn't have called it back even if he could.

As he and Aerielle came within reach of each other, he moved to place steadying hands on her shoulders.

"No!" Screaming this time, she batted his hands away before they made contact.

"Aerielle."

"No!" she screamed again, and raising her fists she began to pound on this chest. "How could you let him die? How?! It was your job to save him!" Angry tears ran rivulets down her cheeks. "It's your fault," she accused. "Your fault, your fault!"

Ignoring her relentless assault upon him, Phoenix stretched out his arms again and wrapped them tightly around her. He crushed her to him even as she battled him, even as she damned him. Her balled fists, unable to move, were caught between them. Her tears dripped from her face and on to his bloodied sweatshirt and tangled hair, and into his agonized soul. Unable to move, Aerielle let out a roar of fury before she began to sob with abandonment as she pressed her forehead to his shoulder.

"Idaho. My Idaho," she mumbled against him, followed by something garbled and then "wolf."

Had she just called him Wolf again? Before Phoenix could think about it further, her words continued. "He was too young to die." More wrenching cries escaped her lips, and Phoenix could feel the sounds wherever his body touched hers as if they were coming from inside him.

"He was all I had," she cried out in a hoarse whisper. "All I had." And then there was no sound except her muffled sobs.

Phoenix continued to hold her, feeling her devastating pain, wishing he could take it all upon himself. He expected her torrent to ease, but when it did not, he raised a worried hand to her hair, and stroked it as she had stroked Tyler's. "For what it's worth, Aerielle, You have—can have—me."

Her reaction was violent and unexpected as she jerked out of his arms.

"No! You left me. Just like my parents. Just like, like he did. With Idaho gone, I have no one left. Every living being in my life leaves me!"

The last words were a shriek, and then she was running for the door. She was through it before Phoenix could think to move. Shaking off his astonishment, he went after her. In her condition, she could get herself hurt, or worse.

She was already rounding the house when he cleared the back vet entrance. Just as he reached the same corner, he heard the screech of tires. For a moment, for the seconds it took him to clear the front of the house and see the street, Phoenix thought he would die, too.

Suddenly it was as if he ran into an invisible wall as he came to an abrupt stop, a moan welling within his own throat. It was Hawk's car that had made the noise, and Aerielle was climbing in to it. She reached for Hawk as she had not reached for Phoenix, wrapping her arms around his brother's neck recklessly, willingly, even as Hawk's arms took the place where Phoenix had forced his. Phoenix felt a roar of his own attempting to escape. He bit down on his lip as hard as he could as the silenced sound ripped through his chest tearing his heart asunder.

Suddenly, Sofia was there, grabbing his arm and hauling him back beside the house before he could be seen from the street. Phoenix would have collapsed if not for the firm century-old walls of the stately Victorian behind him.

Sofia was shushing him like a child even though he made no sound. "It's alright, Phoenix. It's going to be alright." She placed a hand against his chest, over the spot where his heart lay. Was it even still beating?

She replied as if she'd heard him. "It's pounding like a freight train. You can't have a heart attack, Phoenix. I'm not even a licensed vet tech, yet."

Phoenix raised his own hands, covering her one, holding it tight to his chest as if it might still the pain.

"It will be alright, Phoenix," she assured again as he began to slow his breathing. "It'll work out between you and Aerielle. Just give it some time."

He looked at her incredulously. "How can you say that when she's in *his* arms right now?

"Because she isn't in love with Hawk. She's in love with you."

Phoenix went from taking deep breaths to not breathing at all. What had Sofia said? But he didn't need it repeated. He could see the evidence all over her face. "What makes you say that?"

"When she was attempting to kick in the front door, with the love of her dog-life in her arms, it wasn't Hawk she was screaming for, it was you."

The moment in time she described came instantly to mind in full clarity. Earlier Phoenix had unconsciously noted Aerielle'd been hollering his name. But now, he remembered all the words she'd spoken. "Phoenix...Phoenix help me...Yellow Wolf, please." Silence followed except for the pounding, and then,

"Blast you, Half-breed. It's Meyui. Open the door. We need you."

"Yeah," said Sofia watching his face. "I've never heard you called Yellow Wolf. As for half-breed, somehow it didn't sound like an insult."

"It wasn't," exhaled Phoenix, suddenly breathing again for necessity's sake. *It was an endearment. She only called me that when we were alone.*

Sofia smiled gently and with such tenderness, that even in his current state, Phoenix was touched by it. If she ever looked at Hawk that way and his eyes were even half open, his brother wouldn't be able to help but notice.

"We should go in," Sofia murmured. "I'm sure if you look behind me over at the Wellington's, that old lady's probably at her window getting an eyeful at the very least."

Phoenix couldn't stop himself. He glanced across the spread of perfect grass and the hedges that divided the properties and spotted Mrs. Wellington indeed at one of the windows.

"Tyler," he suddenly exclaimed. "What must he think about Aerielle's reaction? I think he must have seen what happened to Idaho. I should talk to him."

They reached the door, now wide open, and entered the clinic waiting room. "I'll clean up and make myself scarce while you talk two talk," said Sofia, "if he's still here," she added glancing at the empty room.

Phoenix's gaze went straight to the operating room door. It was open by a handful of inches. "I didn't leave it open," said Sofia having seen it, too.

Abruptly the front door bell chimed. Sofia glanced at Phoenix. "That'll be the pizza. I'll take care of it."

She left him then, and Phoenix headed toward the second storm of the night.

Tyler was calm, at least on the surface. He stood in the dimmed lighting next to the table and the mostly covered body, his hand stroking Idaho's head in a way that reminded Phoenix of the way Aerielle had been stroking Tyler's earlier. Tyler had also been speaking to the dog, but stopped when he heard Phoenix.

"Saying goodbye?" asked Phoenix

Tyler looked over at him, and Phoenix swore the boy had aged a few years since they'd been in the kitchen planning the evening.

"That, too," agreed Tyler, adding nothing more as he removed his hand from the dog.

Phoenix didn't know where to start,and the two stood staring at each other.

"Tyler—"

"Aerielle—"

They both spoke at once, and Phoenix was instantly worried because Aerielle's name had been the first word out of Tyler's mouth. He stopped speaking immediately as Tyler continued, words suddenly pouring out of him.

"I've never seen anyone lose it like that. I mean I could tell she was upset, but she was getting edgier by the moment. First she was playing with my hair and reassuring me. At first it was kinda weird, but the next thing I knew I was reassuring her. I thought if I played along like she was helping me, she might be okay. But she wasn't. And then...."

"She will be okay," assured Phoenix. "People handle grief in very different ways, Tyler. For her it was anger. It will pass, eventually. I'm sorry you had to see her like that."

"She was hitting you," announced Tyler as if Phoenix hadn't noticed.

"Yes," agreed Phoenix. "I have to admit, her reaction was extreme. But I have a feeling there was more to it than Idaho's death."

Tyler's eyes filled with understanding. "You mean the lie you mentioned telling her?"

"Yeah," said Phoenix, chagrin in his voice. "Did it frighten you?"

"No. Shocked me more like it. I mean she did ramp up there at the end, but for a little while she was as normal as you."

That's not saying much.

"She must have thought something was wrong with me because she started asking me a bunch of doctor questions. After I answered them all correctly, she went and got me some water. And then she fixed up my knee. It wasn't until she was done fixing me up that she—uhm—she ran out of things to do."

"Your knee?" replied Phoenix dumbly, glancing down. "What happened to your knee?"

"I'm right, aren't I?" asked Tyler, ignoring the question

Phoenix quickly noted the torn bloody section of denim and then the white bandage hiding in the shadow beneath. Reassured, he looked back up. "Most likely. While she was worried about you she probably went into doctoring mode. I hate to say it's probably a good thing you hurt yourself, but she might have come apart sooner if not for the delay."

Tyler winced, closing his eyes.

"I'm sorry," said Phoenix. "That was a stupid thing to say," he added backpedaling.

"Stop," demanded Tyler abruptly, his eyes filled with misery and his lips pressed together as if in pain.

Phoenix stared intently at this older, more serious Tyler

"You asked me if I was saying goodbye. I said, 'That, too.' But I really came in to say I was sorry and to face up to what I did."

"Tyler what—"

"I'm the reason he's here," stated Tyler without inflection, glancing at the dog. "I'm the reason Idaho is dead and Aerielle is miserable."

Phoenix didn't bother to ask Tyler what he meant. He just waited in silence for the boy to continue.

Tyler fixed on Phoenix's face while he gripped the table for support. His teeth were gritted as he continued. "When I was home reporting in, Grandma insisted I get the mail. It couldn't wait. She wanted it now, and I was mad. But I raced out to the curb and began hauling all the crap out of the mailbox and the paper box. At some point the wind came up off the lake and the stuff went flying into the street. It was *so stupid.* I was so mad, I didn't look. I just ran into the road. I didn't see or hear the car in time, and when I did hear the brakes slam on, I knew instantly I was dead. And then someone was screaming, "Stop." A second later I was flying just like the mail. I landed on the sidewalk.... There was this horrible thump, and I realized whoever had pushed me out of the way—"

Tyler's voice broke, and Phoenix fisted his hands, controlling his urge to reach out and comfort him.

"I didn't know it was Idaho until I saw Aerielle and heard her screaming. She didn't see me in the dark, and I was partially hidden by the car. The driver started to get out, and I didn't know what to do. Believe it or not, I was still holding some of that crappy mail. I ran back to the house as fast as I could and practically threw it at my grandmother before coming over here. When I came in, Aerielle was just standing there staring as the door closed behind you and Sofia. I didn't notice my knee until Aerielle pointed it out. I killed her dog and she fixed my knee!"

His last words were filled with all the emotion he'd been holding back, and Phoenix saw tears pooling in his eyes while he tried to fight them.

"Tyler," began Phoenix as calm as he'd been in the waiting room with Aerielle.

"I deserve to suffer," demanded Tyler. His voice shook this time and a single tear threaded its way down his face. He backhanded it away almost painfully.

Phoenix winced, stepping forward. "It was an accident, Tyler you didn't—"

"It was stupid! *I* was stupid."

At this point, Phoenix didn't care how Tyler responded. He pulled him close like the hurting child he was. Unlike Aerielle, he didn't resist. He just buried his face against Phoenix's chest and began to cry. "I shouldn't even be allowed to cry."

"Hush," murmured Phoenix. "Tears are a way of cleansing the soul. Even Jesus wept."

Tyler made no audible response, but his shoulders began to shake with his pain, an agony that matched his silent tears.

I call him [the Indian] a savage, and I call a savage something wholly desirable to be civilized off the face of the earth.

Charles Dickens as quoted in Chief Joseph of the Nez Perce by Robert Penn Warren.

13

Aerielle awoke on Sunday morning with a terrible sinus headache. In the first glimpses of consciousness, she thought she had the flu, but then the horrifying reality returned. Idaho was dead. Her sinuses were still clogged from all the tears she'd cried. Rolling over, she buried her face in the pillow, the emptiness at the foot of her bed seemingly heavier than Idaho had been. And then there was the pain. She recognized it too well, only this time she knew she was not having a heart attack, just a heart break. Even that wasn't exactly right, for the pain—this agonizing, deep, wrenching pain—felt as if someone had thrust a hand through her flesh and bone, just below her ribcage, and squeezed. It was difficult to breath.

Since she'd suffered this all-consuming agony before, she knew she'd live. She would only *feel* like dying, long for the kind of relief it brought. The only alternatives for Aerielle were sleep and prayer, and sometimes they were harder to accomplish than she thought they should be.

Aerielle got out of bed, stumbling to the bathroom, grateful she didn't have to work today. She tried not to look in the vanity mirror, but it was next to impossible to avoid. She not only *felt* like dying, she *looked* like it, too. And in addition to her puffy shadowed eyes and her ghostly appearance, she saw guilt in her expression.

How was she going to explain herself to Phoenix? She'd

literally gone ballistic on him, unleashing her fury and her fists. Had she injured him? Physically? Emotionally? In spite of his detached, often silent Indian affectation, she knew him well enough to know he was very good at hiding what he didn't want others to know.

Whatever his thoughts and/or feelings, he had gone well beyond the doctor/hysterical pet owner relationship. He had been Hemene Moxmox—Yellow Wolf—to her, not reacting negatively to her abuse, only holding her until the storm had, well, turned into a hurricane and left the area. And briefly, just briefly, he'd slipped up and called her Meyui, his Morning Light, just as she'd accidentally called him Half-Breed. Aerielle had noticed neither at the time, but the realization came in her sleep. She'd woken around three with both endearments—both words of love—like a whisper of sweet memory against her lips.

→→→

Despite having gotten four to five hours of rest, when Phoenix woke Sunday morning, he felt as if he hadn't slept at all. He wondered if Hawk felt as bad as he did. His brother hadn't come home until midnight, many hours after Phoenix and Sofia had cleaned up the clinic, and the fresh unwanted pizza had been paid for and delegated to the fridge. Maybe Phoenix would have some for breakfast, if he could get out of bed. Groaning, he rolled over, burying his face in his pillow to stifle the sound, just in case Hawk was still home. Phoenix knew his brother had committed himself to helping someone move today. Phoenix wished him good luck with that. As for himself, he'd have enough trouble getting to church. But there were people counting on him.

Phoenix had never been one for mirrors, but 10 minutes later as he stood before the bathroom sink, he couldn't help himself. He looked like he'd partied all night, and then gotten mugged on his way out of the bar. His eyes were bloodshot, and black and blue marks were beginning to form on his chest where Aerielle had punished him. He had no doubt there was more to her explosion than the loss of Idaho, as horrible as that was. She'd been remembering another Idaho and the day he had left her. He'd had that pounding coming for a lot of years, and he would have willingly suffered worse from her.

Compared to the scars.... Phoenix twisted around so he could see the web of white lines crisscrossing his back in the mirror. Nothing could hurt him as those had, and not just physically. The loss of Aerielle as a result of that bloody day, those scars had hurt worse than the whipping itself. There were only a handful of people who had seen the scars, Sofia being one unexpected addition in the last few years.

As for his current injuries, Phoenix only needed a black eye to complete the impression he'd been in a barroom brawl. At least the bruises could be hidden. There wasn't much he could do about his eyes.

As Phoenix pulled out a brush and began raking it though his hair, he wondered if Aerielle was working today. He should call and find out when he got back from church.

Not many hours later, Phoenix tried calling Aerielle at home, but there was no answer. *Would* she answer if she was home? He then tried the hospital and ended up speaking with someone named Heather. When he'd asked for Aerielle, Heather had thought he was Hawk. It figured. But she had started volunteering info before he could correct her, saying Aerielle was off today. So she *was* home and she *wasn't* answering her phone.

After changing into well-worn jeans and an old T-shirt, Phoenix jumped into his truck and drove the short distance to Aerielle's place. Her truck was there. He pulled up to the curb behind it, got out, and headed for the door. Phoenix was glad there was no security type setup, for she'd have had to let him in, and he doubted she would've obliged. She wasn't aware she *needed* to see him, but Phoenix was fairly sure she did. Since the two-story home had been divided into just two apartments, Phoenix headed up the stairs to her door.

There was no sound coming from her apartment, and Phoenix's knock sounded louder than he'd expected. He waited, leaning against the door jamb as the seconds ticked by. He wondered if he'd have to knock again. But then the door started to open, her voice raspy as she spoke. "Hawk, I thought you were—Oh. Phoenix."

"Morning, Aerielle." She looked as bad as he'd expected.

"Phoenix if this is about what happened yesterday and what I did—

"It's not," he said, cutting her off as her voice shook. "It's about Idaho."

Her face blanched and Phoenix was surprised she could get any whiter than she already was. "The dog," he added swiftly, distressed at the extra pain he'd just brought her. "I thought you might want to see him."

Her sky blue eyes, now shadowed and swollen, widened in confusion. "It's not too late?"

Phoenix had to concentrate on keeping his face an emotionless mask while he fought the urge to touch her, comfort her, with more than just his arms this time. "No, it's not too late. I wouldn't do anything with Idaho's body without talking to you. I thought I could bring you over so see him."

"I'm not dressed," she mumbled, glancing down at her disheveled winter pajamas and robe.

'I can wait—in the truck, I mean."

"No. No, you can come in. I'll just be a couple of minutes."

She shut the door behind him as he entered, but offered nothing else, leaving him alone to do as he would.

And so Phoenix waited, using his time to take in the surroundings. Aerielle was somewhat of a minimalist, for there was little to see, and what there was, was extremely neat and organized. This included the few small pieces in the living room, a small sofa being the only place to sit. As for what he could see of the kitchen, Idaho's food dish and full water bowl were lined up neatly on a small mat. There was a hook next to the front door, attached to a plaque that read, "Idaho's Car Keys." There was a leash hanging on it, but not the one the dog had been wearing last night. Phoenix had removed that one, as well as the dog's collar when he'd started CPR. The place was quiet. Too quiet, decided Phoenix. The only sound he heard was Aerielle brushing her teeth.

She rejoined him shortly, her clothes as worn as his, her long hair brushed carelessly. They said nothing as Phoenix escorted her to the truck. He opened the door for her, but didn't help her up. It was too familiar a memory of times past. She hoisted herself in without comment and Phoenix closed the door. The ride back around the lake was silent, Aerielle huddled close to her side of the cab, her head resting against the window.

Aerielle clung to the door handle, stunned by the deluge of memories, which poured over her when she found herself in the cab of Phoenix's truck like so many times before. She was afraid if she let go, she might slide across the bench seat and close the distance and the years which separated them. All so she could curl up at his side and know the comforting strength of him. Yesterday's anger was long gone, unlike the gentleness with which he'd treated her. He confused her, or maybe she confused herself. She shouldn't want to close the distance between them. And if she did, what was to keep him from rejecting her all over again.

The very short trip seemed much longer than it should, and the silence didn't help. When they arrived at the house, Aerielle got out of the cab as quickly as possible, fearful if she let Phoenix open the door for her, she'd jump off the running board and straight into his arms, risking everything.

Phoenix brought her in through the back door, nicely avoiding the path from the front they had taken yesterday. Aerielle slipped out of her coat, laying it over the back of a kitchen chair, watching as Phoenix removed his as well, and hung it on a convenient hook.

He turned, their eyes meeting, and Aerielle looked away. "Come on," said Phoenix heading for the hallway leading to the clinic. "I put him in one of the rooms for you before I came over, just in case. Stay as long as you want." He paused, motioning to the room Aerielle had retrieved medical supplies from the previous evening.

"If you need anything...anything at all...I'll be in the kitchen."

Aerielle nodded and Phoenix left her. Slipping into the exam room, Aerielle found Idaho laid out on the table, his body covered by a soft blanket, looking as if he'd gone to sleep. He was as Aerielle had expected, and she felt gratefulness wash over her at Phoenix's forethought and planning. Pulling a chair up to the end of the table, Aerielle sat down next to the dog, reaching up to stroke his head. He was cold, and Aerielle felt the finality of his loss sweep over her anew. The tears she thought should have run dry by now, returned in a flood and she wept, reliving his loss and those in her life who had gone before. Eventually she began to pray, speaking softly, her head bowed almost as if she spoke in Idaho's ear. "My sweet, Jesus. I knew he wouldn't live forever, but I didn't expect to lose him now. And of all the circumstances, I never would have imagined his last breaths would be taken in the hands of the man I once loved.... I guess of all the places he could have died besides in my own arms, Phoenix's would have been my own choice, too. Maybe you knew that. Oh, God. I treated Phoenix horribly last night. Forgive me. Let *him* forgive me."

When no more words or tears remained, Aerielle stroked Idaho's soft fur one more time, pressing a kiss to the side of his muzzle. "I'm gonna miss you, but I *will see* you again. If Heaven is perfect, then you have to be there. God, you know where he needs to be and with whom. Take care of him. Find him some sheep to herd."

Leaving the exam room, Aerielle wiped at her face. She knew she looked like crap, but then, she'd looked like crap when she'd come in. Silently, she approached the kitchen, and Phoenix was indeed there. His back to her, he stood at the counter, looking very domestic as he dried some dishes. This was the man she'd seen last night, Hemene Moxmox, the man she knew as Yellow Wolf in addition to his given first name, Phoenix. From behind, she was unable to see the signs of ageing, and for a moment, she could pretend the last fourteen years had never happened and she saw him for the young man he'd been, her Half-Breed, her love.

But he was no longer her man, and she was no longer his woman. He was, however, the person she'd abused last night, and she owed him an apology. Gathering her thoughts, Aerielle opened her mouth to speak, only to have Phoenix speak first.

"You don't need to apologize, Aerielle," he said, turning around and meeting her gaze with his. Hands empty now, he leaned back against the counter, resting his palms on the edge. "I deserved the pummeling you gave me."

"But you weren't responsible for Idaho."

They both heard the irony in those words. Phoenix even smiled halfway. "But I did lie to you. And I did desert you."

Phoenix's bluntness had not dissipated with the years, but using it now showed his vulnerability, which *had* been something he'd struggled with in the past. The warrior he'd thought he should be wouldn't have been vulnerable to anything. It was like a salve on an old wound. Seeing his willing defenselessness, hearing him offer himself up for more rebuke touched Aerielle to her core, stripping her of her own defenses. How could they possibly share the same world again, knowing what they'd had, wanting it back. At least Aerielle did, or thought she did.

His compelling gaze never left her's, and Aerielle knew he was wondering what she was thinking that slowed her response. Forcing her mind back to the matter at hand, Aerielle folded her arms across her chest, noticing for the first time, the shadows under his eyes. "You did lie. And you did leave. But what happened in Idaho doesn't make you responsible for Minnesota. And I really am so sorry about the way I treated you. Did I hurt you? If I could have hit you any harder I know I would have."

Now, Phoenix's familiar memorable smile spread to a full grin, lighting up his eyes. "I'm *sure* you would have. Not to worry, though, I've suffered worse."

The laughter in his eyes was like sunshine after the storm.

"But as I told you, you have nothing to apologize for. As far as I'm concerned there is nothing to forgive."

"I'm sorry, anyway."

"Well, then, if it will make you feel better, I accept your apology."

"It does make me feel better, thanks. And so did seeing Idaho again. Thank you for that, too."

"Would you like some coffee?" Phoenix asked, pushing away from the counter.

"That would be nice."

"You still take it with a shot of cream?"

"Yes."

"Why don't you sit down before you fall down. I'll bring it to the table."

As he turned his back to prepare two mugs of the hot liquid, Aerielle shuffled over to the kitchen table, grateful for his suggestion. Suddenly her exhaustion was back. He'd clearly seen it even if she had momentarily forgotten it.

Moments later, Phoenix set two cups on the table and took the seat across from her. "Before I forget," he began, pausing to reach into his back pocket and pulling out a folded piece a paper. "The driver of the car left a note. I guess we were too busy with Idaho to care or notice the rest of the world. We probably shut the door right in her face."

Phoenix slid the paper across the table. "Anyway, she left a number if you want to call."

Aerielle stared at the note, not sure she even wanted to take it. It hadn't been the driver's fault after all.

"She wasn't responsible," said Aerielle aloud, sipping at her coffee and ignoring the paper. "I was. I should have been paying more attention. He was walking by my side, when all of a sudden, he just lunged. So hard in fact—" She broke off, holding out her right hand palm up, revealing a severe rope burn, or in this case, leash burn. It started at her wrist and ran down across her palm.

Before he could stop himself, Phoenix took Aerielle's hand in his, inspecting the angry marks. It was as if he'd grabbed hold of an electric current, and he wondered that Aerielle didn't pull back in surprise. Phoenix tried to ignore the effect of the contact as he examined her injury.

"That looks very painful," said Phoenix, barely above a whisper. "This doesn't look like *your* fault either Aerielle. I'd say Idaho had a mind of his own when he broke free."

Contact already made, Phoenix used his other hand and touched a finger to the edge of the burn. "How bad does it hurt?"

He glanced up at her, wondering if she'd voice a complaint either way. She said nothing, but her expression spoke volumes.

"Let me help you with that," said Phoenix, willing to let go, only because he knew he could touch her again.

"No. I mean it's fine," said Aerielle. "I should know. I'm a doctor."

Phoenix rolled his eyes. "I may only be a veterinarian, but I wouldn't let any of *my* patients go home this way."

"Phoenix, I—"

"Indulge me. Please," he pleaded with his eyes as well as his voice.

"Oh, all right."

Phoenix left the room briefly, returning with some aloe, gauze, and self-sticking material to wrap her hand in. He noticed immediately that the note had disappeared from the table, but he made no comment.

Phoenix began to apply the gel as delicately as possible to the marks on Aerielle's wrist and palm, feeling as if he'd just added an extra conduit to the electrical connection that was already there. Trying not to hurt her, he was careful as spread the aloe and wrapped the gauze. While he would have wrapped anyone's hand with equal care, it was Aerielle's hand he held, her delicate fingers he longed to caress. It was *her* pulse in *her* wrist, which he desperately desired to press against his lips before taking her into his arms and kissing her until the pain of both the dog and the injury were forgotten.

With steel resolve, and the muscle in his clenched jaw beginning to throb, Phoenix let go of Aerielle and reached for his coffee with both hands. "There's uh...one more thing we need to finalize. About Idaho—" Blast, he'd done it again. Why'd she have to choose that name for the canine? Phoenix took a swig of his coffee as Aerielle slowly looked up from her hand. "Would you like Idaho cremated?" asked Phoenix. "So you can have his ashes?"

When she stared at him for a moment without answering, Phoenix continued. "It's not for everybody—"

"Yes. Yes I *would* like his ashes. Thank you. Again. And my hand *does* feel better as well. Is there anything you haven't thought of?"

Yes, how am I going to win you back, away from my brother, away from the past.

→→→

Aerielle woke for the second time that day, only it was much later, and she was already dressed from her trip with Phoenix. This time, there was no cushion before reality hit home. Idaho was gone, and Phoenix was back in her life—as if either of those by itself wasn't difficult enough.

She was suddenly aware of an urgent pounding on her front

door. Aerielle realized it was the knocking that had awakened her. She struggled out of the blanket entangling her, wondering how long the knocking had been going on.

Sock-footed, she did a form of slip-sliding to the door, the pounding coming again as she reached for the door handle.

"Aerielle?" Hawk's voice demanded from the other side. "Aerielle, are you—Oh, thank God," he said as she opened the door to his imposing figure, his face drawn with concern.

"I have this feeling I just saved my door from imminent destruction."

Hawk sagged with relief. "Aerielle, don't scare me like that." And then he roughly hugged her, pinning her arms to her sides, and Aerielle found her face pressed to his icy coat, her access to oxygen cut off. "Crap, Aerielle, I was worried. Phoenix said you'd been over to see the dog. When you didn't answer right away...."

Aerielle attempted to answer now, her voice nicely muffled. Raising her arms at the elbows, she slapped at his shoulders like a floundering bird.

"What is it?" he demanded, loosening his hold.

Aerielle gasped. "I might die yet if you smother me."

"Oh, man, I'm sorry." He let out a short laugh as he let go of her.

"Besides," remarked Aerielle meeting his eyes, "you're cold."

One glance at her face and Hawk took on his worried look again, but he didn't attempt to smother her this time. He peeled off his offensively cold jacket and tossed it onto a kitchen chair as Aerielle closed the door. Turning back to her, he put a hand on her shoulder and pushed her toward the loveseat. "Sit down before you fall down," he ordered, sitting down beside her.

Aerielle briefly smiled at the irony of his words before closing her eyes. "I must really look bad. You're the second person to say that to me."

Hawk grunted with irritation. "The last person I want to sound like right now is my brother."

"Does that mean I *don't* look like I've been sucked dry by a vampire?"

This time Hawk let go with a dry laugh.

"While I know there's no competition," continued Aerielle, "you don't look up to speed yourself. Both you and Phoenix look like you got a half night's sleep combined.

"I'm not complaining. And I doubt Phoenix is either. You on the other hand, look worse than you did when I left last night."

"You sure know how to cheer a girl up."

"For what it's worth, the dark circles under your eyes actually make them look bluer and brighter."

Aerielle turned to stare at Hawk. "Oh, sure, that helps," she said sarcastically, but inside she cringed. Is that what Phoenix had seen today, too? He'd always loved her eyes, and her hair, but there was no way her hair was going to pass for corn silk gold today. But he'd spent a lot of time looking at her eyes earlier...looking *into* them. As for his, she'd found them hauntingly compelling this afternoon, as though if she looked in them long enough, she would have been able to see inside and know what he was thinking...and feeling.

When he'd taken her hand to examine it, she'd been shocked. Indeed, almost literally, as his very touch seem to electrify her skin. And then when he'd applied the aloe to her injury, she'd actually forgotten Idaho for brief seconds while a wildfire she hadn't known in fourteen years, enveloped her and pierced her heart. It consumed her with its memories, and taunted her with that which was out of reach.

How could he still have that effect on her after more than a decade and after all he'd put her through? How could her pulse race so, just being in his presence? Why? Why had he come to Minnesota? Of all places, why here?

If he hadn't come, Idaho might have died anyway, but Aerielle wouldn't be suffering twice the agony, as she was now. She had lost Phoenix once. If there was no future for them, how would she survive losing him again, for she couldn't continue to live here, so close by, her torment growing by the day. She could feel the pressure well up from inside. She tried to suppress it yet again. She didn't want to make a scene. She failed.

"Why?!" Her question exploded from her of its own volition as her hand tightened into a fist.

"I must have missed something," said Hawk puzzled. "Why what?"

Angrily, turning her back to the pillowed arm rest of the loveseat, Aerielle pulled her knees to her chest. She glared at Hawk over the top of them. "Why are you here? I'm talking about you and Phoenix, or maybe *just* Phoenix. What are your doing in Minnesota of all places? I've been meaning to ask you since the day we ran into each other. Why is Phoenix here? Didn't I suffer enough the first time around? Why am I faced with him all over again?"

Hawk looked at her, confused. "Phoenix said Minnesota was the only safe place. He said you'd sworn never to live in the same state twice. Minnesota was the only option. It was the only place he knew besides Idaho.... Oh, horse dung. He lied to me, didn't he?"

Aerielle stared back in mute surprise. What she had told Phoenix was that her one dream was to *return* to Minnesota and work at the Minneapolis Children's Hospital, a wonderful healing hospital where Aerielle had spent a small amount of time as a child. A place that had planted the dream of becoming a nurse, like the ones who had spent so much time with her back then.

"I'll take your silence as an affirmative. I suppose then, when he said he didn't mind me taking you out, he was lying about that, too. That explains the look he gave me when I kissed you at the clinic."

"I wish it had worked," admitted Aerielle.

"You wish what had worked?"

"That kiss."

"*That* kiss, or the other one?"

Aerielle shrugged. "Either or. Life would be so much easier if I could just fall for you."

"Phoenix thinks all women fall for me, and I use them and toss them aside."

Aerielle stared at him in amazement. "Is that what Phoenix thinks? That you're a skirt-chasing womanizer?"

"They don't necessarily have to be in skirts, according to Phoenix, just women," laughed Hawk bitterly. "I have to admit, I've been through my share of girlfriends."

"I would suspect it's because you haven't found the right one."

Now it was Hawk's turn to stare at her with wonder. "How do you do that? How do you have me figured out so well, and yet my own brother doesn't have a clue?"

Aerielle actually laughed. "And since when has Phoenix been the trusting or believing type? He always assumes the worst. It's his nature, his mixed blood if you will. As for myself, I've always been a good judge of character, with one obvious exception."

"Jim Peterson?"

Aerielle nodded. "Jim Peterson. He was very good at hiding himself, unlike Phoenix who was an open book."

"Well, don't tell *him* that. His powerful Indian mojo would be offended. For what it's worth, you're the only outsider who saw through him."

"I think that has a lot to do with growing up in a deaf home. When you listen to somebody by watching their hands, you're more attuned to *all* their body language. After all, there is no tone of voice to distract you."

Hawk's expression turned to admiration. "You're a remarkable woman, you know that? Phoenix never stood a chance against you. I always wondered how you managed to get through his defenses. I mean he's tough as nails. I remember watching the way he changed around you. I was so jealous."

"You? What for?"

"What do you think? I was 15 and hormonal. You were hot

and available, and God knew my brother wasn't going to take advantage of the situation."

"I guess I'm glad I didn't know all this back then," Aerielle blushed.

Hawk chuckled. "Wow, Aerielle. I didn't think anything could embarrass you."

"I don't think my all-seeing white girl mojo can handle it."

Thoughtfully, Hawk turned toward her, resting an elbow on the back of the love seat, and pulling one leg up partway. "You asked if he hadn't made you suffer enough. I knew he hurt you horribly when he disappeared. But after everything you went through, you went and named your dog Idaho."

Aerielle smiled wistfully. "As I said before, despite everything, much good came from Idaho. You know the saying. 'Better to have loved and lost than to never have loved at all.' And I *did* love him. In more ways than I could have dreamed possible. More than my own life, even."

"Then how did you stay? How *could* you stay? I always wondered why you didn't just up and leave."

Aerielle smiled softly. "Sparrow needed me. And I desperately needed to be needed, and since *he* no longer needed me.... As long as he stayed away, I figured I would get through it.

"Now it makes me wonder, though," she remarked, glancing away. "With big brother out of the way, what happened to the 15-year-old and his hormones?"

"Oh, he was still around. But he had no idea what to do for the fragile beauty who cried herself to sleep at night."

Aerielle rested her forehead on her knees, hiding her face. "I tried so hard to be quiet. I didn't know anyone could hear me, especially with Phoenix's bedroom so far from the others."

"I don't think anyone else did. I certainly never heard you from my room, which was closer than the others. It was only a fluke that I heard you the first time. After that I spent a lot of nights sitting outside your door until it got quiet."

Aerielle lifted her head in surprise. "How long did you do that?"

Hawk shrugged. "Until you stopped crying yourself to sleep."

"You sat outside my door every night for.... Hawk, that must have been at least a month."

"Sounds about right."

"You never said anything.... So why did *you* stay? Every night. Outside my door."

"I don't think I really knew. At the time it was the only thing I could *think* to do. I guess I hoped if you were never alone, you would eventually be okay. Maybe in some ways, it was the same reason you did. Sparrow needed you. Hence we all needed you. In the end, watching over you, however unhelpful to you, it changed me, straightened out my priorities. All three of us grew up some that year."

Aerielle reached out, placing a hand on Hawk's arm. "I'm glad you were there, just as I'm glad you're here now."

Hawk's eyes sought hers, his expression questioning. "You don't cry yourself to sleep anymore, but being around him again...it's hell, isn't it?"

Aerielle's grip tightened on Hawk's arm, and she closed her eyes as if the effort would hold off the pain, refute the truth of Hawk's words.

"I keep thinking I should hate him," she admitted, sounding as if something was caught in her throat. "Or at the very least I shouldn't have any feelings for him at all. Instead it's like I'm trapped in a malfunctioning time machine. One moment I'm here in the present, the next I'm in the past. Then for one brief second, I seem to be in both, and it's all I can do not to throw myself into his arms...."

"I'm sorry, " murmured Hawk, taking her hand from his arm and squeezing it tight. "I shouldn't have asked."

Neither spoke for a moment, and then Hawk released her hand and got to his feet. "Can I get you something to drink?"

"Isn't it my job to play hostess?"

"Not today. I have expanded my comfort repertoire beyond just sitting outside your door at night."

Aerielle smiled. "You didn't sleep out there last night?" she queried, nodding toward the front door.

"Not this time."

"Glad to hear it. And I would love something to drink."

Aerielle rested her head against the back of the loveseat again, grateful for Hawk and the friendship they had formed.

When he returned with two glasses of sparkling water, Aerielle reached for hers with both hands, and Hawk winced when he handed her drink off. "I wish I'd noticed your hand yesterday. Doesn't say much for my observation skills."

Eyeing him as he sat down again, Aerielle sipped at her cold beverage. "You sound as if you believe Phoenix noticed. He didn't. I just happened to show him the injury. Is everything a competition with you two?"

"Only most everything. Hey, if I'm going to find my *own* Aerielle, I have to master Phoenix's technique. There's more than one reason I've had so many girlfriends."

Aerielle sipped her drink thoughtfully. "Have you and Sofia ever connected?"

"Sofia!? No. Not that she isn't nice. Actually, she's more than nice. But she's so "good girl" and with my reputation…."

"Can't you just tell her your reputation isn't all it's purported to be?"

"Like, Hey, Sofia, I'm not really a womanizer? I'm not sure I could do that."

Aerielle let out a laugh. "You just got through telling me how you wanted to jump my bones when you were fifteen, but you can't talk to Sofia?"

"Why, Aerielle. I'm stunned by such language."

"No, you're not."

"Yeah, well, Sofia would be. Have you even met her?"

"No. But you talk about her a lot."

"I do? I suppose. She's a big part of our lives. She's also a traditional Italian girl with a watchful matchmaking grandmother."

"You know, it is possible she doesn't know of Phoenix's thoughts concerning your reputation."

"Yeah, maybe. But I think if she were interested in me, I'd have noticed it by now. Anyway, enough about me. What can I do for you? Would you rather be alone? Or is it your desire to put up with my sorry company?"

"I'd rather have you stay, if you can take any more of *my* sorry company."

"I'd put up with just about anything from you. It might make me feel better for not knowing how to help you back when all I did was sit outside your door. Did you have something specific in mind?"

"Actually, I thought maybe some movies would help me forget for a while."

"Hmm. It just so happens I have movies in my car."

"Well, that's convenient."

"I don't have food, however, and I suspect you haven't eaten much today."

Aerielle paused to think about it and finally said, "Actually, I think the only thing I've had is a cup of coffee and this water."

"That will never do. I know of this little Asian place not far from here. I can call in an order and it'll be ready when I get there."

"Sounds good," replied Aerielle, wondering how much she'd actually eat. "Get some cream cheese wontons, and whatever else you like. I think I'm going to get cleaned up a bit while you're gone."

Hawk wasn't gone more than 20 minutes, but by the time he returned, Aerielle had managed a fast shower, put on some clean clothes, and brushed out her wet hair. The least she could do was be presentable if he was willing to stay and put up with her. She was getting plates out when Hawk walked in, movies and bags of delicious aroma in tow.

It wasn't long before they were back on the love seat, an ottoman pulled up in front to serve first as a table, and later as a footstool. They started with a comedy, slowly working their way through the movie and a surprising amount of food. They cleared the remnants of dinner for the second movie, which was a western.

As the thermostat kicked back after nine, Aerielle pulled a throw over herself for warmth. Because they were sharing the footstool, Hawk ended up with his feet covered, too, but otherwise, the change in temperature didn't seem to bother him. It was ten when Hawk put the last movie into the VCR. It was Star Trek IV, The Voyage Home, one of Aerielle's favorite Trek movies. Its familiar cast was comforting, and Aerielle found herself relaxing. Hawk kept her laughing as he quoted upcoming lines and told the occasional Star Trek joke. If she could get this relaxed and comfortable when he had gone, she might actually get some much needed sleep.

→→→

Tires and burning rubber smothered Aerielle's senses as she clung to Idaho for dear life and screamed for Phoenix over and over and—

"Aerielle, wake up. I'm right here."

Oddly it was Hawk's reassuring voice she heard. It penetrated her nightmare and Aerielle opened her eyes to a strangely lit room.

"I have you, Aerielle. It's okay. You were having a nightmare," soothed Hawk, his comforting arms around her.

"Hawk." Her voice was emotional as she released his name, grateful to find herself at home. "Hawk, why is it blue in here?"

Gentle laughter filled one ear. "We fell asleep and the VCR shut off. We are currently viewing the line channel blue screen.

When I first awoke with you screaming, I thought we were having a 'red alert,' only it was the wrong color."

Aerielle managed to laugh and whimper at the same time. It was an odd sound and must have sounded the same to Hawk, for he stroked her hair. "Shhh. I'm sorry I'm not Phoenix, but you can hang on as long as you need to."

What was he talking about? Why did he think she wanted Phoenix, and what could she continue to hang on to? Aerielle's senses grew in awareness as she adjusted to the strange blue light and Hawk's voice. She struggled to put it all together, when at last she realized she was clinging to Hawk, her arms encircling his waist as if for dear life. In her efforts she had also managed to throw herself halfway on top of him.

"I'm sorry," she rushed, loosening cramped hands and returning to a more appropriate location beside him. "I thought you were Idaho," she continued, rubbing at the cramps in her hands.

"Idaho!? You thought I was the dog?"

"That's why I was hanging on to you so tight. I was trying to keep you—him—from getting hit by the car." The tears she'd managed not to shed since dinner instantly brimmed and spilled, despite her efforts to hold them back. "Crap," she exclaimed, reaching up to pinch the bridge of her nose.

"Crap is right," agreed Hawk, reaching for a spare napkin and handing it to her. "I sure know how to put my foot in it. I have to admit though," he continued, humor tingeing his voice, "I'm glad I ended up being the dog. I was sure you thought I was Phoenix."

Aerielle shook her head. "Why?"

"You were screaming for him."

Not again. "It must have been because he was there when I brought in Idaho. I guarantee you it turned out much better that way. I screamed some other things at him, too, which weren't all that nice. I even accused him of letting Idaho die on purpose."

"Ouch," said Hawk, leaning back into the cushions while

watching her. "As much as Phoenix and I disagree at times, he is an excellent vet. I wondered why he asked me to examine Idaho when I got home last night. He insisted I check the dog out and make sure he'd done everything he could."

"Ouch is right." Aerielle rubbed her face with her hands. "I feel terrible. Did he tell you I was physically abusive, as well?"

"Really?! Gosh, no, though I might've liked to have seen that."

"Hawk!"

"Especially since I now know how strong you are," Hawk added, rubbing at his ribs. "You are a force to be reckoned with."

"Great," said Aerielle rolling her eyes. "I wonder if I did any real damage to Phoenix. He claimed he'd suffered worse, but he never did say whether I hurt him or not. I suppose he wouldn't, anyway."

"No, he wouldn't," agreed Hawk. "He will, however, comment if I get home too late." Leaning over the arm of the loveseat, Hawk switched on the lamp.

"You're kidding, right?" demanded Aerielle, reaching for the blanket on the floor and beginning to fold it. "Is he really that obsessed with your reputation?"

Hawk laughed. "Heck, no. It's not *my* reputation he's worried about. He figures that's a lost cause. It's *your* reputation he's worried about, or rather what I may do to it."

"I don't know whether to be insulted or grateful. But, um, does this mean you haven't told him we're just friends?"

"Are you kidding? You're not the only one participating in some form of punishment. I just haven't taken to beating up on him—Oh no! Aerielle, it's 6:45."

"In the morning?!"

Aerielle's obviously stupid question didn't seem to register. "The sun's gonna be up any time, now," added Hawk.

"I'm sorry!"

"Why?" asked Hawk, grabbing his coat and digging for his keys. "Did you drug my chow mein?"

He was grinning when he turned to her. "I gotta fly. I'll get the movies later. Sorry to eat, sleep, and run."

Aerielle barely got out a goodbye before he had the door open. "I'll be lucky to get home before Sofia arrives," she heard him muttering as the door closed.

And I'll be lucky to go back to sleep now. Suddenly alone in the empty silence, Aerielle's grief returned. Grabbing a pillow, she hugged it to her chest and moistened it with tears.

→→→

Phoenix slammed the bathroom vanity mirror harder than intended and was grateful the glass didn't shatter. It was 6:48 on a Monday morning with surgeries scheduled, and Hawk wasn't home. His anger brewing, Phoenix was hard on his hair as he braided it at least halfway down before cinching a leather band around the thick coil. All the while he'd been studying the bruises that were visible where his scrub shirt didn't cover them. The remnants of Aerielle's anger had grown darker with time.

Suddenly he heard the back door open downstairs, and he stepped into the upper hallway to listen. Two voices. Great. Sofia and Hawk had arrived at the same time. Phoenix waited as he heard his brother hurry up the stairs.

"Phoenix," Hawk exclaimed, reaching the landing and heading for his bedroom. "Sorry I'm late. I'll be ready in a—"

Phoenix grabbed his brother by the arm, bringing his forward momentum to an abrupt stop. "It's 6:50."

Hawk rolled his eyes at him. "In the morning!?"

"Of course in the morning. What kind of stupid question is that?"

"It's no dumber than telling me what time it is like I don't know."

"Coffee's brewing, boys," called Sofia soothingly from down below.

Phoenix opened his mouth to speak and then closed it. Switching to sign language, his hands moved in a rapid staccato. "You were gone all night," he accused.

Hawk stared at him, and then had the audacity to smile. Actually it was more like a smirk.

The blood thundered in Phoenix's veins. His hands sliced short angry arcs through the shrinking space that separated him from his brother. "You are no good for Aerielle."

Hawk's eyes narrowed into slits. "*I'm* no good for Aerielle?!" he demanded in rapid sign, slamming the "I" into his chest for emphasis. "What about *you*?!" he continued, this time slamming the word "you" into Phoenix's chest. "*You* willingly took Aerielle's love—her heart—and broke it. And then *you* left Aerielle faster than our father left our mother!"

Hawk's hands blurred with the motion of his silent speech, and then so did one of Phoenix's as he punched his brother in the face. Hawk stumbled backwards, but if he was surprised, he hid it in a single step and a swing that cut across Phoenix's cheekbone and sent him slamming backwards into the wall. Hawk followed the motion forward, getting into his brother's face. And then in a voice so low as not to be heard by Sofia, he bit out harsh angry words. "I should have hit you fourteen years ago when you finally came home. You crushed Aerielle, Phoenix. But you didn't even have the guts to stay and see the results of your handiwork. I, however, lived it, nearly every night for at least a month as I listened to her cry herself to sleep. So don't you ever tell me which one of us isn't good for her."

Phoenix felt horror wash over him. He'd known it must have been bad, but….God help him.

"Okay you two," came Sofia's voice again, filled with warning this time. "I may not be able to 'hear' what you're saying, but I know what fighting sounds like. Get it together. Smoke a peace pipe. I don't care what you do. But you need to operate, and your patients, four legged or not, need your heads in the game and the soothing presence of Doctors Doolittle. Get moving. Now!"

Phoenix took a deep painful breath, and Hawk stepped back, wiping at the blood trickling from his split lip. Phoenix could see the anger leave his brother even as his own melted away in profound regret. "I'm sorry."

"So am I. But we can argue over which of us is the bigger idiot later. I need to change, and you better put something on that eye before it swells shut."

Hawk turned then, once again heading for his room, and Phoenix desperately wished he hadn't stopped his brother the first time he'd gone down the hallway.

We came from no country, as have the whites. We were always here. Nature placed us in this land of ours--land that has been taken from us. I am telling my story that all may know why the war we did not want. War is made to take something not your own."

Yellow Wolf, as quoted in *Yellow Wolf, His Own Story*

14

When Phoenix entered Mr. Danvers' kitchen, the old man was taking a pie out of the oven. "Nothing like hot pecan pie," he announced.

"Smells wonderful," agreed Phoenix, wiping his snow covered boots on the entry rug.

Mr. Danvers glanced in his direction, his eyes widening. "That's quite a shiner you got there, Doc. You have a run in with one a yer patients?"

Tossing his coat over a chair, Phoenix headed for the sink. "Hawk and I had a discussion concerning Aerielle."

"Must a been mighty powerful words."

Phoenix grimaced, scrubbing his hands under hot water.

"What's yer *brother* look like?"

"Oddly enough, considering how hard I hit him, better than I."

"Well, it's a mighty purty color on you, son. So, what's the news with Mildred, Doc? I suspect somethin' ain't right. She's been off her feed."

Reaching for a towel, Phoenix dried off his hands. "In medical terms, she has a displaced abomasum. In English, one of her stomachs has flipped over on itself, causing an obstruction in the GI track. The food can't go anywhere. It'll require surgery."

"Seems to me I heard a that there problem a few years back. Operation's fairly routine, ain't it?"

"That it is," agreed Phoenix. "Don't give Mildred any food or water for the rest of the day. Hawk and I'll be out first thing in the morning to take care of her."

The old man nodded. "Sure thing, Doc, Don't you be worryin' none. I'll foller yer instructions."

When Phoenix didn't move to sit down for coffee, Mr. Danvers eyed him observantly. "Got somethin' else on yer mind? Is it related to yer fight with yer brother?"

Phoenix shook his head, leaning his hands on the back of a kitchen chair. "Not really, though it has to do with Aerielle. You still doing some woodworking?"

Mr. Danvers nodded, setting two cups on the table. "Now and again, when I find somethin' interestin'. You got somethin' interestin' you want done?"

"Aerielle's dog, Idaho, was hit by a car on Sunday and died. She wants him cremated. I was wondering how difficult it would be to make her a wooden urn shaped like a dog. I'd pay you of course."

"Wouldn't hear of it, Doc. I know I owe ya. I think yer idea is a fine one. Just let me know what kind a dog and what color you want the box."

As Mr. Danvers poured the coffee, Phoenix finally sat down. "Actually, do you have anything with a red tint? She had a red merle Australian shepherd." Phoenix found himself smiling. "Idaho had one ear up and one ear down."

"You let me know how old he was, and I'll put the years on it fer her."

"Thank you. This means a lot to me."

"It's only right," assured Mr. Danvers, sitting down. "Mildred means a lot to me. We do for each other."

⟶⟶

The next day dawned silent. Phoenix and Hawk had not gotten around to the "idiot" discussion or any other since their long day of surgery. Mostly they talked shop, and yesterday that had included Mildred.

The ride over to Mr. Danvers' place in Phoenix's truck was quiet, the slamming of the doors upon arrival eerily loud in the brittle morning.

The farmhouse door opened, Mr. Danvers stepping out onto the porch to greet them. "Mornin' boys. You be needin' any help?"

"Thanks, but we should be able to manage just fine," said Phoenix.

"Well, I'll have a pot of hot coffee waitin' fer ya both, and maybe some fresh pumpkin bread."

Phoenix grinned, his mouth beginning to water. "We'll be looking forward to it," he replied, speaking for his brother as well.

Silently, Hawk trailed him to the barn where the lights were already on. They would be able to see just fine. Staying warm was another matter. November was reaching for snowfall.

After properly restraining the cow, who didn't appear to notice the lower temperatures, Phoenix pressed his stethoscope to Mildred's side while Hawk began arranging their instruments.

"I need to ask you something," said Phoenix suddenly, breaking the sterile silence as he pulled the stethoscope from his ears.

"So ask."

"Lytocain, please."

Hawk responded silently.

Phoenix reached for the hypo, and his brother handed him the anesthesia. "It's about Sofia," said Phoenix.

For the first time his brother's eyes met his. "What about Sofia?"

"She talk to you yesterday? About her grandmother?"

"Yeah.... Said she was still trying to do too much and that the old lady was starting to show serious signs of exhaustion."

"I thought maybe there might be something we could do," said Phoenix, swabbing a spot on Mildred's side with antiseptic.

"Like what?"

Phoenix inserted the needle, releasing the local that would quickly numb the cow. "Thanksgiving's almost here. Maybe if we had Sofia and her grandmother over for dinner, it would keep Mrs. Bendetti from wearing herself out with preparations."

Hawk didn't reply right away, the noise of the battery powered razor forestalling conversation as he shaved the hair from Mildred's side. The cow shifted only slightly, and Phoenix knew the anesthesia was taking affect. When Hawk was finished with the hair removal, Phoenix was ready with more antiseptic.

"Neither one of us can cook," said Hawk, returning the razor to its case and pulling on a pair of surgical gloves. "Who did you have in mind to fix dinner?"

Phoenix stared at his brother's profile. "Aerielle."

Hawk picked up a scalpel, his gaze meeting Phoenix's expressionless eyes. "You want to ask Aerielle over for dinner and have her fix it, too?"

"Actually, I thought *you'd* want to ask her.... She is *your* girlfriend."

"About that," began Hawk, turning the knife over in his gloved hands.

"Look, let's call a truce," said Phoenix interrupting, resignation clear on his face. "Sofia needs our help, and in the case of dinner, maybe Aerielle's too. If you explained it to her, I'm sure she'd understand. Besides, Aerielle has no family here, either. She might really appreciate the invitation."

"Yeah, I guess," acceded Hawk, his face still revealing his dislike of the situation. "I'll call her today."

Phoenix nodded. "Good. Now are you gonna hand me the blasted scalpel, or cut me open with it?"

Hawk made no reply. Working in silence once again, he

reached out and slapped the handle into Phoenix's outstretched hand.

→→→

It was a dark, dreary afternoon a day later when Tyler showed up at the clinic. Phoenix had been waiting for him, knowing what he wanted to ask Tyler today would be difficult. Just like what he'd asked his brother to do yesterday had been difficult. This seemed the week for it, and the weather appeared to agree.

"Let's go for a drive," suggested Phoenix, pulling his coat on before Tyler had a chance to remove his. "Maybe get a burger and fries. You hungry?"

"I'm always hungry," replied Tyler. "What's the occasion?"

"Thought it might give us an opportunity to talk."

"When adults say that, it's not usually a good thing."

Phoenix felt a smile tug at his lips. He used to feel that way, too.

"Well I do have something I wanted to talk with you about, but we can discuss it over a meal."

Tyler eyed him warily.

"In the meantime," said Phoenix, placing a hand on Tyler's shoulder and guiding him toward the door, "I'll let you choose all the topics of conversation. Whatever you want to talk about, we'll talk about. Girls. Cars. Boba Fett...."

"Can we go to Busters? They have awesome milkshakes on top of great burgers."

"Sure," said Phoenix, shutting the door behind them. "What's your favorite?"

Aside from telling Phoenix he liked Butterfinger shakes, Tyler surprised him by not saying another word. This was not what Phoenix had had in mind. Pulling out from a stop light, Phoenix glanced at Tyler who sat thoughtfully, his expression hidden in the dimness of the cab.

"Is something wrong?" inquired Phoenix.

"No, I was just thinking."

"About?"

There was a long pause before Tyler continued. "Would you mind if I asked you something?"

"Well. I did say anything. What's on your mind?"

"Um, well...." Tyler glanced out the window. "How old were you the first time...well, you know."

Phoenix was so surprised by the question he nearly missed a stop sign and had to stomp on the breaks. Good thing Tyler's grandmother wasn't watching...or listening for that matter. "Maybe I do know. But if you can't say it, you're not old enough to talk about it. Would you care to make another attempt?"

Tyler looked as if he wished the darkness were more complete, but he began again as Phoenix pulled into the intersection. "How old were you the first time...you had sex?"

"Are you planning on doing something I need to know about?"

"No!"

"Did Nicole recently ditch your competition?"

"No on that one, too, but it *is* about her.

"How so?"

Tyler sighed. "There's a rumor going round that she and Eric are...uhm...having sex."

Phoenix didn't say anything immediately, knowing something of the kind had been coming, but still not prepared for it. Were kids ever kids anymore? "Wow. So what do *you* think about that?"

"Well, some of the kids, mostly the guys, think it's cool. On the other hand, most of the girls think she's nuts and he's a jerk."

"Interesting. Back to my original question, however. What do *you* think?"

"I keep thinking I should feel the same as the other guys, but I don't. And then I wonder what's wrong with me."

Phoenix smiled in the darkness. "Maybe what you *should* be asking is what's wrong with *them*? There's all kinds of issues at stake, Tyler, from the risk of disease and pregnancy, to the loss of something you can never get back, like innocence and a one time commitment to one woman."

"Are you like saying sex should be saved for one person?" pursued Tyler, managing to say the "S" word without pausing this time.

"That's what I'm saying."

"Really? You mean you've never slept with any of your girlfriends? You really believe in this wait until marriage stuff?"

"Tyler, Hawk and I were fatherless for enough years before our mother remarried. I have no desire to risk putting a child of my own through the same. And yes, I happen to be one of those people who believe God planned sex to be between one man and one woman."

Tyler grew thoughtful, and Phoenix let him be. He knew if the boy had more questions, he'd get around to asking them. Eventually, Phoenix grew lost in his own thoughts, remembering the night he slept with Aerielle, only not the way Tyler had intimated.

→→→

It was raining. Not a brief summer shower, but a steady downpour, and as Phoenix made his way to Aerielle's room after midnight, he regretted the rain. It meant no stargazing, or even riding. He and Aerielle had been fortunate so far, with most of the rain the area had received arriving during the day. But there was nothing for it now. The weather tonight forbade even the adventurous to challenge its fulmination.

Aerielle's door was wide open, and Phoenix silently stepped into the room. She was there in the dark, sitting on the edge of the double bed, facing the rain spattered window and watching the driveway turn to mud.

"It's raining." Her pronouncement reached out to him, and Phoenix wondered how she'd known he was there.

He crossed the room, settling on the bed behind her, his hands on her shoulders. "Does it bother you?" he asked, wanting to know if she mourned the weather as much as he.

Aerielle glanced back at him, smiling sweetly. "Only if it interferes with our time together, Half-breed."

"I'm not going anywhere, Meyui" he replied, squeezing her shoulder's in reassurance. She winced, pulling her right arm away.

"What is it? Did I hurt you?"

"No, I'm fine. It's nothing."

Phoenix recognized a subtle change to Aerielle's tone of voice. "It's nothing, huh? Then you won't mind if I take a look at it."

Rolling over and stretching out on the bed, Phoenix reached for the reading lamp he knew rested on the headboard. The lamp's familiar shape came to his hand and he flipped the switch, light flooding the immediate area around the pillows.

"Really, it's nothing," said Aerielle, turning her face away from the light now invading the room.

"Me thinks the lady doth protest too much." Still lying on his side, Phoenix reached up and took Aerielle's arm. And then like the recalcitrant filly she was, he gentled her down beside him. "Let me see."

She seemed about to argue once again, but then gave in, pushing up the sleeve of her T-shirt.

Phoenix's eyes widened, his hand reached out. Gently, he ran his fingers over the peculiarly patterned bruises. "That's a hand print!" he exclaimed. "Who did this?!"

Nervously, Aerielle pulled her sleeve down over the tell-tale marks. "Jim Peterson saw us at the feed store this morning."

"Son of a witch," said Phoenix, slamming his fist into the bed. "What exactly happened, anyway?!"

Aerielle took a deep breath, staring fixedly at the ceiling before responding. "When I went back out to the truck to get the shopping list, he pulled me aside."

"'Pulled' you aside?! What else did he 'do?!'"

"...He told me to stay away from your kind. I told him if he touched me again, I'd call the sheriff."

"I'd like to...."

Phoenix's sentence trailed off as Aerielle placed a gentle hand against his jaw. "Please. Must we waste our time together talking about him?"

Anger was replaced by compassion as Phoenix sensed the pain in Aerielle's voice. Who had gentled whom. Reaching for the lamp, he switched it off, sealing them in darkness lit eerily by the heat lightning. Brushing Aerielle's hair with his hand, Phoenix then cupped her chin and turned her face toward his. Leaning forward, he pressed his lips to her forehead and then her cheeks, tasting the salt of tears she had been unwilling to shed in the light.

And yet despite her tears and her delicate state, Phoenix wanted to make love to her.

Getting close to Aerielle was like dry wood being placed next to hot coals—eventually the wood burst into flames.

Pulling away, Phoenix buried his face in the coolness of a pillow, ordering his heart to cease the fierceness of its beating. Forcing his hand away from Aerielle's hair, he placed it on the space of bed between them. Aerielle's hand came to rest on his, and the sound of rain surrounded them. Phoenix knew if he wanted anything more, he'd have to marry her, follow through with commitment...prove the love he longed to proclaim.

It was hours later when Phoenix woke abruptly, sunrise filtering into the room. His brother was standing at the foot of the bed, his long hair tangled from sleep. Hawk smacked the side of Phoenix's jean-clad leg again to make sure he was fully awake.

Phoenix shifted to a sitting position, the movement waking Aerielle who'd been asleep on her stomach beside him.

She rolled over and eyed them both. "Good morning," she said matter-of-factly, as if she was used to waking up with the Stargazer brothers in her room.

"Yeah, it's morning," Hawk agreed. "And I don't care how innocent this looks, Phoenix, or that you're a year older than the age a Nez Perce becomes a warrior. If Nevin catches you in here, he'll be forming his own war party with you on the opposite side."

"Yeah, I'm coming," mumbled Phoenix, not so casual as Aerielle about finding his brother in the room. "I don't suppose Nevin'd believe I forgot this wasn't my room anymore."

Hawk snorted and left them alone, shutting the bedroom door behind himself.

"He's right," said Phoenix. "If Nevin finds me in here, I'm dead."

"Then what are you still doing here?"

Phoenix glanced down at Aerielle where she continued to lie beside him. Her sleep filled eyes also held amusement, and a teasing smile beckoned from her lips.

Phoenix grinned in return. "What I'm doing here is finding it awfully hard to leave you. I like waking up next to you—preferably without Hawk as well."

"Preferably," agreed Aerielle. "Meanwhile, I have to get up. I have to go to the little girls' room."

Aerielle promptly stood up, climbed over Phoenix, and jumped off the bed.

"I got news for you, Miss Buchanan," he said as Aerielle stepped away from the bed. "You are anything but a little girl."

She turned and looked at him, her eyebrows raised. "Why, Yellow Wolf, how forward of you."

Phoenix suddenly grew serious, his thoughts tracing the bruises hidden on Aerielle's arm. "Don't go anywhere alone."

Aerielle appeared shocked. "Not even the little girls' room?"

→→→

"Remind me why I'm doing this again?" asked Tyler an hour or so later. He and Phoenix were getting out of the truck in front of Aerielle's place.

Phoenix slammed his door shut, locked the truck and met Tyler on the sidewalk. He knew Tyler understood the reason, but knew, also, Tyler needed to hear it again.

"Because by telling Aerielle the truth about the accident, it will bring her some closure, and it will make her feel better about her loss."

Tyler ran a nervous hand through his hair, the wind helping along with the results. "Okay. I get the tell the truth stuff. If she knows I killed her dog she won't feel responsible. It's the part about how this makes her feel better, I'm still struggling with.

Phoenix turned to face the November breeze, as the wind played havoc with his own hair. He glanced to his side and down into Tyler's concerned face. "Knowing Idaho died to save a life will help give his death meaning."

"Even if that life shouldn't have needed saving? At least it will put the blame where it belongs."

"Tyler, it was an accident. So you weren't giving your full attention to your surroundings. That requires an apology, not a punishment. It wasn't as if you meant for the accident to happen. On the other hand, Idaho meant to save your life, which he did. Knowing Aerielle, *this* truth, *his* sacrifice will ease some of her pain. Aerielle needs this as much or more than you needed your knee fixed up afterward. There were three beings hurt that day, not two. The only difference is, Aerielle's injuries are on the inside.

Tyler nodded, his expression reflective. "You know, sometimes you actually make sense in a weird sort of way."

Phoenix turned toward Tyler despite the wind. "*Sometimes* I make sense?" he demanded indignantly.

Tyler laughed at him and Phoenix grinned back.

"You sure you won't go in with me?" asked Tyler.

Phoenix reached out, placing a hand on his shoulder in

reassurance. "You're old enough to handle this on your own. Besides, I'll walk you to the landing. And I'll be in earshot when she opens the door."

"In case she decides to beat me up like she did you?"

"Aren't you a smart mouth today," remarked Phoenix, raising a hand and smacking him lightly across the back of his head. "Come on, let's go before she decides to change her plans and goes out earlier. I don't plan on asking Hawk for Aerielle's schedule more than once."

When they cleared the door on the lower level, Phoenix paused to comb his fingers through his tangled hair. Watching him, Tyler reached up and brushed his own into place.

"That may not be necessary," teased Phoenix.

Tyler's hands stilled on top of his head. "You mean she might rub my hair again?" He grinned. "Jealous are we?"

Phoenix cuffed him on the head again, harder this time. "Get going."

Tyler was laughing as Phoenix followed him up the stairs, but by the time he was face to face with Aerielle's door, all humor had gone. Phoenix kept back, hiding himself around a corner wall encasing the stairwell. Tyler was on his own.

When Aerielle heard the knock, she was surprised. Hawk wasn't due for a couple of hours. Could Phoenix...no that made no sense. But who— "Tyler," she said stating the obvious as she opened the door. But she couldn't have been more surprised if it had been Phoenix.

"How are you? How's your knee?" she asked, glancing down as if she expected to see something.

"Uhm. It's fine," he said absently, "Aerielle."

He said her name with such seriousness, that when Aerielle's eyes returned to his face, she wasn't surprised to see the unflinching expression of a boy doing his best to look like a man.

"What is it, Tyler?" she asked, giving him her full attention. Or she *thought* it was her full attention. It took all her effort to keep from looking up when Phoenix appeared about a dozen feet behind Tyler, a silencing finger to his lips. Then both of them began to speak at once, Tyler with words, Phoenix with his hands.

He needs to talk to you. "I need to talk to you."

About something important. "It's really important."

He's scared, but treat him like a warrior. "It's about—" Tyler's voice trembled. "It's about Idaho."

Phoenix stepped back behind the wall and Aerielle stepped back into her apartment, inviting Tyler inside.

"Would you like to sit down?" she offered, closing the door.

"No. Thank you." Instead the boy seemed to stand straighter. Young warrior indeed. For a moment he reminded her of—

"I was the reason Idaho ran into the road."

Aerielle took a second to wrap her thoughts around what Tyler had just said. "And what makes you say that?"

"It's like this." And Tyler told her. Everything. And Aerielle let him. Never interrupting.

"Again, I'm sorry," finished Tyler, repeating words Aerielle had longed to silence many repetitions before.

"That's the last time I want to hear you say those words," she said, breaking in at last. If he said he was sorry one more time, she would break into tears, for clearly Tyler was suffering as much guilt over Idaho's loss as she was. Wasted guilt. Both of them. "Never again, do you hear me?"

"Yes, I understand," said Tyler, his nervous voice from earlier now filled with courageous acceptance. *Oh, God, he reminds me so much of—*

"I'll leave, then," continued Tyler, sounding resigned. Resolutely, he stepped toward the door.

"Tyler, no. That's not what I meant," declared Aerielle, the unwanted tears spilling over. She ignored them. "What I meant, Tyler," she said as the boy watched her cautiously, "is that you don't *need* to apologize about Idaho again. He did what he was supposed to do. As much as I loved that dog, you are more important. You are your mother's child. If anything had happened to you...." Aerielle stepped toward Tyler and then caught herself. Treat him like a warrior. "Thank you, Tyler. For telling me what really happened. That took a lot of courage."

"Your welcome," said Tyler, eyeing her speculatively. "If it would make you feel better, you can rub my hair if you want to."

"Oh, Tyler." Aerielle laughed, and stepping forward gave his head a good rub, thoroughly messing up his hair.

→→→

Hawk was lost in thought, and had been since he had picked Aerielle up for a late meal at McDonalds. Neither of them had a lot of time this evening, each with work at home requiring their attention. Aerielle had suggested they skip dinner, but Hawk had insisted, saying he needed to talk to her—only now he wasn't talking. If it was anything like the talk she'd had with Tyler earlier, Aerielle didn't think she was up to it. She'd used up her quota of emotional stamina for the day.

Munching on a McRib, minus the pickles, Aerielle reached across the table and tapped the surface where Hawk's attention was currently focused. He glanced up as Aerielle pulled her hand away, knocking her french fries onto the floor as she did so.

"Well, I *wanted* to get your attention," said Aerielle swallowing, while staring at the scattered fries.

Hawk's face lit with laughter. "There are easier ways. You really like to throw your food around, don't you?"

Aerielle used her foot to brush the remnants under the table. "I suppose I could send them home for...."

"For Phoenix?" jumped in Hawk. "He deserves them I'm sure."

Aerielle studied Hawk's expression. "Are things worse than they usually are?"

"You could say that," Hawk nodded, turning his fries around. "Have some."

"Did he say something when you got home at the official crack of dawn the other morning?"

"You could say that, too. We had quite a row, which Sofia put a stop to. I thought she was going to come up the stairs and hand us our heads. It's been a little tense since then. I did enjoy the moment leading *up* to the fight, though."

Aerielle chewed on one of Hawk's fries. "How so?"

"You left bruises on Phoenix Sunday night," said Hawk grinning.

Aerielle paused with another french fry halfway to her lips. "Nooo. You saw them?"

"They were turning a nice shade of blue. Now before you go feeling bad and all, I have something else to tell you. More like ask you. I don't think you're going to like it, and if it wasn't for Sofia I wouldn't even ask, but—"

"Hawk, stop. What are you blathering on about?"

Hawk grunted, picking up his milkshake and taking a long sip. "I guess I'm saying the bruises you left might be a form of consolation for what I'm about to ask you. What Phoenix wanted me to ask you."

Aerielle's expression turned pensive. "And what is that?"

"Sofia's worried about her grandmother. Phoenix thought it might be helpful to have the two of them over for Thanksgiving to keep Mrs. Bendetti out of the kitchen. However, neither Phoenix or I can cook anything more complicated that macaroni and cheese. And so...."

"And so he wants me to come over and cook. What color were those bruises turning?"

"If it helps, I gave him a black eye, too."

'You hit him?!" she stared wide-eyed, wondering how she'd missed the black eye that afternoon.

"Guilty as charged."

"What did he say to make you hit him? Or don't I want to know?"

"You don't *need* to know, and I'm not sharing anyway, except for my french fries."

His attempt at food diversion failed to recapture Aerielle's attention.

"Hmm, an entire day with Phoenix," she mumbled, thinking about how difficult that would be.

"Aerielle, I'm sorry. I shouldn't have agreed to ask—"

"I'll do it."

"You will?" said Hawk, watching her over their forgotten food.

"For Sofia. It's the right thing to do, Hawk. It's the God thing to do." Besides, she owed Phoenix something for bringing Tyler over. Both Tyler and she had needed the moment. Especially Tyler. That kind of unnecessary guilt at his age could be life changing. Aerielle knew it, and so had Phoenix.

Hawk was studying her as if he too had been lost in thought. He shook his head, seeming to come to a conclusion. "Clearly my brother was an idiot when he left you. Still is an idiot, come to think of it."

"Hawk," she pleaded, not wanting to come between them.

"Don't worry," Hawk assured her. "He *is* my brother. I love him despite everything we've been through. Always will."

Aerielle, too, seemed to care for Phoenix despite everything. Would she always? *Oh, God, how will I endure if I do?*

→→→

It was the Wednesday before Thanksgiving, and Aerielle glanced around the Stargazer kitchen one last time, making sure she'd put everything away. The two cats who had watched her since her arrival over an hour ago strutted through the room again, checking to see that Aerielle had not disturbed anything permanently or perhaps dropped any tidbits while preparing the stuffing.

It had been Hawk's idea for Aerielle to start preparations for Thanksgiving the night before, therefore making the holiday more relaxing. He, however, had been unable to be here, and Aerielle had the house to herself, Phoenix being absent as well. Her only interruption had been one message on her pager.

Confident she was leaving the kitchen as she'd found it, Aerielle shut off the lights and walked through into the softly lit dining room. She'd left the dimmer switch at its lowest setting, and the large room had a distinctive welcoming quality with the hard wood floor, the antique-like wallpaper, and the beautiful polished wood molding. On top of that, Aerielle had set the table, grateful they'd only needed five matching sets of dinner wear. Any more than that and she would have had to bring her own, were it to match. The dining room would do, however, and Aerielle found herself looking forward to the holiday rather than dreading it.

Just then, Aerielle's thoughts were drawn to the black cat as the feline paraded out of the kitchen and started up the stairs. Aerielle followed the cat with her eyes until the animal reached the bend in the stairwell and disappeared. She thought about exploring the upstairs since the moment she'd arrived, and up until now had managed to resist. Now, however, her curiosity got the better of her and she reached for the handrail.

The first room Aerielle entered was a bedroom in general disarray, a trademark she recognized as Hawk's. Not that he was a slob by any means, but the room failed to have the order characteristic of Phoenix's domain. And unlike his older brother, Hawk used to make his bed about half the time. It was unmade now, and spread out on it were several veterinary magazines.

Aerielle quickly moved on, wondering how much time she had before risking discovery. Stepping out of Hawk's bedroom, Aerielle discovered the black cat watching her from across the wide landing. It turned, disappearing into another room, and Aerielle followed.

She stopped abruptly in the doorway to what was obviously Phoenix's place of rest, a familiar Indian headdress commanding her attention. The piece of Nez Perce history was no less awe-inspiring now than it had been the first time Aerielle had seen it, the long double tail of eagle feathers beautiful and commanding. So what if it had been inspired by the Sioux? Wasn't imitation the sincerest form of flattery?

The room itself was immaculate as Aerielle had thought it would be. Glass framed star charts hung on the walls and every inch of the room proclaimed this to be Phoenix's territory. Drawn in by all she remembered, Aerielle moved forward, pausing in front of the largest star chart. Her memories stirred to life at the constellations displayed there. It had been so long. Aerielle had forgotten many.

There was a sudden loud "meow" behind her, and Aerielle turned to see which of the two cats was speaking. But this was a different cat, a calico, residing on the floor near the foot of the bed and staring intently at the edge of the mattress above its head. The calico glanced at Aerielle, revealing two black rings around its eyes. Aerielle stared in disbelief. "Esmeralda?"

Turning away, the cat leaped onto the bed only to turn and look at Aerielle again.

"Esmeralda," Aerielle repeated, reverently taking the greying cat in her arms. Holding the pet against her chest, Aerielle sat perched on the edge of the bed. "Oh, my sweet little girl. I never thought I'd see you again. You were just a little bitty kitten the last time I held you. I wondered what had become of you. You cannot know how happy I am to see you."

Esmeralda purred as if in agreement.

→→→

Aerielle leaned over the renovated cardboard box, looking for that yet unnamed calico she'd picked out for Phoenix weeks earlier. There she was, the one with the black rings around her eyes. Aerielle scooped up the seven week old kitten, pressing its face to hers. "It's time to say good-bye, precious. Aerielle's taking you to your new home."

Aerielle glanced around The General Store just to be sure Phoenix hadn't followed her in here. He rarely let her out of his sight these days with Jim Peterson haunting her, and Aerielle had had to insist he wait by the truck behind the small clump of buildings making up "downtown" Shaman Prairie.

Standing, Aerielle walked across the wood planks to the counter of the old country store. Setting the kitten on the counter top, Aerielle pulled a red ribbon out of her pocket and tied it in a bow around the kitten's neck. It wasn't easy, as the kitten was more interested in playing with it. "You have to wear it, just for a couple of minutes."

Stepping out onto the boardwalk, Aerielle was filled with excitement. It was the perfect day for gift giving, the late September afternoon filled with sunshine and autumn colors. It was the kind of day that crept into one's soul and made up memories. Aerielle knew even now that this was a day she would never forget, if just for its beauty and simplicity. And she had something which would make the memory even more lasting, for in her arms she carried a gift that was a symbol—a symbol of her love.

Glancing around just outside the The General Store, Aerielle looked for signs of Phoenix—or Jim Peterson. But aside from the usual bunch jawing in front of the Feed Barn, Aerielle saw no one she recognized.

Hurrying down the wooden walk running between two of the stores, Aerielle headed for the backside of the Feed Barn where the truck was parked. The big loads were always picked up behind the store rather than in front.

Coming around the side of the building with the cat tucked behind her back—not an easy feat—Aerielle found Phoenix pacing beside the truck, his cowboy boots kicking up the dust.

"There you are," he exclaimed, as if he'd been waiting an hour instead of five minutes. "I was getting worried—what do you have behind your back?"

Aerielle grinned. "Close your eyes and hold out your hands."

Phoenix gave Aerielle a wary glance.

"You do trust me, don't you?" she asked.

Phoenix sighed and then did as she'd instructed. He wasn't a moment too soon. The lively kitten was not easy to contain in its present position. Gently, Aerielle brought it forward and set it down in Phoenix's waiting hands. His fingers closed over the squirming ball of fur as his eyes opened.

"It's alive," he said in amazement "It's a cat."

"She's not just any cat," explained Aerielle as Phoenix held the kitten up and looked at her tiny little face. His eyes grew tender. "She's adorable."

"Before you go asking why I got you another cat when you have a barn full of them, let me explain. This little girl is not to be a barn cat. She's to be a house cat. She'll be yours and yours alone—your best friend."

Phoenix grinned. "I thought you were my best friend."

Despite his smile, Aerielle felt the deep feeling in those words and found herself tongue-tied because of it.

"I think I'll call her Esmeralda," continued Phoenix, his gaze returning to the kitten. "So why the gift?" he asked without looking up. "It's not my birthday or a holiday."

Aerielle stared at him, his head bent as he stroked the kitten, his hair cascading forward over his shoulders, cloaking the warrior's heart within. A heart so tender at times, Aerielle was overwhelmed, just as she was now. "For those times when I won't always be around." she managed to choke out. "You should never have to be alone."

Phoenix rubbed Esmeralda's ears, the kitten's small body rumbling in response.

Aerielle continued. "She will be a constant reminder, a reminder that...that you're loved. By me."

Phoenix's head came up, his dark eyes searching hers and leaving her breathless. And then he was reaching for her with his free hand, crushing her body to his, his lips to hers, in a moment so passionate Aerielle wondered how he could continue to hold the kitten so gently.

But the thought was instantly lost to the kiss as Aerielle's pulse was jumpstarted by Phoenix's mouth on hers, telling her very deftly without words, he loved her, too.

Time began again when Phoenix relented and tore his mouth from hers. He was breathing as hard as she. Yet instead of pulling away, or removing his hand from her neck, his lips found their way to the racing pulse at her throat.

"Marry me, Aerielle. Then we won't *have* to be apart."

→→→

Aerielle was crying—again. Disgusted, she wiped a hand over her face while still holding Esmeralda with the other. What a crybaby she was turning into these days. Pretty soon she'd have to start prescribing Prozac for herself.

Hugging Esmeralda close, Aerielle hurriedly left Phoenix's room. She needed air, and she needed it now. Aerielle headed directly for the pair of French doors she'd seen leading to the second floor balcony overlooking the lake. She couldn't get the doors opened fast enough as she practically burst onto the balcony.

Aerielle sucked in a deep breath of surprising, cold evening air, at the same time offering comfort to the cat in case she had been frightened by their flight from the house. However, Esmeralda seemed immune to Aerielle's emotional state. Instead, she shifted comfortably; her purr humming in rhythm with Aerielle's blood, which roared through her veins like a stampede of horses.

Stepping up to the wrought iron railing, Aerielle studied the sky as she tried to get her emotions and her breathing under control. How she thought she could do either while looking at the heavens was beyond her. Though there was little breeze, Aerielle began to shiver, and she held the cat just a tad closer, absorbing the warmth of her body. And then with her gaze fastened on the firmament, she began speaking the names of the stars visible in the cloudless canvas above as she had not done in years. She saved the Pleiades for last, the names belonging to the star cluster slipping from her tongue with a desolation that reverberated off the reawakened emptiness inside.

And then, halfway through those final names, as if from the air itself, came the voice of the Phoenix, low and husky, joining hers. Aerielle thought her heart might rip in two. In the momentary silence which followed, she fought the tears that came with the pain. She would not let him see.

"You speak the names of the Pleiades with such sadness," murmured Phoenix, "as if their immutable light had died."

Aerielle took another breath of cold air, letting it out slowly, the vapor visible in the night. "It does seem like they have grown dimmer with each year that has passed since you introduced them to me."

Behind her, Phoenix winced. Even without seeing Aerielle's face, he could hear tears in her voice, feel the hurt in her words. The knowledge that she was currently in pain because of him made him feel as if his insides were being pulled asunder.

Seeing her with Esmeralda peeking over her arm brought back an onslaught of memories. Memories of the day Aerielle had given him the gift of her love. Memories of him asking her to marry him. *Dear Lord, how could so much have gone wrong? How could I have left her? How could I have not?*

"And what would make the stars bright again?" he asked, wondering if she's actually tell him.

You. Aerielle's thoughts proclaimed the word with such certainty she wondered they didn't explode aloud into the darkness. But instead of speaking her all-telling thought aloud, Aerielle spoke instead of Esmeralda who was currently peering over Aerielle's arm at her master.

"I was stunned to find Esmeralda. I didn't know she was still alive, or even that you still had her."

"She's been the friend you said she would be," admitted Phoenix. "She kept me company all the years we were apart."

His words tore at her memories, pulling Aerielle about. Her thoughts from the past collided with the present as her attention was drawn directly to what remained of a black eye. "Oh." The exclamation escaped unwillingly, even as her hand moved of its own accord to his temple, her thumb gently tracing the bruising. "He must have hit you *very* hard for the bruising to have lasted this long."

Phoenix could barely breathe, let alone speak, with her caress upon his face and her breath visible in the air. "I deserved it," he managed, his throat constricting. "Besides, I did hit him first."

"What?!" Aerielle asked, jerking her hand back, tearing his very heart away with it. "Hawk didn't mention you hitting *him*."

"Really? I'm surprised."

But Aerielle was no longer listening as she studied Phoenix's every feature, from his cheekbones, to his lips, even to his hair. He must have been working, for his mane had been pulled back and braided. She longed to unplait it, run her hands through its familiar length. Finally, her scrutiny was unfailingly drawn to his obsidian eyes.

What she saw stole her breath away. The dark pools of his eyes were filled with an intensity that would have lit the heavens on fire if he'd but looked up. Instead, it reduced Aerielle to ashes. Phoenix looked as if he wanted to—no—*was* going to kiss her. Would she stop him? Could she stop him? Did she *want* to stop him? Apparently none of the above. For as his head lowered, Aerielle titled her face upward in acquiescence. She could see his breath just as she closed her eyes, felt it warm against her lips just before they met his.

Beep, beep, beep, beep. The obnoxious sound of her pager rent the air, startling them both, stealing the moment. Unwillingly Phoenix pulled back, retrieving Esmeralda as Aerielle reached for the intrusive device at her waist. Frustrated nearly beyond reason, Phoenix swore if he had the pager, it would darn well reach the lake with one furious throw. He did his best to conceal his reaction, hiding his face against Esmeralda's, stroking her ears, and planting a kiss on the top of her head.

Devastated, Aerielle fumbled with her pager, first to turn it off and then to read it. Her hands were shaking, and she nearly dropped the despicable piece of plastic when Phoenix stroked the cat. What she wouldn't give to be the cat right now. It should have been her Phoenix was holding, caressing, kissing. If ever she had hated the pager, it was now. She studied the readout anyway.

"There's a phone in the study," offered Phoenix, heading for the other end of the balcony to another set of French doors. Phoenix opened the glass doors into a dark room. Stepping inside, he took Aerielle's arm, guiding her through the outline of furniture shrouded in darkness.

Moments later, light invaded the room, chasing away their brief pause in time but not the knowledge mirrored in each other's eyes. Reluctantly, Aerielle turned away and forced herself to the job at hand.

"You have to go," said Phoenix minutes later, as Aerielle hung up the phone.

"Yes."

Silence followed, Aerielle having to wrest her eyes and thoughts away from those masculine lips that had nearly claimed hers. "They need me at the hospital."

"I hope it won't be a difficult night for you."

"Thank you. So do I. At least I won't be on call tomorrow."

"Call me if you need anything."

I need you to kiss me. Aerielle wondered what Phoenix would say or do if she called him when she got home and told him just that. She wasn't about to find out.

As it turned out, she didn't get home until well after midnight. But despite her weariness Aerielle lay awake until nearly dawn, having stared at the phone much of the time, wishing for the courage, or stupidity, to call him.

Across the lake in his own bed, Phoenix, too, lay awake wishing the phone would ring, wishing he had the courage, or the stupidity, to call Aerielle.

If only the pager hadn't gone off. Then again, maybe he should be thankful. Just because they'd both gotten caught up in the moment didn't mean things were okay between them. Far from it. And when and if he got the chance to kiss her again, Phoenix didn't want Aerielle to be regretting it later. There was way too much at stake, too much she didn't know.

The earth, my mother and nurse, is very sacred to me: too sacred to be valued, or sold for gold or for silver...and my bands have suffered wrong rather than done wrong.

Chief Joseph to the Commissioners of 1876 as quoted in *Chief Joseph of the Nez Perce* by Robert Penn Warren.

15

It was snowing, great big white flakes, casting a quiet enticing beauty over Thanksgiving day. Drawn by the snow's simple splendor, Aerielle decided to walk to the Stargazer home. It was eleven when she left, her only regret being the lack of Idaho beside her. She tried to put aside her thoughts of Phoenix. She'd spent too much of the night dwelling on him, their past, their present, their relationship, however one would describe it.

Aerielle's knock on the Stargazer door was answered by Hawk, who grinned at the sight of her. "It's the abominable snowwoman."

"And I've come to eat you out of house and home," she announced, stepping into the foyer.

"I can well believe that. But, you'll have to cook the food first."

"I hope you put the turkey in."

"Right on schedule as per your instructions. Should be ready at three on the dot," assured Hawk, taking Aerielle's coat. "And I was just working on the destruction of a head of lettuce."

Aerielle laughed. "I've never heard salad making described so eloquently."

"Wow." Hawk paused looking Aerielle up and down. "You're dressed up, quite nicely in fact. I'm afraid Phoenix and I aren't going to measure up."

Aerielle had worn the red sweater dress Hawk had seen on

their first official date, only with boots instead of shoes. The boots she peeled off and left in the foyer. "Hey, you can dress anyway you want. I, in fact, am going barefoot, but I thought I needed something cheery to wear. Now why don't you show me what you've done to our dinner so far."

Phoenix glanced up as Hawk and Aerielle entered the kitchen, and was momentarily entranced by the vision in red. Man, she was beautiful. Purposefully, he pulled his gaze away, fearful of what his eyes might give away, to her, the all-seeing, at least. He was afraid she would recognize the love his heart could no longer contain. Last night, knowing she had wanted that kiss as much as he had, let loose a storm of emotions he had been desperately trying to keep in line.

God help him, thought Phoenix, things couldn't go on this way. At the very least, at the very point of a beginning, he had to tell his brother of his continued feelings for Aerielle and beg him to get out of the way. What Aerielle's feelings were for his brother, Phoenix wasn't sure, but he couldn't believe they were too serious. Aerielle had been calling Phoenix's name that horrible night, and then there was last evening.

"Late night?" asked Phoenix, rereading the instructions on the back of a frozen pie box.

Aerielle stared at his bowed head, cloaked by the mantel of hair. Was he hiding? "Not bad," she hedged. She wasn't about to admit that after the hospital she'd lain awake most of the night thinking about him.

"Aerielle?" said Hawk, pulling her attention away. "Got a question."

"You better help him," encouraged Phoenix, glancing over at his brother with a sardonic look. "He's liable to chop the carrots using the blender."

Aerielle laughed while Hawk grinned thoughtfully, and

Aerielle realized it was the first time in fourteen years the three of them had been happy while together, however briefly.

→→→

"I don't believe it," laughed Sofia, standing beside Aerielle in the kitchen. "Who cut the cranberry sauce into turkeys?"

Aerielle grinned, checking the pop-up button in the real turkey, the smell of the traditional bird filling the room as she cracked the oven door. "Hawk sliced it and then cut it with a cookie cutter. I'm sure he'd appreciate the admiration of his handiwork."

"I put the flowers on the table," announced Mrs. Bendetti, entering the kitchen from the dining room. "Now, what can I do in here?"

Aerielle glanced at the old woman. Her black hair, tied into a bun, was generously sprinkled with gray. A gray almost matching the pallor of her face. "Nothing. You go sit down and relax. That's what guests do at the Stargazer house."

"Aren't you a guest?"

"At the moment I'm on temporary duty as hostess. Now out of my temporary kitchen."

Mrs. Bendetti smiled and reluctantly left the room. "You go, too," said Aerielle to Sofia. "She's not going to relax if you're in here helping."

"She's not well, is she?" asked Sofia.

Aerielle's expression sobered. "I have to admit, her color's not healthy. I brought my medical bag with me. Maybe we can talk her into an impromptu physical later."

"I'd appreciate it," said Sofia, her fear lessening only slightly.

"Go on now. Sit with your grandmother and don't worry."

Don't worry. As Sofia left the kitchen, Aerielle could have kicked herself for using those words. Sofia had every reason to worry, and Aerielle no right to tell her not to.

"What's next?" questioned Phoenix, returning to the kitchen with an empty tray. "Aerielle?"

"Oh, uhm, I'd say it's time to carve the turkey and pour the drinks."

Drinks included a gift from the Bendetti's, two bottles of wine, which everyone was soon sipping and discussing as they seated themselves in the dining room.

It was an oval table, and Aerielle thought it made the seating decidedly less awkward. She was seated between Phoenix and Hawk, while the Bendettis were seated together, Sofia on Hawk's left, her grandmother on Phoenix's right.

"Maybe we should all take turns saying what we're grateful for," suggested Mrs. Bendetti, glancing around the table.

Aerielle sensed Phoenix's sudden tension without even looking at him, knew it was because Mrs. Bendetti was effectively a stranger. Though he'd changed, he obviously still had difficulty opening up before people he didn't know well.

"I think sharing what we're grateful for is a wonderful idea, Mrs. Bendetti," said Aerielle. "Would you care to go first?"

The old woman smiled. "Certainly. I'm grateful for my wonderful granddaughter, Sofia," a tender look was exchanged, "and all the time she spends with me. I'm also grateful she has such wonderful friends."

"Sofia?" prompted Aerielle, arranging the rotation so Phoenix would be last.

"*I'm also* glad I have so many wonderful friends." Sofia glanced around the table, but her gaze came to rest on Hawk. "I'm thankful, too, to be about finished with school, so I can work more closely with you—both."

Instantly Aerielle's radar came to life. So Hawk didn't think Sofia would be interested. Clearly he was as blind as a bat. Aerielle glanced at him to be sure, but he wasn't looking at Sofia. Instead he was studying the content of his wine glass. He appeared contemplative, as if trying to decide what to say as it was his turn. "I'm grateful Aerielle did us the honor of making sure we weren't eating frozen dinners." He paused, waiting for the laughter to die down. "I'm also grateful Phoenix and I made it through another year without managing to kill each other."

Sofia glanced at Aerielle, rolling her eyes, and Aerielle nodded her head in return.

All eyes shifted to Aerielle, and she realized she hadn't thought about what *she* was going to say. "I'm thankful I've been reunited with old friends." Despite her rollercoaster ride of emotions over Phoenix, Aerielle truly was. "I'm thankful I had someplace to go for Thanksgiving. And I'm thankful that though I lost my four-legged soulmate, two very special people have been there to help me through it." Aerielle first looked at Hawk, but then her attention lingered on Phoenix, hoping to reassure him she did not hold him accountable for the dog's loss.

Everyone took her glance to mean she was finished since Phoenix was next to share, but his eyes met hers briefly, and she saw he understood.

"What I'm thankful for..." he said thoughtfully, his face grave as he glanced around the table. "...I'm thankful for mercy... forgiveness...and hope." At that point he raised his goblet. "A toast...to God."

The clanking of glasses resounded and then everyone was drinking and passing dishes. Dinner was a success. The conversation was relaxed, though Phoenix said little, and the food delicious. Aerielle even managed not to drop any items in her water glass or knock anything over. Hawk even teased her about it as he later helped her carry some dishes into the kitchen.

"I'm glad you managed to control yourself," he grinned.

"Watch your mouth, Hawk, or you may be wearing your pie."

"I'd like to see that," announced Phoenix, entering the kitchen with the leftover salad and stuffing.

"Maybe *you'd* like to try the salad," offered Hawk.

"Can I leave before the food starts flying?" asked Aerielle.

Suddenly, they were interrupted by a scream coinciding

with a loud crash. The only one with hands free, Aerielle ran for the dining room, Hawk and Phoenix tossing dishes on the counter behind her.

Bolting into the room, Aerielle stared in dismay. Mrs. Bendetti lay on the floor, buttered New potatoes rolling around her on the floor between splattered cranberry turkeys. Glass was everywhere from the crystal bowl and platter, which had shattered on the polished hardwood. Sofia, delayed by shock, was just getting to her grandmother.

"Call 911, Sofia," ordered Aerielle, rushing over to the old woman who appeared unconscious. Aerielle knelt beside her, resting her knees on the woman's full skirt spread out over the glass. She felt for a pulse at the neck, which she failed to find, and then leaned close to see if the woman was breathing. She wasn't.

Aerielle heard both Phoenix and Hawk behind her, and then there was the sound of crushed glass as Phoenix squatted down beside her. "Hawk and I know CPR, too," he said, as if reading Aerielle's intentions.

"We have to get her out of this glass, first."

It took three of them to lift the robust Italian woman out of the mess while Sofia called for help. As they carried the old woman to the foyer and set her on the runner, Aerielle felt her own shock settle in. She didn't handle too many heart attacks in the cancer ward. Mrs. Bendetti's skin was cold and clammy, her mouth hanging open in what appeared to be a silent plea for help. It was awful. But this was part of what Aerielle had been trained for. Kneeling beside her patient, she tilted the old woman's head up to check the airway and then began breathing for her.

Phoenix knelt opposite her and waited to start the chest compressions.

Sofia returned to the room, phone in hand, mumbling something about her grandmother clutching at her chest.

"Heart attack," murmured Aerielle.

While Sofia remained in contact with 911, Phoenix and Aerielle got their technique in rhythm, but Mrs. Bendetti had yet to take a breath on her own. Time dragged as they waited for the sirens signaling the arrival of help. When Aerielle *did* hear them, it was from far off, her senses tuned to the slightest sound, the slightest touch—the slightest change in Mrs. Bendetti 's condition. There was none.

Minutes passed, Phoenix switching to the breathing, Hawk taking over the chest compressions. The dogs had been banished to the kitchen, and the weeping Sofia with the cordless phone sent to watch the door. The police arrived first, and Sofia disconnected the phone while the officer immediately began helping with CPR. At last the paramedics were there, hurrying through the door, their hands full of equipment.

"I'm a doctor," announced Aerielle, grabbing for the ambu bag just retrieved. Aerielle placed the bag over Mrs. Bendetti's nose and mouth, the job of breathing for the old woman now made easier.

The paramedics went into action, one hooking up a saline IV, the other attaching a heart monitor.

"What rhythm is she in?" demanded Aerielle, handing the ambu bag to Phoenix.

"Looks like V-fib," came the reply.

Aerielle reached for the defibrillator. "All clear."

Everyone pulled back from making contact with the unconscious woman, and Aerielle applied the paddles to Mrs. Bendetti's chest. The shock from the defibrillator raised the old woman from the floor, but the paramedic watching the monitor just shook his head. "No change."

"Again," said Aerielle. "All clear."

Mrs. Bendetti lifted from the floor a second time, Sofia wincing.

"We have normal sinus rhythm," announced the paramedic. "And she's breathing on her own."

Aerielle nodded. "Then let's get her out of here."

Quickly, Mrs. Bendetti was lifted onto the stretcher by the paramedics. Aerielle rose to follow, but Phoenix's voice stopped her.

"Aerielle, you're bleeding."

He was looking at her feet. Confused, Aerielle glanced down, stared at her bare feet, now lacerated from broken glass and stained with blood. *Her* blood. Aerielle promptly passed out.

→→→

Phoenix paced the hospital emergency waiting room like a caged animal. Thankfully, it was fairly empty, as he was drawing enough attention as it was. Not that it mattered. He would have drawn attention had he been sitting calmly reading a magazine. Maybe it was the hair, maybe the face, but people tended to notice him. Some were more discreet with their glances, other's outright stared. Let them. Pretty soon, he'd really give them something to watch as he stormed into the emergency room where Aerielle had disappeared well over two hours ago.

Earlier, when she'd fainted, she'd hit her head and knocked herself out but good. The police had insisted on calling another ambulance. Hawk and Sofia had followed the first such vehicle to the hospital—Sofia had requested Hawk drive her, which left a grateful Phoenix to follow the second. By the time he had raced through the Emergency Room entrance, he'd found only his brother, his face ashen. Sofia's grandmother had coded on the way to the hospital, and they hadn't been able to revive her. She had died in the ambulance. Hawk would wait for Sofia and take her wherever she needed to go.

The pair had left what seemed like days ago, leaving Phoenix, his fears, and his imagination, alone. He'd bothered the woman at the desk so many times, he'd begun to worry she'd call security. Turning abruptly to begin pacing the opposite direction, Phoenix nearly ran down a nurse. She quickly stepped backward so as not to be run over, and for a brief moment, she simply stared up at Phoenix. For one brief moment, Phoenix was tempted to raise one hand up and say, "*How.*" Gratefully, the odd compulsion passed.

"You must be one of the Stargazer brothers?"

Not are you, thought Phoenix, but you must be. "Aerielle's awake. Is she okay? Can I see her?"

"She's doing fine. She sent me to come get you or your brother."

"He had to leave. It's just me now."

"I'll take you to her, then."

The short trip was a blur of doors, another hallway, more doors, and then a plethora of blinking, beeping machines, and healthcare personnel, all of whom ignored them. That was a switch, thought Phoenix.

"She's in there," said the nurse, motioning to one of several small curtained off rooms. She left him, then, and Phoenix slipped into the room, rattling the curtain rings as he did so.

"Hawk?" demanded Aerielle, turning toward the sound, her eyes questioning.

Phoenix winced, stepping toward the narrow bed. "Sorry. Afraid you're stuck with me."

"She didn't make it, did she? The staff wouldn't tell me, so I assumed.... Tell me I'm wrong, Phoenix."

Phoenix's joy at seeing Aerielle was swept away. "I can't."

"Oh, God." Aerielle's voice broke and a sob slipped out. "And I told Sofia not to worry. I know better. It was stupid of me."

"Aerielle," Phoenix began, while dragging a chair up close and sitting on it backwards. "Aerielle, I.... Dang. I don't know what to say."

"It's been a pretty shitty couple of weeks, hasn't it?" she asked, surprising Phoenix with her word choice.

But he agreed with her. "Yeah, pretty shitty." And after a brief pause. "How do you sign that anyway?"

Aerielle let out a laugh that rang with a touch of hysteria.

Phoenix was afraid he might join her. Feeling overwhelmed, he bowed his head, resting his forehead on clasped hands in an attempt to keep his thoughts private.

From the short distance that separated them, Aerielle stared at his glorious hair, knew he was hiding for sure, this time. Her own emotions were running rampant, slamming around inside like a pinball machine. In the course of just a few seconds, her thoughts went back to the dining room table and circled around to each face of those who'd been seated there. She knew fear, grief, and loss, as well as hope. Despite the hope, she felt as if she might shatter any minute.

"Have I ever told you I can't stand the sight of my own blood?" she asked casually, attempting to hold it together.

Phoenix shook his head but didn't look up. "No. Is that why you passed out? I knew it couldn't be from not eating enough."

Aerielle couldn't help it, she let out another snort of laughter, this time leaning even more toward the hysterical side.

"Phoenix? Yellow Wolf look at me."

He did, raising his head and revealing eyes filled with concern. And she knew, he knew, she could see it. "What can I do Aerielle?"

"Take me home."

Phoenix was startled by the request. "Can you even walk? And what about your head? Aren't they worried about a concussion?" Phoenix took her in from head to toe, or rather toe to head, starting with her bandaged feet, to the IV in her hand, to the icepack her blond hair nearly covered.

"I'm sure they are. That's why they're talking about keeping me here for observation. But I can't stay. I hate being here even more than I hate the sight of my own blood."

"You spend your life in hospitals. You're a doctor."

"No. I'm not. Right now, I'm a patient."

"But the doctors are right. Even if you could walk, which I doubt, you need to be monitored for a concussion."

"You're medically trained. You can monitor me."

"Me? Not Hawk?" Aerielle knew the instant he said it he regretted the words. She also remembered well the look Sofia had graced Hawk with earlier that day. Once Aerielle'd confirmed Mrs. Bendetti's passing, she'd had no doubt where Hawk was.

"Yes. You. Now, please take me home."

Phoenix stared at her for an endless moment, while Aerielle stared back, undeterred. At last he spoke. "You will do everything I tell you to do. Everything."

"I promise."

While Phoenix could see the instant relief on Aerielle's face, he was already shaking his own head at his decision.

"Hey, hey!" he snapped as Aerielle began working at her IV.

"It has to come out," she hissed back in a whisper.

Phoenix lowered his voice. "I know that. But at least let me do it."

Aerielle sighed with impatience, but let Phoenix do as he wished. He was a lot kinder about the removal than she probably would have been, but she worried about any seconds lost. Someone might not come back for 20 minutes or they might be back in five. And she wasn't up to fighting with doctors. She knew what they were like.

"Now what?" asked Phoenix. "Do I throw you over my shoulder and run off with you like an Indian stealing a white woman?"

Aerielle rolled her eyes. One never knew when Phoenix's humor might make an appearance. "First give me my clothes and then go find a wheelchair."

"Won't someone notice?"

"Probably, but not enough to question it. They're all working their own cases. Unless you're stealing drugs, they're not likely to question it. Now go, so I can get dressed.

By the time Aerielle had finished getting her red dress back on without the ability to stand up, she was out of breath, and her head was pounding like a drum at a powwow. At least her feet were still numb from the local anesthesia they'd given her.

"Aerielle?" murmured Phoenix above the electronics from the other side of the curtain.

"I'm ready," Aerielle called, hoping only he could hear her. As he pushed the wheelchair in, she did her best to slow her breathing and look like she had no drums in her head, however one did that.

Phoenix parked the wheelchair next to where she sat on the side of the bed, her bandages encasing her dangling feet like white ballerina slippers. If only she could dance her way to the wheelchair. However, there was no way she was getting into it by herself. Determined and resolute, Aerielle raised her arms, and without hesitation Phoenix reached for her, lifting her into his.

Maybe if she hadn't been so medicated, she would have felt more self-conscious. Instead, Aerielle wrapped her arms around his neck and relaxed against his chest as if there was no place she'd rather be. Briefly she closed her eyes, She wasn't positive, but she was pretty sure Phoenix stood there holding her longer than was necessary before depositing her into her waiting getaway car. She savored every second.

Relief flooded over Aerielle the moment Phoenix pulled away from the hospital curb and into the darkness. She didn't care about the pain in her head, her tangled hair, the dress she'd never wear again, or even the freezing temperature of the truck. She was out of the hospital.

"I feel like Bonnie and Clyde," muttered Phoenix, pulling into the street.

Aerielle laughed, and her teeth chattered at the same time. She hadn't been in any condition to take her coat to the hospital, and it appeared Phoenix hadn't remembered his.

"Aerielle?"

She glanced up to find him looking at her, his face set as if he was expecting her to argue over something.

"Yes?"

"Slide over here. At least until the heat's up and running. I'm not gonna have you freeze to death on top of everything else."

So, thought Aerielle, there would be no clinging to the door this time. Without a word, Aerielle slid across the seat of the cab as if she'd done it yesterday. Phoenix raised his arm to welcome her in, wrapping it around her shoulders. She snuggled in, her head to his chest, her right arm across his waist. Oh, but he was warm. "Thank you. For getting me out of there, for taking me home."

"Speaking of home," he said, his voice firm. "We're going to mine."

The sweater Phoenix was wearing was soft under her cheek and smelled like him. "Alright."

"Alright?" asked Phoenix, briefly glancing down at her. "Did you hear what I said?"

Aerielle nodded against him, while reaching up to stroke a strand of his hair that had fallen over her. "You said we're going to your house."

"And you're not arguing about it?"

"I did promise to do everything you said."

Phoenix grunted. "Like I believed you."

"Right now I'd go just about anywhere with you besides the hospital. The airport, the zoo, your house. Besides, if I'd been thinking clearly, I would have known we had to go to your house. The place is a mess, and from what I remember before I disgraced myself, the dogs are locked in the kitchen. Do you suppose they've eaten everything in sight?"

Aerielle swore she felt Phoenix smile. "I wouldn't blame 'em, but they're too well trained. The cats on the other hand...."

They rode the rest of the way in silence, and in fact, when the heat filled the truck, Aerielle remained silent, pretending to be asleep. She had no wish to leave Phoenix's side, nor did she want him to know how much she longed to stay.

He must have become worried, however, for he brushed her

hair with his hand and spoke her name with urgency. "Aerielle, you still with me?"

"Uh huh. Just listening to your heartbeat."

"I may only be a vet, but I'm pretty sure my heart's on the other side."

"I'm sorry I ever accused you of not having one." The last remark brought back the silence, but only a couple of minutes passed before they pulled up behind the house, near the back door. Some of the lights in the kitchen had been left on, and the glow shown through the windows and reflected off the snow.

Phoenix was sorry the trip was over. He hadn't expected Aerielle to stay by his side any longer than she had too. The moment the truck had started to heat up, he'd assumed she'd retreat back to the other side of the cab. But she hadn't, and he had felt her every movement against him, from the nod of her head, to the movement of her lips when she spoke. It seemed with every move, his heart pounded harder. Maybe she *had* been listening to his heartbeat. Reluctantly, Phoenix turned the key, shutting off the engine. Suddenly everything was silent.

"Are we home?" Aerielle inquired, her voice soft and sleepy.

"Yeah, were home."

"What time is it?"

Phoenix glanced at the clock on the dashboard. "Just about nine."

"Would it be rude of me to go to sleep now? I was awake till five this morning," she admitted.

"You, too, huh? Course it wouldn't be rude." *If it wasn't so dang cold out, I'd let you sleep right here in my arms.*

It took some maneuvering of steps, doors, and dogs, but with Aerielle's help with the doors and Phoenix's command of the dogs, they made it to the front foyer and the bottom of the stairs without mishap.

"I can sleep downstairs somewhere," offered Aerielle, studying the stairwell with sleepy eyes.

"You are not sleeping on a couch."

"Well, if you need a break, you can set me down."

"Take a moment, Aerielle, and stop worrying about everyone but yourself. Now, just wrap your arms closer around my neck and hang on tight. We don't want you hitting your head again, either on the railing or the wall.

Phoenix shifted her in his arms, and Aerielle leaned in, wrapping her arms completely around his neck and into his hair, while she buried her face against his neck, her breath warm against his throat.

How wonderfully cruel, thought Phoenix, as he started up the steps. He had the woman he loved cradled in his arms, her warm breath leaving him breathless, and he was taking her to bed. So she could sleep. By the time they reached his room and he'd laid her on the king size bed, she was nearly there. She managed an unnecessary "Thank you" and was gone. Grabbing a quilt, Phoenix covered her. He left the room quickly, fearful he might not leave at all.

He glanced at his watch as he headed back down the stairs. He needed to make sure he checked Aerielle's neural responses at the correct time. Once he had taken care of the shepherds, he'd put one in his room to watch over Aerielle while he took care of KP duty. There was plenty of that. Despite the work which lay ahead, the air was still filled with the festive scent of turkey and pumpkin pie. He supposed if one left it out in multiple rooms and dumped it on the floor, the aroma would last for a while.

Phoenix focused all his energy on cleanup and did his best not to think. Too much had happened today. He wasn't sure he could trust himself with his own thoughts or emotions. If only he could put them on hold for a while, forget for a moment the loss Sofia must be enduring, forget for another how it felt to cradle Meyui in his arms as if she belonged there. So Phoenix concentrated on cleaning as if nothing else mattered.

With the dishwasher *and* the washing machine humming along, and the scent of thanksgiving now replaced with the smell of cleaning products, Phoenix headed for the stairwell. It was back to real life and time to wake Aerielle. With him, he took a glass of water, and the strongest "humanly" safe pain meds he could lay his hands on. Tomorrow would be soon enough for some antibiotics.

This should be "fun." Didn't they say doctors made the worst patients? She certainly hadn't wanted to stay at the hospital. Phoenix suspected if he'd refused her request, she would have found a way without him, leaving herself unmonitored in the process. At least this way he could keep an eye on her.

Using the light from the hallway to see, Phoenix crossed to the side of the bed. Spock stood with a tail wag, as if to say, "See? She's still asleep and she's still breathing."

"Good boy," Phoenix whispered, patting the dog on the head after setting the water and meds on the night stand.

Turning his attention to Aerielle, Phoenix was relieved to see at some point she'd roused enough to turn over. She was now lying on her side, facing away from him. Using the space created, Phoenix sat on the bed beside her.

"Aerielle," he said, his voice quiet yet firm. There was no response, and Phoenix called her name louder. He sure hoped he wouldn't have to shake her awake, or worse yet, take her back to the hospital. She would then have one more reason to be angry with him.

God knew he'd given her plenty of reasons to hate him. The worse reason, of course, was leaving her, a note his only explanation. The second reason would be the lie he'd told her in the note. Only it wasn't the lie she thought it was. And that was the crux of the matter. The only lie he'd told was that he'd lied. He'd literally lied about lying.

Unthinkingly, Phoenix ran a hand across the delicate skin of her cheek before gently caressing her hair back from her face. As if following the warmth of his hand, her head turned, revealing her exquisite sleeping face. Phoenix froze, both in fear of being caught and, by the vision of her beauty. And then Esmeralda poked her head out from beneath the quilt. She'd apparently climbed under the cover and nestled in. Phoenix's breath caught as he moved his hand to stroke the cat, desperately trying to regain his composure and force his mind to the here and now.

But his gaze was locked on Aerielle's face, and the memory of the last time he had seen her in Idaho. The past and present melded together, for she had been asleep on his bed then, too, wrapped in a similar quilt, Esmeralda, just a kitten, snuggled against her. While it was the last time he had seen her, he hadn't *known* it would be the last time. That was the trouble with last times. You never knew they were the last until there were no more. And on that morning, Phoenix had just come in to kiss her delicate lips with a brief goodbye before heading out on Steel. It was always best to start early with fence repair, before the heat of the day. Yet that simple goodbye kiss had become the long goodbye, and one of his most treasured memories.

Phoenix heard a grown of agony and realized it came from him. "Oh, Meyui, Meyui, if I'd only known." Then he was leaning down, his hands on either side of her pillow, one cradling her face. He kissed her then, kissed her as gently as a butterfly stealing nectar from a flower.

All the emotion he had felt that day returned, the indescribable joy of loving her and the deep pleasure of knowing she loved him. All of this filled to running over by the sheer happiness of knowing their life together was at a new dawn.

Aerielle's unexpected response to his kiss hauled Phoenix back to the present, even as her lips parted beneath his. He pulled away from her, cursing under his breath. What was the matter with him? He froze in place like an ice sculpture, staring down at her. Was she awake? Did she know? What would she do?

But her eyes stayed closed and she remained still. Only...had her mouth curved into a hint of a smile?

Sweet Jesus, give me strength. The last thing he wanted to do was wake her now. And in fact, he longed to run from this glorious vision in red, lock himself away from temptation. For once, when Aerielle was here, he actually wished Hawk was, too. Hawk, at least, would not be haunted by his memories of her.

Taking a deep breath, Phoenix calmed himself. "Aerielle,' he said, more matter of fact than he felt. "Aerielle, it's time to wake up."

She moaned something which sounded like dissent and rolled her head back and forth in slow motion.

"Aerielle."

"Go away, Half-Breed. I'm too tired for stargazing tonight."

So she had visited the past just as he had, thought Phoenix. Was she there before or after he had kissed her.

"Aerielle, it's Phoenix. Wake up."

This time her eyelids struggled open. "Phoenix?" There was confusion in her eyes.

"It's time for your neural check."

"I fell," she said, glancing around the room. "And then I fell asleep. I don't even remember making it up the stairs."

Hearing her voice, both Spock and McCoy came over to the bed to inspect her, their eyes observant, their noses busy. Aerielle turned to see them, and stuck out a hand towards them, but they were too far away.

"How do you feel?" inquired Phoenix

She seemed to think about it for a moment. "Well, aside from my head and my feet, everything in between feels fine."

"I'll give you some pain meds after I shine a light in your eyes and you answer some questions."

"You make it sound as if I'm being interrogated."

Phoenix couldn't help but smile.

"You should do that more often," Aerielle said groggily as she gazed up at him. "I forget how good a smile looks on your face."

"I'll make you a deal. You pass this checkup with flying colors, and I'll try to do it again."

She passed her tests easily. Then, after telling her what medication he had procured, Phoenix handed it over and offered her the water. She was working at keeping her eyes open as Phoenix tucked the quilt back in around her and Esmeralda. "Relax. Stop fighting it."

"Smile first," she mumbled, her eyes just slits.

"I did. You must have missed it."

"Liar."

Phoenix froze, but Aerielle seem too far gone to realize what she'd just said. He gave her the requested smile.

Her eyes closed, but her lips managed a few more words. "You...out of practice...need to work on it."

It seemed like the middle of the night when Phoenix checked on Aerielle again, but it was just shy of 1:00 a.m. He was exhausted. The day had taken its toll. Aerielle awoke easier the second time, though she was a tad grumpy. She closed her eyes the moment he was done asking the last question, and she didn't request a smile. Phoenix switched out the dogs, leaving McCoy to keep an eye on her this time.

Retreating to Hawk's room, Phoenix cleared a spot on the bed and plopped down face first on to one of several pillows. Bunching it into place so he could breath. Phoenix went instantly to sleep.

→→→

Aerielle was getting sick of her own name. She was sleeping so well, why couldn't Phoenix just leave her alone?

"Wake up, Blondy, or I may have to resort to extreme measures."

"Leave me alone," Aerielle grumbled. "I know who I am. I'm an idiot doctor who passed out at the sight of my own blood only to hit my head. Now there's some idiot vet interrogating me for my lack of panache."

"I'm offended," replied Phoenix, not sounding as if he were. Aerielle heard the lamp switch on, felt the light invade her eyelids as he sat down on the edge of the bed. "Come on, show me those baby blues."

"Phoenix," Aerielle complained.

"Now I'm really offended," came the sarcastic response.

Aerielle opened her eyes with reluctance, but instead of Phoenix sitting next to her it was Hawk. Of course it was Hawk. When had Phoenix ever called her Blondy? And where was Phoenix?

Hawk answered her unspoken question. "He's sound asleep in my room. And since I haven't gone to bed yet...."

"What time is it? I'm starving. How's Sofia?" Aerielle tried to sit up as she spoke, but Hawk immediately pressed his hands to her shoulders. "Hold on. Not so fast."

Aerielle groaned with her effort and settled for the extra pillow Hawk stuffed underneath her head. He picked up the flashlight on the nightstand. "Now show me those baby blues."

Aerielle tried to keep her eyes open as Hawk shined the light at them, looking for normal dilation. "Hmm, your eyes are fine...but do you know your name?"

"Hawk...."

"No, that's not it."

"Haaawk."

"Well, you did call me Phoenix."

"Hawk!"

He grinned. "You whine with such lovely petulance. And in answer to one of *your* questions, it's three o'clock in the morning As for food, what are you hungry for that doesn't require great cooking skills? I am sure I can find something you can easily throw on the floor."

Aerielle ignored his jest. "First, tell me about Sofia."

"Well, unlike you, I tried to get her to go to sleep, but without much luck. Her oldest brother will be flying out first thing and the others will follow."

"I wish I could have done more. How is she handling it?"

Hawk shrugged. "It's too early to tell. She can be rather matter of fact about life, but she was very close to her grandmother. I guess we'll see. If she's going through what you've been going through..."

"Christmas is coming up," blurted Aerielle. "It's a horrible time of year to be alone."

"Her brothers will stay for a while."

"She'll need the company."

Suddenly, Aerielle wakefulness retreated, and her eyelids began to flutter their way closed. "I'm not hungry anymore, Hawk."

"Aerielle?"

"Hmm?"

"How many Christmases have you been alone?"

"Enough." And then Aerielle knew nothing more.

The Indians throughout displayed a courage and skill that elicited universal praise; they abstained from scalping; let captive women go free; and did not commit indiscriminate murders of peaceful families...they fought with almost scientific skill.

Sherman as quoted in *Chief Joseph of the Nez Perce* by Robert Penn Warren.

16

It was a Maxwell House kind of morning, the smell of coffee waking first Aerielle's nose and then her body. Her ears quickly tuned into the murmur of voices in the kitchen below her—Phoenix and Hawk. Esmeralda was curled up at Aerielle's side, and Aerielle drew comfort from her presence.

"Good morning, precious. Guess it's time to get up. One thing about sleeping in your clothes, there isn't much to do, except get out of bed, and I can't even do that by myself." Not like she wanted to. Aerielle's feet were still painful, and she knew the bandages would have to be changed.

Reaching down to the floor vent that allowed heat to rise from the first floor, Aerielle banged against the grate. "Room Service."

The voices stopped below. Aerielle pushed herself back up onto the bed and waited for her "escort." It was Hawk who appeared.

Friday continued on in its out of the ordinary way with Aerielle spending the day at the Stargazers, mostly alone since the clinic was open as scheduled. During the morning, she called Heather who brought her a wheelchair and some clothes and things from her apartment. Heather's interest in Aerielle's temporary hosts was evident. "There's more to this than you're telling me," she remarked at one point. "I can't wait until you decide to share it all."

Aerielle had remained silent on the subject, changing the direction of the conversation to her work schedule. She was expected in on Saturday. She would have to manage it in a wheelchair. Sunday, also a work day, she'd be back on her feet as long as she took it easy. It wouldn't do to have the stitches rip out.

When dinner hour arrived at 6:30, no one was interested in leftovers. Stains from the potatoes and cranberry sauce, spilled the day before, plainly marked the wood flooring in the dining room. It was unsettling, almost painful. Instead, the threesome ordered pizza and ate in Phoenix's room, talking of Sofia. Phoenix decided to go over and check in and see if she or anyone else needed anything.

Hawk found some Carol Burnett reruns on the TV in his bedroom and made Aerielle comfortable with extra pillows he'd borrowed from Phoenix's room. Aerielle was relieved to have something distracting to watch. Carol, Harvey, and Tim were just as hilarious the second time around. Aerielle laughed so hard she cried. It was a relief to cry tears of laughter for a change.

Hawk was equally entertained, so much that the cats had given up using him as a resting spot.

"Oh, so sad," said Aerielle, wiping at her eyes as Hawk used the remote to silence the TV. "I would have loved one more episode."

"One. How 'bout ten? I could have stayed up all night watching."

Aerielle giggled again, unable to turn the laughter off.

"You, are slaphappy," grinned Hawk, laughing himself.

"I have to work tomorrow. I suppose I should get some sleep. At least I'll *be* allowed to sleep," giggled Aerielle.

"Why don't you grab a couple of pillows, and I'll haul

you back to Phoenix's room. I don't think he'd appreciate you sleeping in here even without me."

Aerielle did her best to hang on to Hawk and the pillows at the same time without blocking his view. Thankfully it was a short trip across the hallway. However, it was an even shorter trip onto the bed when Hawk tripped over McCoy, and lost his balance and his grip on Aerielle. Hawk said something, but Aerielle's cry of surprise drowned it out as she was dumped on the bed like a sack of oats. Her landing was soft, but the only thing that kept Hawk from crushing her as he followed were the big soft pillows she still clutched.

It was comedy of errors, thought Aerielle. For even as Hawk was struggling to find an unoccupied piece of real estate, McCoy had jumped to his feet and began barking. Spock, sure he was missing something, leaped onto the bed knocking Hawk aside, and began lapping at Aerielle's face. She fought the dog's affectionate attention as she began to giggle uncontrollably.

Regaining his balance, Hawk pushed himself up on his knees and grabbed hold of Spock's collar. "Get off the bed you dumb dog. You know you're not allowed up here."

Spock turned and leaped off the bed, narrowly missing McCoy, who had stopped barking as he became a spectator. Aerielle turned her attention to Hawk where he remained on his knees beside her.

"Are you alright?" His questions ended with laughter as Aerielle continued to giggle, tears spilling from her eyes and rolling back into her hair. She struggled to sit up, and then began shoving the pillows at Hawk since he was closer to the head of the bed.

"I'm fine. Really," she added as he turned away with the first one. When he turned back for the second, she hit him over the head with it.

"So that's how it's gonna be." Retrieving the pillow he had just moved, Hawk defended himself and an all-out pillow fight ensued. He was relentless in his return attack, and Aerielle crawled around the bed trying to get away from him. She took swings at him whenever she could, some more successful than others. All the while, she continued to laugh. But gosh, it was getting hard to breath.

It was hard to see, too, with her hair in her eyes. Beside her, she barely saw Hawk raise his pillow again, and Aerielle whirled hers at him in defense. Suddenly he slipped backward and fell off the bed with a resounding thud. "Hawk," she cried, scrambling to the edge of the bed. She leaned over the edge in time to see him shoving his pillow dramatically beneath his head.

"You win," he gasped, looking the worse for wear.

"You're alright, then?"

"I'm fine. But you should see yourself."

Aerielle was kept from responding by the sound of the back door slamming closed.

"Phoenix," announced Hawk. And then they heard a truck door slam. "Leaving."

"Leaving? But he wasn't...but he hadn't—."

"Come home?" finished Hawk. "There's no way we would have heard him. But he would have heard us."

Still leaning over the side of the bed, Aerielle saw as much in Hawk's eyes as she heard in his voice. "You don't think he thinks that...."

Hawk sat up, sighing in frustration. "He's too smart for that. On the other hand, I have given up trying to read my brother."

Aerielle pulled herself up, the brief reprieve from reality over. She dragged frustrated fingers through her hair, raking it away from her face. "It's time you clarified our relationship for him."

"The moment he gets home...again," offered Hawk, getting up off the floor. "I'll go down and wait for him."

→→→

Phoenix stared out at the partially frozen lake from the vantage point of his truck. He was only a few blocks from home. A home which had been invaded by Aerielle's presence. Not that Phoenix minded her being there. It was having her there with his brother. They shared such an easy camaraderie. It tortured him to watch them, listen to them, despite the apparent casualness of their relationship. He wanted to be anywhere else than where they were, together.

He hadn't thought to let his brother go to Sofia's tonight. He had been in too much of a hurry to get away himself. And then to come home to their shared laughter.... Phoenix doubted anything questionable had been going on, but just the thought of his brother making Aerielle laugh the way *he* wanted to make her laugh, just the idea of them being together in *his room*.... Most of all, just the possibility that Hawk might kiss Aerielle good night drove Phoenix crazy, stirring the jealousy he strove to deny. It had to end—his brother dating Aerielle—even his brother would agree if he knew the truth. Tonight, he and Hawk would talk.

→→→

A half our later, her hair brushed, her pajamas on, her medications taken, and herself tucked in, Aerielle stared into the darkness. She was no longer tired, no longer slaphappy, just wide awake and confused. Why *couldn't* she have fallen for Hawk? He was so much easier to figure out. Of course, he'd have been a little young if she'd fallen for him fourteen years ago. Phoenix on the other hand, she just didn't have a clue. "Oh, God, I am so confused. Please give me direction. I don't know what's in that man's mind...or his heart. I'm not even sure I know what's in mine. I did mention I'm confused, didn't I? At least I know you aren't."

Aerielle tossed and turned, wondering when Phoenix was coming back. What would Hawk say to him? What would Phoenix say? Would they get into a fight? Did Phoenix really think she and Hawk had been.... He couldn't. He knew her better than that, didn't he?

It was nearly eleven when Aerielle heard Phoenix's truck. She leaned over the side of the bed, listening through the air vent. The back door opened and closed, but no Phoenix. Blast it all, he'd gone into the clinic reception room and who knew where else. Suddenly, Aerielle saw Hawk pass through the kitchen below her, headed for the clinic.

Well, where there was one floor vent, there was another, asserted Aerielle. Moving to get out of bed, her bandaged feet glared at her. She glanced at the wheelchair. It would be way to noisy. Determinedly, Aerielle slipped to the floor onto her hands and knees. Making as little noise as possible, she crawled her way to Hawk's room, finding the vent just as she'd expected. Stretching out on the floor, Aerielle peered through the openings, Hawk's voice carrying up to her.

"You were gone a long time. Is everything okay at Sofia's?"

"She seems to be holding up. Most of the immediate family's arrived.... How did you and Aerielle fair this evening?"

The question was caustic and Aerielle winced. Phoenix was still upset. She wanted to shout through the vent that he had no reason to be. Instead, she bit her tongue.

Below her in the reception room, Phoenix, too, was biting his tongue. Had Hawk noticed the change in his voice? Phoenix couldn't seem to keep himself in check since the morning he and Hawk had exchanged injuries. His feelings were all over the place, his control gone. He was losing it, whatever *it* was.

"Well, you ought to know. You came in and then left in the middle of an epic pillow fight."

"A pillow fight?!" demanded Phoenix. Showing a calm he didn't feel, he set down the appointment book he'd come to check before seeking out his brother for that necessary discussion. It seemed the "discussion" had already begun. "Do you think a pillow fight was conducive to healing with her injuries?!"

"She started it...and finished it.... Hey, we both heard the door slam. Aerielle's under the impression you might actually think something else was going on. I told her you were too smart for that. Especially after the fight you and I had recently. Am I wrong?"

Phoenix shook his head, attempting to get his anger under control and his erratic thoughts together.

"Look," said Hawk, "there's something I need to tell you about Aerielle and me, something I tried to tell you the day we operated on Mildred."

Phoenix stiffened, the steel in his spine reflected in his voice. "And what's that?" he gritted out, unable to meet his brother's gaze. What didn't Phoenix know? Oh, God what didn't he know?

"Aerielle and I are just friends."

Phoenix's head snapped up as he looked straight into his brother's eyes. Not three feet apart, it was easy to see his brother was being completely honest with him. "But that day at the clinic...you were...kissing her."

Hawk laughed. "That was actually the beginning of the end of a very brief dating experiment."

"But, you guys are always together, including the night before you blackened my eye."

"Like I said, Phoenix, we're friends, very *good* friends, which is why we spend so much time together. With her schedule at the hospital, I'm one of the few friends she has. And hanging out with her is a lot more fun for me than hanging out with you."

"I suppose so," grunted Phoenix, letting out a sigh of relief. Hawk and Aerielle weren't together. Hadn't been since— "Blast you Hawk, why didn't you tell me this back then?! Why did you let me go on thinking you and she...."

Hawk shrugged, regret on his face. "I was being a jerk. I'm sorry, now, but at the time I was angry. I wanted a little payback."

"Payback? Payback for what? What were you so angry about?!"

"That's part of it right there!" declared Hawk, said anger filling his voice. "You haven't got a clue. I don't know if it's because you're dense or because you want to believe the worst of me."

Not waiting for a response, Hawk continued. "You had the one perfect woman, and you let her go. When *I* try to find someone, do I get support? No! I get accused of being a love 'em and lose 'em kind of guy. The worst though, was realizing you thought I'd treat Aerielle that way.

"As for the payback, you wanna know why I really went through so many girlfriends? Because of you."

"Me?!" demanded Phoenix, a look of total confusion on his face.

Hawk laughed at his brother's reaction. "Do you have any idea how many of the women I dated lost interest in me after meeting my 'moody and mysterious' brother with the 'gorgeous hair' and the 'chiseled features?' After a while, I intentionally introduced them to you early to see if I was wasting my time."

Phoenix stared in disbelief. He didn't know what to say. He was having enough trouble accepting what he was hearing.

"And so it went," continued Hawk. "I guess when I had a chance of getting something I knew you wanted, I went after it, or her, as the case may be. That, of course, is also why I didn't let on the status quo had changed. Just so you know, Aerielle had no idea until about a week ago I hadn't said anything."

"Hawk, 'sorry' isn't a strong enough word, but it's all I have. I had no idea."

"How could you? I didn't say anything."

"You should have."

"I suspect there's a lot of things we should have said to each other over the years."

Phoenix lowered his eyes, acknowledging the truth in those words. "You're more right than you know."

There followed a heavy silence, and then Hawk asked, "You still care about her?"

Phoenix looked him in the eyes. "Yes."

"When were you gonna tell *me*? Or weren't you?"

"Actually, I had planned to tell you tonight."

Phoenix felt his brother's penetrating gaze. "There's more, isn't there?"

Phoenix winced. "Yes. But I can't tell you about it, not yet anyway. Aerielle—"

Hawk waved him off. "I get it. It'll wait...for now anyway."

"I'm sorry, Hawk. About everything."

"Me, too."

"Can we...can we start over?"

Hawk nodded. And then he hauled Phoenix into a bear hug. "Always. You're my brother."

Briefly, they pulled apart. "I don't know about you, but I'm exhausted," said Phoenix.

"You can share my room, again. You're even allowed to sleep *under* the covers this time."

Phoenix smacked the back of his brother's head. "Are there any pillows left, which haven't been destroyed?"

Hawk laughed as they headed for the stairwell.

Aerielle was still reeling after hearing Phoenix tell Hawk he still cared for her, and now she needed to escape. She scrambled to her knees. How was she going to get back to Phoenix's room before they got upstairs? She wanted to jump to her feet and run for it, but tearing out her stitches was a high price to pay for eavesdropping. Resigned, she made her "run" for it in four wheel drive. She almost made it, too. Phoenix's room was only a knee length away when the two brother's crested the stairs and flipped the landing light on.

"Aerielle?"

It was Phoenix's voice, and filled with questions. Aerielle glanced back toward the stairway, encountering two sets of curious eyes.

"Oh, hi. You're home, I see."

Phoenix wasn't side-tracked. "What are you doing?"

You mean besides listening to private conversations and crawling around in my pajamas that I'm grateful are not in the least revealing? "The wheelchair seemed like a lot of work just to go to the bathroom. I figured this was quicker." Aerielle's conscience rebelled at her deception, but she clamped her lips together.

"Would you like a hand getting back into bed?" asked Hawk.

"Oh, no, I'm fine." Aerielle proceeded into the bedroom on all fours while Phoenix and Hawk stared after her.

Abruptly, they both followed her into the room, and Aerielle found herself being put in her place, the bed that is, by the two of them. She was sure she was blushing as they both left the room without a word.

→→→

It took a long week after Mrs. Bendetti's funeral for Phoenix to strip and refinish the floor in the dining room. And while he sanded away at the stains and the memories, while he carefully applied a fresh shining layer of stain, he thought of Aerielle. He thought about what it would take to remove the stains in their relationship and restore it to its original luster. Certainly, it would take more than a week. It would also take wisdom, and Phoenix needed all he could get. His thoughts kept straying to the next holiday coming up—Christmas. Christmas and Aerielle's lack of family. He also thought about Sofia, living alone now in her grandmother's empty house.

Phoenix was still thinking about the situation with Aerielle and Sofia well into the second week of December as winter snows descended. They came in an all-out blizzard that even brought havoc to those well accustomed to the white stuff. As Phoenix stared out the balcony window from his office, the snow globe outside reminded him of the record breaking Halloween blizzard last year. The clouds had dropped at least eighteen new inches since early last evening, and they were expecting two to four more. Even the schools in the city and its closest suburbs had been canceled, most of the vet clinic appointments had been rescheduled, and the snowplows were behind in their routes. And who knew when the service would be around to clear the sidewalk and the driveway. Because of the clinic, Phoenix and Hawk didn't usually have time to clear their own snow. Right now, Phoenix couldn't tell the front walk from the yard.

He was grateful he'd put the plow on the pickup the last day of November. He never knew when he might need it to get to one of his larger patients, such as Mr. Danvers' cow. Oddly enough, he was scheduled to pay the old man and Mildred a visit today. It might be fun to test out the four-wheel drive. Maybe Tyler would like to go, too.

The aroma of fresh brewed coffee wafted into the room via a vent or perhaps the stairs. It was a little later than usual, but Sofia had followed the usual routine and made the coffee. Turning away from the French doors, Phoenix followed his nose.

When he arrived in the kitchen, Hawk and Sofia were just sitting down at the table.

"We poured you some already," said Sofia, pointing to a third mug at the table.

Phoenix sat down next to her, wondering what they were going to do today.

"I was just telling Sofia she doesn't need to be here," said Hawk. "In fact, I'm surprised you didn't call first and avoid the trip with the roads the shape they're in."

"It wouldn't have mattered anyway," replied Sofia, glancing down at her coffee as if there were leaves to be read inside. "My grandmother's house isn't that far, I do have four-wheel drive, and I couldn't stand the idea a being home all day, alone in that house."

Phoenix felt the rawness of her pain and placed an arm around her shoulders. Hawk, in turn, reached across the table and took hold of one of her hands. “Hey, you can stay here all day if you want,” he assured.

“Yeah,” said Phoenix, “and you can do whatever you want. There are plenty of books to read, or you can help me bathe the dogs,” he added with an attempt at humor.

“Bathe the dogs?” repeated Hawk as if that was the dumbest idea he’d heard.

Sofia looked up and smiled wanly at him. Her gaze held a familiar fondness. Phoenix couldn’t believe his brother continued to fail to notice. “Or,” said Phoenix, “you can lounge around and watch TV. If that’s not exciting enough, you can count the socks under Hawk’s bed.”

“Hey, those are my spares.”

→→→

Aerielle awoke to the sight of one inch snowflakes spilling past her bedroom window. She jerked up, excited. “Idaho, it’s a blizzard out there. We should….” Her sentence trailed off unfinished. “This was one of your favorite kinds of days, wasn’t it boy?” Aerielle spoke the words reverently, wishing he was there to hear them. Tears welled in her eyes. *Oh, but grief clings like a wet cloak*. She should know. How many times had she lost a loved one beginning with Phoenix and ending with Idaho? She supposed five in fourteen years would be considered acceptable numbers if they hadn’t all been the closest ones to her. She had never been more alone in all her life than she was now.

Sliding off her bed, Aerielle walked to the window of the second floor apartment and looked out. She was stunned by the depth of the snow which had already fallen. The world was white, pristine, like a Christmas card without the holiday lights. She wondered if this first official snowstorm of the year out did the Halloween storm from last year that everyone talked about. The famous Halloween snowstorm of ’91. Would there be a famous storm of ’92? Probably not. It wasn’t just the snow that made last year’s famous, but the fact that it came in October.

So, not only was she the most alone she had been in all her life, she was "stranded" by a thick blanket of the white stuff, the worst of which she'd slept through. Aerielle walked to her dresser and started pulling out clothes. Idaho may not be here, she herself might be lost in a wave of self-pity, but the weather called her forth nonetheless. Aerielle loved snow, had missed it dearly living in Texas. She would not waste the day. Maybe the snow and some prayer could pull her from the brink.

An hour and a half later, having eaten and readied herself, Aerielle was now an hour into her trek. She had discovered early on that the only way of getting around was pretty much the roads. The snow was too deep for just any path, the evidence in her boots proof of that. The road itself was thicker than the fluffiest of down blankets, but the plows must have made at least one pass in the middle of the night for the pristine whiteness in the road was just halfway up her calves. The world was muted by the heavy snow continuing to fall, but here and there Aerielle could pick out the sound of someone starting up a snow blower or wielding a shovel. Thank the Lord it was a Saturday. Despite how hardy and familiar Minnesotans were with the tumultuous conditions, this was an unusual amount of snow even for this state.

As Aerielle trudged her way down the street, she saw others braving the out-of-doors. Some came out to fight the snow, others to explore, and many more to play. Aerielle was passed by a couple on skis, saw at least three snowmobiles, and experienced the bright color of snow-suited children playing and making snowmen and other sculptures.

Deciding some fun activity might lift her spirits, Aerielle lay down in the center of the unused road and made a snow angel. Her work complete, she continued to lie there in the depression while white flakes made an effort to cover her. Closing her eyes to the wet crystals, Aerielle felt encased in the comforting wings of an angel. "Oh, Lord," whispered Aerielle, "I need your comfort as well. There are times when my heart feels so empty and my soul so alone, I think I will die of loneliness. My first Christmas back in Minnesota is coming up, and even if I didn't have to work, I have absolutely no one to spend it with, not even my Idaho. Sofia has her brothers she can fly out and visit. The Stargazer's are going home. And I....I'm digging my hole of self-pity deeper. Father I'm sorry. I know you are always with me, always listening, but I wish I had someone or someplace to go to, even if it's just for dinner."

Climbing out of her angel, Aerielle moved on. While it wasn't exactly a conscious decision, she wasn't surprised when she ended up standing in the road facing the Stargazers' home. She'd bet their Saturday clients had probably canceled or been canceled, because not too many people would be capable of getting around. Maybe later people would, if and when the snow tapered off and the legion of snowplows could catch up with the snow. The highways of course, were their number one target with gang plows staggered to clear two to four lanes at a time.

Aerielle studied the Victorian Christmas card before her. It was not as pristine as many properties. The front walk appeared to have received a partial effort at clearing before a small stampede of horses had made a mess of the yard. If Aerielle had to guess, she'd say it was two or three dogs, and maybe two men and a teen that had romped through the snow. Remnants of snowballs still held their shape where they'd missed their targets.

The driveway, which led past the side to the back of the property, had been clear three to four inches ago, but Aerielle could not guess if anyone was home or not.

Her gaze was drawn up to the balcony at the doors that led to Phoenix's study. Was he there? Was he watching her? His desk did face the lake.

So much had happened since Aerielle'd stood on that balcony with Phoenix, Esmeralda in her arms, her whole being poised for a kiss which never came. And then there was the conversation Aerielle had overheard—listened in on—through the heat vents. Phoenix had said he had to talk to her. And he'd said it in such a way that Aerielle had no doubt he would. He just hadn't said when. The patience Aerielle had clung to was gone with the sight of the snow and the renewed pain of Idaho's loss. If Phoenix had something needing to be said—good, bad, or ugly—it was sure to give her something else to think about.

The more we can kill this year, the less will have to be killed the next war, for the more I see of these Indians, the more convinced I am that they will all have to be killed or be maintained as a species of paupers.

William Tecumseh Sherman, as quoted in *The Nez Perces, People of the Far West*

17

Aerielle trudged the ten or so feet to the driveway and then marched her way across the snow covered surface, heading for the backdoor leading to the kitchen. She wrapped on the door with the back of her mittened hand, hoping it was loud enough to get their attention, or at least the dogs. When she heard no barking, Aerielle was crushed. Were they gone or had they just not heard her? She hit the door again, pounding this time. Now that she'd determined to talk to Phoenix, she was afraid to retreat, afraid the wait would be more than she could bear.

And then the door opened and Sofia was standing there. Somehow Aerielle wasn't surprised. The last time she had seen her was at her grandmother's funeral. Aerielle had felt the need to go, if for no other reason than she'd been unable to save Mrs. Bendetti for more than a brief amount of time.

Sofia didn't seem surprised to see Aerielle at the door either. "You look like a snowman, Aerielle. Come in and thaw out."

Aerielle glanced surreptitiously at Sofia as she stepped into the kitchen beside her. She looked better than she had. "How are you doing?" Aerielle asked, brushing snow from her hair.

"Better, thanks. You want some coffee?"

"That would be delightful."

While Sofia poured, Aerielle hung up her coat. She then stomped as much snow off her boots as she could before removing them.

"I suppose you've figured out they're not here," said Sofia, reaching the kitchen table before Aerielle. "Cream and sugar?" she continued.

"Um, yes. I mean, yes I noted their absence, and yes, cream please."

"In case you're wondering why *I'm* here," said Sofia, "I came over because my house is too quiet without my grandmother there talking nonstop about something."

"And I'm here because my apartment is too quiet, and I wanted to talk to Phoenix. I figured the clinic might be closed."

Sofia turned away from the counter. "Well, you were right about the clinic being closed, but those yahoos decided it was a good day to test out the four wheel drive and the plow and go visit Mr. Danvers and Mildred."

"They left you behind?"

"Oh, they invited me, but the men will have more fun by themselves."

"What about Mr. Danvers' wife Mildred?" asked Aerielle, now brushing back the wet tangled locks of her hair.

Sofia laughed. "Mildred's the cow. Mr. Danvers is an old farmer, and I suspect a bit lonely. He ought to be in heaven today, though. Actually, I bet they all are. Phoenix and Hawk stuffed Tyler and the shepherds into the back seat of the truck cab. Mr. Danvers' kitchen must be flowin' with testosterone."

Aerielle grinned at the image filling her thoughts just as the phone rang.

Looking at the caller ID, Sofia pulled it off the hook. She spoke briefly, and Aerielle recognized who was on the other end just by the smile that lit her face. Hanging up, Sofia turned to Aerielle. "That was Hawk. They just got done helping Mr. Danvers plow the driveway. Now they're making a hot breakfast. Hawk just wanted me to know they were going to be awhile. Actually, I just got a fire started in the family room. Should we take our coffee in there?"

"Are you kidding? Coffee in front of a fire sounds divine.

You know, I don't think I knew they had a family room." She'd certainly become familiar with some other rooms of the house, thought Aerielle wryly.

"Actually," replied Sofia as she led them toward the front of the house, "I think the original term was the parlor. Once in a while after a long day at the clinic, Phoenix and I rent movies and unwind."

Aerielle felt a wave of jealousy, not concerning Sofia herself, but of the time she'd spent with Phoenix hanging out. "I thought Hawk was the real movie fan."

"Oh, he is. I ought to know. He's always quoting copious amounts of lines while we're working. He has a memory for that kind of stuff."

Aerielle glanced up the front stairs as they passed the landing.

"But," continued Sofia, "when not working, he is usually out with friends or someone of the female persuasion. He's certainly had his share of girlfriends."

Aerielle heard the longing in Sofia's voice and was instantly feeling guilty about monopolizing so much of Hawk's time. "I'm sorry," she blurted out.

Sofia stopped at a closed solid pine door, but instead of opening it, she turned to Aerielle, careful not to spill the coffee she carried. "Sorry about what?"

"About monopolizing Hawk. You know we're friends, right? I mean we dated a few weeks, but nothing came of it."

Sofia's expression softened in the muted light coming through the windows on either side of the foyer. If Aerielle were to guess, she'd say the woman looked relieved.

"Why do you think it would matter to me?"

Aerielle felt a pang of sympathy for Sofia. "I saw the way you looked at him at dinner," she said, attempting to avoid the word Thanksgiving. "The fact that he hasn't noticed is beyond me."

Sofia's eyes met hers. "I was jealous of you that day, at

first, anyway. I mean, I'd never had dinner with one of Hawk's girlfriends before."

"You said 'at first?'" questioned Aerielle, before hiding behind her coffee and taking a sip. "When did you figure out Hawk and I weren't a couple?"

"Not long after my grandmother and I got here."

Aerielle glanced back up, eyebrows rising.

"You weren't acting like a couple. I mean you never touched each other, there were no private looks, no indication you were anything but friends. And...while I was watching what was *not* happening, I noticed what *was* happening and how you looked at Phoenix when no one was looking. I must say, you were more stealthy about it. I probably wouldn't have noticed at all if I hadn't been watching you guys so closely."

Aerielle wasn't sure what to say. What did Sofia know? What had she seen when Aerielle looked at Phoenix? Did Aerielle want to know what she saw?

Clearly Sofia saw hesitation, for she turned and opened the door. Warm air and the smell of wood smoke wafted out to greet them before they even cleared the doorway.

The family room was like stepping into a different reality, for it looked nothing like the rest of the house. This was a hideaway. The wood floor was mostly covered by a huge braided rug in warm rustic hues. Floor to ceiling bookshelves lined one wall, while a huge leather sofa with built-in arm chairs on either end was the focal point of the room, positioned in the middle at an angle facing a huge fireplace and what appeared to be the latest in TVs. On the other side of the fireplace was a stereo system. Bracketing the fireplace and modern technology, were a pair of huge windows with drapes open revealing the lake through the artificial curtain of snow. In the back of the room, as if forgotten, was a desk with a computer. The room was a parlor no more. It was contemporary, comfortable, and masculine, down to the beat up coffee table, which encouraged one to put their feet up, shoes and all.

All three cats were there, clearly taking advantage of the comfortable furnishings and cozy warmth. Esmeralda was on the couch. Her head lifted as she watched them from her nest in a beautiful quilt that had to have been made by Elizabeth Stargazer, Phoenix and Hawk's mother. The work and design were familiar, as Aerielle had a similar one on the closet shelf in her bedroom.

After placing her coffee on the table, Aerielle scooped Esmeralda into her arms. She held her close so she could press her cheek to the cat's.

"You sweet girl. You're just as soft as the first time I held you."

Esmeralda purred, the rumble loud in Aerielle's ear. "Idaho would have loved you. He had a fondness for cats. He might have tried to herd you, but he would have loved you while he did it."

"That's the look you had in your eyes on Thanksgiving when you regarded Phoenix," said Sofia in a hushed voice.

Aerielle met Sofia's gaze, feeling the carefully constructed walls begin to collapse. "I gave Esmeralda to Phoenix as a kitten. Before...." Aerielle momentarily lost her voice.

"Hawk mentioned you and Phoenix had been inseparable once upon a time."

"He did?"

"Hawk told me you'd all known each other in Idaho...and that Phoenix had once stolen your heart."

The crackling fire filled the empty places of the room as Aerielle and Sofia stared at each other in silence.

"And what did you see on Thanksgiving?" asked Aerielle, setting the cat back on the couch as if shedding her armor. "What do you see in my eyes now?"

"You look haunted, as if the emotions of your heart have been reduced to a combination of pain and love, each warring for control."

Aerielle closed her eyes and swallowed hard, attempting to

keep her emotions from overflowing their banks. Is this what Phoenix felt like when Aerielle read his mind? Sofia was way too gifted in observation. "The day I gave Phoenix Esmeralda he asked me to marry him."

"No joke!" said Sofia in wonder.

Aerielle's eyes widened in shock. "Oh, God, no," she pleaded, lifting a hand to cover her mouth. *As if that would help now.* "Please, you mustn't say anything to anyone, especially Hawk. No one left alive knows besides Phoenix and me."

"I promise I won't say anything to anyone," assured Sofia, and then her lips twitched as if she was trying to stifle a smile.

Suddenly Aerielle realized what she'd said. "Did I just threaten to end your life?"

"That's what it sounded like." Another twitch.

Abruptly Aerielle began to giggle, and so released Sofia from her attempt at composure. She began to laugh as well. Aerielle felt the tension leave her body, and when their laughter finally died away, Aerielle was smiling. "Mr. Danvers' kitchen might be a testosterone stronghold, but it only takes two of us to have an estrogen run gynecocracy."

"Is that something like a female democracy?" asked Sofia.

Aerielle laughed again. "Very good. It means government by women."

"I like that. And while we're having meaningful and intelligent conversation, they're probably trying to best each other on who will eat the most pancakes."

Sofia's response created an image both gave thought to and in unison they announced the perceived winner aloud. "Hawk!"

"I don't think it takes near as much energy to be the strong silent type," said Sofia. "I think that's one of the traits that drew me to Hawk. He's not the silent type. He talks. I listen. My grandmother talked nonstop my entire life, so I ended up being the listener.

"But that's enough about me and them. What should we do right now?"

Aerielle knew just the thing. "Eat chocolate, make popcorn, find a movie on cable, and forget the boys for a while."

"Well, I guess that rules out chick flicks."

→→→

Four men, or three men and an adolescent, along with two shepherds made Mr. Danvers' kitchen feel full for a change. And the old man seemed as happy as a fox in a hen house, thought Phoenix. He hadn't stopped smiling since they'd met him halfway down the driveway, the Stargazers plowing their way in, while Mr. Danvers plowed his way out.

"Table is set. Juice is poured," announced Tyler behind the row of men at the stove and counter doing the "hard work." "What else?" he asked.

Phoenix glanced up from the scrambled eggs he was working on. He couldn't get enough of the boy's eager joy any more than the old man's happy smile.

"Why don't you get the jug of milk out of the icebox and put it on that there table," suggested Mr. Danvers.

"Icebox?"

"That would be the refrigerator," Phoenix supplied.

"Hey," said Hawk, slapping Phoenix with his free hand. "Watch those eggs. They're supposed to be yellow, not brown."

Phoenix returned his attention to the frying pan he was in charge of, but he couldn't help teasing his brother. "You should talk. The last time you made bacon, you cooked it so long it disintegrated into a pile of crumbs."

Hawk grunted, carefully maneuvering the thick-sliced applewood bacon Mr. Danvers had put him in charge of. The old man himself was making his wife Mildred's famous banana pancakes in an electric griddle. Mr. Danvers glanced into Hawk's frying pan. "Yer doin' fine, son. Don't worry. I won't let that bacon come to harm."

"Maybe you should have put <u>me</u> in charge of the eggs and bacon," said Tyler, once again behind them, "and let you two be in charge of things you can't destroy."

"And what do you know about cooking?" demanded Hawk.

"I know how to cook breakfast. Every Sunday after church my dad made brunch. He taught me everything he knows, like cracking two eggs at the same time, flipping pancakes in the air, and making eggs over easy."

Phoenix looked at Hawk. "Maybe for his next job at the clinic he can demonstrate his breakfast skills."

"The maple syrup is warm and ready to go on the table," chuckled Mr. Danvers. He nodded towards a glass bottle of the real stuff he'd just set on a small plate. "The cakes are on their last side, Phoenix's eggs are done, and Hawk's bacon looks perfect."

Phoenix studied his frying pan and then Hawk's. *So this is what bacon and scrambled eggs are supposed to look like.*

Forty-five minutes later, they were still gathered around the table with the shepherds lying contentedly underneath, using various human feet for pillows. The plates were empty and almost as clean as when they'd come out of the cupboard an hour ago. The milk pitcher was empty, and the only piece of food remaining on the table was a lonely pancake left on the platter. There had been an argument over whether it remained because no one had any room left, or if they were saving it for the dogs. The four of them were full up, but Hawk had scarfed down the most pancakes. Now they sat sipping coffee, including Tyler, while they waited for the food to settle a bit before seeing if they could stand.

Tyler was the first to move, but not far. Grabbing the last pancake and ripping it in half, he stood up and stepped away from the table. Neither dog waited for an invitation, as he was looking straight at them. Tyler ordered them to offer their paws. He shook them and the pancake halves disappeared. "Maybe I should buy you guys some pancake mix for Christmas. On the other hand," said Tyler sitting back down and eyeing the Stargazers, "maybe I should *make* you pancakes instead."

"So what do *you* want for Christmas? asked Phoenix.

"Assuming we don't *cook* for you," added Hawk.

Tylor's face lit up, his brown eyes widening with excitement. "Mom and I are gonna see my dad on Christmas. The counseling seems to be going pretty good. I'm hoping they get back together. That would beat any kinda Christmas gift, though a Cris Carter Viking's jersey would be kinda awesome. I know what you want for Christmas," added Tyler, looking back at Phoenix.

"Aerielle," came a chorus of voices as everyone except Phoenix said her name.

Phoenix was not comfortable with the scrutiny he was under from the three looking at him. Tyler looked like he was enjoying himself way too much, Mr. Danvers appeared happily contemplative, and Hawk studied him warily. "Yeah, well, even if that's true, Hawk and I are expected in Idaho for Christmas. And yet…."

"You gonna finish that there sentence?" inquired the old man.

"And yet," continued Hawk, to Phoenix's relief. "We're worried about leaving Sofia and Aerielle. It's likely to be a tough Christmas for both of them."

"And you can't be in both places at once," finished Mr. Danvers.

Both Phoenix and Hawk nodded, their expressions glum.

Tyler stared at the brothers, then to Mr. Danvers and back again. "Am I the only one who sees a solution?"

There was a short silence before Hawk spoke. "Well. Maybe."

"What's your solution?" asked Phoenix, wondering with just a bit of hope what Tyler's response would be.

"You take them with you. If they don't have anyone to stay

here for, then you don't have to leave 'em behind. You all go to Idaho. Didn't Aerielle used to live there, too?"

Phoenix turned and looked at his brother, not caring whether the hope struggling from the ashes of his heart was revealed within his eyes. He knew his brother saw it, for Hawk's expression softened, and a half smile appeared on his lips. Then Hawk spoke using his hands, using the language no one present but Phoenix could understand. Aerielle's language. *Who's to say this isn't God giving you a second chance? Nothing ventured, nothing gained.*

→→→

As the movie ended, Sofia muted the TV. "That was really good. I've always liked Tom Cruise."

"It was good," agreed Aerielle, "but it just occurred to me, in our avoidance of chick flicks, we picked a movie to watch which only tricked us into thinking we were avoiding the guys."

"What makes you say that?"

Aerielle smiled at Sofia. "We just watched *A Few Good Men*."

Sofia shook her head. "I didn't even think of that. But, if you're up for another, Hawk's got a small collection of movies in the cupboard below the TV. We'll have to screen the titles of course."

"Ooh, that might be entertaining in itself."

"Well, while you appease your curiosity, I'm going to clean up and get something else to drink. Do you want anything? More coffee? Pop?"

"I'm fine at the moment, thanks."

Aerielle moved to the TV, kneeling in front of the cupboard below as Sofia gathered the remnants of their snack. As she reached the door of the family room, she paused. "I know I'm risking my life, but am I allowed to know what you said in response to Phoenix?"

Aerielle paused, her hands resting on the open cupboard

doors. Looking over her shoulder, she studied Sofia's inquiring expression. "I said yes."

Minutes later, when she heard Sofia return, Aerielle had a selection of movies laid out on the floor. "This is an odd mix," Aerielle began, "but it's quite the collection. We have all three Star Wars movies, the whole Planet of the Apes series, and The Princess Bride. Now that's a chick flick if I've ever seen one, but I bet the guys like it because it's funny and has lots of sword fighting."

"Aside from the bangs, you look a lot like the Princess Bride."

Aerielle jerked around in surprise. "Phoenix. I thought you were Sofia."

"Hello, Aerielle. I was just about to call and see if you were home when Sofia told me you were already here."

"Maybe I read your mind?"

"Not likely. Not this time anyway. I just thought of this an hour ago. Actually it wasn't my idea. That sounds like I didn't like the idea. Actually I loved the idea, it just wasn't mine, but I'm asking anyway—"

Phoenix stopped abruptly as if he'd just realized he was rambling. Aerielle was stunned. Phoenix did not ramble. Was he actually nervous? What was this idea, that wasn't his, that he wanted to ask her about?

"Just let me put these video tapes away and you can explain," she replied.

"'As you wish.'"

"I thought it was Hawk who was the movie line aficionado."

"'As you wish' isn't much of a line, and it's only one line repeated multiple times in the same move."

"Do you really think I look a lot like the Princess Bride?"

"Not just me. Hawk pointed out the resemblance as well."

Smiling, Aerielle shut the cupboard door and moved to get up.

Phoenix offered his hand to assist her. Aerielle took it automatically, forgetting how his touch affected her these days.

Once she was up, he didn't let go, but led her to the sofa where he released her as she sat.

Phoenix took a seat opposite of her on the coffee table, pulling one leg up so the heal of his foot rested on the beat-up surface. He rested his clasped hands on his knee and studied her. "This idea Hawk and I talked about…we want you and Sofia to come to Idaho with us for Christmas."

Aerielle was momentarily speechless. "Why?"

Phoenix's stalwart façade softened just a bit. "From what I know of you Aerielle, you have no family left. Even Idaho is gone. I suspect you've spent way too many Christmases alone."

The loneliness Aerielle felt upon waking this morning washed over her. Was this God's answer to her prayer from earlier today? If so, it was a darn quick response. But Idaho? How could she return to Idaho with so much unsaid?

As if sensing her hesitation, Phoenix continued. "Aerielle, we need to talk, at least I do. There are things I need to tell you. If my word is worth anything to you anymore, I promise you, whether you come to Idaho or not, we will talk. On the other hand, I would rest easier if you came."

Still rattled, Aerielle shook her head in confusion. "Even if I want to come, I don't know if I can get the time off. Right now I'm scheduled to work over Christmas."

"Understood. Clearly I'm not expecting an answer this minute."

He said the words calmly and confidently, but Aerielle could read Phoenix well enough. If he hadn't thought it might push her away, he would have begged her to come. She could see it in the staccato of muscle in his jaw. It implored her in a way his words did not.

"Speaking of Idaho," said Phoenix, "a different Idaho this time, I have something for you."

Phoenix picked up a cardboard box that had been sitting on the table next to him. Aerielle hadn't noticed it until then. He must have brought it in with him. Gently, he handed it to her. "It's Idaho's ashes. The box they're in was carved by a client of mine."

Aerielle slowly opened the flaps on the box and then pushed a protective shield of tissue paper aside. She gasped. "It's beautiful."

As she struggled to remove the Aussie-shaped urn, Phoenix reached out to pull the box and tissue away, leaving Aerielle with an artfully carved dog-shaped box.

It was amazingly detailed, and Aerielle couldn't help but stare at the clearly defined shape of an Australian Shepherd. Even one of the dog's ears stood up. A collar was carved around his neck with the name Idaho inscribed.

"I had no idea he was going to get this meticulous," said Phoenix setting aside the cardboard box. "I didn't even know it was going to be shaped like a dog. Here, let me show you the extra features." Removing his foot from the coffee table, Phoenix leaned forward and placed his hands on the box beside Aerielle's. "You can open the box if you want to, either to remove some of the ashes or if you decide to scatter them. It works like a puzzle." While he didn't actually open the box, he showed her how it worked and explained how to seal it up again. "There is also a little built in drawer carved along the back. You press it and it springs open, like this."

A small rounded drawer popped open, revealing a tuft of fur inside.

A startled "Oh!" escaped Aerielle's lips, and Phoenix heard so much pain in that tiny word.

"I saved a little bit of his fur in case you wanted it," explained Phoenix. "If you saved any of his baby teeth, you can put them in the drawer as well."

With her head bowed, Phoenix couldn't see Aerielle's face, but he watched with empathy as she removed the fur and caressed it with her fingers. Gently, she placed it back in the box and closed the drawer. As the miniature hiding place disappeared, a single tear landed on the back Phoenix's hand.

"It's perfect," said Aerielle in a hoarse whisper. She raised a hand to wipe at her face, currently hidden by the fall of her hair.

Getting up from the coffee table, Phoenix walked to the desk and retrieved a box of tissues. He walked back to the couch, and this time, sat next to Aerielle. When he offered her the box, Aerielle set the Idaho "urn" aside and took the tissue box. Immediately she pulled out multiple tissues and pressed them to her still hidden face. Her shoulders began to shake even before the sound of her sobs reached Phoenix's ears.

The sound broke Phoenix's heart equally as much now as it had the night Idaho died. This time, however, he wasn't sure how to respond. For some reason when Aerielle'd pounded on him, comforting her had seemed the natural thing to do. Was it because she had made the first move? Was she waiting for him to make the first move this time?

Aw, heck, what would she do if she didn't want his comfort, hit him again? "Aerielle?" he soothed, reaching out and stroking her hair. Phoenix didn't know if it was the sound of his voice, the touch of his hand, or both, but Aerielle turned to him without hesitation. Phoenix wrapped his arms around her even as she pressed her face to his chest and her broken heart to his.

→→→

Aerielle sat on her bed, nestled against her pillows, Idaho, now in a wooden sanctuary, sitting in her lap. Despite the fact the lights were out, the moon was full and reflecting off the snow, filling the room with enough light that it was easy for Aerielle to read the dog's name carved into the collar. Aerielle couldn't count the number of times she'd wished Idaho were small enough to hold in her arms. How could a life having been lived so large have been reduced to something so small?

While Phoenix hadn't done the carving of the dog shaped urn, he had clearly wanted Aerielle to have something special to hold Idaho's remains. The gift alone told her what he hadn't actually said at any time in the recent past. He cared for her deeply. And as he'd wrapped her grief shaken form in his arms, she knew without a doubt what she'd been questioning for nigh on the same amount of time. She cared about him with the same intensity. Even when her grief had subsided, she hadn't wanted to leave those arms. Now sitting in her moonlit bedroom, with his gift in her arms, she was suffused in memories of the many nights they'd spent riding under the night sky.

He deserved a second chance. She'd always believed this. Now she believed they both deserved one, together. And what better place to explore the possibility than in Idaho. Aerielle knew without a doubt she was going. She didn't know how, but she wouldn't be stopped.

They will teach us to quarrel about God, as the Catholics and Protestants do on the Nez Perce reservation. We do not want to learn that. We may quarrel with men sometimes about things on this earth, but we never quarrel about God.

Chief Joseph to the Indian Commissioners, 1873 as quoted in *Chief Joseph Country, Land of the Nez Perce* by Bill Gulick

18

"So, how'd you manage it?" demanded Heather with a grin, bursting into Aerielle's office.

Aerielle glanced up from the report she was working on. "How'd I manage what?"

"Getting Christmas off, you sneak."

"Oh, that. Word sure does get around fast."

"So how'd you do it?" repeated Heather, leaning with both hands on Aerielle's desk.

"A lot of horse trading, most of it with Dr. Ginsberg who happens to be Jewish. And since I was already scheduled off the first week of January, I got myself a two week vacation."

"You lucky dog, you. Why do I have the feeling this sudden change of plans has to do with Phoenix?"

Aerielle smiled up at Heather. "Because it does."

"Is that all you're going to tell me?"

"Let's just say we were once very much in love."

"I gathered something like that," replied Heather, "And then you dated his brother."

"I was foolish."

"And getting involved with Phoenix again, isn't?"

Aerielle shook her head. "Did anyone ever tell you you're nosy?"

"It's not something I needed to be told. Is this trip the kind

I think it is? The soul searching, heart wrenching, what's in the future kind?"

"Do you blame me?"

"If your feelings for him are as strong as I suspect, you've already started packing."

Aerielle played with her pen guiltily.

Heather laughed, grinning from ear to ear.

"I'm scared, Heather," said Aerielle abruptly.

Heather's smile faded. "You *should* be. Merry Christmas, Aerielle."

→→→

He was dreaming of *her* again. Aerielle. Her eyes were wide with terror, the imaginary night filled with her screams. Phoenix struggled to get to her but found himself pounding uselessly against an invisible wall.

The phone woke him, startling him into a sitting position. His flesh was aglow with sweat, his hair clinging to his skin. Throwing the covers off, Phoenix slid off the bed. McCoy was sitting up as Phoenix stepped into the hallway to get the phone. His watch said it was early yet, only 11:00. He'd only been in bed an hour, then.

His "hello" was greeted by, "Phoenix it's me."

Surprised by her voice and still caught by the webs of his dream, Phoenix blurted. "Aerielle are you all right?!"

"I'm fine. Why?"

Phoenix bit his lip, wishing consciousness had completely returned before he had spoken, especially when his brother opened his bedroom door and looked on with concern, using sign to ask what was wrong.

Phoenix signed, "Nothing," back as he spoke into the phone. "Um, nothing. I don't know why I said that." Talk about lame.

"Phoenix, you sound tired. Did I wake you? I did, didn't I? I'll can call back tomorrow."

"No. Please. I *want* to talk to you."

Hawk remained in his doorway, crossing his arms and leaning against the jamb.

"Well, I'm sorry I called so late, but it's been a long day and this was the first chance I got."

"It's no problem."

"It's about Christmas," she abruptly announced.

She sounded terrified. What if she was about to tell him no? Phoenix gripped the phone tighter and leaned against the wall for support. "And?"

"I got Christmas off—"

Yes!

"But I can't leave till the 23rd."

"The 23rd," repeated Phoenix, his thoughts racing ahead as he began pacing the hallway. "How long can you stay?"

"Till the 8th, if I'm wanted."

Thank you, sweet Jesus.

"Is that gonna work out at all?" asked Aerielle. "I know it's not ideal—"

"We'll *make* it work. Hawk and I will figure out the details," assured Phoenix, turning and looking at his brother. "You just have your bags packed and ready at the crack of dawn on the 23rd."

"I'll be waiting with bells on." Her voice was filled with nervous laughter, and Phoenix understood how she felt.

"You do that," he replied with a calm he didn't feel.

Phoenix hung up the phone under the watchful scrutiny of his brother. "She's coming?" asked Hawk.

Phoenix nodded, brushing a hand through his hair. "But she can't leave until the 23rd."

"When does she have to be back?"

"Not until the 8th. I told her we'd make it work," said Phoenix, knowing Hawk had already heard him say that.

"But?"

"But I don't know if you're going to like my solution."

Hawk's eyes narrowed.

"I was thinking you and Sofia could leave for Idaho the 19th and start back the on the 2nd. Aerielle and I can leave the 23rd and return by the 7th.

"You're right. I don't like the idea. Who knows what you might say or do with that much time alone with her."

"I know you're worried because I already broke her heart once."

"You're darn right I'm worried. But it's really up to Aerielle. Also," continued Hawk, dropping his arms to his sides, "I don't think you can hurt her worse than before."

Phoenix winced. "A couple of weeks ago you asked me if I still cared for her and I said yes. The truth is, I love her, Hawk. I never stopped. I just want a chance to win her back."

"Well, the fact that she's agreed to come tells me she's willing to let you try. If you're both willing, who am I to stand in the way?" Stepping forward, Hawk placed a hand on Phoenix's shoulder and squeezed. "For both your sakes, I hope you succeed."

→→→

It was a clear day in Minneapolis on the morning of the 23rd, clear in that the sky was clear of clouds. On the other hand, it was still dark out at five in the morning. Despite this, Phoenix felt like the sun was shining anyway. As soon as he and Aerielle pulled out of the driveway, he would have her all to himself for most of the next two days. They hadn't talked much since the night she'd called. Her schedule had been hectic with the coming holiday. Phoenix grinned. Things were about to change.

"Think you got enough stuff?" asked Tyler standing amongst the luggage and other paraphernalia piled in the kitchen.

Phoenix smiled at the boy. "Wrapped presents take up a lot of space. It's a good thing Hawk and Sofia took some of them in my truck."

Stroking Esmeralda, content in his arms, Tyler grinned

impishly. "What if Aerielle gets here and her truck is full up of her own stuff? If she packs like my Mom...."

"I'll just send you out to load, and if something doesn't fit, you can toss something of Aerielle's out."

Tyler laughed. "Wish I was going. Never been that far west."

Phoenix studied Tyler, this young man he'd grown so fond of over the months. He'd changed since they had met, in part because he'd grown two inches. In addition he'd matured as a result of Aerielle and Idaho. Phoenix couldn't have been more proud of him had he been his own son. Even the idea of taking Aerielle back to Idaho had been Tyler's.

"I'll make you a promise, Tyler. The next time I make a trip home, I'll do everything in my power to take you along. If anyone deserves to go, it's you."

"Really? That'd be awesome."

"In the meantime," said Phoenix, "I want you to know how much Hawk and I appreciate you coming over every day and spending time with the cats while we're gone. If anything comes up—"

"Yeah, yeah, I know the drill," interrupted Tyler. "You left me a pile of instructions, and I have the phone number for your parents and the emergency vet clinic, and I gave my mom copies of everything."

"Sorry," said Phoenix, "It's just that I worry about Esmeralda."

"Because she's old or because she was a gift from Aerielle?"

"Smart Alec. You know it's both. But speaking of gifts, what can I bring you back from Idaho?"

"Something made by the Nez Perce? Something cool I can hang on my wall."

"That shouldn't be a problem. As long as it fits in the truck."

They laughed in unison. The movement woke Esmeralda, and she escaped from Tyler's arms. At the same time, there was the sound of a large vehicle pulling up the Stargazer driveway.

"Good luck with Aerielle," offered Tyler, "I hope it works out."

"Thanks, Tyler. Hey, am I allowed to hug you goodbye?"

Tyler shrugged. "I suppose. But you better do it now. If Aerielle sees you, she might take it upon herself to rub my hair."

Phoenix hugged Tyler and slapped him on the shoulder, and then just to get a rise out of him, tousled his hair.

"Hey!" said Tyler, batting at his hand.

"Hey, what?" asked Aerielle, abruptly appearing in the doorway from outside, a draft of cold air following her into the crowded kitchen.

Both Tyler and Phoenix stared at her. "Is it my imagination or is she wearing jingle bells in her hair?" asked Tyler

Closing the back door, Aerielle grinning mischievously and shook her head. The gold and silver bells in her hair tinkled with Christmas cheer. "I did say I'd be waiting with bells on. Instead I'm *arriving* with bells on."

Phoenix smiled back. "I like it."

"I'm sure glad you and Hawk decided to leave the dogs with friends. We need a lot of stuff for two weeks, not to mention bringing Christmas presents," she added, glancing around the kitchen.

"You want to help load?" Phoenix asked Tyler.

"Heck, yeah."

The three of them had the truck loaded for bear in no time. With the packing complete, they locked up the house, leaving Tyler with the spare keys. It was 5:45, but there was still no sign of the sunrise. Standing beside the truck in the chill winter air, Tyler gave Phoenix and Aerielle a satisfied look. "I think you guys have everything you need. My work here is done."

Phoenix bit back a smile. If it were up to Tyler, he and Aerielle would return to Minnesota married and with child.

"Unh, unh," said Aerielle eyeing Tyler. "I would like a proper goodbye. After all, I won't see you again until next year. And gosh, by then you'll be fourteen."

Tyler eyed her warily. "And what is a proper goodbye?"

"How about a hug?" she asked, holding out her arms.

Phoenix watched as the almost 14-year-old Tyler swaggered over to her as nonchalantly as you please and hugged Aerielle like he did it all the time. Grinning, he looked at Phoenix and winked. The little snot. He was deliberately teasing him about the fact that Aerielle was hugging him, when he knew darn well Phoenix was wishing she would hug *him*.

Phoenix pretended to glare at Tyler and then nearly burst out laughing when Aerielle finished off the hug with a hand to his hair. "Sorry, Tyler," he heard Aerielle say, "but you'll be too old for that when I get back. You have a good Christmas. I hope you get whatever it is you want from 'Santa.'"

Stepping back, Tyler nodded, his grin now a gentle smile. "I hope you get what you want, too."

→→→

If they ever made it to Idaho, who knew when they'd get there. They certainly wouldn't arrive at their halfway point as planned. It was growing harder to keep their speed up as each hour of the day wore on and they drove into snowfall. They'd covered nearly six-hundred miles, both Phoenix and Aerielle taking turns at the wheel. Their conversation had remained light and companionable until the snow began to get so thick that driving took too much concentration.

"We're never gonna make it to Billings," said Phoenix, peering over the steering wheel into snow-pelting darkness. "Doesn't look like we're even going to make the Montana border. It's already eight o'clock, and with the way this storm is going, we won't get much farther."

Aerielle nodded in agreement, unconsciously gripping the arm rest as she, too, attempted to see out. "We should probably find a place to stay while we can. We'll just have to call the Best Western in Billings and cancel our reservations."

"About a mile back I think I saw a sign for a motel up ahead. It should be coming up soon."

Phoenix's memory served them well, and shortly they were

pulling into a semi-truck-lined parking lot next to a small motel and diner. Neon signs and twinkling Christmas lights glowed warmly in the windows of the diner, welcoming weary, hungry travelers. Phoenix pulled Aerielle's truck in front of the motel office, and the two of them hurried inside carrying a bit of the storm with them as they brushed snow from their clothes.

"Well, you're just in the nick of time," announced the smiling gum-snapping woman behind the counter. Before either Aerielle or Phoenix had a chance to say anything, she added, "We got one room left. That'll be forty-five dollars."

She received no response as Phoenix and Aerielle instantly glanced at each other, the words "only one room left" repeating themselves over and over again. If there'd been something to trip over or spill, Aerielle was sure she would have.

"We could try farther up the road," suggested Phoenix, motioning towards the door.

"You won't find anything here abouts," cautioned the woman behind the counter.

Aerielle didn't know what to say. She glanced at Phoenix. "What do *you* think?"

He wasn't. Spending a night alone in a motel room with Aerielle was not something Phoenix had planned on *needing* to think about, for whatever reason. Now that circumstances had decided otherwise, Phoenix felt himself torn between logic and emotion. Logic won. "I guess I think maybe we should be grateful for what's available and deal with it."

"I agree."

"Number 5," said the woman, slapping a key down on the counter. "Will that be cash or charge?"

Phoenix and Aerielle exchanged few words as, minutes later, they unloaded what luggage they'd need. Setting the bags down in the green and yellow room, Phoenix glanced nervously at the single double bed. How was he supposed to *deal* with *that*?

"You hungry?" he asked. Turning to Aerielle, he found she, too, was staring at the bed.

"Ravenous," she agreed, nodding her head vigorously, the bells chiming in her hair.

"Then let's see what the diner has to offer."

The diner. Aerielle clung gratefully to the word as they made their way through the snowy parking lot.

"Ellie's Diner" greeted them in pink Neon at the door before they stepped in out of the cold. The place was busy, mostly with truckers, many likely heading home for the holidays.

"Come on in, you two," called a blond fiftyish looking woman in a pink waitress uniform. "I'll get this table cleared and you can have a seat. Busy night, but there's always room."

"You got room anywhere else, Ellie?" demanded a large man with a baseball cap tipped back on his head.

"You watch your mouth, Bill Andrews, or I'll see that your room is rented out from under ya."

"Aw, Ellie."

"Don't 'aw, Ellie' me, and no more kissing my waitresses under the mistletoe."

Sitting down at the table indicated, Aerielle glanced around, noticing the mistletoe Ellie spoke of. There was also a Christmas tree blinking away in one corner and holiday music playing joyously in the background.

"Roads must be gettin' meaner out there," remarked a gray haired man at an adjacent table.

Phoenix nodded, sliding his coat from his shoulders. "It's pretty wicked out there all right. We were hoping to make it to Billings tonight."

"You're lucky you got as far as you did. May not even get outta here till noon tomorrow. The wife'll just have to keep dinner warm."

"Coffee, you two?" inquired Ellie, arriving with a pot and two cups.

Both Phoenix and Aerielle nodded.

"Here's your menus. The special tonight is meatloaf, mashed potatoes, and green beans with jingle bell cookies. Only my bells are edible," she added, nodding toward Aerielle's hair. "Take your time deciding, and I'll be back."

Phoenix suddenly realized he wasn't hungry, but he went through the motion of studying his menu anyway. In the end he decided on the special. Aerielle ordered an egg salad sandwich and french fries with gravy.

"Want some?" she offered several minutes later, sliding the plate in his direction.

Phoenix suspected she wasn't really hungry either. He helped himself to the offering, wondering why it was so hard to think of something to talk about after not having any problem all day.

"How's your meatloaf?" asked Aerielle, unknowingly rubbing at her eyes.

"It's fine. And your egg salad?"

"Fine."

Aerielle yawned, picking at the food on her plate.

"You seem tired," said Phoenix, forgetting himself.

"Tired? Oh, no," assured Aerielle, "I'm not tired...I'm not bored either, I'm just...yawning. Is that White Christmas playing now? I really like that song. It's one of my favorites."

Phoenix paused, a french fry halfway to his mouth. "Your favorite is Oh Little Town of Bethlehem."

The tension suddenly increased, becoming almost tangible. Aerielle stared at him, forgetting the music. "Your memory serves you well."

Phoenix's eyes were dark pools of memory, the past revealed there. "That's debatable," he said. "Some things are better forgotten."

Aerielle smiled sadly. "And what of the other things? Are they lost forever?"

"Jingle bell cookies, anyone?" asked Ellie, plopping down a plate.

Aerielle looked away, wondering how they'd let the conversation get so serious. Grateful for the interruption, she busied herself with her sandwich and prayed for another reprieve. It came as the man adjacent to them engaged Phoenix and Ellie in conversation.

The evening dragged on, their barely emptied plates taken away, and their coffee refilled innumerable times. The conversation, having become stilted once again, had been made easier by their friendly neighbor who seemed to enjoy a good chat. But it was getting close to ten o'clock. Both Phoenix and Aerielle were tired though neither were willing to admit it. Having downed too many cups of coffee, Aerielle escaped to the bathroom.

"That's a mighty pretty woman you got there," said the older man, glancing at the departing Aerielle.

Phoenix nodded. "She is at that."

"You mentioned you were heading to Idaho. What's there?"

"My family."

"Hmm, *Your* folks, huh?" said the man, looking thoughtful. "You and her just get married or something?"

Phoenix nearly spilled his coffee. "What makes you say that?"

"Just watching you two. You can't keep your eyes off her. She can't take her eyes off you. Yet, here you sit nursin' your coffee, glancing at your watches, and rattlin' on about nothin'. You're actin' like a pair of old-fashioned virginal newlyweds afraid of being alone together."

Phoenix swallowed hard, grimacing. "No. We didn't just get married."

"That's too bad."

Turning back to his paper, the man left Phoenix to his thoughts. If the old guy only knew.

One thing was for sure, he and Aerielle weren't gaining anything but more stress the longer they sat in the diner. They were only putting off the inevitable, whatever that was to be. Phoenix pulled his wallet from his back pocket, determined to end this. Tossing enough bills on the table to more than cover the bill and a healthy tip, Phoenix stood and slid his coat on. He was waiting with Aerielle's coat in hand when she returned. He saw a glimpse of panic in her eyes for just a second before she turned and allowed him to help her on with her jacket.

Snow was still falling as they crossed the parking lot in silence. Neither said a word as they entered the motel room. Aerielle switched a light on and Phoenix shut the door behind them. Sliding her coat off, Aerielle's jingle bells rang almost discordantly.

"I guess I better take these out or neither one of us will get any sleep."

Phoenix could tell she regretted the words the moment she spoke them.

Phoenix ignored her remark. "Can I hang up your coat?"

Without looking back at him, Aerielle held it out to him before marching into the bathroom, her hands already working on her hair. She shut the door with her foot, clearly eager to escape.

Phoenix couldn't blame her. He wasn't quite sure what to do with *himself*. He tried turning on the small TV to gather some weather information, but whatever form of reception the motel used, was also under attack by the storm. Phoenix shut off the fuzzy TV, noting it's age. It hadn't even come with a remote. In fact, the whole room looked as if it hadn't changed at all in the time since Phoenix and Aerielle had met. Even by the one light Aerielle had switched on, he could clearly see the carpet was worn and discolored and the bed itself looked tired with its threadbare spread. There was only one chair in the room, straight backed and wooden, and it looked like a spare from a dining room set. If Aerielle and he had stayed together for the last fourteen years, would their relationship have deteriorated like this? Somehow he doubted it.

With nothing else worth looking at except the view, Phoenix flipped off the light Aerielle had turned on and went to stand in front of the window by the door. Even with the curtains wide open, there wasn't much to see, except a cascade of snow backlit by the diner's steady light and the twinkle of Christmas bulbs.

It was beautiful, even soothing, but it failed to ease Phoenix's anxieties. What kind of situation had he and Aerielle gotten themselves into? Being alone in the truck was one thing, being alone in a motel room was another.

Even the guy at the diner had figured out they were avoiding coming back here. What exactly were old-fashioned virginal newlyweds, anyway? Was that supposed to be a couple who'd just gotten married and hadn't consummated it yet? One thing was for sure, he and Aerielle weren't virgins. As for the newlywed part, Phoenix wondered if spending six hours together out of fourteen years of marriage constituted as newlyweds, especially considering Aerielle wasn't even aware the marriage was valid.

Aerielle. Phoenix sighed as his thoughts went back to the night they'd exchanged their vows.

→→→

> Midnight. A clear sky lit with thousands of stars. Stars Phoenix barely noticed as he stood by the barn with Morning Dew and Steel, waiting for Aerielle.
>
> Aerielle. The woman who was to be his wife. Phoenix was awed by her consent of not twelve hours ago. She had instantly suggested a marriage beneath the canopy of night that had brought life to their love, while he had shared his desire to experience the ceremony of his ancestors. Their decision to marry tonight had been one made out of conviction and out of love. Having agreed to join their lives, it seemed only appropriate to limit the days and hours of what remained of their aloneness.

There was no thought of the past or of the future. They were living for today, for each other. One man, one woman, who loved.

Phoenix watched the darkened house with a mixture of anticipation and anxiety. How else did one feel when one was about to exchange those vows that would tie him to another for a lifetime?

Phoenix was eager to see his bride, who like himself had chosen to wear native clothing for the ceremony. Phoenix was dressed in a set of fringed buckskins. Aerielle would be wearing a dress he had borrowed for her.

There was the whisper of footsteps. Phoenix turned. Aerielle was a vision, the soft white elk skin dress with elk's teeth fitting her graceful form perfectly. Fringe brushed her moccasin clothed calves. Her corn silk hair shimmered in the moonlight and the scent of hyacinths carried to him on the gentle breeze as she approached. He'd never seen her so beautiful.

"Aerielle," his voice filled the stillness as Aerielle stopped before him.

She smiled.

Less than thirty minutes later they stood upon familiar ground, the place they'd witnessed so many sights within the heavens, the place they'd shared so many secrets and dreams.

Phoenix gazed at Aerielle as she stood before him, unable to believe she was here. It had all happened so fast, without planning or forethought. But what was there to plan? They loved. She would be his. He would be hers. Their lives were to be reborn.

"Phoenix?" murmured Aerielle, her eyes questioning.

Phoenix reached out, taking her hands in his, her skin warm and soft against his calloused flesh. "Tonight, Aerielle, you will call me *Hemene Moxmox*, Yellow Wolf."

Aerielle's eyes glowed. "I would be honored."

His heart ready to burst with love, Phoenix continued. "And I will call you Meyui, Morning Light, because you brighten each of my days and have done so since the day you arrived."

"Even when you thought you hated me?" teased Aerielle.

Phoenix grinned. "Even then. You were a challenge I looked forward to despite myself."

Aerielle laughed. "You fooled me."

"But not God," said Phoenix. "And you were praying."

"So what does it take to become a Nez Perce wife?"

Phoenix shifted, his expression thoughtful. "Many of our ceremonies are not meant to be shared with other than our people, Meyui. Promise me you won't tell anyone the details of what takes place here tonight."

Aerielle squeezed Phoenix's hands, her eyes wide and as open as her soul. "I promise."

At that moment a cloud passed before the moon, dimming the light of night as if in acquiescence to Phoenix's wish for privacy.

It was not a long ceremony, or a complicated one. Standing before God, they pledged their lives together, and the night soon echoed with age old words, *Inepne hanisa. Hama hanisa.* I take you for wife. I take you for husband.

> Where there had been two, there became but one, in word as well as in flesh. Hemene and Meyui consummated their marriage beneath the stars that night, wrapped in the warmth of blankets and each other's arms.

→→→

Aerielle stared into the bathroom mirror, knowing that despite how tired she looked and felt, getting to sleep was going to be difficult tonight, and she couldn't stay in the bathroom forever. Nor for that matter did she want to. She just wanted the awkwardness between Phoenix and her to go away. If they could just shut off the memories until they arrived in Shaman Prairie. Both the good and the bad, for first he'd loved her... and then he'd left her. Aerielle covered her face with her hands wanting to scream. How could someone who had hurt her so profoundly and angered her for so much time, elicit the same feelings from her now as he had in the innocence of their youth?

Pulling her hands away, Aerielle stared at her reflection. She looked awful. Her makeup had worn off, her eyes looked haunted, and the dark circles underneath made her look like she was dying. And then there was her hair. Getting the bells out had been a lot harder than putting them in. In fact, one lone bell had refused her entreaties to let go. It was on the only part of hair that wasn't spiraling in one direction or another from the abuse it had endured today.

Not having brought a brush into the bathroom, Aerielle used her fingers to comb through the mess as well as she could. She then took a deep breath, slapped off the light switch, and yanked the bathroom door open.

Darkness greeted her, but it wasn't complete, for as her eyes adjusted she saw Phoenix standing in front of the window watching the snow whisper past. The changing lights of Christmas flickered across his face, and in the perfect profile she could see the bump in his nose where it had been broken. The fortifying breath of air Aerielle had taken wooshed out.

"The snow's mesmerizing," said Phoenix not moving. "Kind of like you."

Kind of like her? She was the one staring at *him*. Shaking her head to free herself of said desire to stare, Aerielle heard the minute tinkle of the remaining bell in her hair.

She walked over to him, saying, "Can you help me get this one bell free? It appears to be trapped."

Phoenix turned as she joined him at the window. "Hey," he smiled. "Love the hair."

"Don't tease."

"I wasn't. I like the way it curls." He reached out, pulling a strand straight and then releasing it. Looking at him in the soft light of the window, Aerielle wished she had a reason to reach out and play with *his* hair.

"So where's that bell?" asked Phoenix.

Aerielle turned sideways, raising a hand to touch the offending item. Phoenix stepped closer, his fingers brushing hers as their hands traded places in her hair.

"Do you need a light on?" she asked, while at the same time closing her eyes at his touch.

"No, there's plenty from the window. What did you do, sew these bells in with surgical stitches?"

"You bet. I wanted to show off my skills."

Phoenix was concentrating on her hair, so Aerielle was not surprised when he didn't respond. Responding was what *she* was doing. He was standing so close she could feel his body heat, as well as his breath against her hair. Occasionally his arm would brush against her shoulder sending shivers everywhere. Worse yet was when he leaned just so and his hair brushed the side of her face.

What had she been thinking asking for his help. She'd have been better off if she'd taken a pair of scissors and hacked the bell off. They hadn't even spoken of the past yet, uncovered the truths which lay there. Phoenix'd told Hawk he needed to talk to Aerielle about things, and that he still cared for her. But just how much did he care? What couldn't he have said in Minnesota? Why invite her to Idaho?

"Got it," said Phoenix, but he didn't sound pleased.

"Why?" asked Aerielle, taking a step back so she could see his face.

Surprised by her sudden movement, Phoenix dropped the bell, but he didn't look to see where it fell. He was silently cursing the distance Aerielle had just put between them. He had taken as much time as he could to get that bell out of her hair just so he could be near her. Had he been that obvious? Was she asking him why he'd done it?

"Why...." he began, stretching out the word and hoping she'd fill in the rest.

"Why did you ask me to come?"

Phoenix met her gaze squarely, taking in her beautiful face. He did not pretend to misunderstand. Her question was as clear as a mountain spring, as simple as the answer that lay in his heart waiting for release. "Because I love you. Because I've always loved you and I always will."

The answer was more than Aerielle had expected, more than she was prepared for. She looked away, besieged by his overwhelming honesty, unmitigated joy and absolute confusion fighting for control of her emotions.

Phoenix suddenly wondered how he had kept those words inside all these months. He felt as if he had been mute and just gained the ability to speak. But in reality, it was his heart which had spoken. Exposed, he reached for Aerielle, longing to know what she was thinking.

Gently he placed his hand beneath her chin, turning her to face him. Their gazes collided, stealing Phoenix's breath and annihilating his better judgement. Without thought, Phoenix lowered his mouth to Aerielle's, his lips brushing hers in gentle reverence. He kissed her as if he'd never kissed her before, tasting, testing, teasing. Aerielle's mouth parted tentatively beneath his and Phoenix was lost. The kiss was no longer gentle, but fervent. Aerielle's hands tangled themselves in the thick mass of his hair as Phoenix at last pulled her into his long-empty arms.

Aerielle thought she'd be crushed by Phoenix's embrace, yet was willing to die there. He loved her. He always had. The pain from the past was not due to lack of love, and that was all Aerielle needed to know at that moment.

Several more impassioned kisses followed, or was it just one long kiss with no beginning and no end. Phoenix and Aerielle's longing for each was only magnified by the years of separation after having loved so hard and hurt so long.

It was unclear who ended the timeless kiss first, or if it was in accord, but unwilling to let her go, Phoenix began pressing kisses to the golden spirals of her hair.

Aerielle buried her face against Phoenix's mane cloaked shoulder, her heart pounding in her ears, or was it his. They stood thus, holding each other, until at last the relentless pounding of their hearts began to slow, and the breathless quality to their breathing dissipated.

"Aerielle...." Phoenix began, at last releasing her. "I'm gonna go back to the diner for a minute and see if anyone's gotten an update on the weather.

"Yeah, okay," she murmured, her thoughts racing as fast as her heart had been.

She was glad when Phoenix left, for she was overwhelmed by all the emotions crashing onto the shores of her heart.

Suddenly realizing she was still standing in front of the window, Aerielle quickly moved away. Heaven forbid she was still standing there when Phoenix returned.

Aerielle had no idea what to do next. There really wasn't anything *to* do next. And if there was, she was too exhausted to do it. Overall, it would probably be the least awkward if she just went to bed before Phoenix got back. It wouldn't require anything other than removing her boots, and maybe, just maybe, her socks.

In the end, she tucked her socks inside her boots, leaving them lined up under her coat, and crawled into the one and only bed. She crossed to the other side, farther from the door, a whole knees length away farther. Sliding under the covers, she lay on her side facing the door. Surprisingly the mattress was not as bad as she'd expected, and the sheets were soft and smelled like, well, like fabric softener.

Aerielle inhaled deeply of the pleasant scent, trying to calm her mind and emotions, the one thought she'd had when Phoenix kissed her seared into her brain. He loved her...still. That meant there was still a chance...a hope...for a future. Aerielle closed her eyes, the taste of Phoenix's kiss still upon her mouth, while his declaration of love engulfed her heart. She'd wanted to hear from his own lips why he'd asked her to come. His lips had definitely told her.

"Oh, God, please," Aerielle whispered. "Let it be so. I've spent enough of my life without him. Let us get through the past so we can have a future. Just as you forgive, let Hemene and I find that same forgiveness from one another."

Aerielle grew lost in prayer, and it was the sound of the key in the door that abruptly silenced her. She peered into the darkened room through the sweep of her lashes, hoping he'd think she was asleep. His back was to her, his hair blanketed in snow. Taking off his coat, he hung it on a hanger, and then brushed the snow from his hair.

He turned and Aerielle closed her eyes again. She felt the movement of the bed as he sat down, and listened as he removed his boots. Would he leave his socks on or off? Aerielle suddenly found the question ridiculously funny. She bit her lip to keep from laughing. Was she getting slaphappy?

She barely noticed as he got into bed and pulled up the covers until suddenly there was no sound at all. Minutes ticked by, loudly, Aerielle listening for the sound of his breathing. She heard nothing, and in the end opened her eyes again. He was on his back, but as if drawn by the simple movement of her lashes, he turned his head to look at her.

"Can I ask you something," he said simply.

Aerielle couldn't help herself. "You want to know whether I'm wearing socks or not?"

Phoenix stared at her a moment and then actually chuckled. "*Are* you?" he asked rolling onto his side so he was facing her.

"No. You?"

"Uh huh."

"So," said Aerielle, studying his handsome visage in the near darkness. "What did you really want to know?"

There was still enough light coming in from the window for Aerielle to see his expression grow contemplative.

"I guess I wanted to ask you almost the same question you asked me. "Why did you agree to come?"

Aerielle glanced away, knowing full well what he was asking, but wondering if she dared be so honest.

"If you're not ready to answer, it's okay. I realize what I'm asking you goes a lot deeper than what you asked me. After all, I was the one who walked away. I was the one who hurt you."

There was such pain in Phoenix's voice, he sounded physically injured. Aerielle jerked her head up, studying his face, which for a change was not unreadable, but naked with pain and regret. Aerielle sucked in a deep breath at the sight of it. And then she spoke.

"I came because I want to have those conversations we should have had fourteen years ago. I came because I want to offer up the past for healing. I came, because despite how angry I was at you, despite the fact I may have even hated you at times, I still have feelings for you."

Phoenix didn't know what to say. The hope rising in him was near to bursting. The only thought he'd had while kissing her had been the fear she'd pull away, maybe yell at him, even slap him. Instead it had been nothing like that. She had kissed him back with as much ardor as he had pursued those soft, delicate lips of hers. All this despite the fact she'd just admitted to having hated him at times. She was seeking healing, seeking truth, wanting to have the discussion she didn't know the half of. Actually, she had said conversations. Plural. Well, they could have as many conversations as she wanted, if he could only find absolution. Dear sweet Jesus, he wanted her forgiveness.

God, she was looking at him with such angst. Phoenix thought to speak, but he didn't have words. "I...don't know what to say, Aerielle," he admitted, feeling utterly helpless.

Instead of the hurt he expected to see, her expression blossomed into one of sheer tenderness, and reaching out with her hand, she gently caressed his face. Phoenix was humbled to the depths of his soul.

"I like what you said earlier," whispered Aerielle, her voice a rasp of emotion, "and I wouldn't mind hearing it again."

What was she saying? What had— She wanted him to declare his love for her?! Again?! Phoenix was overcome with disbelief.

Taking a moment to unlock his voice, Phoenix took her hand from his face, and placed it against his mouth, kissing her palm. Then pressing her hand to his heart, he spoke the easiest words in all the world. "I love you, Meyui. I always have. I always will."

She spoke no words in return, but the look in her eyes spoke for her, and Phoenix couldn't get enough of them. Couldn't get enough of her. He wanted to make love to her, this woman, his wife. But as far as she knew, he had never been her husband, and this was definitely not a good time to disavow her of her truth. So instead, they lay there in silence, their gazes locked, Phoenix, at least, unwilling to look away or release the hand he still held.

Aerielle finally broke the passage of electrified time. "We're never gonna go to sleep, are we?"

"Not likely," grimaced Phoenix, freeing her hand at last

and rolling onto his back, putting another whole eight to ten inches between them. Reaching up, he ran his hands through his tangled hair in aggravation.

"I could go sleep in the bathtub," remarked Aerielle, smiling despite the tension that had gathered.

Laughter tugged at Phoenix's lips and then he sobered. "You could sleep in the truck Aerielle and it wouldn't matter. The only place I want you is in my arms."

Phoenix had no idea what he'd expected her to say in response, but he hadn't even considered she would *do* something in response. Before he could react, she'd slid over and settled against his side, placed the hand he'd just been holding on his chest, and rested her head upon his heart.

His hands still in his hair, Phoenix momentarily froze. Then with a deep sigh he expelled the breath he'd been holding, and lowered his arms to cradle his precious Meyui. He closed his eyes tight against the tears that suddenly pooled there. This—was the farthest from Hell he'd been in fourteen years. "*Taz ziketin*, Meyui. Sweet dreams."

As long as the sky is blue
and the grass is green
and the water flows
this land is ours.

Nez Perce Treaty of 1855

19

It was nearing ten o'clock the next evening when Phoenix brought Aerielle's pickup to a halt in front of his parents' home. This night was as clear as the last had been obscured. In addition, all the outdoor lights were lit up in welcome. Phoenix glanced at Aerielle who remained unaware, lost as she was in the world of sleep. She sat almost facing him, one leg curled up on the seat, the back of which had been reclined and a small pillow placed beneath her head. She looked exceedingly peaceful, and Phoenix felt almost guilty waking her.

He called her name and patted her leg. "It's time to wake up Aerielle. We're here."

She awoke instantly, most likely waiting for just such an announcement. "We're here," she said, repeating his words, her eyes alight with excitement. "I can't wait to see Sparrow. She said she'd be waiting no matter how late we were."

"I can't wait to see her either," said Phoenix, reaching for his door handle. "My little sister. Pregnant. I guess she's not so little anymore. She's all grown up."

"You were here for the wedding," teased Aerielle, raising her seatback.

"Yeah, well, I had trouble processing that, too."

Before either of them could say anything else, the back door of the house was thrown wide. Three men, dressed for the cold, stepped out with warm smiles, ready to welcome them and assist with the unloading.

Aerielle recognized all of them, though she'd only seen Sparrow's husband Jared in photographs. Nevin and Jared headed for Phoenix, his stepfather wrapping his arms around Phoenix and giving his back a good slapping. Aerielle saw nothing more as Hawk pulled her up off the ground and into a bear hug. "Who'd have thunk it, but I've missed you. No one around here's been throwing food on the floor."

"I'll see what I can do," laughed Aerielle with difficulty, just having had the air crushed out of her.

Hawk promptly planted a friendly kiss on her forehead and set her down, though he didn't release her right away. Instead he leaned his head down to hers, his mouth to her ear, his demeanor serious. "So how was the trip?"

Aerielle smiled in appreciation of his concern and whispered back. "It went well."

"Phoenix didn't hurt you? I mean your feelings? He didn't say or do anything stupid, did he? I mean, I can punch him again if I have to."

"He was...perfect. We saved the difficult stuff for when we got here."

"Good, because I was kinda worried the state of your hair was a result of you sticking your finger into a socket because of him."

Aerielle giggled, pulling back to look Hawk in the face. "I braided my hair up with jingle bells for our Christmas departure."

Hawk was grinning. "Why does that not surprise me?"

"Quit hogging her, Hawk," came Nevin's voice, as he approached them with Jared beside him.

Both Aerielle and Hawk looked up and over, over Nevin's shoulder where they could see Phoenix, who did not look in the least pleased.

"I think I've just been daggered," said Hawk, just before releasing Aerielle and stepping back. He headed for Phoenix despite the look, and Aerielle was the recipient of a much more traditional hug from Nevin. He hadn't changed much except his hair. Where he used to wear it long and tied back, it was now cut short. It did nothing to diminish the evidence of his lineage.

"Good to see you Aerielle," he said, stepping back. I couldn't have been more surprised to find out you were in Minneapolis, even though I knew my daughter and you'd been writing for years. Speaking of which, this here is—"

"Jared," finished Aerielle, smiling at the young man beside Nevin. "I would recognize you anywhere, with all the photos Sparrow has sent."

"She likes her pictures," agreed Jared somewhat shyly, his eyes slightly hidden by a sweep of brown hair that fell over his forehead.

Shyness aside, he held out his hand and Aerielle shook it.

"I don't mean to treat you like the sideshow, Jared, but Sparrow is here, isn't she?"

Jared smiled and nodded. "You're all she's been talking about. Labor pains couldn't keep her away. She's inside with her mom and Sofia."

"They're laying out a late Christmas eve feast," assured Nevin. "Figured you two would be starved."

"Definitely," agreed Aerielle. "Since we got such a late start this morning, we barely took time to stop. We were both in agreement we wanted to arrive on Christmas eve. We didn't want Christmas day arriving before we did."

"Guess you cleared it by two hours," said Jared.

"Why don't you go on in and gab it up with the ladies," Nevin added, pointing toward the door. "The boys and I'll take care of the unloading."

Aerielle's eyes lit up, and after a hurried thank you, she headed for the door.

Phoenix watched her go, feeling a touch of disappointment that his time of having Aerielle to himself was over.

"Glad you made it home safe," said Hawk. "You encountered all the snow Sofia and I never saw."

Phoenix glanced at his brother, mild annoyance in his eyes. "Looked like you were *really* glad to see Aerielle."

Hawk nodded knowingly. "I saw the look you were giving me. Hang it, Phoenix, I wasn't flirtin' with her. I missed her, that's all. Well, that and I wanted to find out how the trip went."

"How the trip went with me, you mean," Phoenix grumbled.

Hawk shrugged. "Had to find out if I needed to slug you again."

Phoenix felt a smile begging to escape, and he let it go, surprising Hawk by the change in his demeanor. "You know, Hawk. You're a better brother than I ever gave you credit for...I'm sorry about that."

"Well. Apology accepted. Now don't go getting all mushy on me." His last word came out strangled sounding as Phoenix bear-hugged his brother.

"Darn it, Phoenix. I said—"

"Shut up," insisted Phoenix, slapping his brother on the back of the head as he let him go. "I happened to have missed you. Just be grateful I don't plant a kiss on your forehead."

"Call me grateful, then" said Hawk, raising his hands in surrender.

"Okay, boys," came Nevin's voice. "Let's get this truck unloaded."

Inside the house, Aerielle had just managed to leave her boots behind in the entry way before Ellie Stargazer, Sparrow, and Sofia were upon her with smiles and greetings, the ladder spoken, as well as signed. Her coat was quickly taken as she was led into the aromatic kitchen filled with mouthwatering dishes.

Sparrow was the first to sweep her into a hug, if somewhat awkward due to the child between them. "Oh, Aerielle, to see you again after so long."

Aerielle longed to say something in return, but knew even though *she* could hear *Sparrow*, the other woman wouldn't hear *her.* She settled for hugging her harder and received a kick in the ribs for her effort. Both woman started laughing at once as they broke apart.

"That's a greeting I've never gotten before," Aerielle signed, speaking aloud as well.

Sparrow grabbed Aerielle's hand and placed it on her belly, and Aerielle felt the distinct pressure of a tiny foot. Joy welled inside, and she felt the tears that came with it slip down her cheeks. Sparrow, her dark hair spilling around her face, smiled so big it would have lit up the room had there been no lights to do so.

"I don't think that baby sleeps," laughed Sofia from the counter where she was pouring Aerielle a glass of wine.

Aerielle pulled her hand away from the hidden child so she could speak to Sparrow. "Do you have names picked out for this little miracle?"

"Not yet. He's not due until early March. Jared says we'll know what his name will be when we see him."

"It's a boy?! When did you—"

"Just this week. We weren't sure we wanted to know, but I convinced Jared before my last ultrasound. We are thinking of possibly giving him a traditional name. He will after all be full-blooded Nez Perce."

Unlike Phoenix and Hawk, thought Aerielle, whose father was white.

Elizabeth, known to everyone as Ellie, interrupted them so she could welcome Aerielle with her own hug. Pulling away she looked Aerielle over. When she spoke she signed as well so Sparrow wouldn't be left out of the conversation. "Aerielle Buchanan. I would say you have not changed, but I would be lying. You have grown as beautiful as Sparrow has with the years."

"But what have you done with your hair?" demanded Sparrow, pulling a strand of Aerielle's hair straight before letting it go.

Grinning, Aerielle explained, and then they were all laughing. "Remind me to never get a perm."

There was a lot of noise behind them as four men entered the house, arms full.

"I have to direct traffic," said Ellie. "Sofia, do you mind keeping an eye on the biscuits?"

"Don't worry, I'll watch them all the way into my stomach and then onto my waistline." Sofia attempted to sign the words, and Aerielle was amazed at how much she had picked up in a week.

"Come," said Sparrow, urging Aerielle out of the kitchen and into the small alcove where a phone still sat on the same little table. There was still just one chair, but neither sat.

"What is it?" said Aerielle.

Sparrow signed for her not to speak aloud. "I must speak to you in private, quickly, before the others come in."

"Is something wrong?"

"I hope not. But Aerielle, I know you must think I broke my promise and told Phoenix about you. How else would you end up living in the same city? What you must think of me, but—"

"No, no," assured Aerielle. "I know you didn't break your promise."

"But how?"

Aerielle explained how Phoenix had tricked Hawk into moving to Minnesota, saying that was the one place he would never see Aerielle, when the opposite was true. "He knew what hospital I wanted to work at, how I'd dreamed of working there from when I was a child, at least until....never mind. That part doesn't matter. Just know—I know—you didn't do anything wrong."

"Oh, Aerielle. You have no idea how relieved I am. I would have been heartbroken if something had come between our friendship after all these years."

"Our friendship is fine." And this time, Aerielle hugged Sparrow. Once again she got kicked in the ribs for her effort.

An hour later found all eight of them jammed in like sardines around the crowded kitchen table, but loving every moment of it. More than a couple of bottles of wine had been consumed and the wild pheasant picked clean, yet no matter Sofia's efforts, there were two biscuits left, and not a person with room to put them, unless it was a pocket for later.

The conversation had been nonstop, and not a little confusing as people attempted to sign, eat, and speak all at the same time. Sofia finished eating first only because she wasn't as fluent at sign language and had eventually given up in the melee. There was a lot of discussion around horses and babies, and the house Jared and Sparrow had built on a piece of Stargazer land. It seemed the two, soon to be three, were taking up the family's side business of breading and selling appaloosas in the absence of the brothers. As the group wound down, Nevin, Ellie, and Sofia began to clean up. Jared had an arm around Sparrow whose head was nestled against his shoulder.

Phoenix leaned back in his chair, while beside him, Aerielle had just noticed Hawk was watching her intently and tapping his wine glass. For a moment, Aerielle didn't have a clue as to why. And then she remembered. She hadn't spilled or dropped anything yet. Casually picking up one of the remaining biscuits as if she planned to eat it, she suddenly whipped it across the table. She would have hit Hawk right in the head if he hadn't shifted out of the way in time. Sparrow let out a surprised yelp, while Jared's eyes widened and he eyed Hawk to see if there was going to be a return assault.

Phoenix shook his head. "You two and your food."

"Hey, I didn't throw anything."

"Yeah, but I bet you're the reason it got thrown."

"Whose throwing what?" demanded Sofia, laughing over by the counter.

"I'm throwing something," announced Phoenix, signing with a flourish. "I'm throwing the towel in. All I want is a shower and some sleep."

"Oh, a shower sounds wonderful," agreed Aerielle.

"Ladies first."

"No you go first. I'm not as tired."

"Why don't you guys just shower at the same time?" interrupted Hawk, and then clearly realizing what he'd just said, "in different bathrooms, of course."

But it was too late. Sparrow was laughing, Jared had a grin on his face, and Sofia was patting Hawk on the shoulder. "You stepped in that one."

"I just meant, that since Phoenix and I helped Nevin install that new water heater the last time we were home, hot water is not an issue. I've taken a shower while the dishwasher's been running without a problem."

"Were you alone?" teased Sparrow.

Grapping the last biscuit, Hawk began breaking pieces off and hurling them in his sister's direction.

Somewhere behind the group at the table, Ellie was heard asking Nevin, "How old are they now?"

→→→

Fresh from her shower, Aerielle tied the belt of her robe over flannel pajamas, and plopped down on the end of the bed she was sharing with Sofia.

"Oh, that felt good," she said, staring at her reflection in the mirrored dresser. Her hair was a mass of wet, uncombed strands, but the kinks and curls were gone. "I wonder where my hairbrush is. I couldn't find my shower bag. I think I used your shampoo."

"Then use my brush" offered Sofia, handing over her own.

"That'd be great." Aerielle took the proffered brush and began working it through her hair.

As she brushed the tangles from her now straight hair, she couldn't help thinking how different tonight was ending compared to last evening when her hair had been wild and so had the company. Her wild Half-Breed had gone and kissed her. And it had been...what? Memorable? Fabulous? How about intoxicating and about as addictive as any drug. She wouldn't mind some of that drug right now.

"You're awfully quiet all of a sudden, Aerielle. Where'd you go?"

Aerielle glanced at Sofia, moving the brush in her hand to the another section of her hair. "Last night. When Phoenix and I stopped for the snow. The place we stayed at. They only had one room left."

Sofia's eyes widened. "Don't tell me, there was only one bed, too."

Aerielle felt herself flush. She hadn't planned to mention that.

Leaning forward, Sofia demanded, "What happened?"

"Not what you're thinking," assured Aerielle.

"You spent the night alone in a room with one bed with someone you agreed to marry at some point, and nothing happened?"

"Well, not nothing. He, well, he kissed me. And I kissed him back. But not in bed," she added.

"What happened in bed?"

"Nothing. I mean, we slept, with our clothes on."

"Well, you guys are a model of restraint. Not that that's a bad thing, of course. I'm actually impressed."

"If you'd seen that kiss, you wouldn't think so, I mean about being a model of restraint."

"So what brought about this amazing kiss?"

Setting the brush down in her lap, Aerielle looked Sofia directly in the eyes, and her tone serious, she said, "He told me he loved me."

Sofia gaped. "Wow. You didn't even make it all the way to Idaho before finding out how he felt."

"He also said he'd never stopped loving me."

Understanding settled in Sofia's expression. "He's been holding a torch for you all this time."

"So it would seem."

"So what did you say when he told you all this?"

"I was too stunned to say anything. And then he kissed me and I forgot just about everything."

"And while you forgot just about everything, what was it you remembered?" Sofia asked gently.

Aerielle blinked in surprise by the question. "I...I remembered what it was like to be loved by him. I remembered what it was like knowing we were meant to be together. But most of all, I remembered what it was like *loving* him."

"Wow, all that from a kiss."

"'Since the invention of the kiss there have been five kisses that were rated the most passionate, the most pure. This one left them all behind.'"

Sofia stared at her. "Are you quoting *The Princess Bride*?"

"'Well done, Grasshopper.'"

→→→

"Darn it, Hawk, I can't find them," Phoenix groused, looking through the various bags lying around the bedroom floor.

"You talking about your clothes?" asked Hawk with a smirk, for Phoenix was looking through the luggage dressed in a towel, his long wet hair dripping down his back.

"Found those," said Phoenix sarcastically, tossing a handful of items onto the bed. "I'm looking for my hairbrush, my toothbrush, my shampoo, any and all such items. I managed to find shampoo in the shower, but unless you want me to use your toothbrush—"

"Not a good idea," laughed Hawk from the bed where he lay on his stomach reading a magazine.

"Then maybe you should get off your butt and help me."

Hawk grunted, and slid his magazine aside. Moving to get up, he paused, spotting a travel bag on the floor next to where he was lying. Quizzically, he pulled the bag up, setting it in front himself. He unzipped the bag carefully, lifted the lid, and looked in with great curiosity.

Pulling a brush out of the bag, he admired it momentarily. "Is it pink?"

"Is what pink?" demanded Phoenix, shuffling through another bag.

"Your brush."

"Of course it's not pink," Phoenix snapped, "What's the matter with you?"

When Hawk didn't respond, Phoenix glanced back at his brother, who was smiling like an idiot and holding up a pink hairbrush.

"That's not mine," said Phoenix, stepping over to the bed and taking it from Hawk.

"You think?" asked Hawk. "What gave it away? Was it the color of the brush or the roses on the bag?"

Without waiting for a response, he reached into the bag again and pulled out a stick of deodorant. Pulling off the lid, he sniffed. "Mmm, that's nice."

Phoenix sat down next to his brother just as Hawk put the lid back on and handed him the deodorant. "This must be Aerielle's," Phoenix remarked, looking at the bag.

"Of course it is," said Hawk "Look, she has a purple toothbrush. You could use hers."

"Smart alec." Phoenix took the toothbrush Hawk handed him, adding it to his collection. "I really don't think we should be going through—"

"Oh, man. Perfume."

"Let me see" demanded Phoenix, taking the bottle away from Hawk before he could open it. Setting everything else down, Phoenix unscrewed the flower shaped top. Pullng the lid free, Phoenix held the bottle up to his nose. The scent exploded from his memories, and he closed his eyes as if to keep them from escaping. "Hyacinth," he said at last. "This was all she wore back...." Phoenix's voice trailed off and he was unable to speak.

Gently, Hawk took the bottle and its lid from Phoenix. He sealed it up without smelling it. Gathering the rest of Aerielle's things, he placed them back in the rose bag and zipped it up. Setting it aside, he pulled a similar bag off the floor, only this one was black.

"Here," he said, handing it to Phoenix. "Now you can brush your teeth *and* your hair. And hurry up with it, would ya? Your hair's drippin' all over the bed, *my* side to be exact.

"Grumpy, aren't we?" ribbed Phoenix, taking the bag and getting up.

"'We' would be the key word, Phoenix," said Hawk. "You were the one who came in here after your shower all angry like. What was that all about, anyway? You fall down and hit your head in there?"

Phoenix shrugged. "I had too much time to think in there." And then gathering the clothing he'd thrown on the bed, the bag his brother had just handed him, and the blow dryer, he disappeared back into the attached bath.

⟶⟶

Phoenix was still thinking close to an hour and a half later as he lay on the living room sofa staring through the floor to ceiling windows at the stars. He had tried to stop thinking several times, had even gone through all the stars in the sky visible to him and named every last one he could. Anything to make him sleep, but the moment he closed his eyes...all he could think about was Aerielle and what had happened last night.

It was because of this that when she actually walked into the room he thought for a moment he was imagining things. But there she was, looking like an artist's depiction of an angel. Her robe was completely white, and her hair, having been washed, lay like a gold silken mantel down her back as she turned to gaze out at the stars. There had to be a metaphore there somewhere, he thought, watching an angel studying the stars. Apparently she hadn't noticed him in the dark.

For a second, Phoenix thought to get up and join her at the window when reality pinned him in place. He may have been thinking of Aerielle for a while now, but clearly he'd left his brain at home. Everyone in this house had seen the scars on his back, everyone except Aerielle. And here he was wearing sweats with no shirt and not one of his mother's quilts in sight. There was no chance he could leave without being noticed, and no flippin' way he was going to explain the scars in the middle of the night on Christmas day. He just had to pray she left the room as unaware of him as she had when she'd come in. However, Phoenix hadn't drawn a single breath when she turned around.

Aerielle nearly jumped out of her skin when she turned and found Phoenix lying on his side watching her from the sofa. "Good grief, Phoenix. Why didn't you let me know you were there?"

"Sorry. I was too busy admiring the view, I guess."

And he wasn't talking about the stars, thought Aerielle. She had to admit, the view wasn't so bad from this direction either. Phoenix was bare-chested revealing muscles which had only hardened and matured with the years. Even in the darkness there was enough on display, Aerielle found herself wanting to explore the plains of his exposed flesh.

"So what are you doing up?" asked Phoenix. "I thought you'd be sound asleep by now."

"I'd like to be. But somebody let me sleep too long in the truck. At least that's what I'm blaming it on. What about you? You should be exhausted."

"Hawk kicked me out of our room because I was keeping him awake."

"Keeping *him* awake. Why weren't *you* sleeping?"

Phoenix gazed at her without speaking, and Aerielle cursed the expressionless warrior's face he was giving her now.

"I was thinking about what happened last night...about that kiss...about what I said."

"You didn't mean it?" gasped Aerielle.

"Aerielle, no! I mean yes!" Phoenix swore and then moved as if to get up, but changed his mind. "Aerielle, come here," he said, patting the available real estate still open on the sofa in front of him.

Confused, Aerielle followed his instructions, sitting down in front of him.

"Lie down, would ya," he said, his eyes pleading. "I need to see you when I talk."

Aerielle thought it odd he didn't just sit up, but she did as he requested anyway. Would he really say anything that bad if she was lying so close?

It turned out to be the perfect fit, and they weren't actually any closer than they'd been the night before. But that's what he wanted to talk about, wasn't it? Last night? The real reason she hadn't been sleeping either.

Still on his side, he looked at her, no longer expressionless, but regretful. "I meant everything I said to you last night Aerielle. Everything. No regrets. But what I did, kissing you, was wrong"

"But—"

"Aerielle, I asked you to come home, not *just* because I love you, but to explain what happened fourteen years ago, to work out the past, to ask forgiveness. Instead, I skipped right over all the important stuff and made a move on you."

"Hey, I was there, too," retorted Aerielle, gazing up at him. "And that was no 'move.'" That was one heck of a kiss, and I happen to remember kissing you back. And I'm not sorry. In fact…just the opposite."

Phoenix looked away, unable to face the trust in her eyes. How could she possibly trust him again after what he'd done? He forced himself to look back at her, meet her gaze. "Aerielle, I don't want to put your heart at risk again. Hawk's been very clear I did more than just break it last time. I put you through Hell."

"Hush," she whispered, and put a finger to his lips, a finger he longed to kiss. "It's already too late, Half-Breed," she continued, the endearment like a caress. "My heart was put at risk the day you opened the pantry door and found me inside. Besides, what if I end up breaking *your* heart?"

She pulled her finger away with the question, awaiting his response. She had no way of knowing nothing could equal the broken heart he'd suffered when he left her. "I would say I got what I deserved."

"Oh, Phoenix, that's not true."

"So, if I've already put your heart at risk, what am I to do Meyui?"

"Kiss me, unless you don't want to?"

Phoenix eyed those lips so close to his and knew he was lost. "I haven't stopped wanting to kiss you since I *opened* the pantry door."

"Then kiss me, Hemene. Kiss me like you did last night. I want to remember."

Hemene. She'd called him Hemene—Wolf. It was the first time she'd used the Shahaptin translation of his name since their wedding night. Not questioning what it might mean, Phoenix did as she'd commanded and kissed her.

This time it was Aerielle who cradled his face, her thumbs following his cheekbones, as familiar to her memory as his kiss upon her lips.

He wrapped his arm around her waist, holding her secure. As he did so, his long hair slipped forward, creating a veil around Aerielle's face, and suddenly, the memories were so real, she would have sworn she could smell that long but not forgotten scent. But she wasn't remembering. Was she? Aerielle pressed a hand against his shoulder and gently broke off the kiss.

"What is it?" he asked concerned.

"That's my question," she said, and gathered a handful of his hair and pressed it to her nose and sniffed.

"Only you could make this seem oddly normal."

Aerielle smiled. "But your hair, I remember this scent. What is it?"

"You're going on about my shampoo choice? It's just some local brand I used to use. Found it in the shower."

"It's fabulous," grinned Aerielle, and lifted her face to kiss the smirk off his lips. "What's it called?"

"Something like Earth, Wind, and Fire. Oh wait, that's a band. Maybe Earth and Fire? I can get you some for Christmas," he joked, for it was clearly a masculine scent.

"I'm glad that wasn't what was in *my* shower. That would have been strange indeed, considering I couldn't find my own shampoo."

"That reminds me," said Phoenix, watching indulgently as she continued to play with his hair. "Hawk found part of your luggage in our room."

"So that's where it went."

"Yeah, and Hawk was pretty tempted by your purple toothbrush."

"You must be feeling a tad better, now. You just made two jokes within seconds of each other."

Phoenix's eyes, barely visible, narrowed in thoughtfulness. "While my kiss helps you remember, your kiss helps me to forget."

Aerielle brushed her lips against his again, and then turned on her side, her back cradled to his chest as they both lay facing the window. His hair spilled over her shoulder along with her own, and Aerielle absorbed the scent of it even as she drank in the night sky. "Maybe we should take a few minutes not to forget or remember, but to just be who we are, and where we are, right now."

"Well, then, right here, right now, I'm having the best Christmas I've had since childhood."

"Oh, Hemene, it's definitely at the top of my list, too." Following her words, Aerielle took one of Phoenix's hands in hers and signed "Merry Christmas" into his palm.

→→→

Aerielle was startled awake, and at first had no clue where she was, only that she was having trouble breathing. And then she remembered she was on the sofa with Phoenix, and his grip around her had tightened painfully. She could hear his ragged breathing, and feel the shake of his head. He was dreaming.

"Phoenix," she cried, pulling at his arm.

He awoke with an explosive gasp, his breathing ragged. "Aerielle! Aerielle are you alright?!"

"I will be," she squeaked, "if you would allow me to breath."

It took him a second as if he was orienting himself. "Oh. I'm sorry." Instantly his grip loosened. "Did I hurt you?" he questioned, his voice filled with concern.

Aerielle shifted onto her back so she could see him. His eyes were wide with fear. "It's okay, I'm fine," she assured. "What about you?" Placing a hand on his face she discovered it damp to the touch.

"A bad dream, that's all."

"You sure?"

"I'm sure."

Aerielle didn't believe him, but decided not to pressure him. The way he'd asked her if she was alright reminded her of his response the night she'd called and woken him from sleep.

As for sleep, "As much as I enjoy being here, Half-Breed, the last thing I want is to be found here with you come morning. I think I'm going to head back to bed."

"I'm gonna stay a little longer, clear my head."

"You're sure you're okay?"

"Me big tough Indian brave. Yes I'm fine."

Aerielle giggled. "You sound like Tonto from *The Lone Ranger.*"

"Guess that makes you the ranger. Sleep tight, Kemosabe."

→→→

The Indians survived our open intention of wiping them out, and since the tide turned they have even weathered our good intentions toward them, which can be much more deadly.

John Steinbeck, America and Americans, as quoted in *The Nez Perces, People of the Far West*

20

It was the next morning, and Phoenix was examining his appearance in the bedroom mirror one last time. He barely recognized himself. The brand new v-neck sweater he was wearing was not something he would have picked out in a million years. First of all it was white. Second of all it was cashmere. But when your mother wrapped it in Christmas paper along with a pair of new blue jeans and left you a note to wear them, you did as you were told. It was odd, thought Phoenix, while his hair was clearly brown, it looked a heck of a lot darker against the white than it did other colors he wore. He couldn't help wondering what Aerielle would think.

Leaving the bedroom, Phoenix headed for the kitchen. Before he got that far, he ran into his brother coming in through the back door escorted by a breath of Idaho winter.

"Hey, big brother," said Hawk. "You done sleeping the day away? It's near on ten, and I've already mucked out some stalls and fed some horses."

"Hope you did my share," grinned Phoenix.

Taking off his coat, Hawk eyed his brother suspiciously. "Someone is sure in a good mood this morning. Where'd you go last night when I tossed your butt?"

"I went down to the girls room and spent the night with them."

Hawk stared at him, one boot on, one boot off. "Humor?

From you? Okay what did you do with my brother? Speaking of which, you sure are all duded up this morning. Even for Christmas, what you're wearing is dressy by your standards. You trying to impress someone?"

"Not sure. It was a gift."

"From who?"

"Mom."

"So you gonna tell me where you really went last night? You didn't come back to bed until nearly dawn."

"Nope. So, you gonna have a second round of breakfast?"

"I guess that's *all* I'm gonna get, so yeah."

A moment later, they ran into Sofia on her way out of the kitchen. "Morning, boys, I—Wow. Don't you look drop dead gorgeous this morning, Phoenix."

Phoenix looked at his brother using his eyes to say, *I impressed her.*

Hawk glanced down at the clothes he'd worn to the barn. "I sure hope Mom left me a gift like yours."

"Enjoy breakfast, you guys," said Sofia. "I'm gonna go check on Aerielle. When I left the room she was still dead to the world. We can't have her sleeping through Christmas."

"Somehow I don't think she did," mumbled Hawk, just loud enough for Phoenix to hear, or so he thought.

"What'd you say?" asked Sofia.

"Yeah, I didn't hear you either," said Phoenix.

"I um, I said I can't wait till dinner. With my encouragement, I got Mom and Sofia to fix us up a nice Italian meal today. We are having Sofia's wonderful lasagna, among other things."

Phoenix groaned. "Oh, man, maybe I should skip breakfast."

"Well, dinner's not until 2:00," said Sofia. "Just keep breakfast light."

"I offered to help with dinner," Hawk informed his brother as they entered the kitchen proper. "I was rebuffed."

Their mother was standing at the kitchen island where there was an odd assortment of food items, from a jar of homemade jelly to a can of diced tomatoes. "You were rebuffed because we ladies want to gab up a storm and talk about you men."

"Did you hear her?" demanded Hawk, pretending aggrievement. "They're going to talk about us."

"Well, you've actually been behaving yourself," teased Phoenix. "So what are you worried about?"

"And then after dinner, you males can clean up and talk about all those things men talk about," added Ellie.

"We could talk about women," suggested Phoenix.

Ellie looked up from slicing mushrooms and stared at her eldest son. Then she glanced at Hawk. "Who is he, and what have you done with your brother?"

Hawk laughed. "You did it now, Phoenix. Using humor. They'll be talking about *you* when they're fixing dinner."

Phoenix suddenly felt uncomfortable, and he knew the moment his mother knew it. "Don't worry about it, you two," she said, talking to both, but looking at Phoenix. "If we really were going to discuss the men in this household, Jared makes an excellent topic.

"Now sit down and let me make you some English muffins. We also have juice, coffee, hardboiled eggs—"

"Mom, we can feed ourselves," interrupted Hawk.

"Yes, you can, but not this morning. Now sit."

After Ellie set two black coffees in front of them at the table, the brother's caught up on vet business and then moved onto horses. "So how's my stallion?" asked Phoenix, wondering how soon he would have a chance to ride him.

"Nimipu is as fit as a fiddle," said Hawk. "I've ridden him a few times. I guess Jared rides him the most. He says Sparrow reminds him not to get too attached, because he's your stallion. But he has his own horse, one of Nimipu's offspring. None of the foals Nimipu's fathered are quite as big as he is, but big enough that Nevin is making a lot of money on stud fees."

"We should all go riding together," suggested Phoenix, "You, me, Aerielle and Sofia, and Sparrow and Jared. I'm assuming Sparrow's still riding?"

"Yeah, she is. That'd be fun."

Their discussion was interrupted by the aroma of English muffins with warm butter and jelly as their mom stepped between their chairs and set a plate in front of each of them.

Their, "Thanks, Mom," came out in surprising unity.

Her hands now empty, Ellie put one on each of her son's heads, gently caressing their hair. "Do you know how good it is to have you boys home? Nevin and I've missed you both so much."

Leaning down to Hawk first, she kissed him on the temple. Turning to Phoenix, she pulled lightly on his long hair, tilting his head back a bit. She kissed him on the forehead.

"It's good to be home, Mom," assured Phoenix.

Ellie moved her lips from his forehead to his ear and whispered, "You make all the jokes you want, Hemene Moxmox. I won't draw any more attention to it. I can tell you're happy. And that makes me happy.

"I have a surprise for you boys," Ellie announced, straightening up. "We are having a special guest for dinner. Your father is coming."

Hawk nearly choked on the bite of food he'd just taken, and Phoenix almost spilled his coffee. "You invited Larry?" asked Phoenix for the both of them, as Hawk was still attempting to chew and swallow.

"Well, he misses you, too. Besides, I can't hold my anger towards him forever, especially when I am so happy married to Nevin, and Sparrow is about to produce my first grandchild. If your father hadn't left us, many things would have been different for you boys. You wouldn't have become Stargazer's for one. But most importantly, none of us would have Sparrow in our lives, and I can't imagine life without her."

"Neither can we," agreed Hawk.

Phoenix felt a rush of joy. "I've missed Larry. I'm glad you asked him."

"Good. I'm happy. I see you found the clothes I bought for today. Hawk, there's a similar package waiting for you. I hope you don't mind. I know you traditionally dress better than Phoenix, but I plan on taking pictures today, so I bought you two clothes which would complement each other. Sparrow and Jared will also be dressed similarly. I want some Christmas pictures of my children including my son-in-law."

And Aerielle? What of her, thought Phoenix. For in all the world, he alone knew the truth.

→→→

When Aerielle arrived in the kitchen a while later, she was surprised to find it empty. Where was the women's brigade she'd been told would be fixing dinner? Hearing a voice from the direction of the dining room, Aerielle headed that way. She soon discovered the voice was actually coming from the phone alcove, and it was Phoenix. Catching sight of her, he waved her in, speaking into the phone as he did so.

"Yeah, I'll see you later. Merry Christmas."

Hanging up the phone, Phoenix reached out for Aerielle's hands and pulled her toward him.

"Why doesn't anyone ever turn the light on in here?" asked Aerielle into the dimness surrounding them.

Phoenix smiled. "Because it's much easier to spy on a pretty girl making cookies if she doesn't know you're here. It also makes it cozier when *kissing* a pretty girl in here."

"Do you speak from experience?"

"I will after this."

Even without the light on, Phoenix's lips found Aerielle's unerringly. Her mouth greeted his, while their fingers twined together in their own embrace.

It was a leisurely kiss, and when at last they broke apart,

Aerielle sighed as she nodded her head. "That was definitely an improvement over kissing in a well-lit room."

"Makes it harder for Hawk to walk in on us."

As if having been called forth, Hawk's voice came to them from the kitchen. "Hey, where did everybody go? Mom? Sofia? Sparrow?"

Afraid she might burst into laughter, Aerielle buried her face against Phoenix's shoulder.

Releasing her hands, he wrapped his arms around her and pulled her in closer, holding his breath.

They hadn't long to wait for just as quickly as he'd appeared in the kitchen, Hawk could be heard heading out of the room.

Pulling away, Aerielle ran her hands over Phoenix's arms. "What are you wearing? You're as soft as a...."

"Cashmere sweater?" suggested Phoenix, stepping back so she could get a better view.

"Wow."

"That's what Sofia said. Am I to intuit that 'wow' is a good thing?"

"You're teasing me."

"A little. I have to admit to being a little unsure if I could carry this off."

"You can not only carry it off, Hemene, you can carry me off while you're wearing it. Did Hawk pick this out?"

"Ouch."

"Don't pretend you're surprised by the question," Aerielle teased back.

"Actually, my Mom bought both the sweater and the jeans."

"So that's where Hawk gets his fashion acumen."

"I never gave this fashion stuff too much thought, but maybe I should. I like the way you're looking at me right now."

Aerielle smiled at him. "Did Sofia look at you this way this morning?"

"Not exactly. Her expression was more one of shock...but

after she said 'wow' she also said I looked drop dead gorgeous. I just figured she said that to make Hawk jealous."

Aerielle laughed. "I doubt that's why, but did it work?"

"Actually, I think it did. We'll have to see if she likes what Mom picked out for him.

"Speaking of parents," continued Phoenix, "my father's coming over today."

"He's what? Since when? I didn't even know you had made up. Did Hawk, too? I guess he wouldn't be coming if he wasn't welcomed by everyone, including your mother. What does Nevin think of all this?"

"You gonna let me get a word in edgewise?"

"Sorry," grinned Aerielle, making the motion of zipping her lips.

"You'll be happy to know, I took your advice and gave my father a chance. It was good advice. We've become friends. It also led to Hawk meeting Larry halfway, too. He'll never be 'Dad,' but that's what Nevin is for."

Joy lit Aerielle's face. "So what's he like? And when did this happen?"

"Larry wasn't, and thankfully still isn't, the same man he was when he was married to my mother. I can't say too much without breaking his confidence, but I will say it's been a change which has lasted at least fourteen years."

"Fourteen years?" repeated Aerielle, the lightness leaving her voice.

Phoenix could hear her unasked question. Familiar regret welled up inside, and he made no effort to hide his emotions from her. He did his best to let her read his face before responding. "When I left that day.... When I left *you* that day...I went to my father's. I was there about nine months. Didn't come home until the 4th of July."

"When did you say?"

"The 4th of July."

The 4th of July? Of all the days on earth, he came back on the

4th of July?! Inexorable joy and raging pain battled for Aerielle's memories as she fought to hide the effect of his words from the man standing before her.

"I'm glad you and your father made up," Aerielle thrust into the silence.

Phoenix didn't seem to notice how lame her response was.

Before she could think of something else to say, the sounds of women's voices could be heard coming from beyond the dining room.

"Let's get out of here while we still can," said Phoenix, ushering Aerielle from the alcove. "I'll leave you here to join the rest of the ladies and see what the guys are up to."

Aerielle had about six seconds to shove the 4th of July back to 1979 where it belonged and she used every last one.

®®®

Christmas went by faster than Aerielle wanted it to. This was the first Christmas in too many years that she'd actually enjoyed the day. After their Italian dinner in the formal dining room, a casual gift exchange had taken place in the living room. No one was left out, and in fact, even Hawk and Phoenix's father Larry had gifts waiting for him. Once they'd cleaned up the masses of ribbon, bows, and wrapping paper, the sun was setting.

The men took a break to feed the horses. Afterward, more wood was added to the huge fireplace, Christmas cookies were brought out, and games dug out of a closet. Sparrow insisted on starting with Twister. She thought it would be fun to see everyone do contortions while she watched, seeing as it would be too difficult for her to play being six months pregnant. She also gave anyone over 35 permission to forego this "wonderful opportunity."

"I've always wanted to be the spinner," she announced, settling on the loveseat next to Jared.

"You just like to torture your brothers," accused Hawk, signing as he lined up next to Sofia on the plastic mat decorated in colored circles.

"Don't worry. I like to torture Jared, too. You'll get a break, Hawk. I wouldn't want you to hurt yourself."

"It's the old folks here, Phoenix and Aerielle, that are most at risk of falling," Hawk replied.

Aerielle glanced at Phoenix. "You taking him down, or am I?"

"Left foot yellow," called Sparrow, followed by, "Right hand blue."

Several games followed, the true older generation fully entertained by the antics of the younger. Jared was rotated in just as Sparrow said he would, and both Hawk and Phoenix got a chance to talk to Larry when they were relieved. Showing off the most flexibility, Sofia and Jared outlasted everyone else.

"I had no idea you were so skilled," said Hawk at one point, as he went down second to last to Sofia. It was the third time she'd outlasted him.

"I guess you need to start paying more attention," she smiled, victoriously.

"My turn to sit out," declared Aerielle, signing emphatically.

"I think we should see how the guys do without us," agreed Sofia. "Can I spin?" she asked conspiratorially, sitting down next to Sparrow with a hand out.

Aerielle joined Larry on the sofa. They had been introduced earlier, but hadn't shared any direct conversation. "Phoenix was very happy when he found out you were coming today," she said studying him. It was clear to her where Phoenix had gotten his thick wavy hair. While Larry's identical dark chestnut hair was just below the collar, there wasn't a straight lock to be seen.

"I think he's happier *you're* here," replied Larry with a smile, his voice nearly drowned out by the sudden laughter in the room. "You know, you're the spittin' image of his description of you all those years ago. Doesn't seem like you changed much."

"Phoenix talked about me?"

"He didn't *not* talk about you. You were all he thought

about. He also made it clear you were the reason he took a chance on *me*."

"Really."

"I've wanted to thank you for nigh on a decade and a half. I never thought I'd get the chance."

Aerielle didn't know what to say. "I…um, I'm glad, I mean about you and Phoenix."

"After Phoenix, eventually came Hawk. You brought both my sons back to me, Aerielle. That makes you pretty special."

Aerielle glanced back at the game and the oddly arranged trio, then back at Larry. "I'm sorry. I'm at a loss for words."

"It's alright. You needn't say anything. When I left my family, I never expected to see any of them again. I was married to the drink. When I finally found my way out of the bottle, Elizabeth had remarried and my sons were nearly grown. I knew I didn't stand much chance with the boys, but I had to try. But you were the reason it finally happened. So thank you."

Aerielle didn't feel like she'd done that much, and she wanted to say it was nothing. But clearly it wasn't nothing to Larry or to Phoenix and Hawk. "You're welcome."

Any embarrassment she may have felt was forgotten as the lighthearted banter in the room exploded as Sofia called, "Right foot yellow."

It was almost a race as the three men all aimed for a yellow circle at the same time. "No," yelled Phoenix, as he and Hawk started to go down. "Not alone," Hawk declared and the brothers reached out in unison to pull Jared down with them. There was a chorus of thuds and laughs and even a groan or two. By now everyone in the room was laughing.

"Okay," declared Sparrow, "one or two more sets. First round will be Jared, Hawk, and Sofia. If there is no clear winner, then we'll do the highest ranking two against each other to find a winner."

"I hope there's a prize for the winner," said Jared rubbing at his shoulder after signing the words.

Sofia gazed fondly at her husband. "Don't worry, sweety. If you win I'll give you a kiss."

Jared actually looked embarrassed.

"Don't you worry, either, Sofia," continued Sparrow. "If you win, I'm sure Hawk will oblige."

"I will?"

"You are, after all, the only unattached male here," Sparrow explained.

"I am? Hey, you're assuming I don't stand a chance of winning."

Sparrow grinned at her brother. "At least I'm *giving* you a chance."

"Well, since I'm out for the moment, I'm getting something to drink. I'm dying of thirst," said Aerielle.

"I'll join you," agreed Phoenix.

In the kitchen, Aerielle downed a full glass of water and then placed her glass under the water dispenser in the fridge once again. Phoenix leaned back against the center island, admiring her as he sipped from his own glass. Aerielle, beautiful as long as he'd known her, was even more so today. And it wasn't just the red and silver she was adorned in. Nor was it her delightfully disheveled hair, which like his, had become unruly from game play. She seemed…happy.

Sensing his study, she turned to him. "What is it? My hair's a mess, isn't it. I should go brush it."

"That would be a waste of time, as I'm going to mess it up some more right now."

Setting his glass aside, Phoenix stepped away from the counter.

"Hey, we don't have time for this," said Aerielle, despite the smile on her face.

"And why not," he asked, removing the glass from her hand and putting it on the counter.

"I don't want to miss Sofia beating Jared at Twister."

Crowding Aerielle against the fridge, Phoenix raised a hand

to Aerielle's face, running a finger along the line of her jaw. "And what makes you think she's going to win?"

"Oh, she will. She'll stop at nothing to get that winner's kiss from Hawk."

"Ah, is my sister also involved in this matchmaking attempt?"

"Not by request."

"That won't stop Sparrow," chuckled Phoenix, brushing his nose against Aerielle's.

"There's no stopping you either, is there?" murmured Aerielle in acquiescence, her lips so close to his, Phoenix could feel the cold radiating from them as a result of the ice water.

"It's your own fault. You wore your Hyacinth perfume today, and it's been teasing me through that endless game of Twister."

His lips brushed hers for the briefest of moments.

"I didn't know you'd noticed."

"What would you have me do? Ravage those lips of yours in front of everyone?"

Aerielle blushed. "Is that what your intentions are now?"

"Unless you stop me."

Aerielle's response was to slip her hands around Pheonix's neck and under the tangle of his hair.

He grinned rather wolfishly before his mouth took possession of hers.

"Break it up you two. Neither of you won the game. It's up to Jared and Sofia."

At the sound of his brother's voice, Phoenix released Aerielle and sighed. "Your timing has always been impeccable," he remarked, turning toward Hawk.

"I have to be good at something, even if it is accidental. Besides, if you wanted privacy, the kitchen is not the best location for playing kissy face. I ought to know. That's where Dad caught me and Lily."

"Man, you were so grounded," agreed Phoenix.

Aerielle's eyes widened in surprise.

Hawk grinned. "That was in the spring after you left Idaho. You see, we weren't officially allowed to date until we were sixteen."

"And you weren't sixteen?" guessed Aerielle.

"Oh, I was sixteen, if barely. Trouble was, Lily wasn't."

"Lily was fourteen," Phoenix added. "Not only were we not allowed to date until we were sixteen, but we weren't allowed to date girls *under* sixteen. Neither was a problem for me."

"That's because you avoided girls," said Hawk. "Until Aerielle, anyway."

"I *tried* to avoid her."

"But I'm so irresistible," Aerielle joked.

Phoenix laughed "Irresistible? You were a force to be reckoned with. I had no hope against you."

"So what happened to Lily?"

"Her family wasn't as strict," sighed Hawk. "By the end of the school year she was dating a senior, and I was dating nobody. It's hard to get a girlfriend when you're grounded."

Laughter erupted from the living room.

"Hey, we're missing the final match," exclaimed Aerielle, grabbing her water. "Come on, guys."

"Be right there," said Hawk. "I'm thirsty, too."

A minute later, Hawk joined Phoenix and Aerielle just inside the living room watching the showdown. Hawk was sipping eggnog, while Aerielle was still working on her glass of ice water.

"Come on, Jared," Hawk encouraged along with all the other men in the room.

The women were all cheering on Sofia, even the spinner, Sparrow. "Sorry, Jared, but I have to side with the women on this one. Right hand red. Left hand red. Left foot green. Oh, no. Right foot red."

Since there were only two playing, the rules stated a circle could not be shared. However, both players went for the same red circle. Sofia barely beat Jared to it and in his attempt to avoid stepping on her foot, he lost his balance and fell.

"Chivalry may not be dead, but occasionally it loses its grip," said Phoenix to Aerielle as the room filled with varying responses.

"You go, girl!" exclaimed Sparrow. Getting to her feet with surprising agility, she hugged Sofia amongst the cheers and laughter from the onlookers.

"Give me your eggnog," urged Aerielle, placing a hand on Hawk's arm.

He gave it to her willingly. "Something wrong with your water?" he asked, leaning down so she could hear him.

"No, silly. Your kiss is the prize for the winner. You're going to need both hands to kiss Sofia."

"I am?"

"If you do it right, you will. What are you planning? A polite kiss on the cheek?"

"Well, I—"

"If that's all you do, she'll be devastated."

"She will?"

"Of course. She'll think you find her unattractive. That's not true, is it?"

"Of course not. I'll kiss her on the lips then."

"Hawk!" Aerielle exclaimed in a whisper.

"Yes, ma'am," responded Hawk, knowing he was in trouble if not why.

"Sometimes you can really be dense," scolded Aerielle. "I want you to think Lily. Now, go out there and get yourself grounded."

Hawk stared at Aerielle, his face just inches from her own. "If I kiss her like that, she may slap me."

"You're up, Hawk," came Sparrow's voice through the noise. "Time to kiss the winner."

"You're sure about this?" mouthed Hawk, glancing back and forth from his sister to Aerielle.

"Yes."

"Okay, but my life is in your hands."

"Hawk, quit yappin' and get over here. You're keeping Sofia waiting."

"Yeah, yeah," he muttered casually, moving away.

His gaze remaining on the room, Phoenix bent his head to Aerielle. "What were you and Hawk in conference about?"

"I was giving him kissing advice."

Phoenix blinked. "I know I didn't understand what you just said."

"You understood just fine. I told him to go out there and get himself grounded."

Phoenix jerked his head around to look at her. "What—"

"Pay attention or you're gonna miss it."

Biting his tongue, he turned back in time to see his brother put an arm around Sofia's shoulders and raise his other with a flourish as if making an official announcement. "All hail to the reigning queen of Twister. Your prize m'lady." And before anyone suspected what he was about to do, he dropped his arm to her waist, bent her over his other arm, and kissed her thoroughly. When he didn't release her right away, there was general laughter from the audience.

"I wonder if there will be prizes for Pictionary," remarked Nevin.

Ellie smiled at her husband. "Considering it's a team game, let's hope not."

"I swear he didn't get that audacity from me," voiced Larry.

Hawk gradually returned Sofia to an upright position, gently letting her go, as she didn't seem too steady on her feet. Her face blossomed with color at the sight of her audience, but she raised her chin as if that was exactly the kind of kiss she had been expecting.

Taking pity on her, Sparrow clapped her hands to get everyone's attention "There will be a 30 minute intermission before a rousing game of Pictionary."

Greater love hath no man than this, that a
man lay down his life for his friends.

John 15:13

21

The day after Christmas turned out to be the perfect day for riding. By early afternoon when they departed, the sun shown off the white crystalline landscape like a glorious beacon, while temps were in the mid-twenties. Aerielle and her five companions had taken the horses out with the ultimate goals of getting in a long leisurely ride and collecting pine cones from one of Sparrows favorite spots. Later the pine cones would be loaded up with peanut butter and birdseed and hung in the trees near the ranch.

All three of the Stargazer siblings road bareback, even the much pregnant Sparrow who headed the pinecone-birdfeeder delegation. The afternoon was a rush of fresh air, breathtaking views, and the muted pounding of hooves as various riders let their eager mounts out for a run.

For Aerielle, her favorite view this afternoon was Phoenix. Whether he was riding beside her, his legs guiding the great Nimipu with effortless ease, or racing ahead, one with the horse, his long hair caught by the wind, Aerielle was unable to take her eyes from him. If anyone belonged on a horse, it was Hemene Moxmox—Yellow Wolf. He rode as if born in the saddle or lack thereof, and he was mesmerizing. Of course, Aerielle had found him mesmerizing off a horse as well, had fallen in love with the stubborn young man he had been. Hard to believe they'd both been just out of high school when their lives had crossed. They'd seemed so grown up at the time. But young love or not, it had been love, and Aerielle had not known its like since—until now. Yes, now. She was as much or more in love with the man he had become than the one she had loved back then. He had changed in ways she'd least expected, his compassion magnifying over the years as some of the anger seemed to have dissipated. He also seemed to have acquired a sense of humor.

Oh, Lord, how could she have allowed herself to fall in love with him again? Yet how did one keep from falling in love? She could have stayed home, not come to Idaho. Yet, Aerielle doubted that would have kept her feelings from engaging. Delayed them maybe. But what was her love going to cost her *this* time if things didn't work out? The price of her previous loss had cost more than her heart, nearly her soul. There'd been times she'd wanted to die. Drawn to the instigator of her thoughts, Aerielle glanced at him again. This time she found herself getting caught in the act.

"What is it?" asked Phoenix, gazing back at her.

"Well, uh, I was just enjoying the view," she quoted, using his own words from Christmas Eve.

Phoenix raised an eyebrow. "Well, don't let me interrupt you." And then with smugness tugging at his lips, he turned his attention forward again as if she'd said the most natural thing.

Yes, thought Aerielle, a sense of humor.

They'd been riding on and off for more than an hour when they came to a familiar rise leading down to a camas prairie. In the spring and early summer the land would dance with stalks of beautiful blue flowers stretching from horizon to horizon. In years past, the camas bulbs were a large source of food for the Nez Perce, serving a purpose more important than that of nature's artwork. It was one of the many sights Aerielle missed from her brief years in Idaho. She could picture this very section as it had been in the summer of '78.

Phoenix must have been doing some remembering as well, for he reached out and took her hand, squeezing it gently. She could imagine the feel of his flesh without the gloves they both wore as easily as she could picture the blue and green camas waiting beneath the white winter carpet extending down and beyond. Beside them in the row of horses, Hawk was telling Sofia about the camas that grew in this part of the country, their various colors, and even about the deadly camas masquerading as the real thing, at least until they bloomed. Sparrow had pulled her horse out of the line and around to face him, so she could see what her brother was saying with his hands.

"That reminds me of New Year's Eve," announced Sparrow, animation lighting her face.

"What's the connection between camas and New Year's eve?" asked Sofia, Hawk signing for her.

"It's not the camas," said Hawk, "it's the masquerading part. I assume the Gilberts are holding their New Year's Eve masquerade party?"

"It's a costumed barn dance," Sparrow explained to Sofia. "You've all been invited. Jared and I have been planning our costumes for weeks now. Masks are expected, unveiling allowed at midnight, in case you're unsure who you're kissing in the New Year with."

"Sounds like a blast," said Sofia. "The *party* sounds like a blast," she restated, as everyone laughed.

"I love costume parties," agreed Aerielle. Grinning, she glanced from Phoenix to Hawk mounted on either side of her. "You two could go as Indians."

Hawk winced and Phoenix groaned. Ignoring them, Aerielle continued. "Sofia and I can throw something together for ourselves. There's plenty of time for shopping or sewing. Ellie's got a great Singer."

"What do you think, Phoenix?" began Hawk. "Maybe we should go. It appears we'd be disappointing these ladies if we say no. Going native may not be such a bad idea. No costume creation needed."

How well she knew, thought Aerielle. All three of the

Stargazers had artfully hand-crafted clothing made by their mother. Phoenix was the only one she'd seen in his buckskins—the night they'd married, at least the night Aerielle'd thought they had. *Not now!* She shoved away the memory.

"I can make you guys some masks," she suggested. But before her words had even completed themselves, she felt Phoenix's hand tighten painfully over hers. Was he dueling with the memory she herself had just fought off?

Seeming to realize he was hurting her, Phoenix let loose her hand. He glared at his brother, clearly frustrated he had suggested going. "You can go if you want to. I don't do costume parties."

"You used to," pleaded Sparrow.

"Things have changed." With but subtle pressure from his thighs and a light touch of the reigns, Phoenix headed his horse back in the direction from which they had come. "It's time we get moving."

Without hesitation, Aerielle urged her own mount to follow. As she headed down the rise, her eyes on Phoenix, she wondered if *things* had changed, or if *Phoenix* had.

By the time they arrived at Sparrow's favorite pine grove some twenty minutes later, the tension had dissipated. Even Phoenix seemed to have let go of his momentary frustration. When they began to dismount, they had essentially been divided into three groups of two.

Aerielle wasn't sure if the division of couples was intentional, but she didn't care. More like grateful. Riding the Stargazer land today with Phoenix had brought back more than memories. The emotions that overcame her the last couple of hours had grown relentless since they'd left the camas prairie and she'd been reminded of Phoenix's stubborn pride. The past had stolen her unto itself, romancing her with the simplest of memories and the most intimate. She wanted nothing more than to be alone with Phoenix, but would have to settle for the yards that lay between them and the others.

Phoenix slid from his mount like a wraith. Seconds later he stood holding Aerielle's horse's bridle gazing up at Aerielle with an intensity, which made her wonder at his thoughts. "May I assist you, Meyui?" he murmured softly.

In response, Aerielle pulled her feet free of her stirrups and swung one leg over her mare's neck so that she was facing Phoenix from the saddle. His arms reached for her and she slipped into them. In but a moment she was standing before him, his hands at her waist, his gaze cleaving to hers. It was the kind of look that would normally have left her immobile. However, Aerielle's posterior was suddenly proclaiming how long it had been in the saddle.

She groaned and reached back to rub at her backside, essentially locking Phoenix's arms in place at her waist.

His eyes glinted. "Need help with that?"

"Phoenix Yellow Wolf Stargazer. That sounds like something Hawk would say."

"Hmm. It does. Maybe I've been living with him too long."

"Well, maybe that's a good thing—living with Hawk that is. Not your offer to…assist." Flushing, Aerielle glanced over the back of Nimipu to see Sofia laughing at something Hawk had said.

"So, did your brother say anything about that kiss he planted on Sofia last night?"

"Only that he was surprised she didn't belt him."

"He's not very perceptive where Sofia is concerned, is he? I told Sofia she may have to be more obvious. Say ten ponies tied at his teepee or something."

Phoenix chuckled. "Let's hope I'm a little more perceptive when it comes to you."

As he spoke, the wind caught his hair and it reached out whispering against Aerielle's face. A familiar scent caught her attention.

"You smell like that shampoo again." Reaching out, she

greedily gathered up a portion of his mane and drew it to her nose.

"You seemed to like it, so I figured, waste not, want not."

Before Aerielle could respond, she was struck by a snowball. Or Phoenix was. Or they both were, as close as they were standing. She groaned. Phoenix pulled away, looking past Nimipu at his brother. "Hawk!"

Aerielle had never experienced a snowball fight like the one that followed. Despite growing up in Minnesota, she had no recollection of exchanging shots with this many people at once, every man and woman out for themselves. Even Sparrow got into the fun. The males dominated, determined to annihilate each other, especially the brothers. Aerielle was already sore from laughing so much the night before, she wondered if she'd be able to breathe without pain by the morrow. But she didn't care. She was exhilarated, joyous, and…and intoxicated. Intoxicated with the day, intoxicated with the joy of the moment, intoxicated by the love she could barely keep from declaring.

Suddenly the fear she felt at risking her heart was gone. Despite everything she'd gone through in the past, her gain had outweighed her loss. As a result, she was willing to risk her heart again.

The certain knowledge of this brought Aerielle to a standstill. Like a statue, she could do nothing but stare after Phoenix as he battled his opponents.

Some fifteen feet away, Phoenix was about to release his latest snow-packed creation in Jared's direction, when he felt certain he was about to be hit from behind. He jerked around to see who hunted him, but found himself looking at Aerielle instead. She stood staring at him, seemingly immobilized, a look of surprise on her face. Was something wrong?

The snowball he held slipped from his hand, and Phoenix hurried toward her over the now well-trampled snow. "What is it? Are you okay?" he asked urgently.

Abruptly she smiled, her eyes alight. "I'm fine. But you

look like the abominable snow-Indian." Reaching up, she began brushing snow from his hair. Her gloved hands were surprisingly gentle, as if she were caressing his hair more than anything. "What did I do to make you think something was wrong?"

"You were staring at me." Now didn't *that* sound stupid.

"I like staring at you," she teased.

"That's not what I meant exactly."

"What are you doing?!" he demanded with a grin as she slid her hands from the ends of his hair into the deep pockets of his jacket.

"Warming up my hands. My gloves are soaked through from making snowballs."

Phoenix raised an eyebrow. "Might be more effective if you remove your gloves before putting your hands in my pockets."

"I don't know about that," she intoned sarcastically. "There's snow in this one," she said, pulling a handful of the white stuff from his left pocket. "And in this one—" Her expression grew thoughtful and Phoenix immediately attempted to stop her, but he was too late. "—in this one there's a present, which from your reaction, I wasn't supposed to see."

They both looked down at the blue foil wrapped gift about six inches long by an inch and a half wide. Phoenix didn't try and take it back from her.

"Is this for me?"

"Yes...I meant to give it to you before we left the stable today, but we were interrupted by my perfectly-timed brother."

"Which means you probably intended to give it to me when we were alone." Aerielle reluctantly moved to put it back, but Phoenix put out a hand to stop her. Glancing at the four still playing like children with a snow day, he said, "You can open it now."

She looked up, studying his face. "You sure?"

As far as Phoenix was concerned, he hadn't wanted to be alone for Aerielle's sake. It was himself. He never was big on giving or receiving personal gifts in front of others. But he wouldn't make Aerielle wait. "I'm sure."

"Looks like a pen and pencil set."

"I assure you it's not," he replied sardonically. "It's not even a Christmas present, which is why I didn't give it to you yesterday. It's something to remind you of Idaho."

Aerielle glanced back down. "A souvenir collector's spoon?"

"I'm gonna open it myself if you don't get on with it!" Phoenix feigned an effort to retrieve the gift, but Aerielle reeled it in, hugging it to herself. "Don't you dare. Help me take these wet gloves off first."

Quickly removing his own, Phoenix pulled Aerielle's off one hand at a time, while she held her gift like a prized treasure in the other. Not wasting another second, she eagerly ripped off the paper. Balling it up, she shoved it into his pocket where the wet gloves had gone.

Carefully, she lifted the lid. "It's a ring."

"I didn't want it in a ring box for obvious reasons. It's Idaho. Your dog, Idaho. I had it made from some of his ashes. It's a red diamond because he was a red merle...."

Phoenix's voice trailed off as Aerielle glanced up at him, shock filling her expression. "This was made from Idaho?"

"Yeah, they take some of the ashes, remove the carbon and compress them until they form a diamond."

Tears pooled in her eyes. "And you did this for me? It must have cost a small fortune."

"It wasn't about money, Meyui. I saw what that dog meant to you. I had to find a way to keep him with you."

"It's stunning," said Aerielle lifting the ring and admiring the white gold band with its simple stone setting. "I've never seen a red diamond."

"Here, let me take the box so you can try it on. It should fit the ring finger on your right hand. I measured one of the rings you wear on that finger when you took it off prepping for Thanksgiving."

As Aerielle slid the ring on, Phoenix wished he was putting the ring on *for* her, her left hand of course. They'd had no ring fourteen years ago. Technically hadn't a need for one. Yet maybe if there had been something more tangible to their exchange of vows, he would have made a different decision. Emotion caught in his throat.

Aerielle seemed to be having the same problem as her tears spilled over. Was she thinking about their lack of ring, too? Or was she contemplating her loss of Idaho? What an amazing day it had been so far, and he had made her sad. What was he thinking, letting her open the gift, now?

"I'm so sorry, Meyui."

She glanced up at him, seeing raw emotion on his normally unreadable face. "Whatever for? It's beyond perfect."

"Yet I've made you cry."

"Oh, Hemene. These are tears of joy. I keep thinking I know you, but you continue to amaze me. I haven't been this happy in, well, let's just say a long, long time. And it's all because of you. I'll cherish this gift forever."

Phoenix wanted to cherish *her* forever. Wanted to take away any and all of her unhappy days. He'd have found a way to buy her a ring for each finger if it were but possible to return to her all that had been stolen, starting with his love.

Oh, God, what a fool he was. What wasn't he willing to do for her? How could he deny her a simple costume party? "I'll go."

Wiping the tears from her cheeks, she stared at him, his expression full of tenderness. "Okay, I missed a sentence there. Where are you going?"

"To the Gilberts' New Year's Eve costume party."

"What? Where in the world did that come from?"

"I want to *keep* making you happy."

"Oh, Phoenix, I—" Cutting off the rest of her sentence, Aerielle leaned toward him and promptly kissed him.

"I'm gonna go tell the girls about the party," she continued, stepping back, her face radiant, "and show them my ring of Idaho."

Phoenix said nothing as he watched her run off. Just stood there and stared. Had she been about to admit she loved him? Would she want to say those words when she knew everything? Phoenix longed to think so, for he could love no other than his Meyui. He longed to see his Morning Light *every* morning for the rest of his life.

"I can't believe what I'm seeing," Hawk remarked as he approached, catching his brother off guard.

Phoenix glanced around. "What? Where?"

"You *love* her."

Confused, Phoenix turned back to his brother.

Hawk nodded toward Aerielle, now in a huddle with Sofia and Sparrow. "You really *love* her."

"You sound surprised. Since when is this news to you?"

Hawk studied Phoenix. "Since I saw it on your face as plain as day."

Phoenix's jaw tightened, but he didn't speak, not knowing what to say.

"Don't worry," assured Hawk. "You're back to total inscrutability. I guess hearing you *say* you love her isn't the same as actually seeing it written on your face. How long have you felt this strongly about her?"

Phoenix shrugged. "Can't say when I knew I loved her exactly. I just know I started falling the moment Sparrow's new sign language instructor walked into the barn and offered to help me muck out the stalls."

"I had no idea. Not really. If I'd known—"

"I was always good at hiding things."

"Except from her."

"Except from her," agreed Phoenix.

"You need to tell her the truth, Phoenix, the reason you left. If she cares half as much for you as you feel for her, she deserves to know."

"I know. One of these days, Hawk. But not today. I won't ruin today."

→→→

Dinner turned out to be a come as you are when you are, as six bedraggled riders arrived in various states of dryness and warmth. Both Sofia and Aerielle had pulled out dry clothes to put on, but Aerielle had also chosen to take a hot shower followed by a quick blow dry to her hair. She thought she'd be last to dinner, but saw Hawk ahead of her in the hallway striding toward the kitchen and the sounds of laughter.

Despite the appealing aroma of well-seasoned food beckoning from that direction, Aerielle glanced back toward the room the brothers were sharing, wondering if Phoenix remained. The door was open and muted light emanated from within. Was he still there? She really would like to thank him again for the ring—alone this time.

When Aerielle neared the door, she hesitated. This was Phoenix's former bedroom, the one she herself had occupied for nigh on six months. It was full of memories, some happy, some so heart-wrenching, the memories still pained her. How long had Hawk said she cried herself to sleep? A month? Yet despite everything, she loved again the man who'd caused that pain.

Taking a deep breath and releasing it slowly, Aerielle proceeded to the doorway and looked in. The room was dimply lit, the only light coming from the attached bath and the clear night of countless stars showing through the window. The window Phoenix was staring out of, his back to her, his freshly brushed hair cascading down his back. She found him as beautiful a figure as the sky beyond.

Aerielle must have made a sound, for Phoenix spoke. "Do you ever miss the view of the night sky, Hawk? From Idaho?"

Clearly he thought she was his brother, but Aerielle answered him anyway. "More than you know."

She thought for a moment he stiffened, but then as lithe

and graceful as he mounted his horse, he turned to face her. She could well imagine him as a warrior of old moving through the wilderness, a silent ghost blending into the trees. The thought shot spirals of desire through her. It didn't help that he was barefoot and bare-chested, his fresh jeans transforming into buckskins to form the warrior image. Tendrils of his hair had slipped forward, trailing down his chest, drawing her attention to his sculpted sinewy frame.

"What are you doing here?"

Good grief, thought Phoenix, as the words slipped from his tongue. The one person he'd rather see than all others and he was demanding to know why she was here. "I'm sorry. That came out wrong. You just surprised me. I thought Hawk had come back."

"Disappointed?" she smirked, walking toward him.

Despite his disinclination to show the scars he bore, no man, let alone Phoenix, would be disappointed when the woman he loved was looking at him the way Aerielle was looking at him now. "Not in the least," he said, desperately aiming for casualness as she approached him. "Am I late for dinner?"

"I don't think you can be tonight. Actually, I thought I might catch you alone, or at the very least, minus Hawk."

"Specific reason?"

"Well I—Why? Do I need one, Half-Breed?" Reaching upward, she traced the strands of his hair from his temples to his shoulders and then down his chest. Surely he was going to burst into flames. Just as her hands reached the bottom of his rib cage, Phoenix wrapped his arms around her, crushing her against him. He lowered his head, molding his mouth to hers, seeking the sweet nectar inside.

Her honeyed lips opened to him, even as her arms wrapped around his waist and her hands slipped up his back beneath the mantel of his hair. As Phoenix lost himself in Aerielle, the thought quickly came and went that this would be an excellent time for his brother to walk in.

The moment his kiss claimed her, Aerielle knew this was a wonderful terrible idea. What fire had she started? And the one time she truly would have welcomed Hawk, he would not appear. She should push her Hemene away, stop what they could not finish. But while his mouth demanded her response, she was as greedy as he. The muscles in his back rippled beneath her eager caressing hands even as his long silken hair whispered across the backs of them. His flesh was as hot as if he'd been standing before a fire, and Aerielle's fingertips as sensitive as if reading braille.

"Aerielle." He gasped her name while pulling his mouth from hers, and she knew what it cost him for she knew what it cost her to *let* him.

"I know, I know," she whispered in agreement.

He buried his face against her neck, his breathing ragged, but he held her just as tightly, still not ready to let go. Aerielle bit her lip to keep herself from asking for more. Lessening the intensity, she continued to stroke his back, letting her fingers trace each line of muscle. It was as they held each other such, that she began noticing the flesh beneath her fingertips change in texture wherever she drew them. His back should have been smooth. Instead, it felt...Aerielle couldn't describe it exactly. It was uneven, somehow. Her hands ceased caressing and began exploring.

Phoenix knew the moment she recognized something was amiss. Knew he could not stop her from seeing the scars. Tried anyway. "Meyui, no."

"Oh, yes, Hemene," she deterred, stepping away from him.

"Not today, please."

"Today is as good as any. Turn around."

Aerielle noted his reluctance, but determined the secret needed sharing. He was hiding something awful, she knew it, her hands had felt it. Even as he turned his back to her, Aerielle reached for the nearest light switch, the glaring brightness of the overhead light revealing everything his mane of hair didn't hide.

Stunned into silence, Aerielle reached out, and with a touch like gossamer, she brushed away the waves of hair, her eyes and then her fingers tracing the lines of white scars trailing down the length of his back. She'd spent enough years in the medical field to know how badly he must have been beaten for such scars to remain. How could anyone have done this to another human being?

"Phoenix, why?"

The agony in Aerielle's voice was echoed in that of Phoenix's when he replied. "You know why. Because I'm an Indian." *And I had the audacity to love you.* The last words, spoken only to himself, were filled with silent tears as he wept for the past—not for what might have been, but for what *had* been.

→→→

Indian summer sunlight warmed the vast Idaho prairie, as well as Phoenix, as he labored repairing fence lines and mending gates. Despite the hard work, Phoenix had never felt more at peace. When he and Aerielle had parted that sunrise newly married, Phoenix should have been tired, but instead he felt alive. He had wanted to spend the whole day with his Morning Light, but there was work to be done.

At last, Phoenix finished the gate that paralleled the dusty dirt road which divided two large sections of pasture land. The road was a private one, the land in all directions belonging to his step-father.

It was therefore a surprise to Phoenix when he heard the sound of a vehicle approaching from the road. He straightened before the gate, his hammer hanging loosely in his hand. He didn't recognize the dust-raising truck nearing him, but he did recognize the occupants. Jim Peterson and two of his cronies.

Phoenix's muscles tightened with tension, and he could feel the familiar twitch within his jaw.

The truck came to a stop, the passengers getting out with leisurely assurance, their doors slamming almost in unison.

"You're on private property," announced Phoenix, his face granite as they climbed over the fence.

"So why aren't you on the reservation?" quipped Peterson in response.

He and his two buddies swaggered toward Phoenix as if he were the trespasser.

Phoenix's hand tightened on the hammer. "I suggest you leave."

"Oh, we will," said Peterson, pausing just a few feet away. "Just as soon as we make sure you understand a few things. One of the others grinned, shifting his weight. At that point Phoenix caught a glimpse of something beneath his jacket. It was the handle of a gun which had been stuffed into his jeans.

Without thought, Phoenix raised the hammer and swung at Peterson who was the closest. Peterson deflected the blow and the hammer glanced of his shoulder.

"You damn Indian," Peterson shouted, lunging at Phoenix.

Phoenix landed a punch in Peterson's midsection and then was grabbed from behind. Like the wolf-warrior he was, Phoenix fought ferociously, landing many blows, but there were three of them, and within minutes he was overcome. Immediately he was hauled to his feet, his arms pinned back by the two unnamed, his nose radiating pain. It was then he realized it was broken, and there was blood running rivulets down his face, dripping off his chin.

"Do you have any idea why I'm doing this?" demanded Peterson, standing directly in front of Phoenix. "Do you?!" he asked again, putting his face close to the one he'd bloodied.

Giving in to the need for some sort of response, Phoenix spit at his enemy, enjoying the sight of the blood and saliva leaving a trail on Peterson's face. Peterson responded with a right fist to Phoenix's jaw, explosive pain resulting.

"I'm not doing this because you're a half-breed," continued Peterson calmly, wiping at his face. "I'm doing this because you're a half-breed who can't keep his filthy hands off a white girl. I saw you with Aerielle yesterday morning behind the Feed Barn—saw you kissing her like the savage you are. Now I want you to tell me that you'll be a good Indian and not go near Aerielle again."

Phoenix's eyes narrowed. "Go to hell."

Peterson struck him again. "Say it!"

"Never."

Once more Phoenix was hit, his face taking the brunt of the punishment. "Never," he repeated before his adversary even had a chance to speak.

He was rewarded once again. "I got all day, breed."

Phoenix glared at Peterson through eyes that were slowly swelling shut. "Better get more vacation time."

Peterson hit him again, and then several more times in his mid-section, sending pain to every breath Phoenix took.

"Say it!"

Phoenix didn't even attempt to open his eyes. "I'll never give into you."

"Is that right?!"

Suddenly, Phoenix was thrown forward against the gate he'd been working on, his long hair spilling over the top rail, his arms pinned to the railing by Peterson's silent companions.

"Well, then," continued Peterson, "how do you feel about me payin' a visit to your mama?"

Phoenix glared, and he fought the hands that held him for all the good it did. And then there was a whirring sound. Phoenix cried out as a sharp slicing pain ripped through his shirt and into his back.

"And after I visit your mama, I think I'll chat with your sister."

The whip came again, tearing away at the layers of flesh. Another agonized scream forced its way past Phoenix's lips.

"Now you listen good, breed. You stay away from Aerielle, or I'll be forced to discipline her even before I visit your family."

Breaking the speed of sound, the whip cracked and struck once more. This time Phoenix bit his tongue rather than cry out.

"You can't be everywhere at all times," came Peterson's voice behind him. "You can't protect them all. And don't bother calling the sheriff. We'll deny everything and we got alibis. Now," said Peterson, bringing the whip down for another round, "you got something you want to say to me?"

Phoenix did not reply, for at that moment he slipped into unconsciousness. Sometime during the blackness, Phoenix briefly became aware of a another loud cracking sound, and then the earth trembled beneath him, around him, and he thought only of death.

The sun was setting when Phoenix awoke, surprised to find himself alive. He was cold. The sunlight was almost gone, his shirt was in shreds, and his blood was on the ground. Phoenix tried to move, but pain like fire consumed him. How long had the whip continued to rip away at his back? How much of the pain was caused by torn fabric ground into the wounds? His ancestors had done something right. They'd worn nothing but a loincloth for war, keeping their wounds clean. And what of the damage done with fists? Phoenix couldn't even feel his nose anymore. His eyes, nose, and face throbbed as one.

Forcing one swollen eye open a mere slit, Phoenix tried to tell if his horse was around. There was no sign of Steel from his present vantage point. In an agony of effort, Phoenix lifted his head for a better view. Nooooo! The death he'd dreamed of lay before him in the form of Steel's lifeless body.

Phoenix reached out to touch the stallion, his hand becoming still as his eyes caught something else he could not readily identify but which looked like hair. And then realization dawned. It was his, carefully cut off and laid out for display beside the body of his horse. In their own way his enemies had scalped him. Ironic. The Nez

Perce had never taken scalps. But Phoenix wasn't laughing. For the first time since his father left, Phoenix wept.

→→→

Aerielle called Phoenix's name three times, but no response. He was lost in the past, having left her behind. Stepping closer, Aerielle pressed her face to his shoulder blade, her lips to a ragged scar. Her arms she slid around him and up, so that her hands cupped his shoulders, pulling him near. His body was tight with tension, and she knew he was unaware of her presence.

Suddenly he spoke, his voice distant and without emotion, his thoughts still elsewhere. "After I'd passed out from the whipping, they cut off my hair."

Despite the simplicity of his words, they cried out in the stillness of the room. Aerielle knew what that particular loss must have cost him.

She longed to know more, she wished to know what Phoenix had been remembering—who had done this to him, when it had happened, and why that person or persons hated Indians so, that they had not only whipped him, but cut off his crowning glory. But Aerielle had already asked too much, pushed too hard. Phoenix was hurting. *This* time because of *her.*

"Phoenix." She spoke his name again, bringing her lips as a healing caress to each line of white crossing his back. "Phoenix, I'm sorry."

It was from a great distance that Phoenix heard her voice, felt her lips against his flesh, her breath against his soul. Her kisses whispered, "I'm sorry. I'm sorry it happened. I'm sorry I brought it back."

Inside, Phoenix bowed in acceptance, for despite the agony the memory of that day brought back, it was nothing compared to the fourteen years that had followed—life without Aerielle.

I am going in the morning when the sun *eetetolokt* [pauses on the horizon's edge]. It is then that I will leave you and all others. You, my only son, and my daughters gone, were only loaned to me. Loaned by Ahkunkenekoo [God, Deity]. You are my brother, they, my sisters. I will go with the new sun.

Yellow Wolf, as quoted in *Yellow Wolf, His Own Story,* the evening before he died

22

Later after eating dinner, Aerielle escaped to find some solitude. She wanted—needed—to be alone. Shutting herself in the room she shared with Sofia, Aerielle settled onto the bed, pulling her knees to her chest and wrapping her arms tightly around them.

The past—her past—hung over her, for just as she regretted not being there for Phoenix, she regretted *his* not being there for *her.*

Her memories were filled with nights she'd wept over his absence and sometimes even hated him for it. Their separate paths those fourteen years had not been easy ones for either of them, but Aerielle hazarded to guess Phoenix's pain had yet to rival her own. It would. For her loss was his, though their grief would not be the same when soon the years of silence were broken. He would suffer separately, uniquely, fighting his own set of horrors as she had fought hers.

Aerielle buried herself in the memories as if to prepare herself for what was yet to come. It was not difficult to remember. Some things remained forever as real and poignant as the moment they were inscribed upon the soul.

→→→

Breathe, they said, but Aerielle couldn't breathe—she was too busy hyperventilating. Concentrate, they said, but Aerielle couldn't concentrate—she was too busy screaming. With one last gut ripping cry and an assist from more hands than she could count, Aerielle forced her unwilling child into the waiting world. It's indignant cries were instantly as loud as her's had been.

"What is it?" she demanded raggedly, attempting to sit up despite the nurses' efforts to hold her down.

"A boy. Our first 4th of July baby."

Aerielle grinned. "I knew it. I knew he was a boy. Let me see him."

Within minutes that seemed like hours, the baby was placed on Aerielle's less rounded stomach just like in all the prenatal films. It was the only thing that had happened like she'd been told it would. Aerielle wanted to laugh as her son continued to express his own feelings on the matter.

"He must weigh ten pounds," said one of the nurses.

"I could have told them that," murmured Aerielle, smiling down at her child. "But I certainly can't name you Nimipu like that big colt, now can I? Not to worry, Mommy already has a name picked out for you." And how appropriate it was, thought Aerielle, fondling the moist waves of dark brown hair crowning her son's head. "You will be Wolf Stargazer Buchanan, but I, and only I, shall call you Hemene."

Not caring in the least what anyone chose to refer to him as, Wolf Stargazer Buchanan filled his lungs once more.

Time shifted, three and a half years went by, Wolf grew into a boy, and Aerielle became a mother by experience as well as by giving birth. They were wonderful, horrible years, bringing both joy and heartache. Each moment was precious, each moment quickly lost. Now, once again they shared the same room. Only this time, Wolf occupied the bed, and Aerielle was the one who wept.

She tried not to cry, or at the very least to do it silently lest she waken her sleeping son. It was just one of the many nights they'd spent thus, just a few of the many tears she'd shed. But it was different this time. Their brief journey in life together was almost over, and though Aerielle had known for the last year that she would someday lose her beloved son, she had never given up hoping for a miracle.

Wiping away at a silent stream of tears, Aerielle gazed down at her three-year-old's ashen face, peaceful only in sleep. The beautiful hair he'd had, so much like his father's, was gone. The chemo treatments had seen to that. His closed obsidian eyes had grown dull with pain, and his high cheekbones more pronounced with the loss of weight. Yet even as his life ebbed, he was the spitting image of his father, the likeness uncanny, even unto the magic of his hands, shown now in the way they nestled a sleeping six-month-old puppy.

Of course pets were not permitted in hospitals, one more reason Aerielle had chosen to let her son spend his last days at home. Wolf and his dog were best friends, and the boy found solace in his presence. Aerielle had given the Australian Shepherd to Hemene for his third birthday, the same day which he'd named the dog Idaho. The two had been inseparable ever since, except for hospital stays. If these were to be his last days—if this were to be his last day—Hemene deserved at the very least to have Idaho by his side.

"Mommy?"

His voice startled her, and Aerielle hurriedly wiped at her tears as she stood. Her effort was for naught, as her son didn't open his eyes.

"Yes, honey?"

"I wish you and Nana and Idaho could come with me to see Jesus."

"Oh, Hemene, I wish we could, too. But time passes faster in Heaven and I bet we'll be there very soon, especially Idaho.

"So if dying is like going to sleep, then when I wake up again, Idaho might be there already?"

"I bet he will be sweetheart."

Suddenly Wolf's hand was on her arm, his dark eyes opening to meet hers. "Is it almost over, Mommy?"

Aerielle felt as if her heart stopped beating. Words of response caught in her throat even as Wolf continued. "Will I be with Jesus soon? I'm so tired, but every time I fall asleep I wake up here."

Oh God, if she could only *keep* him waking up here. Biting her lip, Aerielle fought the new flood of tears. "Yes, honey, you will be with Jesus, soon." The tears escaped anyway, slipping down her cheeks unchecked.

Wolf studied them. "Why are you crying?"

"Because I'll miss you."

"Will I miss you?"

"No, Hemene. That's one of the nice things about Heaven. There's only happiness there."

"Then, I wish you could come, too. Now, not later."

Aerielle gripped the railing of Wolf's bed, fighting for the strength to continue. "So do I, sweetheart, but I have to stay and take care of Idaho."

"Mommy, hold me."

Aerielle fumbled with the railing on the bed, lowered it, and then lay down next to her son, the dog nearly squished between them. Reaching for her son, she gently pressed his head to her breast and cradled him like a fragile crysallis, waiting for him to transform from a wolf into a butterfly and be free.

Unable to stop them, fresh tears slipped from her eyes.

"It's okay to cry, Mommy," said Wolf, his eyes closing. "That's what you always say."

Nodding though he couldn't see, Aerielle brushed a kiss to his forehead. "I love you, Hemene."

As Wolf drifted back to sleep, Aerielle fought her body's need to do the same. She wouldn't leave him. She wouldn't miss what time was left, even if it was just to watch him sleep.

It was nearly dawn on that cold January day when her wolf-turned-butterfly left her forever.

→→→

Her cheeks moist, Aerielle reached for the photo hidden in her suitcase. It was the one from her night stand, the twin to the one at work. She gazed down at Wolf and Idaho, the boy laughing, the dog attempting to lick his face.

The picture had been taken on Hemene's birthday, and you couldn't even tell his hair wasn't his own. He'd insisted upon a wig a few weeks or so before the picture, after an older boy had accused him of scalping himself. Aerielle had managed to get him a wig closely resembling his own hair and at the same shoulder length his had once been.

Holding the photograph to her chest, Aerielle tried to picture her son as he would have appeared now. No doubt his hair would have been as long as his father's. But he'd be laughing at one of his mother's jokes, for his sense of humor had shown signs of matching her own. And at thirteen, he'd probably be friends with someone like Tyler and have his eye on a cute girl in his English class.

But it wasn't this version of Wolf Aerielle longed to see standing before her. It was her three-year-old little boy who had told her it was okay to cry, and who now cradled a long lost dog in his arms. Aerielle blinked back tears. "I still miss you, Hemene. Be a good boy and take care of Idaho till I get there."

→→→

"Let's go costume shopping," announced Sofia, popping into Nimipu's stall where Aerielle stood brushing the horse. The stallion snorted at Sofia's presence.

"Beautiful, isn't he?" asked Aerielle, stroking Nimipu's nose. "Looks just like his father, but he has his mother's temperament."

"How come he looks different than the one in the next stall. That one *looks* like an Appaloosa—white, brown spots. Nimipu is brown with white spots on his back end."

Aerielle grinned. "He's a Blanket Appaloosa. Dark all over except a white spotted blanket on the rump."

"Oh, I get it," said Sofia "Kinda like a tortoiseshell cat is the reverse image of a calico."

Laughing, Aerielle shook her head. "There are also Leopard Appaloosas, Snowflake Appaloosas, and Peacock Appaloosas among others. Kinda like costumes. Speaking of which, Everett would be the best place to go for supplies. And now would probably be the best time, with Phoenix off visiting his father.

I'll be done here in just a few minutes. Why don't you see if Hawk wants to go with."

→→→

Hawk did indeed want to "go with" as they said in Minnesota. While the conversation flowed freely between the three of them, Aerielle drove the sixty mile stretch to the large city of Everett, large in relation to Shaman Prairie in that it had a population nearing 40,000. Hawk, seated in the middle of the truck cab between the two woman, was enjoying the undivided attention, at one point referring to his present company as "the most ravishing escorts he'd ever had." Despite his smooth talk, Aerielle and Sofia were quick to send him off during their plunder of a costumes and makeup shop on one of the main streets in downtown Everett. Aerielle also picked up some beautiful red fabric she would ply Ellie's Singer sewing machine with.

When the group met back at the truck, Hawk suggested they get an Italian Soda.

"An Italian soda?" repeated Sofia "What is it?"

"What *is* it?! said Hawk. "You Minnesotans need to get out more."

Aerielle laughed. "What they are is wonderful. A tasty concoction of crushed ice, club soda, creme, and the flavoring of your choice. I like banana."

"Black cherry," put in Hawk.

"I haven't had one in years."

"Then lets."

"Not here," said Aerielle. "Shaman Prairie. The General Store. We haven't shown Sofia around town yet, anyway."

"Well, let's go," said Sofia tugging on Hawk's arm. "With all this talk I'm getting thirsty."

→→→

Sofia was slurping noisily at the bottom of her glass while Hawk and Aerielle grinned over her head.

"You were right," said Sofia, pushing the empty glass away from herself reluctantly. "Italian Sodas are wonderful."

Hawk nodded. "Black cherry."

Aerielle shook her head. "Banana."

"Strawberry," announced Sofia, spinning her stool around from the counter to face the rest of the old-fashioned store. "Mind if I look around?"

"Not at all," said Hawk, following Sofia with his eyes as she started down an aisle. "I think as long as we're here I'll go on over to the Feed Barn and pick up some supplies," he added to Aerielle.

"We'll meet over there. I'm going to see if I can buy myself a wicker basket."

"Please tell me what you're going to the party as."

"If I do, you have to promise not to tell Phoenix. I want to see his reaction when he sees me."

Hawk's eyes lit up. "I swear, on my honor, not to tell Phoenix, or anyone else for that matter."

"I'm going as Little Red Riding Hood."

Hawk burst into laughter. "Red Riding Hood and Hemene Moxmox?"

"Hey, no one said the wolf wasn't yellow."

"That is a hoot. Now I want to see his reaction, too. And what about Sofia? Any hints on her costume?"

Aerielle grinned, shaking her head. "You might as well get going. I'm not gonna tell you."

Hawk left for the Feed Barn only partially satisfied as Aerielle joined Sofia exploring the store. She'd never spent much time in here despite the fact that she'd lived not just five miles away when living with Phoenix's family. Mostly when Aerielle had come to town it had been for fabric.

It wasn't long before Sofia found herself a sweatshirt with Shaman Prairie written across the front, and they continued to wander the aisles like two kids in a toy store, pointing out this and that. Aerielle even found Red Riding Hood a basket.

"Do you know him?" said Sofia suddenly, stopping and nodding towards the end of the aisle they were in. "That guy's been staring at you."

Aerielle glanced up, her eyes coming to rest on a guy with dark hair about her age. He did seem familiar, but Aerielle couldn't place the face. Abruptly, he turned and left, and Aerielle shrugged. "Maybe. Don't remember."

Aerielle shifted her attention to the shelves in front of them, taking in the small selection of Shampoos and Conditioners. And then she started. "It's not possible. I don't believe it."

"Believe what?" asked Sofia. And then she watched in surprise as Aerielle pulled a bottle off the shelf and removed the cap.

Aerielle inhaled and then grinned, an old, familiar scent of musk greeting her. "This is it. I can't believe it. This is really it."

"What is what?" demanded Sofia, as Aerielle proceeded to inhale again with a euphoric expression on her face.

"It's—" Aerielle paused, reading the bottle and then proudly showing it to Sofia. "It's 'Earth and Fire...Musk'".

"Yeah, so, is this a hobby of yours, going into stores and sniffing shampoos?"

Aerielle burst out laughing. If Sofia only knew how many bottles she had smelled over the last fourteen years, many of them in the last month. "It's not even *sold* in Minnesota."

Sofia continued to look baffled. "Yeah, so, take some with you. Buy a whole case. But you might want to know, this is a man's shampoo."

Aerielle grinned confidently. "Yes. I know."

It wasn't long before Aerielle and Sofia completed their shopping experience. Aerielle's bag included a basket containing shampoo and conditioner. Certainly not what the original Red Riding Hood brought her grandmother.

"I sure had fun today," announced Sofia, clutching her own bag with its sweatshirt and other souvenirs.

"Me, too," agreed Aerielle as they headed for the exit.

Someone came through the door in front of them, pausing in their path. Distracted, Aerielle glanced up and then stopped breathing. Shock overcame her. Unable to speak, she just stared. Staring back was Jim Peterson. Fear Aerielle'd thought long forgotten rushed in even as she took a deep calming breath.

He was much the way she remembered him, his wavy blond hair a bit shorter, his face more lined. There was no surprise in his expression, just a sudden grin and a self-assured look. "Mike said you were back. I didn't believe him."

Mike. The guy watching them who had looked familiar.

"I should have, you know," continued Peterson. "I knew you'd come back someday, Aerielle."

The way he said the words made her shiver. Aerielle hadn't seen Jim Peterson since the day he'd left the marks on her arm, but he had written a string of letters, all proclaiming his belief she'd come back to him. They'd only stopped because her father had died, and her mother and she had moved to Texas. Aerielle had just assumed Peterson would have gotten over things when he couldn't write her anymore. Clearly he hadn't.

Aerielle tightened her grip on her bag and stepped to the side. "If you'll excuse us—"

"Aerielle, where are you going?" Peterson asked, his voice icy cold as he moved with her, blocking her path. "You haven't even said hello."

"I'll go start the truck," declared Sofia, brushing past.

Aerielle knew Sofia was going to get Hawk. Knew his "Indian" presence might aggravate things, longed for it anyway. If Jim didn't let her leave, maybe Aerielle'd lam him over the head with a little Earth and Fire. But making a scene wasn't on her wish list for the day, any more than passing out from fright.

"I really need to be going," she tried once more, attempting to go around him.

Peterson cut her off, this time his hands coming to rest lightly on her forearms. Aerielle tensed and resisted the urge to jerk her arms away, recalling the pain of trying to do so in the past.

"You have no idea how much I missed you, Aerielle. But I knew you'd return in due time."

The guy had obviously lost a few more marbles in that same time. "Please let go of me."

Instead, Peterson forcefully raised her free hand to his lips.

Aerielle nearly attempted to pull away and swing then, but schooled herself to be calm and tried one last time. "I need to go." She bit the words out in staccato, hoping she sounded firm and assured instead of panicked.

"Of course you do," Peterson replied much to her surprise. And then he released her as well. "We'll see each other again soon, Aerielle, I'm sure of it."

And then he left through the door from which he'd come, leaving Aerielle to stare at the place where he'd been. She shook her head, attempting to free herself of the undeniable revulsion and fear she felt. She tried to tell herself she was overreacting, but she didn't hear. Trying to pull herself together, Aerielle stepped out into the coldness of the day, which had turned to night.

A worried pair met her on the lighted boardwalk.

"Sofia said someone was keeping you from leaving," worried Hawk

"He's gone," Aerielle mumbled as Sofia snagged her package from her limp hand.

Hawk put an arm around Aerielle's shoulders, swearing as he did so. "You're shaking like a leaf."

Aerielle looked up to meet Hawk's worried gaze. "It was Jim Peterson."

Hawk's face visibly paled. "Not again. Dear God, not again."

He looked as if he was about to say something more but then thought better of it. Before she could question him, Hawk began guiding them toward the truck. "We need to go."

Sofia looked at them both worriedly, but kept her mouth shut. Two minutes later, their tires hit the county road, Hawk driving this time. Sofia rode shotgun with Aerielle in the middle as if they were both determined to protect her.

It was only five miles to their destination, and the road quickly slipped away beneath them. Hawk had the steering wheel in a strangle hold, Sofia sat still and silent, and Aerielle stared out the windshield watching a heavy snow begin to fall, her thoughts tumultuous.

She continued to think on Jim Peterson's outrageous behavior. She'd never expected to see him again. Somehow she'd thought he'd just get over his fixation, maybe move away, possibly get himself in trouble with the law. It never occurred to her he'd still be here—waiting for her.

Though his phone calls had continued until Aerielle left the ranch two months after Phoenix disappeared, the anger that'd been in his voice had been replaced by a cold sickly sweetness—like that which she'd heard tonight.

"I wonder if he spends a lot of time in Shaman Prairie," said Aerielle. The question carried through the oppressive tension, reaching Hawk as he turned the truck into the mile long dirt driveway now dusted in snow.

"I suspect he does. He went into the grain business with his dad, and they move a lot of product through the Feed Barn. Of course, the last I knew, they still don't have any direct dealings with the Indians."

"I'll just have to stay out of town, then," said Aerielle, searching desperately for a solution. "I'll only be here another week or so."

"A lot can happen in a week, Aerielle."

"He doesn't even know where I'm staying."

"Not yet."

Aerielle peered at Hawk in the darkness. "What are you saying?"

"I'm saying he can find out if he wants to know. We have to tell Phoenix about this."

"Please, let's not. It'll only make things worse. Maybe we're making a mountain out of a molehill."

"Do *you* think so?"

Aerielle tried to say yes, but the word wouldn't get past her lips. Her fear of Peterson still clung to her, and the memories of his past threats echoed through time. "All right, so maybe the guy is a little off balance, but do we have to tell Phoenix about this? Can't we just wait and see what happens?"

"The last time we waited it cost us a dead horse and a pound of flesh."

"What?!" Aerielle wasn't sure she'd heard him right, but then she realized that Sofia was staring at him as well. There was a too-long stretch of silence before Hawk continued, the shake of his head making his reluctance to speak evident. "You were never supposed to know about it, Aerielle."

"There've been enough secrets."

Hawk laughed, a hollow sound that echoed Aerielle's own heart.

There was another silence as Hawk pulled the truck up in front of the house, the outside light revealing their faces for each other's review. Hawk's was lined with tension. Turning the key, he killed the engine, and the only sound was the whisper of snowflakes against the windshield.

"Jim Peterson put a bullet into Phoenix's stallion Steel."

Aerielle was stunned. "That's horrible. I'd just assumed that he'd died of natural causes. When did this happen?!"

"The day Phoenix left and didn't come back."

The first day Aerielle had died inside.

"I found the stallion when I went out looking for Phoenix," continued Hawk. "At that point I thought it was best you didn't know. In fact, Nevin was the only one I *did* tell."

"And then you got a phone call from Phoenix late that night." Aerielle's voice trailed off as she fought the surge of pain the memories were bringing back. "You said he only wanted to talk to *you*."

"That's right. It was then he told me Peterson and his buddies killed Steel and there was nothing but his word to prove it. He swore me to secrecy, Aerielle. Said he thought the best thing he could do for everyone was to disappear for a while. Phoenix wouldn't even tell *me* where he was, not for months. He told me that he'd drop you a note, said something about you guys not being serious and you getting over it. God knows it was the worst secret I'd ever been forced to keep." Hawk grunted. "Guess I *didn't* keep it."

Aerielle shook her head, shocked and confused. Nothing made sense. First a dead horse, then a phone call in which Phoenix lied about his and Aerielle's relationship, followed by a note to her with a whole different story, telling her the concocted marriage had been but a ploy to seduce her and he couldn't face her with his guilt. There had to be a piece missing. The entire sequence of events didn't make sense.

In the momentary silence, Sofia opened the passenger door and slipped out. "I think maybe I shouldn't be here for this." Gently she shut the door.

In the brief seconds it took for Sofia to depart, realization dawned and Aerielle turned on Hawk. "You didn't just mention a dead horse. You mentioned a pound of flesh. Were you referring to Phoenix's back?"

Hawk was stunned. "I didn't know you knew about.... How'd you find out about the scars?" Abruptly he looked embarrassed and glanced away. "Never mind."

"Not like that," Aerielle mumbled, her head reeling with revelation. "I didn't sleep with him. At least not *this* time around."

Suddenly Aerielle had the truck door open and was making a run for the brightly lit barn.

I could smell white people, the soldiers, a long way.... My Guardian Spirit instructed that I scout mostly alone. None of the enemies had appeared coming on our last sun's trail...I watched if antelope acted curious. It might be danger. If prairie birds flew up in distance, it might be buffalo stampeding.... The unexpected shadow against a big rock.

Yellow Wolf, Scout of the Nez Perce as quoted in *Chief Joseph of the Nez Perce* by Robert Penn Warren.

23

The distance to the barn seemed like miles as Aerielle rushed toward it—toward the truth. The puzzle of the past was coming together with frightening reality. The dead horse, Phoenix's beating, the call of lies to his brother, the note of...more lies?!

Aerielle's pain and anger spilled forth as she slid open the door. "Phoenix!" Her scream was harsh and insistent.

Horses stirred, but nothing more. He had to have heard her. "Phoenix!" She yelled his name again, marching down the passage between the stalls, the normally calming smell of horses and hay doing nothing to cool her anger. "Blast you, Yellow Wolf, where are you?!"

Horses snorted and Phoenix stepped out of Nimipu's stall, wiping his hands on a towel. "I'm here."

Aerielle stopped a few feet from Phoenix, vaguely aware of the smell of horse lineament. They gazed at each other—afraid. There was much at stake, much to lose. For Aerielle it was the future, for Phoenix it was life itself, and he had every reason to fear. He could hear Aerielle's anger lashing out at him, feel her pain pierce his being. He knew why she had come. It wasn't supposed to be like this. How did he explain? With the truth, an inner voice urged, the whole truth.

Across from him Aerielle fought her own battle, fighting the urge to run, to flee from the truth, to escape from the already overwhelming anguish. Raising her head high, she forced herself to speak.

"Before God, Phoenix, you need to tell me the truth."

Tossing away the towel he still clutched in his hands, he nodded, the waves of his hair rippling against his black sweatshirt, the familiar movement in his jaw revealing his tension. "Nothing but," he said simply.

"Then tell me, Hemene. Are we, or are we not, married?"

Phoenix swallowed—hard. "Not by white man's law."

"But by Nez Perce tradition?"

Silence followed, filled with an agony of soul. "Yes."

Aerielle closed her eyes against the backwash of tears. "Dear Jesus," she pleaded.

Her cry for help was painful to Phoenix's ears and torture to his heart. She must have suffered more than he'd ever imagined.

"Aerielle...." His voice was hoarse when he spoke, and the hand he raised to touch her dropped reluctantly back to his side.

"The scars on your back," said Aerielle, "Jim Peterson did that, didn't he?"

"Yes.... And with every wound he laid open, he promised the same for you...and Sparrow...and my mother...if I didn't leave you alone. I thought to protect you, protect them. I didn't know what else to do. It seemed the only solution at the time."

"Your solution was wrong."

"I know. But by the time I figured that out, it was too late, or at least I thought it was."

Aerielle's anger abruptly fizzled out. The answers she'd waited years to know had finally come, but Aerielle knew not the release she'd expected. Instead she felt the excruciating weight Phoenix had carried—for his family, for her, and unknowingly, for his son. What he had done, he had done out of love. Surely, he must have gone through his own form of Hell, and though different than her own, no less significant.

Aerielle's expression softened, revealing a lingering sadness. "Sometimes I hated you for leaving me, but it had to do with more than just my loving you and feeling betrayed. You see, Hemene....there was a child."

Aerielle saw him stiffen though his expression didn't change.

Stunned, Phoenix refused to believe he'd heard her right. "What are you saying?"

"Just what you think I am. When you left me, you left me pregnant."

No! Phoenix's thoughts screamed. Oh God, no! Aerielle had carried his child?! Not possible! Never! Horror and disbelief fought with Phoenix. He struggled to speak, though no words would come except those which would deny the possibility of that which Aerielle was speaking. "It can't be. We were only together the one night...." His voice trailed off as he realized the stupidity of his words. It *could* be, and it *had* been.

Phoenix reached out, grasping hold of the stable door for support. "The baby...you didn't...."

"You would believe me capable of murdering our child?"

Phoenix winced, shaking his head. "No...course not... stupid of me." Phoenix couldn't believe he'd even suggested it. Then where *was* this child of his? Was it someone else's child now, living out its existence with no knowledge of those who had created it through love? He searched Aerielle's eyes for conformation and was shocked by the sense of loss he found there.

Aerielle smiled tenderly, sadly, her eyes pooling with tears. "While you were coming home on the 4th of July, I was 1500 miles away giving birth to a baby boy."

"A son," whispered Phoenix, still grappling with the reality of his fatherhood.

The tears spilled over, sliding down Aerielle's cheeks. "He looked just like you. I named him Wolf. Wolf Stargazer Buchanan. And I called him Hemene. He was a sweet, gentle, wonderful little boy.... He was two and half when he was diagnosed with Leukemia. He died a year later."

Phoenix felt as if his legs would no longer hold him, felt as if his heart would cease to beat, felt that even when he'd been beaten and scourged he'd never known such pain.

Dazed, he stepped past Aerielle and sought the sanctuary of the night. There he would grieve for the son he'd never known and never would. There he would grieve for the son he'd lost and lost again.

→→→

Aerielle stood alone in the middle of the suddenly lonely barn. Reaching up she wiped at the stream of tears. It was done. After fourteen years it was done. The life and death of Wolf Stargazer Buchanan was no longer a burden to be carried and kept as a secret. A secret known only to her parents, neither of which still lived. If there was to be a future for Phoenix and herself, the secret would have to be shared with his family, for Aerielle could no longer live with hidden truth. But Pheonix would have to be the one to tell all, including the truth of their marriage vows.

"Thank you, God, I didn't marry someone else." It was bad enough she'd dated Hawk, however briefly. Even then, Phoenix had kept his secret, not wanting to bind Aerielle to a life she'd thought long over and so short-lived as to be counted in days if not hours. For that's how long it had been from the moment they'd exchanged their vows until the note came from Phoenix declaring them false.

Aerielle had told her parents everything upon her return home. It had been all her mother and Aerielle could do to convince her father not to confront Phoenix's mother and step-father, seeing as Phoenix was missing. But Aerielle had assumed the blame. Legally, she had Phoenix had been consenting adults, both eighteen, and despite everything, Aerielle did not regret the child, for it was all she'd had left of the man she loved. And when the child she'd loved died, all she'd had left was Idaho, and when Idaho had died, the man she'd loved was back in her life. And now...now she loved him more than she had when the circle had begun.

The question was, what now? She had yet to tell him of her love. She'd been waiting until the secret of their son was no longer hers alone to bear. She'd never expected to find Phoenix held a secret of his own. He hadn't made up those vows, and he'd meant every word.

Taking a deep, calming breath, Aerielle turned and left the barn, sliding the giant door closed. The night was still and silent as the snow continued to fall. There was no sign of Phoenix as Aerielle walked the distance to the house. She worried, hoping at the same time he was in one of the outbuildings. Though it wasn't very cold by winter's standards, Phoenix was without a coat. She glanced around the yard one last time before entering the back door into the kitchen.

Hawk and Sofia were seated at the table, offering no pretense as to why they were waiting there.

Hawk stood. "Aerielle what's going on?"

Now that Phoenix knew the truth, it was all Aerielle could do to keep from blurting out everything. "I think that's something you should ask your brother."

"Where is he, then?" demanded Hawk, glancing past her.

Aerielle looked back at the door, though not expecting to see anything. "Out there somewhere. He needs...time."

Aerielle spoke without bitterness, almost tenderly. Phoenix's abrupt departure from the barn had not surprised her, and she felt no second betrayal as some might have expected. She had had ten years to grieve the loss of their son. Phoenix, too, had earned the right. Aerielle was patient. She would wait.

"*He* needs time?" repeated Hawk. "What about you? You've been crying. And what about what you said in the truck? About not *this* time."

As if suddenly remembering she hadn't been present for Aerielle's confession, Hawk glanced at Sofia.

"Look, if you two need to talk," Sofia began.

"No," declared Aerielle," cutting them both off. "Right now, *Phoenix* and *I* haven't finished what needs to be said.

"Then what's he doing wandering around in the dark?" Hawk demanded.

"Hawk," said Sofia, placing a gentle hand on his arm. "Clearly they need more time alone. Your parents are gone. Let's you and I go out. There must be a bar within 50 miles we can close down."

Glancing at Sofia, Hawk nodded. "You're right. Sorry Aerielle. I guess I keep thinking about my own desire to talk to him. I'll wait my turn."

"I'd appreciate that."

Leaving the kitchen, Aerielle went to her and Sofia's room and changed into more casual attire, warmer attire, in case she had to go looking for Phoenix. It was too cold for him to stay out there very long, unless he went back to the barn. But she doubted he would. She'd made the barn unsafe for the moment.

Aerielle attended to her vigil from the vantage point of the living room sofa. Christmas tree lights and electric candles illuminated the room in festive color, but Aerielle kept her eyes on the hallway leading to the bedrooms from the kitchen, her ears attuned to the back door. And she prayed. For Phoenix, for herself, for their future. Silently but persistently, Aerielle pleaded for her Savior's guidance.

The clock on the fireplace mantel seemed to tick ever louder as each minute passed. It was deafening by the time Aerielle heard the back door open and close an hour later. There were brief thuds as shoes or boots were left on the entryway rug, and then Phoenix passed Aerielle's view and disappeared down the hall. Was he looking for her?

Without a sound, Aerielle made her way to the hallway in time to see Phoenix frozen in place, his eyes locked on to her and Sofia's closed bedroom door. But instead of proceeding to the room, he entered his own bedroom instead, shutting the door silently behind him. Debating on whether she should knock on his door, Aerielle's mind was made up by the sound of the shower coming on. He must be cold to the bone by now.

Disliking the continued silence, but assured Phoenix was safely returned, Aerielle made her way back to the living room and put on some Christmas CDs, allowing the soothing melodies to soak in.

→→→

Clothed in a damp towel, Phoenix sat on the edge of the bed, his head bent forward as he attempted to brush the snarls from his hair. It was being exceedingly stubborn tonight, either that, or Phoenix was short on patience. Anything was possible. Well, maybe not. Phoenix had stood in the shower until the hot water was gone and still he didn't feel clean.

He'd done just what his father had done. Roughly, Phoenix forced the brush through his hair, ripping away at the delicate strands. *He'd left the woman to whom he'd promised his life.* The brush raked the back of his scalp, descending cruelly. *He'd left his own son fatherless.* The last of the snarls broke free, the brush spilling to the floor with its prizes secured within the bristles. Jim Peterson had taken Phoenix's hair and the skin off his back in payment for Aerielle. Phoenix would have given it all again if it would but change things.

His heart breaking for the son he'd never held and the woman who'd suffered through that child's birth and death alone, Phoenix fought the resurgence of tears. Flipping his head back, his long wet hair slapped sharply against his back.

They needed to talk, he and Aerielle. Phoenix needed to face her, face the past. He would not run this time like he had fourteen years ago, no matter how noble his intentions had been. Determined to see things through tonight, Phoenix wondered if Aerielle was asleep. According to the clock it was only eight, but her door had been closed earlier.

Minutes later, dressed in clean jeans and sweatshirt, Phoenix followed the sound of Christmas music to the living room.

There he discovered Aerielle studying the ornaments on the tree. She was singing. Pausing in the doorway to listen, Phoenix realized the song she softly accompanied was Oh Little Town of Bethlehem, the one she'd been amazed he'd remembered to be her favorite.

When the song ended, Aerielle turned from the tree, startled to see him there. Their gazes met, their eyes reflecting similar grief.

Phoenix was beautiful, thought Aerielle. Beautiful, strong, and sad. His damp hair had already begun to ripple into waves, his jaw was clenched in proud determination, and his midnight eyes revealed there'd been a time of tears.

"That was Wolf's favorite song, too, wasn't it?" said Phoenix.

"How did you know?"

"How could anyone hear you sing that song with such love and not have it be so?"

Aerielle didn't know how to reply, but Phoenix spoke instead. "Tell me about him Aerielle, tell me everything."

"Of course," she replied, "I've longed to do nothing but for the last fourteen years. And we have the place to ourselves for a while."

"We do? Where'd Hawk and Sofia go?"

"They went out to give us space, since we were 'fighting.'"

"Great, I suppose Hawk will blame me for that."

"Actually, I might have let it slip to your brother that you and I had been 'intimate' fourteen years ago. I don't think he's too happy about it."

"You what?!" Phoenix collapsed onto the sofa, his back to an armrest.

"I'm sorry. It just slipped out."

Aerielle perched at the other end of the sofa, wondering if she could say anything else to add to Phoenix's nightmare of a day.

"It slipped out?" repeated Phoenix. "Like what? Hey, I had

a great time shopping today. Oh by the way, I slept with your brother way back when?"

"Phoenix, I'm sorry. I'm sure he'll understand. We're not the first two human beings to have sex together—"

"He'll kill me—"

"And if you explain about the vows?"

"I don't know what he'll think is worse. Having taken advantage of you without vows, or having shared vows and then left you."

"You didn't hold me to *my* vows. Won't he have the same compassion about yours?"

"No. He won't. Because I'm not white."

"Yes you are, Hemene. Or have you forgotten?"

"Alright then, I'm only half white."

"Well, I'm all white. And you took my vows as truth that day. Was I lying to you?"

"Of course not."

"Well then if I was married to you in 1978 then I'm married to you now in 1992, because I don't remember getting divorced. I bet you haven't broken your marriage vows, have you?"

Phoenix appeared stunned by her question. "Well, no. Well, actually, I did go out with Sofia twice."

Aerielle felt herself momentarily speechless. His response was almost humorous. "Sofia? That's kinda funny considering how she feels about Hawk. And speaking of which, I went out with Hawk a few times. I guess that makes us even."

Phoenix stared from his end of the sofa. "You never went out with anyone else?"

"I went to college while raising a child and then on to medical school after losing one. Dating wasn't on my radar."

Wolf. The truth struck Phoenix again like a poisonous dart. Why were they arguing over vows when Phoenix had left Aerielle with his child? His eyes on the woman he still loved, he struggled with that truth, wanting to hide his emotions, his thoughts, his failures.

Aerielle's sky blue eyes were warm as they gazed into his dark ones. Phoenix saw not the anger or hatred he'd expected to see less than two hours ago, just sadness, and surprising tenderness. His shoulders slumped in surrender. "What I did was wrong, Aerielle. I should never have left you."

"You did what you thought was right."

"But it *wasn't* right."

"But your *heart* was. Give yourself a break. We were only eighteen."

Sensing Phoenix's resistance to her words, Aerielle chose for the moment to let them go. And so they sat, facing each other with a chasm wider than the few feet between them, Phoenix struggling with his guilt, Aerielle struggling with how to combine the three and a half years of Wolf's life into hours.

She told Phoenix everything she could think of, starting with Hemene's birth on the 4th of July, 1979 and ending with his death, January 23, 1983. In between there were stories of joy and stories of pain. She told Phoenix about the time in her 3rd year of college when Hemene used crayons to color her completed homework and how the professor had given the boy an A. She shared how Hemene had started saving up the hair he lost from chemo and locking it away. Phoenix and Aerielle shared laughter, joy, and tears. And as the story of Wolf Stargazer Buchanan came to a close, the room—the past—was sealed in silence. The music had shut off a long time ago, and though Christmas lights still surrounded them, both Aerielle and Phoenix remained unaware. For the first time, they grieved the loss of their son together.

Phoenix's voice was a near whisper when he spoke, and Aerielle could hear the unshed tears. "I'm sorry, Meyui. God only knows how sorry I am."

Compassion claiming her, Aerielle moved over to Phoenix's side of the sofa, and sitting on the edge of the cushion, she wrapped her arms around him. He buried his face against her shoulder, and Aerielle stroked his hair. "I already forgave you

Phoenix. So did God. Now, you must find the strength to forgive yourself."

Wrapped in each other's embrace, they remained silent for several minutes.

At last, Aerielle pulled away. "Come on. I have something to show you."

Five minutes later found them seated on Phoenix's bed, their backs to the headboard, a leather-bound photo album having just been placed in Phoenix's lap. "Pictures of Hemene," Aerielle explained.

Reverently, Phoenix stroked the grey leather book, his eyes on the black wolf embroidered in the cover and the words inscribed beneath. Wolf Stargazer Buchanan. "You brought his whole life with you."

Aerielle watched as Phoenix's sensitive fingers traced the wolf. "I knew no matter what, the time had come," she explained. "All the pictures are labeled, but let me know if you have questions."

Slowly, expectantly, Phoenix lifted the cover. He stared. His son stared back. It was a later picture, probably one of the last taken. Aerielle hadn't been exaggerating about the resemblance. No one could have seen Phoenix and Wolf and doubted. Phoenix studied every curve and every line of the boy as he held a very small puppy who looked to be squirming in his arms. Phoenix read the notation at the bottom. "Hemene's third birthday with his present—Idaho." Idaho. The name reverberated through his very being. No wonder Aerielle'd been so devastated. The dog *had* been all she had left. The ring Phoenix had given her tied her to her son—their son.

Phoenix flipped to the next page, and found Wolf on his first day of life, swaddled in a blue puppy-patterned baby blanket, his eyes closed in sleep. His head was crowned with whispy brown hair the color of Phoenix's. Phoenix swallowed. His son was beautiful. With meticulous slowness, Phoenix examined every detail, and then every picture following, reading every caption carefully written.

Aerielle leaned over occasionally, pointing things out, sharing more bits and pieces of the boy's life. Mostly, she tried to remain unobtrusive, allowing Phoenix to progress through the album at his own pace. There were an abundance of happy photos, some professionally done, some not. Covering the last six months of the boy's life, most of the photos included a growing Idaho. The last picture appeared to be taken on Christmas as Wolf and Idaho posed next to a grandly decorated tree. The dog was as big as the boy by now, and Wolf had all he could do to wrap his arms around the shepherd.

Reluctantly closing it, Phoenix hugged the album to his chest, grateful for what he had, but wishing for the real thing.

Glancing over at Aerielle, he found her burrowed into the softness of the pillows, watching him with sleepy eyes.

"What did you tell our son about me?" asked Phoenix.

"That I had loved you dearly, and for reasons I couldn't explain, you were unable to be with us. And when he asked what you looked like, I told him to look in the mirror, for the only picture I had of you was within my heart."

Phoenix's wonder left him silent. Unable to take his eyes from this woman he loved, he watched as her eyes closed in sleep, and then watched some more. Did she still love him? Could she still love him?

Phoenix knew the longing to rest next to Aerielle and hold her in his arms as he had the night in the motel. Shifting position, he gave in to the urge to lie beside her. Reaching out, he placed his arm around her waist. It would be but for a moment, he promised himself, wondering if the stolen moment would have to last him a lifetime. "My precious Aerielle, my Meyui, how I love thee."

→→→

Phoenix yawned, pouring himself a cup of coffee. It was early to be up, but he'd had that horrible dream about Aerielle again, the one where he couldn't save her. He would have thought with Aerielle back in his life, the nightmares would have gone away. Phoenix wasn't even sure where he and Aerielle stood. There was but one thing of which he was confident—he'd die before he left her again. Only if she did the leaving would he part with her.

The clock in the living room chimed six, letting Phoenix know it'd be another hour before the sun came up—probably before anyone else got up either. Glancing toward the living room where his brother slept, Phoenix wondered when Hawk had come in. Phoenix certainly hadn't heard him, but the bedroom light had been shut off and Hawk now slept on a couch. Having fallen asleep next to Aerielle, Phoenix's stolen moment had turned into hours, and even when he'd woken from his dream, Aerielle had not stirred. Leaving her to rest, Phoenix had proceeded to the kitchen to warm a lonely cup of coffee.

Taking another sip from his steaming mug, Phoenix decided it would go better with a frosted sugar cookie and pulled a decorated snowman from one of many Christmas tins. Staring down at the chocolate chip eyes and buttons, Phoenix remembered the last chocolate chip endowed cookies he'd eaten of Aerielle's. That day, he had been caught hiding in the alcove because of those cookies.

Biting into the snowman, Phoenix walked to the same alcove and stepped into the shadowed darkness. Nothing much had changed. The telephone stand remained as it had always been, the old wooden chair just a little more aged. Finishing off his cookie, Phoenix recalled how Aerielle had given him a good tongue lashing without Sparrow ever having been aware of his presence. He smiled and sipped his coffee. He remembered wanting to shake her and kiss her at the same time. At least half of that he still wanted to do. Only now...only now he didn't feel worthy.

Phoenix's smiled faded and he gulped his coffee, burning his tongue. Sighing in resignation, he sat down on the chair. After placing his coffee on the phone stand, he pulled his knees up to his chest, resting his heels on the edge of the chair. Where was he going to go from here? And would it include Aerielle? The future had never seemed so hard to grasp, the past so difficult to deal with. He loved his Morning Light. The days would only be dark without her. He could only hope she felt the same even knowing the guilt he bore. His head in his hands and his elbows on his knees, Phoenix began to pray, asking God for forgiveness and, for his help.

I felt the end coming. All for which we had suffered and lost! Thoughts came of Wallowa, where I grew up....Then with a rifle I stand forth, saying in my heart, 'Here I will die.'

Yellow Wolf, Scout of the Nez Perce as quoted in *Chief Joseph of the Nez Perce* by Robert Penn Warren.

24

When Phoenix awoke for the second time that morning, it was to the sound of his mother and Sofia's laughter in the kitchen, and the presence of his brother standing rumpled in the bedroom doorway staring at him. Or was he glaring at him.

Phoenix sat up in bed, still clutching the photo album he'd perused after Aerielle had departed.

Hawk stepped into the room wiping sleep from his eyes as he shut the door with a thud. "You're lucky Aerielle was here earlier, or we would've been having this conversation in the middle of the night."

Phoenix knew where this was going, knew also there was no point in trying to stop his brother. Hawk would have his say.

"Fourteen years ago when you left, you told me it wasn't serious between you and Aerielle and she would get over your absence quickly. We both know how that turned out. Then the other day I find out you've been in love with Aerielle since practically the first day you met her. Then through a slip of Aerielle's tongue I find out you two slept together. And I don't mean the innocent little sleeping arrangement of last night.

"She already is, or was, or is again, your woman. How could you possibly let me go out with her?!"

"You're right," agreed Phoenix, clearly surprising his brother. "I messed up big time. But it's worse than you thought."

"Worse?! How the heck could it be worse?!"

Leaning forward, Phoenix placed the photo album at the edge of the bed. "Have a look."

Eyeing his brother closely, Hawk picked up the album and flipped it open. "What do old photos of you have to do with anything?"

"It's not me, Hawk. Read the cover."

Giving his brother another odd look, Hawk closed the lid and read the name engraved there. He read it and then read it again. Phoenix could see his lips moving as if that was the only way he could be sure he was reading it correctly. His face blanched and he opened the album again. As if on cue, his legs seemed to give out, and he landed on the edge of the bed where the album had so recently lain. "You're right, Phoenix. It's gotten worse."

"Why don't you get comfortable, and I'll tell you the whole story."

"The whole story?" Hawk repeated, still staring at Wolf's 3rd birthday photo. "There's more?"

His voice a monotone, Phoenix poured out an abbreviated version of the story, making sure to cover the highlights, for the first time saying it all without leaving anything out. By the time he was finished, Hawk was wearing a sick expression, which reminded Phoenix of how *he'd* felt just hours ago.

"Geez, Phoenix, how could you let me go out with your wife?! Why didn't you at least tell me what you knew?"

"Why didn't *you* tell me I was making a mess of your love life?" asked Phoenix in reply.

"It's not the same!" argued Hawk.

"You're right. It's not. But how do you tell your brother you left your wife the day after you married her? Besides I figured if I hadn't held Aerielle to the vows, it was like they never existed."

"So these vows you gave her a pass on, what'd she have to say about them?"

"That she's still married to me."

His head in his hands, Hawk shook his head, his shoulder's

slumping as the last of his anger died away. "Some of this happened because we could never talk."

"Maybe we never tried hard enough."

Gently Hawk set the photo album on the bed between them. "Then it's time we changed."

"Agreed," said Phoenix, meeting his brother's gaze with all barriers down.

Abruptly, Hawk himself began to look uncomfortable as if *he* was hiding something. "Phoenix—"

"What is it?"

"It's about Jim Peterson."

"What about him?!"

"He knows Aerielle's back."

→→→

It was midafternoon the following day before Aerielle finished her costume. Glad of the break before dinner, she sought out Phoenix, as usual finding him in the barn. It didn't take but a mere suggestion for him to agree to a ride.

Five minutes later they were on their way into the shimmery afternoon. The sun glittered off the warming snow, and the horses snorted in pleasure. Phoenix and Aerielle shared little dialogue, their thoughts caught up in the wonder of their surroundings and the revelations of the last few days.

They stayed out on the prairie for some time, running the horses and chasing the wind. The horses hooves sounded in rhythm with the riders as they leaned over their mounts, their hair and the horses mains caught in the rush of wind as they raced along.

Cresting a small rise, they pulled the horses up to a prancing halt, stopping to admire the endless horizon of patched white and brown lingering against the blue sky in the distance.

"It's incredible," proclaimed Aerielle, watching as the molten sun's edge touched the line where earth and sky were joined.

"And so like you," murmured Phoenix. "The sky is as deep

as your eyes, the sun the color of your hair, and the breeze like the whisper of your voice."

Aerielle stared at him in awe, overwhelmed by the tender caress of his voice.

Sensing her eyes upon him, Phoenix turned his dark gaze to meet her own. "Don't look so surprised. I've been comparing you to the rising and setting of the sun for fourteen years. I missed you, Aerielle. If only I'd told you the truth from the beginning. If only I'd later tracked you down."

Aerielle sensed his continued self-condemnation, recognizing it's similarity to her own regrets. "If only I'd told you about Wolf. If only I'd come back to Idaho."

Turning his gaze toward the sunset, Phoenix took in a deep breath of cold air. Aerielle continued to stare, unable to get enough of this enigmatic man who had hold of her heart. He looked bold and powerful, sitting his mount nobly, while the angle of the sun's rays highlighted the hollows beneath his cheekbones. He resonated strength, confidence and wisdom, but Aerielle knew the vulnerability that lay beneath his bronze flesh within his Nez Perce heart.

She reached out to him with words even as he, too, began to speak.

"You first," she acceded.

"I was just thinking, if we're to survive this time in our lives, we have to give up our 'what ifs.'"

Aerielle smiled, pride filling her. "I was going to say something similar. I'm glad you said it first."

"We need to move forward," continued Phoenix.

"And what better time," agreed Aerielle, nodding her approval. "In just a few days a new year will begin. Maybe *we* can begin again as well."

Phoenix turned to Aerielle, his eyes absorbing her with an intensity that left her breathless and feeling as if he'd searched her soul. "A clean slate?"

Aerielle nodded. "A clean slate."

"I would like that," said Phoenix.

"Then there's one thing still needing to be said before the new year begins."

"Oh?" Phoenix's trepidation was obvious, and Aerielle rushed to reassure him. "For once it's good news."

"Oh. What is it then?"

"Besides telling you about our son, it's the most important thing I've been wanting to say. I love you, Hemene."

Phoenix was speechless. He hadn't been expecting to hear those words. Longing to hear them, yes, but expecting? "You're not just saying that because—"

"I'm saying it because it's true. Fourteen years ago, I didn't think it was possible to love you any more than I did. But I was wrong, Phoenix. I love the man you've grown into even more than the one I married. You need to know that. And believe it. Tell me you believe me."

Reaching out, Phoenix took Aerielle's hand in his. "When you look at me like that, I would be a fool not to."

"Then don't be a fool. On New Year's Eve at midnight we begin anew."

→→→

The next few days were surprisingly quiet ones. The young people spent a lot of time hanging out with each other, from playing board games and watching movies to riding horses and exploring Idaho. Of Jim Peterson there was no sign, but trips to downtown Shaman Prairie were limited to Nevin and Jared and the women were never left alone. Aerielle kept praying if she stayed out of site it would be the same as out of mind, and all the Minnesotans would return home unmolested.

Finally, New Year's Eve arrived without fanfare, and everyone in the house was preparing for the evening ahead.

"Do you think he'll notice me?" demanded Sofia, staring at her reflection in the mirror as she straightened the curls from her hair.

Applying Wild Cherry to her lips in the same mirror, Aerielle glanced at Sofia and laughed. "Unless Hawk's blind. You make a devastating Cleopatra."

"And you *have* the mistletoe, right?" questioned Sofia for the third time.

Aerielle stood up, the skirt of her voluminous red gown swirling about her red shoes. "Yes, it's in my coat pocket," she assured, reaching up to adjust her hair. "What time is it, anyway?"

Sofia glanced at her bare arm only to discover it devoid of a time piece. "I guess Cleopatra didn't wear a watch. Let's see, according to the clock it's almost seven-thirty."

"Five and half hours," whispered Aerielle.

"Until midnight and your new beginning?"

Aerielle glanced at her new friend, and nodded. Because Hawk had been told everything, Aerielle had brought Sofia in on the rest of the story as well. After Hawk and Sofia went back to Minnesota, Phoenix would bring the rest of his family into the know. One step at a time, starting with a new beginning.

"Until midnight," agreed Aerielle. "Now tell me, honestly. Do I look like Buttercup?"

Sofia turned to her, studying her closely. "You look like the Princess Bride to me. I'm sure a lot of people will know who you are. I can't believe you are so good at sewing. Good thing you bought that material for Red Riding Hood's cape. That dress is just perfect."

"Thank you. I don't get to do much sewing anymore. So do you think Phoenix will get the point?"

"That you're his bride?" laughed Sofia, pulling the straightener from her hair. "Oh he'll get the point, alright. Now how's my hair?"

"Will you hold still?!" demanded Hawk as he attempted to wrap one of Phoenix's braids.

"I can't believe I'm actually going to this party," said Phoenix, shaking his head much to Hawk's aggravation.

"We won't be, if you don't hold still!"

"Here, I'll do it myself." Taking the white Ermine-furred wraps from his brother, Phoenix stepped over to the mirror, the fringe of his buckskins whispering with sound at the slightest movement. Phoenix glanced at the image facing him, unable to believe he'd been talked into this. But he'd gone through with it for Aerielle, and he proclaimed authenticity from head to toe, including the bone handled knife sheathed at his belted waist. His hair, freshly washed and blown dry, hung mostly loose, with just two narrow braids on either side starting near his temples. It was around the bottom section of these braids that Hawk had been attempting to wrap the four inch long strips of fur.

His efforts succeeding at last, Phoenix's stepped back and stared at his reflection. He couldn't help but remember the last time he'd dressed so for Aerielle—the night of their wedding.

"Come on," urged Hawk, dressed in his buckskins and running a quick comb through his too-short-to-braid black hair. "You look gorgeous. Now, we'd better get a move on, or the girls'll actually be ready before we are."

As it was, when Phoenix opened the bedroom door, he nearly walked into Aerielle who was passing. She turned, her long red gown swirling about her ankles.

The brothers spoke in Unison. "The Princess Bride."

Aerielle's face broke into a radiant smile.

"I thought you were going as Little Red Riding Hood," said Hawk.

"I repurposed the fabric."

"I approve," Phoenix stated, his eyes consuming her.

"Well, I approve, too, but I don't think either of *you* care. Where's *my* date?"

Aerielle pointed down the hallway toward the kitchen, her eyes never leaving Phoenix.

"Why don't I just slip by and let you too stare at your leisure."

Hawk was gone before either spoke again.

"You are incredibly handsome," murmured Aerielle recalling the last time she'd seen Phoenix wearing his buckskins.

"And you my dear Meyui, are breathtaking. I'm glad you 'repurposed' your costume, though I must say, Red Riding Hood was ingenious."

"Oh," said Aerielle coming to herself, "speaking of Red Riding Hood and the big bad Yellow Wolf, I had a picnic basket planned for you."

As if by magic, Aerielle pulled a basket out from behind the edge of her dress and held it out to Phoenix. "I'm afraid it's not edible."

Taking the basket from her, Phoenix began to laugh. "A fine collection of Earth and Fire."

"I like the way it makes your hair smell. You should use it all the time."

"Is this where I'm supposed to say, 'As you wish?'"

"Well," said Aerielle reaching out for a handful of his hair, "I wouldn't complain."

"Hey if you get free sniffs, then so do I." Reaching for her, Phoenix pulled her close and buried his face against her neck. "Ah, yes, hyacinth."

"That's Buttercup, Wesley."

→→→

Standing near the punch bowl, Aerielle drank thirstily from her glass as she and Phoenix watched the festive masqueraders. Many of the one hundred or more participants were whirling about on the wooden planked dance floor, while others, sharing conversation and good food, stood about or sat on hay bales. Many of the masks the party attendees wore were as unique as their costumes, and indeed, Aerielle had decorated *her* mask with red sequins and adorned Phoenix and Hawk's with feathers.

Glancing at her watch, Aerielle sighed. Ten o'clock. Even though she was having a good time, she longed for midnight, the unmasking, the new life. "Come quickly," she whispered.

Suddenly Batman and Cat Woman walked past on their way to the food laden table. It was obvious by the body displayed by Cat Woman's too tight outfit that she'd visited her share of food accommodations in the past.

"Hey, there they go," said Phoenix, catching Aerielle's attention as he pointed to the bottom of the stairs leading from the hayloft, a.k.a. cloakroom. Hawk and Sofia, now wearing coats, were headed for the barn door on their way to the house.

"That's the signal," said Aerielle, setting down her empty punch glass. "Time to go up and hang the magic mistletoe."

Conversation, laughter, and live country music followed Phoenix and Aerielle up the wooden stairs to the enclosed loft hidden above.

"I can't remember the last time I danced so much," announced Aerielle, her hand clasped securely by Phoenix's as if he feared she'd stumble.

"There are some similarities to a powwow," agreed Phoenix. "Aside from all the dancing, the costumes are almost as colorful. I can't believe Mom and Nevin came as Little Bo Peep and Wolfman Jack."

Aerielle laughed. "What about Mr. Spock and Guinan. A Vulcan from one Star Trek series and a bar-tending El-Aurian from another."

"Jared smiles too much for a Vulcan. I will say, however, playing Guinan hides Sparrow's condition pretty well."

Reaching the top of the stairs, Phoenix and Aerielle entered the large loft, piled with bales of hay, outfitted with tack and supplies, and in the middle of it all, coat racks. "What's wrong with this picture?" remarked Aerielle and laughed.

"It'd make a great photograph.... So where's this mistletoe you want help hanging?"

"It's in my coat pocket," said Aerielle, searching through some coats until she found her own.

"So this idea of Sofia capturing Hawk with mistletoe, where'd you come up with it?"

"Oh, it wasn't my idea," replied Aerielle, digging into her coat. "It was Sofia's."

Phoenix's eyes widened in surprise. "Sofia?"

"Yeah. I told her you Stargazer men were thick headed and needed a little help to figure out what you wanted."

"Part of the ten horses tied to a teepee?"

"Argue if you will," said Aerielle, returning with the mistletoe and some ribbon, "but it was I who made the first move on you."

Phoenix grunted in acquiescence as he took the proffered mistletoe.

"Sofia said to tie it in the doorway," added Aerielle. "I presume because it's the only place low enough to reach, as well as see, without craning one's neck."

Stepping back to the doorway, Phoenix tied the ribbon first to the kissing token and then reached up and tied it to the open doorframe.

"There," he announced. "Now, where are we hiding?"

"Hiding? Are you insinuating you want to spy on them?"

"With all the times Hawk caught us, as he puts it, 'playing kissy face,' you're darn well right I want to be a fly on the wall."

"Yellow Wolf. I'm shocked...but we could hide behind the coatracks farthest from the door."

"About here?" he inquired a minute later from the strategic location they'd scoped out.

Aerielle nodded from beside a blue ski jacket. "Now all we have to do is wait."

"If you think all I'm doing is waiting," suggested Phoenix, his hands coming to rest at Aerielle's waist.

"Why Half-Breed. I don't have any mistletoe."

Reaching up, Phoenix stroked the satiny mask framing Aerielle's blue eyes. "Don't you know, you *are* my mistletoe, Meyui? I long to kiss you every second of every minute of every hour of every day."

"Oh, Hemene. You can be such a romantic."

They moved at the same time, their lips joining in a tender embrace. After a while, Phoenix followed distraction to Aerielle's tender throat where he found her pulse pounding as erratically as his own.

"I love you, Meyui," he declared, telling her with words what his body longed to prove. He pulled her closer, if that were possible, sliding his hands into her golden tresses just like her hands were bound in the length of his. They were silken shackles willingly worn by each, even as their lips returned to be taken captive by the other's.

Suddenly, there were footsteps on the stairs. At first, Phoenix thought it was the pounding of his heart, but he quickly realized Hawk and Sofia were returning, or somebody else was coming. Aerielle's eyes widened in anticipation as they pulled away from each other and pressed themselves into the row of coats, peering below the top shelf where the hats and mittens were lined up. Thankfully, the noise from the festivities below muted out their cautious movements.

They caught a brief view of Sofia and Hawk as they came through the doorway and moved over to the closest coatracks. The rattle of hangers gave their presence away, though they could no longer be seen.

"I sure hope this works," signed Aerielle, looking at Phoenix without speaking.

"I don't know," he signed back, "you know how thick headed we Stargazer men can be."

Aerielle grinned and turned back to the view of the mistletoe. Sofia and Hawk came back into view, heading for the doorway.

"Check out the mistletoe," remarked Sofia casually.

"Didn't notice it earlier," replied Hawk, nearly running into the woman where she'd stopped while his gaze had been directed upwards.

Sofia glanced up briefly before smiling at Hawk invitingly. Apparently, he wasn't *that* thick headed, for after a brief moment of hesitation, he leaned down and brushed his lips against hers.

Aerielle shook her head, rolling her eyes. Sofia must have felt the same way, for her eyebrows lifted. "Come on. I know for a fact you can do better than that."

Hawk stared at her wide-eyed, and then without a by your leave, he roughly pulled Sofia into his arms and kissed her with such veracity it was Aerielle's turn to raise her eyebrows.

Phoenix grinned. He and Hawk were alike in more ways than one. They both liked to kiss their woman in a memorable way. It was definitely not a Kodak moment but a memory that would last just as long.

Abruptly Hawk released Sofia with almost as much fervor as he'd taken her in his arms. "I'm sorry," he exclaimed.

Sofia's eyes widened once again. "You're sorry? Sorry you kissed me?"

"Well, no—"

"I thought maybe you actually *liked* me," interrupted Sofia. "Liked me well enough to kiss me without prompting from either your sister or mistletoe. I guess I was wrong."

Sofia turned to flee, but Hawk reached out and caught her arm. "Wait!"

Sofia turned back, looking first at the hand on her arm, and then at Hawk's face, tears brimming in her eyes. "What?!"

Determination filling his expression, Hawk reached up with his other hand and ripped the mistletoe down, tossing it over his shoulder. Then cupping Sofia's face in his hands, he kissed her again. This time the kiss was long, thorough, and poignant, as if he'd been longing to kiss her like this for a very long time.

Pulling away at at last, Hawk looked squarely into Sofia's eyes. "I'm not sorry."

"You do like me?" she asked, as if still unsure.

Hawk chuckled. "Blast it woman. It's *me* who should be asking *you* that question. I didn't think you wanted anything to do with me. I mean, why would you. You're such an innocent, old-fashioned girl, and what with you giving me a hard time about my 'surplus girlfriends,' and telling me I'm a ladies man just playing with hearts...."

"Innocent? Old fashioned?" Sofia laughed. And then her laughter ended with a sigh. "Maybe I am. But the only reason I gave you a hard time is because I was jealous."

"Jealous?"

"Yes, jealous. *I* wanted to be the woman you swept off her feet, the one you brought flowers to."

Hawk looked stunned, totally un-nonchalant, thought Phoenix. So much for his lady-killer image. His brother certainly didn't have it all together right now.

"I, um," mumbled Hawk, struggling for words.

Not quite able to hear him, Aerielle leaned in a few more inches. Inches that caused a drover coat to slide onto the floor. That in itself might have gone unnoticed over the music and chatter from below, but the clanging of the metal hanger hitting against the coatrack could not.

"Did you hear something?" asked Sofia, ending Hawk's discomfiture.

"Something suspicious," he replied.

"Humor me," said Phoenix to Aerielle, his gaze mischievous. Promptly, he took up the pleasurable task of kissing her until he felt Hawk and Sofia's presence behind them.

Glancing over at the other couple, Phoenix grinned. "Your timing gets worse all the time, Hawk."

Hawk grinned and shook his head. "Now I know how *you* feel."

→→→

With Aerielle's head resting against his shoulder, her breath warm against his skin, and his own arms cradling her close, Phoenix could almost forget the other couples surrounding them on the dance floor. But soon the music came to an end, and reluctantly Phoenix released her.

Aerielle's blue eyes were glittering more brightly than the red-sequined mask encircling them. "How much longer until midnight, Phoenix?"

Sliding a buckskin sleeve out of the way, Phoenix glanced at his watch, a slow smile making its way to his lips. "Ten minutes."

Aerielle glowed. "Let's welcome the new year beneath the stars. Beneath the Pleiades."

"I'll get our coats," said Phoenix, nodding his approval.

"I'll be waiting outside," replied Aerielle. "I need to cool off. This many people dancing in a barn sure puts off a lot of heat."

As Aerielle headed for the door, she passed Sofia and Hawk having an avid conversation while gazing at each other with new eyes.

Stepping into the night, Aerielle was relieved. The sky was still clear of clouds, the stars of Idaho's open places filling the black velvet sea with their multitudes.

She received the encompassing air with a welcome breath, filling her lungs with its refreshing taste. With her full skirt and long sleeves she hardly noticed the winter temperature touch her skin.

Stepping across the width of the paved drive that led to the house, Aerielle paused at the edge of an open field, the starlit horizon endless before her. Freeing herself of her mask, she sought the Pleiades. "There you are," she murmured moments later, the prize within her view.

"A bit chilly, don't you think?" declared a voice somewhere behind her.

Startled, Aerielle turned to find a pirate lounging against a red pickup some ten feet away, a green satin headscarf matching a long sash around his waist. What Aerielle assumed to be a fake knife was lashed to his side. She was disappointed to discover that she and Phoenix might not be alone for the appointed hour. She studied the man, his visage unfamiliar, his black mask concealing. Despite the flashy costume he wore, Aerielle didn't remember seeing him before.

"I like your costume. I didn't notice it earlier," she said.

"I just got here a few minutes ago."

Aerielle was surprised. "Just in time for the stroke of midnight."

"Just in time to claim you as mine forever, Aerielle. I believe the timing of your return to Shaman Prairie was destiny."

Aerielle thought she was going to be sick as the realization of who she was talking to settled upon her. He was a pirate all right. One who had come to plunder her future as he had her past. Jim Peterson.

Whenever the white man treats the Indian as they treat each other, then we shall have no more wars. We shall be all alike—brothers of one father and one mother, with one sky above us and one country around us, and one government for all. Then the Great Spirit Chief who rules above will smile upon this land, and send rain to wash out the bloody spots made by brothers' hands upon the face of the earth. For this time the Indian race are waiting and praying....

Chief Joseph, as quoted in *Let Me Be Free* by David Lavender

25

"Jim Peterson," stated Aerielle flatly. At the same time, she estimated the distance to the barn door and knew she'd never make it. She hoped she had no need to escape, or fight for that matter, since she carried no bag of Earth and Fire for a weapon.

Jim smiled at her recognition of him and stepped away from the truck, crossing the snow dusted drive. "Were you expecting someone else?" he asked, closing the distance between them and blocking Aerielle's view of the barn door.

Aerielle knew a moment of relief when Peterson stopped just out of arms reach. "As a matter of fact, I was."

"And who could you possibly be waiting for? Your little friend from the General Store? What you need, Aerielle, is a man."

"She already has one."

Jim Peterson whirled about at the sound of the rich ominous voice even as Aerielle breathed its owner's name. "Phoenix."

There was wary anger on her warrior's face as he approached, now divested of the coats he'd carried and the mask that had inhibited his view. He was like an apparition out of the past, and hauntingly beautiful. His steps were languid and yet bold, his face a study in protective fierceness, and Aerielle knew such pride, such love; she felt her fears slipping away.

Phoenix stopped short of Peterson, his expression watchful, his jaw beginning to throb.

"And just what are *you* doing here?!" demanded Peterson, his distaste evident in more than just his words as he eyed Phoenix up and down.

Before Phoenix could respond, his attention was abruptly drawn to Aerielle as she took a step toward him, her face, her eyes, filled with such tender feeling as to melt the snow beneath their feet. "He's my husband," she proclaimed, her voice filled with pride.

Stunned by her proud declaration and the overwhelming emotion that went with it, Phoenix was momentarily caught off guard. He missed the sudden fury on Peterson's face just long enough for the other man to make a lunge for Aerielle.

"You little slut," Peterson spat, reaching for her.

Peterson came so suddenly, Aerielle had no time to react. She heard Phoenix's roar of anger even before Peterson's hands closed about her throat. Aerielle would have screamed if it were possible. She could feel his fingers closing off her airway.

Aerielle abruptly went sprawling onto the ground as Peterson fought against Phoenix's attack. She could hear fists making contact as she struggled to rise, tripping over the long folds of her red gown. Snow slipped into her shoes and melted against her hands as she once again moved to get up.

Without warning, Jim Peterson came crashing down beside her. As they both got to their feet, she could see the bitter hatred in his eyes and then the movement of his hand against his waist and the glint of metal.

"No!" she screamed, grabbing at Peterson's sleeve as he turned from her toward Phoenix, a step behind. The fabric of his pirate shirt slid between her fingers as easily as the knife blade entered Phoenix's flesh.

Phoenix stumbled backwards, confused by the sudden, unseen pain that tore into him. He glanced down, only to discover the hilt of a knife protruding from his chest. Aerielle's horrified screams pierced the night almost as effectively.

"Shut up!" Peterson yelled, turning his fury and his fists on

Aerielle. He slammed a hand hard across her face, and Aerielle heard the crack, felt her nose break. And then he was on top of her, the excruciating pain in her face magnified a hundred fold as he hit her again.

Phoenix heard her scream like he had those endless nights, only this was no dream, and there was no wall separating them this time. His shock exploded into rage as he moved to save the woman he loved from the demon of his nightmares.

Pain racked Aerielle, her vision blurred, and she longed for a knife to bury into Peterson. And then suddenly, his weight was gone, but it was some moments before she was able to fight the pain enough to move.

Aerielle struggled to stand, her eyes focusing on the two whose fight had led them off the drive and into the snow blanketed prairie grass. She stumbled forward to help, to help defeat the enemy that had denied her son a father and tortured the man she would willingly die for. She knew Phoenix couldn't last, and if the knife was moved....

Hurling herself at Peterson, Aerielle was but a brief annoyance as he knocked her aside. The green sash about his waist came free in her grasp as she fought to retain some hold on him. Seeing the snow-covered sash for the weapon it could be, she rose again, gripping it determinedly in her hands.

Aerielle bit back another cry as Phoenix was knocked to the ground. Before Peterson could follow, Aerielle wrapped the sash around his neck, drawing it tight just as he reached up and attempted to free himself. She heard him gasping for air, and then Phoenix was standing before him, his fists like lightning as Peterson's head seemed to snap in two directions at once. Phoenix's blows landed with such force, Aerielle wondered that she and Peterson could still be standing.

Suddenly Peterson shifted hard, hitting Aerielle in the face. She didn't know what happened next, for her world turned momentarily black as the pain all but consumed her and left her lying face down in the snow. She struggled to remain conscious, attempting to concentrate on the cold blanket of white turning red beneath her face. She knew they were still fighting, could hear the grunts of pain. Phoenix. Phoenix. She had to help him. But as Aerielle forced herself up onto her hands and knees, her blurred vision revealed that Phoenix had Peterson pinned down and was pounding him into the frozen snow-covered earth.

Standing, Aerielle faltered before struggling across the short distance to where Phoenix straddled his adversary. An adversary whose defenses were at last gone as he stared at the despised enemy.

Phoenix, still filled with rage, glanced down at the knife in his chest, wishing to pull it free, yet knowing he dare not. He then realized it wasn't the only knife he wore. Caught up in his anger and fear for Aerielle, he'd forgotten the six inch hunting knife at his waist.

Reaching down with a bloody fist, Phoenix pulled free the knife some four generations old.

"Phoenix, no!" cried Aerielle.

Deaf to her words, Phoenix put the knife to Peterson's throat, but it drew no blood.

He stared into the eyes of the man who had robbed him of his Meyui, his son, and his life, and he longed to slit the mongrel's throat.

It was obvious Peterson was in pain, but he glared up at Phoenix, his hatred alive. "You gonna kill me with some ancient ceremonial weapon?" he demanded hoarsely.

"Actually," snarled Phoenix, "I would have liked to use your own knife. Then you would have the blood you hate within you."

Peterson swallowed hard against the knife pressed to his throat. "Why don't you just get on with whatever it is you're gonna do, breed. Maybe you'd like to scalp me."

"The Nimipu didn't take scalps," declared Phoenix bitterly. "What I would like to do, though, is cut out your heart."

Aerielle's cry was instantaneous as Phoenix raised the

knife and brought it down. But Phoenix's "magic" hands had flipped the knife, and with the hilt forward, he struck Peterson unconscious.

Phoenix glared down at his enemy. "Lucky for you I once promised God, if I ever had the chance, I wouldn't kill you. God forgive me, because I want to."

Phoenix sheathed his knife and struggled to his feet, the effects of his wound suddenly evident as he nearly fell. Aerielle reached for him as he stumbled forward, allowing him to lean on her. Wrapping an arm about his waist, she brushed his hair away from his chest and studied the entry point of the knife he wore like a badge and the trickle of blood that ran from it. Thankfully the fight had not lasted more than a couple minutes, for enough damage had been accomplished with the first blow.

"How am I doing, Doc?" whispered Phoenix, glancing down.

How *was* he doing, wondered Aerielle, fear for Phoenix's life no less powerful now that the struggle was over. The blade of the knife had only been about three or four inches long, but there was no way to tell how much damage had been done. And there was nothing she could do, save pray no vital organs had been struck...like his heart. Equally serious was the possibility a major artery had been severed and Phoenix was bleeding to death internally. At that moment, a fresh trickle of blood began to stain a path down the front of his buckskins and Aerielle winced.

"Doc?" questioned Phoenix, hearing the fear in her silence as she began to guide him toward the barn.

"It may have just punctured your lung," she said, quoting the best case scenario she could hope to believe. "Leaving the knife in could, therefore, keep the lung from collapsing."

Phoenix studied Aerielle's face, now filled with worry as she helped him across the trampled snow. He longed to tell her that he loved her, afraid if he didn't, there would be no other chance. She was his Meyui, his Morning Light, in life and in death. For some reason, none of those words came out when he spoke. "That's quite a nose job you have there," he said instead, biting back a cry of pain as he stumbled.

Aerielle grunted. "Do you think it'll be as good as yours?"

"Better—Aerielle, what time is it?"

"What?"

"The time. Is it midnight yet?"

"I don't know, I—"

A loud roar of music and voices suddenly rose from within the barn. "I guess so," she said.

Phoenix stopped, his gaze on Aerielle. "Kiss me."

"Phoenix, this is no time—"

"Kiss me." *Before it's too late. Before our new life ends when it has yet to begin.*

Aerielle sensed the urgency in his voice and recognized his fear, a fear that was her own. He might be dying! Oh, God! She couldn't lose him too! "There's no time," she cried, and then to cover her frightened admission, "I'm a mess." Her voice shook as she wiped a hand lightly across her aching face and then attempted to guide Phoenix toward the barn door nearly within her grasp.

But Phoenix wasn't to be moved. His expression was insistent. "You look beautiful to me."

Aerielle felt her terror in losing him welling into tears despite her effort to fight the panic rising within her. Arguing no more, she leaned forward, her bruised and bloodied lips meeting his in the gentlest of kisses. It wasn't a long kiss, nor a passionate one. It was a simple kiss, a sealing of a bond in love, as well as blood.

"I love you," Phoenix whispered against her lips. And then he promptly passed out.

→→→

As the ambulance brought them ever closer to those who could help, Aerielle huddled next to Phoenix where he lay on the stretcher. She and the paramedic opposite her watched for any signs of change. The ride was taking too long, but then this was the wilderness of Idaho, not the crowded city where Aerielle made her home. Shaman Prairie had no emergency medical facility, and it was sixty miles to the nearest hospital in Everett. In the meantime, behind the ambulance, Hawk's headlights let them know they weren't alone. They had actually met the ambulance halfway between Shaman Prairie and Everett.

For what seemed like the thousandth time, Aerielle checked Phoenix's oxygen mask and, despite the monitors, felt for his pulse. It was rapid but steady. Next, her movements gentle, Aerielle checked the entry point where the knife still protruded for signs of increased bleeding. Overall Phoenix was holding his own.

Suddenly the sirens came on, indicating an increase in traffic, and Aerielle knew they were nearing their destination.

The noise reached past Phoenix's unconscious state, and his dark eyes opened, glazed with pain.

"We're almost there," she told him, placing a hand on his shoulder.

Phoenix made as if to speak, and then, realizing he was wearing an oxygen mask, he slowly raised his hands and began to sign.

"Where's Wolf?" he asked.

Aerielle was confused and it must have shown.

"Where's he buried?" continued Phoenix, using all his strength to sign the words.

"He's...I...." Aerielle stumbled, not knowing how to answer. For Hemene's ashes had yet to be laid to rest. Though it was not Nez Perce custom, she'd had him cremated with the intention of scattering his remains on Nez Perce land when the time had come. His ashes were currently in her suitcase.

Phoenix continued to sign. "If I don't make it—"

"You will!"

"—bury me with him."

"You're not going to die," declared Aerielle, her voice almost pleading as she stared into Phoenix's eyes.

Sensing her resistance, Phoenix reached up, lifting the oxygen mask. "Promise me!" he ordered aloud.

An errant tear slid down Aerielle's cheek. Reaching out, she settled the mask back into place. "I promise."

→→→

Two hours later, a punctured lung now repaired, Phoenix lay sleeping in a sterile hospital room. Aerielle stood beside his bed, breathing in the blessed sight of him. A tube ran to his chest, providing his lung with the suction it needed to stay inflated, and an IV was placed in his left arm. Because other parts of his body had taken the brunt of the punishment, his face had suffered but a few small bruises, one purpling his right cheekbone. There were dark circles beneath his eyes, and his hair was unkempt. Despite all, Aerielle found him pleasing to the eye—he was alive.

Phoenix stirred slightly and then became still. Leaning over him, Aerielle brushed a kiss against his bruised cheekbone and stroked his hair. A familiar longing came over her, this need to hold him as she'd needed to hold her son, but unable to without causing pain. Resisting the urge, Aerielle settled into a nearby chair, taking up her post. For she would not leave him this night. She would remain at his side until he saw with his own eyes that she was there for him in this time of need as she had not been fourteen years ago.

Having seen that Phoenix was stable and knowing Aerielle would call if his condition changed, his family had taken rooms at a motel a few blocks away. Hawk had started for the ranch; the horses would need to be fed in a few short hours. Aerielle would watch and pray, and probably fall asleep, but she would be there when Phoenix woke.

Several times during the ensuing hours, Aerielle was drawn to Phoenix's bedside as he began to toss and turn and even cry out. She could only imagine what nightmares haunted him after the nights events. Many times he called out her Indian name, Meyui, and then something else Shahaptin she was unable to translate. "*Hattia tinukin*," he would say, his voice hoarse with agony and fear.

Aerielle responded with whispered assurances, speaking a few words of his Indian tongue here and there as she remembered them. With her hands she soothed his face, clasped his hands, and sometimes even held him down as he fought his unseen enemy. Eventually, and none too soon, her voice would penetrate the wall of dreams, and he would cease in his travail. After assuring herself the tube to his lung remained as it should be, Aerielle took his wrist in her hand. She felt for the steady beating of his pulse, waiting for it to return to normal before she once again retreated to her station in the chair.

Time went by, Aerielle never wavering in her duty of love. There was a stretch of nearly two hours in which Phoenix did not appear to be caught up by his dreams. It was during these two hours that Aerielle slept, however briefly, however lightly. When she awoke it was nearly 8:30, and Phoenix was becoming restless again.

Aerielle hurried to his side, putting a gentle hand on his arm. It had no effect as he turned roughly, calling out.

"Phoenix, it's okay," urged Aerielle, pushing down on his shoulders as he lashed out at the memories assaulting him.

"Meyui!" he cried, still unaware of her, or his surroundings.

"*Zaain*, Hemene. I am here. *Sepekuse*. Let it be."

The words, spoken in the language of his ancestors, reached for him, soothing and hopeful. But Phoenix failed to hear her words. Reality was lost to him, for he was caught up in a snow-laden world so real, so vivid, that the blood trickling down the front of his buckskins was warm against his fingers as he searched for the anteceding wound. He found the hole in his chest where he knew the now missing knife had once been. And suddenly *hattia tinukin*, the death wind, swirled around him, past him, tossing the falling snow about as it rushed around the side of the Gilberts' barn in search of someone Phoenix could not yet see.

His moccasins heavy with snow, his vision obstructed by the heavy flakes, Phoenix ran after the wind. But he was too late. Rounding the side of the barn, he found his Meyui lying in a bloody pool of melting snow, the knife taken from his own chest now buried in hers. Phoenix's scream was a roar of agony, which not only filled the imaginary night, but the very real hospital room as well. His cry shocked Aerielle, and must have woken himself, for his eyes abruptly opened, the reality of his dream having little time to fade.

"Oh God, Oh God, you're alive," he choked out in relief. Reaching for Aerielle, Phoenix drew her to him, oblivious to the pain the movement caused.

"And so are you," whispered Aerielle. Tears welled in her eyes as Phoenix's lips brushed her forehead with lingering tenderness. Aerielle stroked his hair, his shoulders, feeling his taunt muscles relax.

At that moment, the hospital room door flew open, and a nurse came rushing in. Aerielle drew away from Phoenix, though she remained seated on the edge of the bed, her hands clasping his. "He's okay," she assured the startled nurse who'd come on duty just a short time ago. "He was dreaming."

The nurse glanced at Phoenix and nodded. "I'll let the doctor know you've come around."

"The doctor already knows," replied Phoenix as the door closed behind the nurse. "I have just one question, Doc."

"What is it?"

"If I was just dreaming, how come I hurt so bad and your face resembles a bruised grape?" Phoenix pulled a hand free from Aerielle's and raised it to her cheek. The humor was gone when he spoke again. "What did he do to you?"

"It's just a broken nose and few extra bruises."

"Peterson's gonna pay for it."

Aerielle glanced away, avoiding the answer to the question Phoenix was sure to ask next.

"Peterson is in jail, isn't he?"

"Not exactly—"

"What do you mean, not exactly?!" demanded Phoenix, gritting his teeth in pain as his effort in anger backfired. "The Sheriff was at the blasted party. So was Phillip Bluefeather from the BIA," added Phoenix, referring to the lieutenant from the Bureau of Indian Affairs, the official native law enforcement on the reservation.

"I'm sorry, Phoenix. But when you hit Peterson, it apparently wasn't enough to knock him unconscious for more than a couple of minutes. He got away."

Phoenix shook his head, a new kind of pain evident on his face. "It seems I did nothing right."

"That's not true. I'm alive because of you."

Phoenix grimaced with disgust. "You almost *died* because of me!"

→→→

Phoenix woke to the sound of silence, yet knew without opening his eyes that he was not alone. He could sense their dialogue in the movement of air and the brush of clothing. They were using sign language—they, being Hawk and Aerielle, the only two left without local jobs needing attention. Sofia had flown back to Minnesota in order to handle the minor appointments and reschedule the rest. Hawk, too, would have to return soon to deal with business, but had insisted on waiting until Phoenix was at least out of the hospital. As for Aerielle, well....

It was Phoenix's fifth day, and he'd had it up to the proverbial "here" with lying around and rethinking that which he couldn't change, wondering at a future he couldn't predict, and worrying about the safety of the woman he was unable to protect. Phoenix had never felt so useless, so frustrated, and so without hope. And Aerielle, woven into it all, was due back at work on Saturday. She would be flying home on Friday, leaving her truck to be driven home by Hawk while she used his brother's car. This allowed her an extra day in Idaho, but even so, counting what was left of the afternoon, Phoenix had two and a half days to make everything right in her life and his. Phoenix had never felt so incapable of anything.

Opening his eyes, Phoenix's gaze rested on Hawk and Aerielle where they sat speaking—speaking of him. Aerielle was signing now, and Phoenix read her words. "They'll probably release him on Thursday or Friday, and I think his tube will be removed tomorrow. Physically, he's on schedule, but emotionally...I don't know where he is. It's like he's climbed into himself and disappeared."

"Like Jim Peterson," signed Hawk. "Maybe it would help if he were found."

Aerielle shrugged "Possibly. But I think it's more than that. Phoenix blames himself for what happened, and I don't even think *that's* all of it. I think there's something so deep inside of him, so difficult to face alone, he's having trouble coming to terms with it. I just wish I knew what it was."

Phoenix's eyes closed, hiding a rash of pain and self-directed anger. How did he tell his Morning Light, what "it" was. Her brave warrior of the Nimipu, descendant of Yellow Wolf, was afraid.

→→→

Wednesday afternoon. One and a half days left. Step number one. Get out of here. Whether anyone liked it or not, Phoenix was going home, or at least home in Shaman Prairie. The tube in his chest had been removed earlier in the day, so all that remained was to finish getting dressed. Why hadn't someone bothered bringing in some proper clothing, ones a little less conspicuous and without blood stains? No matter. He'd come into this hospital dressed as a Nimipu. He'd leave the same way, minus the blade in his chest. Phoenix wondered where the knife had gone and then realized the police must have it. He glanced at his own knife, resheathed it, and laid it aside. His shirt was all that was left to put on, but he had no idea how he was going to manage alone.

Frustrated and already tired from his exertions, Phoenix stepped over to the bed and sat down. He would take a short break. As it turned out, it wasn't short enough. Aerielle returned from her and Hawk's lunch earlier than Phoenix had expected. He didn't look up as she entered his room, knowing the disapproval he'd see on her face.

Actually, the first expression to appear on Aerielle's face was surprise. The last thing she'd expected to find on returning was Phoenix dressed in breeches and moccasins, obviously getting ready to go home. His shirt was clutched in his hands, and he was apparently trying to figure out how to get it on by himself.

"What are you doing?" she demanded, disapproving.

"What does it look like I'm doing?" he replied, his face hidden by a wall of hair as he continued to study the shirt.

"It looks like you're trying to kill yourself."

Phoenix glanced up at last, revealing not only his face, but a bandage taped to his chest. Its whiteness was a stark contrast to his bronze skin.

"And I have no intention of letting you do any such thing," continued Aerielle, her worry hidden in her sharp tone of voice. "I didn't work hard at saving your life so you could try taking it again."

"It's high time I got out of here and did something useful!" quarreled Phoenix, standing and grimacing in pain as he did so.

"You *have* been 'useful.' In case you've forgotten, you also saved *my* life less than a week ago."

"Oh, I haven't forgotten. If anything, I haven't been *able* to forget." Phoenix walked stiffly over to the window, his eyes on the snow cascading past the glass. "You see, you had it right the first time. I didn't save your life. You saved mine."

Aerielle was confused. "What are you talking about?"

"I'm talking about the knife I should have seen before it ended up in my chest!" snapped Phoenix not turning around. "I'm talking about the other knife I should have remembered I had and then used. I'm only alive—you're only alive—because you managed to strangle Peterson sufficiently enough for my measly efforts to work. I couldn't even knock the *cultis shoyappe* unconscious."

"What do you think this is?!" demanded Aerielle in frustration. "Rambo part nine? You're not the hero of a movie. We stood up to Peterson together, Phoenix. We defeated him together. Maybe that's the way it had to be. You don't hold some monopoly on the pain he's caused. I lost my husband because of him, and my son was robbed of a father."

Aerielle's voice echoed into silence as further words failed her. Phoenix's head bowed and his shoulders seemingly slumped though he continued to stand as straight and proud as Aerielle had come to expect. Somehow, she had made things worse.

Aerielle continued to watch Phoenix a moment, having lost her way in her attempts to resolve his ongoing struggle. He stood unmoving before the snow-dusted mountain view, the rippling waves of his hair covering the scars on his back in a way time would never do. The scars to his flesh, like the those to his spirit, though concealed at times, were permanent.

Aerielle didn't know what else to say. Maybe there *was* nothing else to say. Crossing the floor, Aerielle slipped up behind this silent Indian of hers. She slid her left arm around his waist and placed the other across the uninjured area of his chest. She clung to him, hugging him as hard as she could without causing pain.

"Speak to me, Hemene," she pleaded, her face pressed against the thickness of his hair, her voice filled with longing. "I love you," she added, knowing that now she really *had* said everything she could.

Phoenix could feel her love flowing from the gentle touch

of her fingertips upon his flesh. He could hear it in the husky pleading of her voice. It was so powerful, so strong, the certainty of it filled his being with an almost painful intensity, causing him to tremble. Raising his dark hands to her fair ones, Phoenix covered them, sliding his fingers between hers in a soothing movement. "I'm afraid, Aerielle."

Phoenix knew instant relief in saying those words, but he also felt Aerielle's surprise as she attempted to pull away in order to get a better view of his face. Phoenix didn't *want* her looking at him. His grip tightened over her hands, and she relaxed, resting her head back down on his shoulder. "There's no shame in fear, Phoenix," she said gently.

Phoenix heard her words, but they brought no relief. "If my faith were stronger, would I not trust God enough not to be afraid?"

"Maybe. Maybe not. We are, after all, only human. And 'knowing' something doesn't always mean we shut out the response of the flesh."

Phoenix sighed. "I don't seem to be shutting out anything today."

"Is it Jim Peterson you fear?"

"Him. And others like him, and the effect they have on our lives…your life. Face it Aerielle. Every time I enter your life, I seem to bring you pain. Forgetting Peterson, who else lies in wait in our future? Enduring by myself is one thing. Putting you through it is another."

Aerielle tightened her hold on Phoenix, remembering the times she had gone through it with Wolf. "There will always be those in this world like Jim Peterson…or Mrs. Wellington."

Startled, Phoenix turned his head, his cheek brushing Aerielle's corn silk hair. "How'd you know about—"

"Hawk told me."

"Hawk. It figures. He fits so well in your world Aerielle. I don't think I ever will. Even my own people don't understand me as they once did. Some consider my religious views to be on the outrageous side."

Aerielle laughed lightly. "Believe me, that statement is true of anyone who gives God more than lip service."

Aerielle could feel Phoenix smile, however ironically. His voice held a hint of resignation when he spoke. "I fit in neither world. Sometimes I wish I could believe in the Dreamer faith and be able to look to a time when Hunyahwat would cause all the Nimipu to be reborn, as well as all the wild game in order to feed my people. And in that time, all would be as it had once been before the white man came—save you of course. In the hear and now I am the 'wrong' color and of the 'wrong' faith. I guess we will be doubly cursed if we stay together, Aerielle."

"Does that mean you've decided to keep me despite the possible problems?" asked Aerielle.

Phoenix felt the warmth of her breath against his neck, the nearness of her body embracing his. He wanted nothing more in this world than to keep her as his own. And why not? Wasn't she his already? Yet the reality of the thought was hard to accept. "I guess it's just starting to sink in that I really don't have a choice about keeping you. You *are* my *wife*."

Phoenix turned in Aerielle's enfolding arms. "Don't misunderstand, Aerielle," he continued hurriedly, their eyes meeting for the first time, Phoenix's filled with fear and self-reprisal. "It's just...I don't think I could live with myself if something happened to you because of me."

Aerielle's expression was compassionate as she rested her hands on his arms. "But it wouldn't be because of you. You can't take responsibility for other peoples' actions, or for that matter, circumstances out of your control. That's something I've been forced to learn repeatedly with each child I've lost, my own *and* those I care for. It's been the hardest with Wolf, of course. I still fight off feelings of guilt for his death."

"But you weren't responsible."

"Exactly."

Phoenix shook his head. "I understand what you're saying, but you didn't put Wolf in danger, and it doesn't feel like the same thing. I just don't know."

Once again at a loss for words, Aerielle raised a caressing hand to Phoenix's face.

"One thing I *am* sure of," continued Phoenix, capturing her hand in his and bringing it to his lips, "is that I love you."

"And I you," she whispered back.

This time it was Phoenix's hand caressing Aerielle's face, followed by his lips taking over hers.

It was a tender but brief exchange as each fought the urge to crush the other close and thereby cause Phoenix pain and possible injury. He was the one to pull away. Leaving a kiss upon Aerielle's forehead, Phoenix pressed the side of his face to hers. "Are you really my wife, Aerielle?"

He felt her smile as she spoke. "Is there any doubt? Is there any question our vows were truly consecrated before God? I don't think there has ever been any question where He was concerned. He knew our hearts, He understood what happened. He then dealt with our lives and returned us to each other."

Drawing back, Aerielle met Phoenix's gaze. "In all those years, Phoenix, I never loved another. And dating Hawk, that was an act of loneliness, nothing more."

Phoenix glanced away, suddenly reminded of his own guilt. "You were innocent of the truth Aerielle, but I wasn't. And I also gave in to loneliness."

"You mean Sofia? And look how that worked out."

Suddenly they were both smiling and then Aerielle spoke. "I can just see God up there with a sad smile on his face, shaking his head, saying something like 'My poor besotted children. It's about time they realized the only thing separating them was a brief moment of eternity.'"

"Let's make it official, Aerielle. By white man's law." Phoenix's tone was serious as he continued. "If anything should happen to me, I don't want there to be any question that what's mine is yours."

"Nothing's going to happen to you!" exclaimed Aerielle, wishing to deny the fears within herself.

"You don't know that, Aerielle. Please go along with me on this."

Aerielle studied the pleading eyes of her beloved and found she could do naught but agree. "When?"

"Right away. Tomorrow. Before anyone, or any law, or any circumstance can separate us again."

Aerielle wanted to argue nothing would ever separate them as before, but from experience, she knew that even horrors unbelieved in could happen. Raising a hand, Aerielle caressed Phoenix's tension marred jaw. "I'll expect a large dowry of horses."

"Thank you, Meyui."

"I'm just a sucker for your native charm."

"Then get me out of this place. Please."

Aerielle once again found herself unable to refuse, knowing how Phoenix had helped her escape similar surroundings a short time ago. He'd been here long enough. It was time to go home, or at least as close to home as they could get, and as close to resolving Phoenix's fears as they were able. God would have to do the rest.

The Great Spirit put it into the heart and head of man to know how to defend himself.

Chief Joseph as quoted in *Chief Joseph of the Nez Perce* by Robert Penn Warren.

26

It was early when Aerielle woke Thursday morning. Her thoughts were filled with the dialogue having taken place not so many hours past. After arriving home from the hospital, Phoenix had gathered his family together and then told them everything. There were moments when Aerielle thought she'd have to practice her medical skills. Hawk provided an added soothing presence, having already survived the shock of their news. It wasn't so much the marriage part, but the beating, the separation, and the loss of Wolf. There had been much discussion, and as things calmed down, Nevin had agreed to help them obtain a short notice marriage license so they could deal with remaining concerns. Though the family was disappointed they hadn't known any of what happened sooner, they were pleased to welcome Aerielle as one of their own.

Despite the previous evening together, Aerielle had yet to tell Phoenix where Wolf was buried, or rather, where he was not. She worried he might be upset she'd had their son cremated, since it was not the custom of his people. But Phoenix needed to know, and Aerielle needed to share. In their new life together, Aerielle wanted nothing left to tell. However, the telling...the telling would be hard. Aerielle had never revealed that part of her life—the "burial" of her son—to anyone.

As for their new life together, Aerielle just wanted to get on with it—together—without Jim Peterson. How many times had she prayed the police would find him and lock him away? Probably more times than she'd prayed for his soul. Aerielle winced with guilt, knowing she'd given into the "response of the flesh," for she had no compassion for Jim Peterson. She fought off the bitterness and hatred, which stormed her emotions after being held at bay by so many years of ignorance. It had been easier to forgive Phoenix thinking he was to blame for his leaving, and even that had taken time. God grant her much *more* time and perseverance to forgive the thief who'd stolen so much of her life. One thing was for sure. Forgiving and forgetting—even living—would be difficult for her and Phoenix until the Jim Peterson story was brought to a conclusion. But Aerielle had learned a lot in fourteen years. This time she would stand and fight. Defeat would not know her name again.

→→→

Not far down the hall, another warrior was having trouble with the concept of sleep. Being out of the hospital, Phoenix would have expected to sleep better and longer, but the plight of Aerielle's leaving on the morrow and the confusion of his own heart, called to him before the dawn. Hawk, hogging up the covers, lay asleep beside him, and afraid of waking his brother by his restlessness, Phoenix rose. He dressed as quickly as he could, which wasn't saying much. Phoenix bit back more than one groan.

Deciding to try and tackle his fears of the future head on, Phoenix sought out his source of hope. Taking his Bible and grabbing a couple of carrot sticks from the kitchen, Phoenix headed for the barn. He was praying for God to hear his prayers even before he reached his destination, Nimipu's stall, Phoenix's prayer closet from ages past.

Phoenix fed Nimipu as he prayed, wishing he had the strength to brush the horse. Instead, he stroked Nimipu's nose and prayed for God's peace and for His wisdom. He prayed for Aerielle's protection from Peterson and others. But most of all he prayed that his and Aerielle's different worlds would not be forever at odds with each other's and Aerielle would not continue to suffer for the life she'd chosen with him in a culture where he would never truly belong.

Exhausted just from standing, Phoenix sat down on an overturned bucket and opened his Bible. Nimipu appeared to doze, and Phoenix ignored the stallion. Thumbing through his Bible, he read bits and pieces of familiar verses, searching for an answer, wishing a page would fall "magically" open to the key to what troubled him. He wanted any response that would remove the fear for Aerielle from his soul.

But Phoenix had never been one to receive visions from God or sudden "thou shalt know the answer" revelations. He'd seen those blessed with prophesy, but he had never prophesied. He'd seen those blessed with miracles, but had never experienced one. Phoenix had struggled through some difficult times with raw faith to hold him steady, but now, this time, he wanted more than to believe. He wanted to see, or hear, or experience God's answer in a way that left no doubt, *He was speaking.*

But no pages miraculously opened, no verse jumped out, no vision claimed him, and no voice spoke. In the core of his soul, Phoenix was alone. Or at least it felt that way. And despite knowing his feelings and emotions were temporal, like the changing landscape on the soil of the soul, Phoenix could not shut out what Aerielle had termed the "response of the flesh." Phoenix felt empty, alone, abandoned, therefore he was. And the only ray of hope that glimmered was knowing his emotional state put him in some mighty good company. For had not Jesus himself cried out, "My God, my God, why hast thou forsaken me?"

→→→

It was only 6:30 when Phoenix returned to the house. Slipping his snow covered boots off at the door, he headed over to the sink to wash up. He wondered if Aerielle were awake. No, he had no answers, no assurances to share with her, but Aerielle didn't seem to dread Phoenix's fears as he did. She would be, would remain, his wife in any circumstance. What had Phoenix done to deserve her?

When Phoenix entered the hallway, the light was on beneath her door. He knocked. She opened it while still tying her red velvet robe over a turquoise nightgown. Her hair was slightly mussed, and Phoenix suspected his own looked about the same.

"Good morning," she said, smiling without apparent surprise and stepping back to let him in.

"I didn't wake you, did I?" asked Phoenix.

Closing the door behind him, she shook her head. "Not at all. I was just vacillating between reading a book and packing."

Phoenix noted the open book lying on the pillow of the unmade bed and the open suitcases haphazardly lined with clothes. It wasn't like Aerielle to be unfocused.

"Having trouble sleeping?" he asked, stepping over to the nightstand by the bed and lifting a musical snow globe left out from the holidays. "Christmas seems like ages ago."

"And Minnesota like another life," agreed Aerielle from behind, ignoring his question.

Phoenix replaced the ornament and turned. "I should be going with you tomorrow."

And I should be staying, thought Aerielle. And she would stay if he asked her to, but she knew not only wouldn't he ask, he wouldn't permit it. She loved him enough to stay and possibly lose her job, and he loved her enough to let her go and keep it.

"I wish you *were* going Phoenix, but you need to give your injuries a little more healing time."

"Veterinarian heal thyself?"

"Something like that. But in the meantime, I get to play nursemaid until the plane leaves tomorrow. Speaking of nursing, it's time I changed your dressing. I have all the stuff right here." Aerielle walked over to the dresser where she'd set the supplies when they'd come home from the hospital. "Let's see. Gauze, tape, antiseptic, antibiotic, gloves—looks like all I need is a pair of scissors. Be right back."

By the time Aerielle returned, Phoenix had managed to remove the zippered sweatshirt he'd chosen that morning instead of a pullover. Despite his selection, the task of removing it was painful. It must have shown in his face regardless of his efforts to conceal it, for Aerielle was quick to comment when she returned.

"Are you all right? Are you in a lot of pain? Did you take your pills?"

Phoenix met Aerielle's gaze with a raised brow. "You sound more like a mother hen than a doctor, but thanks for asking. Yes, I took my pills. And no, I'm not in too much pain, and I wouldn't be in much at all if I had remembered not to put my arm back. Luckily, I only have to put my arm forward to sign the marriage license."

For Aerielle, Phoenix's last words brought to mind her early morning thoughts and the need to tell Phoenix of their son. She continued to think on it as she pulled on gloves and reached for the bandage on Phoenix's chest, working to lift the edge of the tape.

Her hands were sure and gentle, and Phoenix thought how lucky the children were that she cared for. He studied her bent head, wanting to touch her hair, yet having to settle for enjoying the scent of her, mixed with the remnants of hyacinth.

"In the ambulance, you asked me where Wolf was buried."

Her statement came out of nowhere, surprising Phoenix. "That I did," he replied, wishing he could see Aerielle's face.

"He isn't exactly buried. I had him cremated."

At that moment Aerielle tore the remainder of the bandage free. Phoenix inhaled sharply as the tape peeled away from his skin.

"Sorry," said Aerielle, glancing up. "It actually hurts less that way."

"No problem."

"Are you upset?"

"About Wolf?" Phoenix thought about it a moment, reviewing the many practical aspects of such a decision. "No. I guess not. Should I be?"

"Well, I know cremation's not customary," said Aerielle, setting aside the used bandage and picking up a sealed antiseptic swab.

"But it's not unheard of," replied Phoenix. "Besides, you know as well as I, that the body is but an empty shell after death."

Aerielle tore open the antiseptic and began wiping the area over and around the stitches. Her voice took on a note of grief as she continued. "That's what *I* thought, or should say 'I knew.' But it didn't feel that way when the time came. Even though I told myself his soul was gone, I still saw my baby when I looked at him."

Aerielle was still wiping at his laceration, and Phoenix knew it was more than clean by now, but he said nothing as Aerielle went on.

"Suddenly, I wanted everything to be done right—proper. Only I didn't know what proper was. And I wanted him buried on Nez Perce land, and I didn't know how to accomplish that either."

Abruptly Aerielle turned away, disposing of the antiseptic with sharp movements. Her distress was obvious, but Phoenix didn't know what to say. Didn't know if he should say anything.

She turned back to him, roughly tearing open the miniature package of antibiotic. Despite her agitation, her touch was surprisingly light as she began applying the ointment with her fingers. "I dressed him in some native clothing he'd begged me for a few months earlier. But they were made by the Sioux."

"I'm sure they were fine," soothed Phoenix, unable to remain silent any longer.

Mechanically, Aerielle applied more ointment, and Phoenix knew she was not hearing him.

"The burial situation seemed to be so complicated, so I decided to have him cremated in order that later I could bring his ashes home where they belonged."

Phoenix felt her pain constrict his own heart. What an horrendous responsibility to be placed on a single set of shoulders. "You did what you thought was best."

"I brought his ashes with me when I came."

"You did?" Phoenix started looking around and saw it immediately. When you knew what you were looking for it was obvious. The turquoise urn was not as big as he'd been expecting, but neither had his son been big. Another reminder he'd never reached the age of four. "What's your plan?"

"Leave him with your parents until we can bury him or scatter his ashes together on Stargazer land."

"Then that's what we'll do."

By now Aerielle had finished with the ointment and had stepped over to the dresser to wipe her fingers on another antiseptic swab. She then began cutting a section of gauze to the right size and applying strips of tape. Turning back to Phoenix, she laid the bandage over the injured area of his chest and began sliding her fingers over the edges of the tape. Her hands trembled and Phoenix knew she was fighting tears.

"You have no idea what it was like, Phoenix. I couldn't stop looking at him. I couldn't say, okay it's time. I didn't want them to take him away."

Phoenix felt tears building in his eyes as he began to understand what it had been like to "bury" their son and, to have done it alone. "I'm sorry."

Aerielle continued to smooth tape needing smoothing no longer. "And then he was gone and I wanted him back. And then days later they were handing me a container of ashes. Ashes. My son was dead, and all I had were ashes." Stepping back, Aerielle peeled off her gloves and tossed them toward the trashcan. "I never felt so alone. Why did he have to die, Phoenix? He was just a little boy. He had a whole world yet to discover…. I wasn't ready to let him go."

Phoenix reached out, gently pulling Aerielle against him, feeling her tears against his neck even as his own escaped from his lashes. "I'm sorry, Meyui. I'm so sorry." And he was. He was sorry their son had died, sorry for not being there, sorry she'd been "alone."

He hugged her tight, the pain of his injury blending with that in his soul. They held each other, sharing their grief, while Phoenix longed for a way to take Aerielle's from her and make it his own. She had suffered enough. He brushed his lips against her hair and then her cheeks, chasing away the tears lingering there. Her lips parted as he reached them and Phoenix kissed her, tasting her sweetness mixed with the salt of her tears.

They lost themselves to the moment and many more afterward. It was from a great distance that they heard a loud knocking at the door. "Aerielle, is Phoenix in there?" It was Hawk.

With an effort, Phoenix drew his lips from Aerielle's. He swallowed hard, trying to regain his composure. "Yes?" His voice sounded hoarse, and Phoenix did not question the momentary silence which followed.

"I thought you and Aerielle ought to know, Bluefeather and the Sheriff are on their way over."

Normality returning, Phoenix gently released Aerielle and stepped over to the door and yanked it open. "What'd they say?"

Hawk appeared relieved to find Phoenix dressed, at least partially.

"Bluefeather didn't give any information. Just said he'd be here in about fifteen minutes."

"Okay thanks. We'll be out in couple." Closing the door, Phoenix turned. "Did you hear?"

"I heard.... Phoenix, about Wolf, thank you for understanding."

Phoenix walked back to her, gently taking her face in his hands. "There is nothing to understand. I meant what I said. You did what you thought was best. And I don't doubt it was right.... Something else, Meyui. Remember, despite how you or I have felt or feel now, we have never been alone. God's hands were upon us all the way. Only a miracle could have closed the distance between our lives and placed us on opposite sides of the same lake. *You* are my *miracle*, Meyui. God forgive me for asking for more."

→→→

The kitchen was crowded. It wasn't a large one to begin with, and now there were seven people in it, five of them squeezed together on one side for a better view of the two just-arrived lawmen. Phoenix could sense the anxious waiting in the room and felt a familiar throb within his jaw.

"As you probably already know," began Phillip Bluefeather, "we've come about Jim Peterson."

"You found him," said Phoenix, his arm tightening around Aerielle's shoulders.

"That's right, we found him," replied the Sheriff, "or rather the state patrol found him. Peterson drove through a speed trap doing a hundred and five."

"And I suppose he just pulled over," remarked Hawk sarcastically, lacking the patience of those around him. "So what's the next step?"

"There is no next step, not for *you* people, anyway," said Bluefeather. "Peterson *didn't* stop. The highway patrol gave chase for a mile or so before Peterson lost control of his car. He's dead."

There followed a moment of stunned silence. Phoenix felt like he was hearing the words on reverberation delay. Peterson dead? Could this possibly be a second miracle? But, how *could* he be dead? After all these years, after everything he'd put them through, the guy had simply died in an auto crash? No arrest, no conviction, no suffering for what he had done? For a second, Phoenix wished he *had* had the pleasure of putting a knife into Peterson's heart. But almost in the same moment, he regretted the thought, knew that it, just as the act itself, was wrong. Relief swept over him. Peterson's future had been taken out of Phoenix's hands—completely. The burden was no longer his to bare.

"Dead!?" demanded Hawk, speaking as if he too thought Peterson had gotten away.

"Dead," repeated Phoenix, saying the word for what it represented—the end.

"Then all is as it should be," announced their mother with certain calm. Turning away from those too stunned to move, she left the room. Nevin followed her, leaving the three remaining to take up the slack.

"So what now?" asked Phoenix.

"Like Phillip said," replied the sheriff, "There's nothing more *to* be done."

"What you're saying, is, it's over," broke in Aerielle, speaking at last. "No arrest, no trial...no facing him again."

Aerielle turned to Phoenix, her own relief evident in her eyes. "I know I should be sorry, but...."

"Me, too," he said assuredly.

"Make that me three," added Hawk, his indignant anger gone.

"We should be heading back to town," said the sheriff, glancing at Bluefeather.

Phoenix stepped forward, offering a hand to each of them in turn. "Thanks for coming out."

The sheriff nodded and stepped out into the cold. Bluefeather paused at the door, his face revealing no hint to his thoughts. "Maybe you'd feel better if you thought it wasn't an accident."

"What do you mean?" asked Phoenix. "You said he lost control of his car."

"He did. Right into Coyote Gulch. Taz alago, Yellow Wolf."

Bluefeather was gone.

Phoenix, Aerielle, and Hawk all stared at the now empty doorway, the significance of Bluefeather's statement lost on none of them. Many of the Nez Perce would say that Coyote—the creator, the trickster, the destroyer—had had a hand in things. But all present knew better.

"A little more than poetic justice, wouldn't you say?" asked Hawk.

Phoenix's voice was low and solemn when he replied. "'Vengeance is mine, sayeth the Lord.'"

→→→

Moonlight reflected off the snow, lighting up the darkness like a nightlight. For Phoenix, who sat gazing at it from the sofa in the living room, it brought back memories of New Year's Eve. So calm, so still, stars lighting up the heavens where the moonlight failed to reach. Only now, Jim Peterson was dead, and Aerielle attempting sleep in preparation for her journey following their nuptials on the morrow. Judge Candy, a friend of Nevin's, had agreed to see them at eight a.m.

It was nearing midnight, and Phoenix knew, he, too, should be in bed, but his thoughts precluded easy rest. Visions of the moment he'd nearly killed Jim Peterson on the night like this one filled his mind. It had taken everything inside of him for Phoenix to turn that knife around and attempt to knock Peterson senseless instead. Phoenix wondered if at that moment Peterson's hatred could have equaled his own. But now their hatred was gone, Peterson *unable* to hate, and Phoenix left with nothing and no one *to* hate.

Phoenix shifted on the sofa, pulling his legs cross-legged beneath him. If he had killed Peterson he would have been left with the guilt, but this way—God's way—his conscience was free, at least of murder. On the other hand, Phoenix wondered if he had done everything he could have, beginning fourteen years ago. Regrets, reprimands, and "what ifs" plagued him, and though he knew the danger Peterson had posed in his and Aerielle's lives was gone, he couldn't help but wonder about the future opposition they might face, and question whether or not he would handle things more effectively.

Phoenix was growing morose and enough was enough. He should at least try and sleep. After all he was "getting married" in the morning. Phoenix stood and headed for his room.

His brother was looking through Wolf's photo album when Phoenix entered and sat down to remove his moccasins.

"I can't get over the likeness," remarked Hawk without looking up. "Of course, there's something of Aerielle here, as well, but I can't place it."

"I've felt it, too. And it's more than the familiar teasing glow in those eyes."

"Definitely, though that in itself shows a streak of Aerielle's personality."

Phoenix sat up from removing his moccasins and inhaled sharply, placing a hand on his chest.

"You all right?" asked Hawk, glancing at Phoenix and setting the album aside.

"Yeah, just moved too quickly."

"Maybe you ought to pay a visit to your doctor. She'd probably make you forget all about the pain."

Phoenix eyed his blunt brother and wondered how Hawk had managed to end up more like their half-sister Sparrow than he had like Phoenix. "Let's just say the timing isn't right."

Thoughtfully, Hawk leaned back into a stack of pillows on the bed. "And what about this morning?"

"Nosey as well as indecent, aren't you?" said Phoenix. "For your information, nothing happened this morning. The timing obviously wasn't right then either, or why else would you have interrupted as per your usual tendency?"

Hawk had the sense to look sheepish. "Sorry."

"Well, I'm not," said Phoenix, standing up. "The timing really wasn't right, just like it isn't right now."

"You waiting on that marriage certificate?"

"Maybe...partly." Phoenix paused and peeled off a layer of clothing, grimacing in pain. "It would also be nice to be healthy. And alone," he added, his gaze settling on Hawk. "You really do have a knack for timing you know."

Hawk grinned. "Everybody has to be good at something."

"Take up another hobby. But before you do, Aerielle and I are going to need a witness tomorrow. Since you've witnessed practically everything else, would you care to attend the 'nuptials?'"

"I'd be honored."

"Good."

"Maybe you could invite me to the birth of your next child as well."

Hawk didn't bother ducking as a slow moving Phoenix threw a pillow from the chair.

→→→

For Aerielle, Friday morning came with a rush of last minute packing, a hurried shower, and the throwing on of faded jeans, a blue sweatshirt she'd at some point borrowed from Phoenix, and a pair of hiking boots. Phoenix was less hurried, but similarly dressed. There had been an unspoken agreement to play down the importance of the coming ceremony, in that giving it too much credence would lessen the significance of the vows exchanged years ago and repudiate their belief that God had known and accepted their commitment all along. For deep within them both was the knowledge that God, with the hands of a loving father, had patiently, insistently, brought an end to their separation.

They spoke no vows in chambers for similar reasons. They simply exchanged "I dos" following the appropriate questions of whether they wished to be married to one another. The whole thing was over in less than three minutes, the surprised judge keeping his questions to himself. Hawk made a remark about the whole thing being rather unromantic and insisted that Phoenix and Aerielle at least follow up their brief words with the traditional kiss.

But as Aerielle turned to Phoenix and saw the message written in his eyes, she knew there would be nothing traditional about it. His kiss would be a claiming of what was his, a relinquishment of what was hers, and a declaration of what was theirs. They belonged to one another, as they always had, as they always would. Aerielle waited, breathless, as Phoenix leaned toward her. "What God has brought together," he whispered, "let no man, no circumstances, ever put asunder. I love you, Meyui." And then he kissed her, his princess bride, and the world dissolved.

If the world hates you, keep in mind that it hated me first. If you belonged to the world, it would love you as its own. As it is, you do not belong to the world, but I have chosen you out of the world. That is why the world hates you.

John 15:18–19

27

With the passage of time came healing—to hearts, to minds, to bodies. Phoenix was glad for his returned health, but anxious to see Aerielle. Despite their occasional phone conversations, and Phoenix's many calls to check in with Hawk and Sophia, who were managing a burgeoning relationship as well as the clinic, it had been two long year-like weeks since Phoenix had seen Aerielle, and the healthier he grew, the more impatient he became to see her. However, tomorrow he would be heading for home and looking forward to a very private reunion with his wife.

In the meantime, he had to get through the rest of the day. His parents weren't due back from Everett until seven, another four hours, and Phoenix had already mucked out the barn, showered and packed, and cleaned his room. What next?

Brushing his hair, Phoenix sat down on his freshly made up bed, studying the cloudy winter's day outside his window. It wasn't overly cold, but the weather people were predicting snow. Phoenix hoped it wouldn't be enough to slow him up in the morning.

Aside from missing Aerielle, the last couple of weeks had been good for Phoenix, forcing him to slow down and relax, get his thoughts together, and spend more time in prayer. Phoenix still worried about the consequences the mixing of his and Aerielle's worlds might bring, but he had come to accept his fears, trusting God knew best. Phoenix had certainly received his share of miracles in the last several months. He now knew he could live without all the answers or instant assurances. He would, as he had in the past, take strength from his faith.

"Thank you, God, for you sustenance, and let my reunion with Aerielle come quickly."

Phoenix glanced away from the window, noting the photo album he'd set on his pillow. Exchanging it for the hairbrush he still held, Phoenix lifted the cover of the album to reveal Wolf and Idaho. All at once it hit him. Wolf had his mother's smile. Phoenix couldn't believe he hadn't noticed it immediately. He had no doubt Wolf had had his mother's easy going disposition as well, for his eyes clearly did reveal a mischievous crinkle.

Sliding the photograph from its reflective sleeve, Phoenix held the picture close, leaning toward the window, studying the oh so familiar yet unfamiliar face. The boy's eyes were alive with his mother's laughter, while the deep hollows beneath his cheekbones revealed his native ancestry. As for his nose, it was identical to Phoenix's, or had been at least until Phoenix broke his. Unlike both his parents, Wolf's nose would remain straight forever, and his heart would never again be broken.

Attempting to replace the photograph in the album, Phoenix noticed there was writing on the back. He turned the picture over, expecting to find the date it was taken, but found much more written there.

It was Aerielle's handwriting, and unlike many doctors, it was crisp and clear, easily read. It began, "To my beloved son, remember John 15:18–19. 'If the world hates you, keep in mind that it hated me first. If you belonged to the world, it would love you as its own. As it is, you do not belong to the world, but I have chosen you out of the world. That is why the world hates you.'"

Another inch down in a different color ink was written, "Hemene, you have now gone to the world to which you truly belong. In a blink of an eye, at least for you, we will be reunited.

You, me, and your father in a world where there is no white, no Indian, no half-breed, just believers. Until then, I miss you."

Phoenix felt tears spill over, but did nothing to stop their descent. This brief verse, these simple words, were equal to any vision he could have seen, or any voice he could have heard, and truly a gift after he'd accepted no answer at all. God Almighty was a God of timing. That sure knowledge sent a rush through his being like Phoenix had never known. Using something written many years ago, his God had chosen now, this moment, to share it. Phoenix knew without question, that the message had been waiting for him—Yellow Wolf—for a very very long time. And the message was clear. It mattered not what worlds he and Aerielle came from, nor that those worlds were different. The two of them were tied together in Christ, and as a result of their vows, they were joined ever more completely, at least until this life ended.

"Thank you," said Phoenix glancing upward. Reverently, he slid the picture of his son back into its sleeve. A smile touched his lips as he closed the photo album. Only God would have the foresight to use Aerielle to reach Phoenix in the manner that He had.

Aerielle. He had to talk to Aerielle.

Minutes later, Phoenix was standing in the alcove where the phone sat, hurriedly dialing Aerielle's number at work. The call was quickly answered, but not by Aerielle. The woman on the other end told Phoenix she had the day off. Thanking the woman, Phoenix tried Aerielle's apartment. Disappointment mounted as her phone remained unanswered. Phoenix paced the darkened alcove, running his free hand through his hair. "Come on, Aerielle, pick up the phone."

"I would if I could."

Startled, Phoenix turned, dumbfounded to find Aerielle standing in the doorway, her figure silhouetted by the light from the kitchen behind her. She was smiling.

Vaguely, Phoenix heard her voice on the phone as well and realized her answering machine had picked up.

He returned the phone to its hook, his gaze never leaving Aerielle. And then he laughed. "What are you doing here?!" Not waiting for an answer, he stepped forward and unceremoniously pulled her into his arms. He kissed her. She kissed him. And Phoenix was amazed to find he wasn't imagining it all. Her hands tangled in his hair, creating a rumble of desire in Phoenix's throat.

"Thank you," he said at last, pulling back to look at her.

She leaned forward, teasing his lips with hers. "What for?"

"For being here. For allowing yourself to be God's vessel and for being everything you are."

"I don't know what I did to deserve so many compliments, but I'll take them."

Phoenix chuckled and turned her toward the doorway, urging her out of the alcove and into the kitchen. "Come out here and let me get a good look at you." He drew her into the middle of the room facing the light from the window. He studied her, recalling every feature, every brush of light and contour, noting the lack of bruises on her face and the slightly crooked nose. "You're more beautiful than ever."

"Flattery will get you everywhere," she replied, not in the least minding his generous attention.

Phoenix laughed. "As glad as I am to see you, what *are* you doing here? I'm starting home tomorrow."

Aerielle shrugged. "I had the next two days off. I thought we'd make the trip together. Besides," she added, growing thoughtful, "there's something we haven't done yet."

"Wolf's ashes," said Phoenix.

"It's almost ten years to the day. I thought now would be a good time."

"Buried or scattered?"

"I thought we could scatter them on the Camas fields."

Phoenix nodded his agreement, his eyes tender. "You're a wise woman, Meyui."

"And you're confused."

Phoenix reached up and caressed her cheek. "Aside from my faith in God, I've never been more sure of anything in my entire life. Except maybe of how much I love you."

"Then be sure of one other thing," said Aerielle. "My love for *you*."

As one, they reached for each other, their lips and bodies meeting in an embrace that sealed their words, each second that followed a touching of their lives, an exchange of their hearts. Phoenix could not *kiss* her *long* enough, *hold* her *close* enough, or make *love* to her *soon* enough. Her woman's body tortured his, her heated touch forever branded him. But with the last effort of a drowning man, Phoenix released her, forcing space between them. Aerielle appeared as flustered as he was. Phoenix's breathing was still labored as he gathered breath to speak. "There's only a couple hours left of daylight. We'd better get going."

→→→

Heavy-lidded clouds covered the distant mountains when Phoenix and Aerielle rode their mounts onto the small piece of snow-covered camas prairie Phoenix's family owned. The first time Aerielle had been on this land, the camas lilies had been in full bloom. It was a sight she'd never forgotten, wave after wave of blue petals welcoming the heated sunlight. Aerielle tried to picture what it would be like in six months when the flowers blossomed again upon this land her son had only imagined. Despite his never having seen it, he'd lost himself in the stories Aerielle had told him of this place, Idaho, the land of the Nimipu, the land of his father.

Wolf had been proud of his father and his father's heritage even then. Aerielle, too, was proud. She had never seen such a noble man as the one who rode before her now, leading the way, cradling the burial urn of their son in the crook of his arm. His presence was that of a man who had come to accept life for what it was and found peace therein. Part of that peace for both of them had come with setting aside enough ashes to have two small diamonds made to be set in a pair of matching wedding bands. What better way to honor and remember their son.

Minutes passed before Phoenix drew Nimipu to a halt, Aerielle urged her horse up beside him.

"What do you think?" Phoenix asked, turning his sculpted face and obsidian eyes upon her.

Aerielle took a moment to lose herself in that face, in those eyes. Phoenix met her gaze without understanding. "What is it?"

Aerielle slowly shook her head. "Nothing."

Still confused, Phoenix reached out and took her hand and brought it to his lips. "It's all right, Meyui. We'll see this through together."

Aerielle squeezed the hand holding hers and shook her head once again. "No. *You* must be the one to lay Hemene's ashes down. He would have wanted it that way."

Phoenix regarded her for a few all too brief seconds and then released her gaze and her hand with the gentlest of parting. He turned, lowering his attention to the urn. He studied the receptacle a moment with reverent eyes, and then glanced back at Aerielle. "In the past, red face paint would have been applied to the deceased, and his body buried facing east. Now, we have no such customs, nor, in this case, do we have a body. How should I proceed? Is there something Wolf would have wanted?"

Aerielle smiled gently. "Something glamorous. He, like other exuberant children, had grand imaginings about the way Indians did things."

"No doubt. Well, I'll think of something." Pursuing such thoughts, Phoenix turned Nimipu into the light of the clouded sun and urged the horse forward with a slight pressure of his knees.

Aerielle waited and watched. Snow began to fall, and all was silent save for the sound of muffled hoofbeats.

Urging Nimipu on, Phoenix increased the distance between himself and Aerielle. All the while he could feel her eyes upon him, wondering what he was going to do. Phoenix wondered too. He had been given the honor long planned for herself, and he hoped her trust was not misplaced.

He glanced down at the turquoise container in his hand. Its contents were nearly all that remained of his son, and this was as close as he would ever come to holding him. In defiance of the absurdity of the thought, Phoenix felt a terrible wrenching within as he experienced a mere glimmer of the torture Aerielle herself had gone through. This was his son, a bright-eyed little boy who had laughed and loved. Phoenix's grip tightened possessively about the container and in spite of the head knowledge that he held but the remnants of life, his heart clung to a child. A child, who because of the gentle ministrations of a woman of God, had loved the father he'd never known and the land he'd never seen.

"Sweet Jesus. Thank you for the gift of such a woman and the son I have yet to know." The truth was, this life was but a moment, and the time would come when Phoenix would see his son face to face and know him heart to heart.

The falling snow grew heavier while Phoenix's heart grew light. "This is for you, my son." Sharply, he turned the stallion, his back to the sun, his face to the east. "Aiyee!" Phoenix shouted, and raising his burden of love into the air, he spurred the stallion into a gallop. A moment later, lowering the urn, Phoenix released the cover and stretched out his arm, tilting the container toward the ground.

Wolf's ashes whispered out and were intently whisked away by the wind Nimipu created. Phoenix turned to watch as they were caught up into the snow filled air to be spread out over the land. And then the ashes were no more, the vessel carrying the past, now empty.

Several hundred feet away, Aerielle watched, the scene like a vision. Hooves pounded on the snow-swept prairie as Phoenix, intent on his mission, turned to watch the past disappear. Tears of pride filled Aerielle's eyes. Pressing her heels to the sides of her mount, she urged the horse into a run, closing the distance to the man she loved.

Within seconds, they drew to an abrupt halt opposite each other, their horses snorting from the run.

Through the remainder of tears, Aerielle smiled her pride and assurance. Phoenix accepted her approval. Mutual pain glowed in their eyes, mingling with the knowledge they had at last done what needed to be done. Their knees brushing, Phoenix leaned over and kissed Aerielle, his free hand encircling her delicate throat in a gentle caress. Her pulse whispered against his fingertips, and her lips parted in reply. Releasing her at last, Phoenix gazed into the now peaceful blue of her eyes while using his thumb to soothe her tender lips. "Our son is home, Aerielle. Let us go home as well."

→→→

They talked little on the way back except to share a comment about the heavily falling snow. Their thoughts were one and the same. The past was done. Now they longed for the intimacy of those who had waited much too long for their future.

Upon their return, the horses were quickly divested of their trappings and made comfortable in their stalls. Phoenix checked on one of the mares who was due to foal in the next week or so. She looked fine, and Phoenix paused to pat her side. He felt movement within.

"Aerielle, come here."

Her expression filled with curiosity, Aerielle entered the stall and stepped over to the mare where Phoenix motioned her.

"You can feel the foal," he said, nodding toward the mare's swollen belly. Aerielle reached out and Phoenix took her hand, placing it on the horse's side with his hand over hers.

Suddenly, Aerielle felt a ripple against her palm, an undeniable declaration of life. With it came a sudden rush of memories. Memories of her own child stirring within her without Phoenix's hand to feel it too, memories of a swift nine months that brought forth the very special gift of her son. Aerielle longed to know it all again, the feeling of life within her, the joy of such a gift as a child. Though recently, she'd contemplated the possibility of future children with Phoenix, all at once, it was extremely important to her. She wasn't content to live with just memories anymore.

Confused by the overwhelming emotions claiming her, Aerielle made a humorous comment about the foal having to be a male, and then made what appeared to be a casual exit but was really an escape. With a need for fresh air, she left the barn, stepping out into the beautiful snow-laden world, new flakes touching down like angels' wings. She took a few steps and paused, turning in the direction of the camas prairie and the burial place of her son. Hemene would not be her only child, *their* only child. He couldn't be. It was not enough. There were children waiting to be born. And if she and Phoenix upon their first union had produced such a child as their son, what would a second union bring? Most important of all, would Phoenix be willing to find out? Would he be willing to take the same chances they'd taken fourteen years ago? Aerielle needed to know, needed to ask, and prayed for the answer she longed to hear.

She stood there waiting, knowing he'd be done soon. And then she heard the barn door slide open and closed and his near silent step upon the snow.

"You're not wearing your jacket," he murmured against her hair as he wrapped his arms around her from behind.

Aerielle felt herself pulled tight against his chest, liked the protective quality about the movement. She turned her face into his shoulder and the length of his hair. "Neither are you."

"Aren't you cold?" he whispered, lowering his head to nibble at her neck.

Not likely, thought Aerielle, for heat had begun to radiate from everywhere their bodies touched. It wasn't good for Aerielle's concentration and the questions she'd had in mind to ask, but it was hard to think when the man she desired most in the world was forging a trail of hungry kisses across her flesh.

Aerielle attempted a deep calming breath, only to find herself overcome by the annihilating scent of Earth and Fire—the scent of her man. In a moment, she would be lost. Turning her head, she made as if to speak, but Phoenix's lips immediately seduced hers. With a soft cry Aerielle turned in his embrace, giving way to the demand of his mouth as she wrapped her arms about his neck. She forgot her words, knew but the crushing need of her warriors embrace, the intimate desire of his pleasuring kiss, and the sweet caress of soft thick waves as she buried her hands in his snow-dusted hair.

Phoenix felt her surrender, knew he'd known no such joy since their long ago wedding night. He heard himself groan as the kiss intensified. And then, in the back of his mind, he groaned again. There was something he'd wanted to ask before they'd gone this far, this place beyond all thought and reason.

As if by a desperate mutual need, the kiss was abruptly broken off, leaving them each speaking the other's Nez Perce name.

"Hemene."

"Meyui."

"You first," said Aerielle.

Phoenix took a deep breath and jumped right in. "Meyui, let's have a baby."

Aerielle's eyes widened and then filled with hope, and suddenly Phoenix knew she'd been thinking the same thing.

"When?" she asked.

"How 'bout now?" he suggested, a glint to his eyes.

She grinned. "You mean that?"

"As a matter of fact, I insist on it." Phoenix's voice was a growl as he sealed his words against Aerielle's sweet and yielding lips. He forgot everything save the desire to mold her to his embrace, the longing to shower her with kisses, and the need to make her body one with his.

Amidst the soothing backdrop of falling snow, the warrior named Yellow Wolf lifted his Morning Light into his arms and carried her inside.

Nine months, four days, and seven hours later, Meadowlark Stargazer was born.

CPSIA information can be obtained
at www.ICGtesting.com
Printed in the USA
LVHW022116210423
745008LV00003B/482

9 781489 746832